UNSANCTIONED EYES

A NOVEL BY BRIANNA MERRITT

Unsanctioned Eyes
By Brianna Merritt
Copyright © 2017 by Brianna Merritt. All Rights Reserved.

ISBN-13:
978-0998996202

ISBN-10:
0998996203

Cover art by Najla Qambers
Edited by Jennifer Sell
Formatting by Kody Boye
Author Picture by Strength of Atlantis Photography

Leverage Publishing

For God—

Who told me to write "my story."

Part One

Death is just the beginning

Chapter One

I exhaled, the plume of breath lifting into the air and quickly vanishing in the pre-dawn light. Above me, the sky hung heavy, dark, and blue, as if struggling to wake itself from a deep and peaceful slumber. The icy temperatures of the desert night were only just beginning to wane. Tendrils of warmth crept through the sand I stretched out on.

A bead of sweat trickled down my forehead, but I resisted the urge to brush it away. Absolute stillness was vital to blending into the hilly terrain.

Just a little bit longer and you'll have your prize.

Cheek pressed against the stock of my rifle, gazing down the long-range scope, I watched the Afghani village below me. The horizon glowed brighter by the minute as the village slowly began to stir. Men and women emerged out of the mud-brick houses, children trailing in their wake. I didn't stir—didn't twitch a muscle—as small flocks of goats were released from crudely built pens. The children wielded staffs deftly, herding the livestock toward the back of the village where shrubs and greenery grew against the odds. In groups of twos and threes the adults headed after the flocks, trudging toward their fields.

The smell of Afghanistan was dry and savage—lethal—leaving my throat raw and my lips chapped. I ran my tongue over the torn skin of my mouth, focusing on breathing. Training to be a sniper was harsh, but no one had mentioned just how hard the job

1

would eventually become.

Swiveling my Accuracy International L115A3 rifle to follow the villagers walking into their daily activities, I allowed myself a deep breath. Keeping my index finger extended alongside the trigger guard, I took my eyes away from the scope long enough to peer out at the horizon, lightening with every moment. I would have to leave soon for fear of being discovered in the daylight—but not before I had a chance to end my target's miserable life. Not if I could help it.

Come on, you bastard, come out and play.

I laid my cheek back against my rifle, adjusting the scope to point directly at my target's house. The empty bedroom came into focus again after I blinked to clear my eyes. Its ramshackle, dusty splendor shone in the dim light of a sluggish dawn that hid many of the village's defects.

Adjusting the grip on my weapon, I checked the time on my watch. 05:06. Only thirty more minutes before I would be forced to leave my position and rendezvous with the rest of my scouting unit.

Dammit.

If I didn't get the shot now, the Afghani would be free to continue his involvement in the terrorist sect that ruled the Middle East with an iron fist.

I wiggled my toes in the tight confines of my combat boots, fidgeting as the sun climbed higher on the horizon. My shadow cover faded inch by inch as I lay unmoving in the sand.

The villagers were deep into their daily work, tending to field and flock, unaware that an army sniper had their home in her sight. If my plan worked, the Afghanis wouldn't know until it was too late that I had fired a bullet. And the soldiers back at base would never find out that I had carried out an unsanctioned hit. As far as my comrades knew, I was still guarding their backs on the boring scouting detail our base had ordered the night before. Snipers were supposed to remain unseen, so who would notice that I wasn't even there?

The idea of leaving a dead body in the village, five miles from the base, didn't worry me. The natives were always feuding—what was one more bloodied corpse in the sand?

Focusing through my scope again, I surveyed the village, desperately hoping.

Seconds ticked by as I took a patterned three deep inhales. I glanced at my watch again.

He isn't going to show. The mission's failed.

My finger pulled back from the trigger guard of my rifle as I moved to disassemble it. I had already pushed my window of time. My comrades on the scouting detail would notice when I didn't show up at the rendezvous, and then it would be game over for me.

There was nothing legal about what I was doing—not even remotely. I hadn't been ordered to kill anyone. This mission, this target, was of my own making. Unsanctioned.

I hesitated before crawling away from the ledge overlooking the village and spotted movement across the desert.

The early dawn glow illuminated the turban of the lone figure approaching the village from the rock hills surrounding it.

"There you are," I muttered under my breath, settling back down into my alcove among the shrubs and sand.

The Afghani man entered the village and then his house, avoiding the other villagers who were out in the fields. I lost track of him for a moment before he appeared in the bedroom—directly in the center of my crosshairs.

His dark, sun-kissed skin presented a stark contrast to the white turban and robe he wore. My breath caught in my lungs as I tensed. I smiled. My long wait wouldn't be in vain after all.

Closing one eye, I anchored my face against the stock of my weapon as I inhaled deeply through my nose. My wind gauge was set, my training thorough enough to guarantee a kill shot.

Body relaxed, I pulled the trigger.

One .338 Lapua Magnum bullet exploded from the muzzle of my rifle, the suppressor masking the majority of the blast. I felt the kick against my shoulder, a reassurance. The bullet entered the man's temple and shattered the stucco behind him—a definite kill. I saw the man jerk and collapse against the bloodied wall of his home.

I folded up the bi-pod legs, collapsed the stock of the L115A3 and stuffed it into my backpack, in the same motion I scrambled backward from the ledge. Three seconds later I was on my feet and scurrying down the other side of the hill, leaving no trace behind to condemn me.

The man I had just killed made my total number of unsanctioned hits an even thirty-eight.

Thirty-eight times I have flirted with Death and survived.

◇

I was waiting in a shallow cave at the base of a boulder when the scouting team straggled into view. A light breeze caressed my sweat-stained skin as I uncoiled from my seat on the ground.

"Abrams," one man said, the others acknowledged me with curt nods as I walked into their midst.

"I swear you're bloody invisible."

4

I glanced sideways at the soldier speaking. He offered a slight smile, his tanned skin almost the same shade as my former target.

"That's why I'm the sniper, Tyrone," I replied as our leader radioed in our position.

He chuckled, shrugging his backpack higher on broad shoulders.

"I won twenty pounds because no one saw you during the entire mission. Jones isn't too happy about that." He nodded at the mentioned soldier.

"Shut up, Algeria," our leader, Major Kevin Jones, snapped. "We head back now."

Falling into perfect silence, the five-person unit emerged from the shadows of the cave and turned toward Archangel Base. I walked beside Tyrone, my eyes downcast or sweeping the horizon ahead. He didn't need to know that his bet had been won on the sole fact that I wasn't even on the mission.

Dawn reigned pink and golden orange on the horizon as we marched into the military compound. Despite the early hour, life inside the gates was already bustling.

The encampment stretched out over a mile under the shadow of a tall mountain. High fences had been built to keep enemies out and secure a border. I stuck to the back of the pack as the scouting unit headed toward the main building. A group of six soldiers jogged past us in their sand-colored t-shirts and pants. Behind me at the motor pool, several people were cleaning and maintaining a Humvee. Life on the base rolled onward despite itself—despite what we did on our missions outside of the gates.

Slipping away from the unit, I headed for the barracks and a cold shower. After lying in the dry sand all night and toting around enough gear to smother me, I was ready for clean clothes and a nap.

I don't miss much about civilian life, but choosing

5

my own wardrobe, feasting on chocolate, and drinking good tea are at the top of the list.

I crossed the base's yard, passing other soldiers and equipment we kept stowed under tarps. The sun climbed higher in the sky, chasing the memories of moon and shadow away. My sweat increased, as did the heat, cooking me inside of my dirty uniform. Soon it would be unwise to be outside for fear of roasting like a turkey.

I would never understand why anyone lived in the Middle East. It was a land of unforgiving terrain, and if the natives didn't kill you, the elements would.

Opening the door to the barracks, I came face-to-face with my spotter, Major Nigel Payne. I halted in surprise.

He arched an eyebrow, looking me up and down before stepping over the threshold. "Where the hell have you been, Andrea? They just told me you went out on your own again."

"It was a scouting mission, Nigel. Nothing to worry about. I didn't need a spotter, and Major Jones agreed," I replied, desperately wanting to push past him into the shade of the barracks. The relationship we shared had never been entirely friendly; more of a competitive rivalry where duty forced us to watch one another's back.

"Scouting missions get ambushed or go south. You shouldn't have gone alone," he said as he glowered down at me.

There's no way in hell I wanted you along.

"Are you done scolding me like I'm a naughty schoolgirl?"

Nigel growled but sidestepped to let me pass. We both entered the barracks and walked toward our rooms near the back.

I could almost taste a hot shower when a captain dashed past us. "Briefing in the conference room in ten minutes. Be there." Before either of us could reply, he was gone around the corner.

I turned to Nigel. "So much for my shower."

"You'll be lucky to get a shower in the next week by the sounds of that," he said, making an about-face.

I growled deep in my throat. So much for a moment of relaxation—ten minutes was hardly enough time to change my uniform. It would take seven just to walk to the conference room. I ground my teeth together and dumped my gear in my room before hurrying across the base to the briefing.

◇

As soon as I walked into the conference room, I knew that the briefing wasn't being held under normal circumstances. Something serious was going down, as was evidenced by the grim expressions on every face present.

Half of the base had piled into the space that usually sat fifteen people comfortably. The three monitors secured to the back wall displayed a multitude of different graphics and information. Two of the screens had aerial pictures of a village and an Afghani man I didn't recognize. The other monitor played footage of six British soldiers who had been brutally executed three days earlier by the International Free Militia. The horrific news had sent me on my unsanctioned mission to take down the man in the village. My suspicion of his involvement in the execution was clear-cut motivation to end his life in my mind.

Staying close to the wall, I snuck inside the room as Brigadier Wyatt walked to the front to address the crowd. He cleared his throat. Silence followed.

"This is Rafeeq Majeed, leader of the Afghanistan division of the International Free Militia."

Wyatt pointed to the picture of the Afghani, wasting no time on an introduction. "Red Team returned this morning from their scouting detail with proof that Majeed was the man behind the execution three days ago." Wyatt gestured to the footage of the soldiers.

An angry murmur followed his announcement.

My heart stopped at his words. *What? It can't be.*

I had killed the man who had murdered those soldiers. I had shot him dead in a village five miles from where I was sitting. They had it wrong—Majeed wasn't the killer, it was *my* target. I swallowed hard.

I have to remain calm. Wyatt's information is wrong, that's all.

I knew what I had done—I knew who I had killed.

"Also," Wyatt went on, "I was just informed that a man from the Lartay village has been killed. The locals say it was some time before dawn. They suspect one of our men for the crime." Whether on purpose or by pure accident, Wyatt looked at me as he finished speaking.

No, no, no. This can't be happening.

I took careful steps to ensure I was never caught. Thirty-seven times I had gotten away with it. Where had I gone wrong this time?

Calm. I had to stay calm.

"As of now, our orders are to subdue Majeed at all cost," Wyatt said. "I want a team ready to go after him by sunset. Major Jackson will select the team and walk you through your orders. The rest of you are dismissed!"

The conference room began to clear, and my heart began galloping like thunder in my ribcage.

Following the flow of people out, I lifted my eyes one last time to stare in horror at the picture of the Afghani on the monitors. What had I done?

My information had been solid—or so I thought.

The man I killed in the Lartay village was the murderer. He had to be; otherwise, I had just bloodied my hands with an innocent man's death.

"Major Abrams?"

Wyatt's voice stopped me before I could vanish down the hallway. I clenched my hands into fists and turned slowly to face him, coming to rigid attention. His grim expression leveled with mine. The leading officer from the scouting detail stood next to the Brigadier, watching me intently.

"Major Jones told me that you were nowhere to be found on their mission," Wyatt began. "In fact, he states in his report that you're practically a phantom among the men nowadays. You and I both know that snipers are excellent at their jobs, that they have to be, but remaining invisible isn't within the human laws of nature. Would you like to tell me where you were last night, Major?"

I gulped down the rising fear inside of me. If I were convicted of any of my crimes, I would be locked inside a jail cell for the rest of my life.

"I was looking ahead, sir." I lied, willing my expression into neutrality.

Wyatt nodded, greying temples showing as he started pacing in front of me.

"Jones, you are dismissed."

With a curt nod to Wyatt, the officer left the conference room.

"You personally asked to go on the mission alone, without a spotter," Wyatt said, "You've done this repeatedly in the last few weeks. I'm afraid you're trying to win this war single-handedly. You and I both know that isn't a good option."

I said nothing.

His strategy wasn't working on me. By grouping us together, he was trying to win my confidence. But I knew better. He wasn't nearly as kind and loyal as he pretended to be. As a fourth generation soldier, he was in the war business. He didn't have a passion for putting an end to the fighting. Not like I thought I did at least.

"Would you like to tell me where you were last night, Major?"

"I already told you, sir. I was looking ahead. It's not my fault that the others never saw me. Clearly, they aren't vigilant enough, because I assure you I was there all along." It felt good to lie. I had always been an impressive liar—a fault my mother had complained about constantly.

"Then tell me, why do the slugs in your rifle match the one found in the Afghani's body?"

I was startled. Never in all my planning had I expected the Army to investigate the murder of one Afghanistan native. In fact, in the past thirty-seven cases of my unsanctioned kills, no one had even raised an eyebrow.

"I... I don't know, sir," I stammered, caught completely off guard.

Wyatt smiled kindly, but his eyes were as deadly as snakes.

"Are you missing your rifle, Major?"

I said nothing.

"Are you missing a box of ammunition, Major?"

I said nothing. Wyatt's smile dimmed, lips matching his cold gaze.

"I see," he said. "So if you're not missing your rifle or a box of ammunition, then we can both safely say that you were in possession of the weapon all last night and this morning, yes?"

"Is there a point to this, sir?" I demanded, trying to flip the tables back on him.

But the man just chuckled. "Oh yes, there's a point. A very particular one I'm afraid."

I waited, breath held, body tense, for him to say

the dreaded words. My game was over. I had been caught.

"I think you'll want to take a look at this," Wyatt said. He picked up a black remote for the TVs and pressed a single button. With a condescending trill, the screens flickered and started playing a scene I'd lived through but never thought I'd see.

My body lying prone on the rocky incline facing the Lartay village was unmistakable in the video footage captured by drone surveillance. Stunned, I watched as my rifle fired. My takedown was immediate, a blur of motion as I scrambled away. The footage ended as I left the frame and Wyatt clicked the remote again. All three of the screens went black as he faced me, disapproval in his narrowed eyes.

"The man you killed was an informant of ours and had been supplying us with valuable information regarding the movements of the IFM. I'd like to hear you explain your way out of this one, Abrams."

I didn't speak; not because I didn't want to, but because I physically couldn't make my lips move. Whatever information I'd had on the Lartay villager was wrong. He was an innocent man and I had killed him.

This is the end of the line.

"You've got innocent blood on your hands, Abrams." Wyatt glared at me, his words making my heart pound faster. "What do you have to say for yourself?"

Wyatt's casual posture made my spine stiffen in anger. I knew what came next. The security forces would charge in with handcuffs and arrest me. Hushed, private court proceedings and public humiliation would follow. I would be locked away in prison, trapped for as long as the people in charge wanted to keep me there. My freedom was slipping through my grasp as I stood in frozen horror. The taste of iron bars closing in around me was enough to set my jaw—and determination.

Prison was the last place I would ever let them drag me.

They could never lock me in a cage—no matter what that cost. They would have to kill me before handcuffs could go around my wrists.

When I didn't speak up, Wyatt did. "Major Abrams, you are hereby under arrest—"

I cut Wyatt off.

The knife in my combat boot was in my grip a second before the man's blood splattered on the floor between us. A thin line of red across his throat expanded as his body swayed unsteadily. His eyes widened as a sickening gurgling sound escaped his lips.

Stepping backward, I watched as his knees buckled and he dropped to the floor. Wyatt gasped up at me in confusion and pain. He struggled for his last breath, using it to curse me as I turned to run.

My feet carried me halfway across the conference room before the door suddenly opened. I stopped dead in my tracks.

Standing in the doorway was Tyrone, face morphed into an expression of pure shock. He seemed frozen in place as we stared at each other in disbelief.

"You... you... " He trailed off, unable to finish his thought.

I started sidling closer, glancing wildly at my escape just beyond him. We'd been friends since arriving at the base together. But what was friendship when it came to homicide?

"Tyrone, I don't want to hurt you," I said, getting closer and seeing his fingers tighten into fists. "Just let me go."

He hesitated for a moment and I thought he would back down to let me pass. But then he jerked backward and slammed the conference room's door closed—with me on the inside. I swore, lunging after him only to crash against the glass. It groaned under my weight, but did not break. Tyrone's wide eyes stared back at mine as he lifted a radio to his lips.

"Tyrone!" I shouted, pounding against the glass once before scurrying backward. If he was calling who I suspected, I was finished.

Whirling away from the door, I searched frantically for another way out of the conference room. Nothing.

The door behind me swung open. I heard boots on the floor and counted four separate pairs. A quartet of Royal Military Police.

It can't end like this.

I made it as far as the other side of the room before the RMPs could grab my arms. One wrestled me down on the conference room table, trying to pin my arms by my sides. Another RMP grappled with my legs. He earned a bone-breaking kick to the jaw and I was up at once. Tyrone kicked my legs out from under me and I sprawled on the floor, knife skittering out of reach.

Flipping onto my back, I brought my legs up and slammed my boots into the chest of the third RMP, who was bearing down on me. He stumbled backward, crashing into two more soldiers. I scooped up my knife and slashed at the closest man. He jumped back, but not far enough to avoid the blade cutting open his hand.

Droplets of blood hit the floor as I wheeled to find another escape route. I saw nothing but walls and soldiers with guns.

I was trapped.

More RMPs sprinted into the hallway, their guns leveled at my chest. Someone was shouting as I made a final desperate attempt to flee past them.

Unsanctioned Eyes

I felt the pang of bone-jarring agony as the butt of a rifle struck between my shoulder blades. The floor dashed up to meet me and spots danced in my vision. Groaning, I tried to fight back as Tyrone finally pinned my legs down. Something hard struck my temple again, and the black spots expanded to fill my vision.

Chapter Two

Archangel Military Base, Afghanistan

The holding cell the security forces had locked me into reeked of mold and fresh paint. I lay back on a stainless steel cot, arm over my eyes in a desperate attempt to block out the glaring LED bulbs above me. The vents high in the ceiling blew a steady stream of cold air. My skin prickled with goosebumps, the pair of plain cotton pants and t-shirt I wore doing nothing to shield against the chill.

Six days. Six bloody days I had been locked inside concrete walls and metal doors. My only visitors were the men who brought food twice a day and accompanied me to the bathroom just as often. Other than those necessary occasions, I was never allowed to leave the cell, the strain of being confined to one place steadily driving me into restless insanity.

I turned over onto my side, the cot beneath me not giving so much as a squeak. Thick metal bolts secured it and the table and chairs a few feet away to the floor, preventing me from using them as weapons or a means of escape. Sighing, I tried to drone out the sound of silence so that I could sleep. No such luck.

What I wouldn't give for a six-inch stiletto right about now.

At least with a knife I could bargain my way off of the military base by holding the man who interrogated me daily at death's door. I flopped back onto the cot to stare at the ceiling. There were sixteen ceiling tiles. I had already counted them. The wall

15

panels were eight and a half by twelve inches in total. There were ten panels per wall.

What I wouldn't give for a piece of paper. Origami would be a step up from this damned boredom.

Closing my eyes, I listened to my internal clock reach 12:15 p.m. Right on schedule the cell door clicked, the heavy bolt mechanism opening. I smirked. Footsteps approached and a metal tray was deposited loudly on the table.

"Get up."

I peeled open one eyelid to look up at my former spotter, Nigel Payne, standing at attention above my noontime meal. He repeated his command, expression hateful.

"That's no way to greet a comrade, soldier," I mocked, sliding off of the cot and standing tall. My bare feet were silent on the tile floor as I crossed to the chair and plopped down in it.

"Bugger off. You're no comrade of mine, murderer," he hissed as I examined the substance some might call food.

"What the hell is this?" I demanded, gesturing at the piles of *glob* on the tray.

He chuckled slyly and took the chair opposite me. Vaguely, I heard the door lock being put back into place. The foursome of guards outside of my cell returned to their positions, awaiting further instructions.

"Chicken, grits, and broccoli."

"Tosh," I retorted. Since I wasn't given any silverware to eat with, I poked a rubbery object that might have been in the form of a piece of chicken with my finger. I wrinkled my nose in disgust.

"What's the matter? Not hungry today, Abrams?" he spat, arms crossed, watching me with the same distaste I had for the food.

16

"Naff off." I picked up the chicken and took a bite. My taste buds didn't thank me for it.

They're going to starve me before my trial date.

The air conditioning droned on, spewing its frigid breath into the cell. Nigel didn't seem to mind. His heavy uniform was enough to keep him warm while I shivered and tried to choke down my meal. I had just started on the green mush he had called broccoli when he spoke again.

"Your lawyer should arrive tomorrow and a transfer date should be set."

I dropped the broccoli, which bounced when it hit the tray, and wiped both hands on my pants. "Where are they sending me?"

"Somewhere with high security," Nigel said. "Some place where they won't care if you get a few black eyes and broken bones."

My ribs ached at his words. Archangel was still in turmoil thanks to my panicked murder of the Brigadier who oversaw the anti-terrorism base. It was a miracle I'd survived being discovered for his death. There was a reason the soldiers stationed here got the results they did. All of us at one point or another had broken army regulations and been sent to Archangel for the chance to work on discipline. Or as Wyatt had once put it, a chance to discipline our rebellion into good works.

"What are they going to do with Tyrone and the RMPs who found me? Being a witness is serious business." I pictured the look of sick horror on Tyrone's face when he had walked in on Wyatt and me.

"They're keeping them safe and neat until your trial. Then Tyrone will testify you right into a cell for the rest of your life. Which brings me to the only question you haven't answered since your arrest." Nigel leaned forward in his chair. "Why'd you do it? Why did you kill those unsanctioned targets? Why did you kill Wyatt?"

I smirked. "I already told you, Nigel. Waiting for the Prime Minister and Secretary of State to make up their minds about who to kill takes too long. I did it to win the war."

"We're not at war!" he shouted, banging his fist down on the table. My meal tray rattled, the broccoli mush jiggling like jelly.

"The terrorists are attacking us"—I leaned forward too, arms braced on the table—"and they're winning. If we're not at war with them then why are we even in Afghanistan in the first place?"

"We're not at war," he repeated.

I snorted. "Don't you have someplace else to be stupid?"

"Not until four."

We stared at each other from across the table. Two soldiers—one still pinned with medals of honor, and the other awaiting a trial date for murdering a commanding officer.

Nigel exhaled, scooting back in his chair and straightening. I let him take my half-eaten meal and back toward the door.

"You're going to regret everything," he muttered as the door was unlocked.

I shrugged. "What difference does it make?"

With a sneer, he slammed the cell door closed as I returned to my cot.

<>

The sun broke on the seventh day of confinement and my cell door clicked open unexpectedly. I paused halfway down in my push-up, sweat dripping onto the concrete floor beneath me.

It's too early for lunch.

Holding my position, my muscles giving a

18

painful grunt of submission, I looked up at the doorway and frowned.

Two men stood just inside my cell, watching me. One wore an expensive black suit, while his companion had favored a pair of dark jeans, a leather jacket, and a V-neck that had graphic writing on it. Upon closer inspection, I smirked, reading the words: I solemnly swear a lot.

You're not military, that much is obvious. My lawyers then?

I tossed my head, hair sliding back from my eyes as I uncoiled lazily from the push-up. Sinking into a hip and crossing my arms, I silently surveyed my visitors, noting their body language. For being in the same room as a murderer, they didn't seem to be angry or on edge.

In fact, they appeared to be right at home.

I arched my eyebrow and gave the man in the suit a once over. He had the appearance of a leader. The midnight black tie matched the jacket and pants he wore. His dress shirt was a deep grey and matched his steely gaze. The florescent lights of the cell glinted off of his black, close-cropped, and styled hair. His companion, a taller man not much older than me, could have been an Abercrombie model. Standing in my dank holding cell, he looked completely out of place. I noted how his hands stayed by his sides nonthreateningly. He even flashed a smirk at me. Writing him off as a secondary priority, I turned all attention to the suited man.

He watched me take in his body language as if he knew exactly what I was doing. For the first time in my years of service I felt the power in the room shift away from me. I was no longer in control. Something far more deadly had waltzed into my presence.

"When are they moving me?" I asked casually.

The man in the suit smiled, an alien expression on

his stoic face.

"That isn't why we are here, Andrea," he said in a silk-like British accent.

My eyebrow shot up at the familiar tone. It matched my own perfectly. I frowned as he took a seat at the table and folded his hands over the surface of it.

"For the sake of your real lawyer and transfer date, I will make this brief," he continued.

Goosebumps popped out along my arms at his words, the chill of the cell gone. If these men weren't my lawyers, then who were they and what were they doing in my cell?

How did they even find Archangel?

I took a closer look at him as he waited for me to take the seat opposite. His face didn't have any lines or wrinkles around the eyes and mouth, evidence of infrequent happiness or laughter. In fact, his lips had a natural flat line that gave his entire face a seriousness that radiated intimidation. But above all else, it was his eyes that stole my breath right out of my lungs.

People told their stories through their eyes and I could read them like a book. But this man's eyes were onyx and death.

Swallowing, I resisted the urge to look away from them. They were so intense that I felt like I was falling into them, being drawn forward by invisible arms. I tried to search his gaze for anything—any sign of life or emotion. *Nothing.* My skin crawled.

The man, whoever he was, was reading my soul. A connection unlike any other I had ever felt was suddenly tethered between us. Taking a shallow breath, I forced myself to remain neutral and unaffected. Whatever happened, I couldn't let my feelings show.

Cockily, I sauntered over to my cot and sat. The man smirked, settling back into the table's folding chair as if he had read enough through my eyes too.

His companion stayed where he was, leaning against the doorframe, muscled arms folded across his chest. I silently wondered how the two of them knew each other. They were completely different—polar opposites.

"Who are you?" I asked, words clipped.

"Someone who knows that prison is no place for someone of your *talents*," the man replied without hesitation. His voice was a feline purr—soft, cunning, and a promise of immediate violence if provoked. "I've come to offer you a job."

A job?

It seemed highly unlikely that he was being serious since we were standing in a prison cell.

"As you can see, I'm slightly disappointed with my current employment." I smirked, playing along with his game. Neither man reacted like I thought they would. No smiles. No shared jokes or grins. Could they be serious? "Who are you?" I asked again.

"My name is Rourke Andres and I can save you if you agree to one thing, Miss Abrams." The man in the suit spoke up, voice echoing darkly off the walls.

I nodded, breathless. "Go on."

"We have to kill you."

Chapter Three

Archangel Military Base, Afghanistan

Six soldiers? Was that really the best they could do?

I stood in the middle of my cell, holding still as two men snapped a pair of handcuffs onto my wrists. The ice cold metal pinched my skin as they tightened it way past a comfortable position. I winced.

"I think you've got it tight enough, Major." I met Nigel's eyes long enough to see his hatred bloom.

He cinched the cuff on my left arm tighter. My soft gasp made him laugh. "If you want to make it to your trial date with both arms intact, I suggest you shut up. We've been cleared to use any force necessary to make sure you comply. No one will care if you have a couple of broken bones." He glowered at me, and then turned to his men. "Let's go."

Together, the six soldiers fell into their escort positions around me as the cell door was rolled open. I tried to shrug the tension out of my shoulders, but it proved impossible with the handcuffs.

We took a left outside of my cell and marched down the narrow hallway. I kept my eyes forward, attracting little attention from the military police all around me.

I counted the time it took us to exit the main building of the base and emerge outside. Nigel and an RMP took hold of my upper arms, grips vice-like as we stepped out into the crisp evening air. My wrists throbbed from the tight handcuffs and my skin rubbing against the metal. A pink and purple sunset painted the

23

skyline, casting harsh shadows on the world.

Anxiously, I glanced around for any sign of my mysterious visitors. There was none—just the long walk of shame to the waiting helicopter.

Some criminal I must be. They really rolled out the red carpet for this.

"Walk," Nigel hissed when I slowed to look over the rest of the base.

I glared at him, resisting his shove forward.

"*Walk.*"

"No." I twisted to look behind me. Rourke Andres had been clear about where I should be when his companion came to the rescue. Locked inside the helicopter was as good as a death sentence. My breath hitched as I watched the last rays of sun slip behind the mountain to the back of the base.

This is it. The plan happens now or never.

"Dammit, Andrea." Nigel shouldered me forward a step. The RMP on my right joined with him, their combined strength sliding me in the sand. I licked my lips. My palms were sticky with sweat.

Come on... please.

Nigel swore at me again, taking hold of the short chain connecting my handcuffs. He gave it a swift jerk backward and then threw me ahead. I lost my balance and fell forward.

On my knees, I craned my neck to look back at my spotter. His expression was hard, eyes narrowed.

"Walk."

I shook my head. "You'll have to kill me here."

He drew back a fist. "Why you little b—"

The sand dune outside of the base suddenly exploded.

Like a belching dragon, smoke shot upward into the darkened sky. Sand splattered in every direction, raining down like pelting, scratching hail. Men screamed and swore, lunging in all directions as sheer

24

chaos broke out. The RMP tackled me to the ground as the smoke and flames grew steadily higher.

"Get her back inside *now!*" Nigel shouted.

The helicopter exploded next. Black debris and livid flames bathed the horizon in louder screams and blazing heat.

Dense smog flooded across the compound yard, pushed by a stout wind. The smoke converged into a suffocating, burning cloud all around us. I was roughly hauled to my feet as people started coughing and swearing.

Dangling from the belt of my escort, the keys to my handcuffs caught my attention. Years of training kicked in as he hauled me toward the main building we had just left. I skidded to a stop, my combat boots finding purchase on the ground. Throwing my elbow back, I heard his nose crunch and the following grunt of pain. He cursed and reeled away, hands clasped over his nose as it gushed blood. I drew my fist back and struck again. His chin received the full force of the blow and he dropped like a rock. Crouching beside him, I grabbed the keys and in three seconds was free of my handcuffs.

Another explosion went off, this time inside of the barrack's fence. A third followed—the ground quaking in reply.

I squinted through the haze, searching for the gate. Two more explosions went off, sending debris and fire flying. Nigel was a good twenty feet away, rifle in hand as he shouted orders. Out of the corner of my eye, I saw the fender of a Humvee sailing toward the soldier a moment before Nigel's cries were silenced for good.

So much for your patriotic idiocy.

Scooping up the military police officer's gun, I crouched, ready to make a run for the gate. I nearly jumped out of my skin as Rourke's companion

25

appeared next to me. His hair was tousled in the air, eyes wild with adrenaline.

"When I say run, move to the last Humvee and get inside."

I saw the two grenades in his hands and nodded in understanding.

A grin curling his lips, he told me to run.

I tore across the base, sand flying in my wake as the man launched the grenades into the midst of panicked soldiers. The explosions went off on either side of me. Flames rocketed sky-high as I dodged to avoid the plummeting debris. The heat was incredible, hot enough to blister my skin as I raced past.

Reaching the furthest Humvee, I threw open the passenger door and clamored inside as my companion did the same behind the wheel.

"Hold on," he told me, engine roaring to life under his touch.

I gripped the bar attached to the door as we accelerated in reverse, bouncing over the uneven turf.

Gunshots rang out and bullets slammed into the Humvee's armored shell. We stopped suddenly, the man wrenching the wheel so that we were facing the barrack's guarded gate. I knew immediately what he was going to do next and felt my heart stop dead in my chest. It sunk like a stone to the pit of my stomach.

"You'll never make it," I said, gritting my teeth.

He just grinned wider, shifted into drive, and stomped on the gas.

I cursed everything in the world as we shot forward, my body bouncing on the seat. Glancing out the back of the vehicle, I saw swarms of soldiers and military police rushing to the other Humvees or giving chase on foot. They weren't going to let me slip through their grasp so easily.

My companion gestured to the stolen rifle I had lying across my lap.

"When I say so, fire off five rounds," he instructed, depressing the pedal harder.

I gritted my teeth, mentally counting the Humvees.

Five, not including ours.

My blood went cold in my veins, but the man didn't explain further as we reached the gate going sixty miles an hour.

"We're not going to make it," I said again, bracing against the door, teeth gritted.

The front of our vehicle hit the obstacle, snapping it apart with the force, and continued through. I lurched and my hand locked around the overhead bar, the only thing keeping my forehead from colliding with the dashboard.

"Made it," he said.

I glanced sideways at the driver, eyes wide. He just chuckled, knuckles white as they gripped the steering wheel.

"My job is to get you out of here alive," he said. "Your job is to perform one last sniper mission."

We started climbing a sand dune away from the base.

"I attached an explosive charge to the front of each Humvee. TNT and a little C-4. Hit it and say bye-bye to all your troubles."

Cresting the dune, he throttled our getaway vehicle into park and threw open the hatch above.

"Don't miss."

"I never miss," I said, unsnapping my seatbelt with a click. Hands tightening around the rifle's stock and barrel, I stood up through the vehicle's roof hatch and braced my feet on our seats.

Bringing the gun to my shoulder, I stilled my nerves, aiming at the tactical vehicles below. Through my sight, I saw the soldiers in various states of battle dress rushing for the Humvees—some already seated inside and pursuing. True to my companion's word, there were, what looked like, explosive charges secured to the front fenders of each vehicle. In their haste to pursue us, no one seemed to notice the ticking time bomb they were riding inside.

Definitely not an amateur's Molotov cocktail.

I sighted down the rifle's scope, took a deep breath, and squeezed the trigger. The gunshot went off and the first Humvee in line exploded. Then four more times and gunpowder and smoke filled the air as I dropped back into my seat.

"What are you doing?" I demanded when I saw my companion wiring a bomb to the steering wheel of our vehicle.

"Don't ask questions, just follow me." He opened his door and jumped out. It didn't take a second invitation for me to follow suit.

Rounding the front of the Humvee, he took my arm and led me away at a dead sprint. We took refuge behind another sand dune, both breathing quickly. I barely had time to duck my head before he detonated the explosive.

The vehicle shot heavenward, flames spewing out of its doors and windows hot enough to melt the metal. I looked away, eyes tearing up from the heat.

As the smoke began to clear, the man grabbed my arm and dragged me along behind him.

"You're going to want to see this." He chuckled as we crawled out from behind the sand dune to peer down at the military base. I wasn't prepared for what happened next.

He produced a small black box from a pocket and typed in a quick code on his phone, before pressing a button on the object. There was a loud rumbling noise and then the ground caved. The military base imploded inward, the ground thundering in reply. My arms splayed as I tried to catch my balance. At my side, the man let out a loud whoop, fist pumping the air in delight. But there was no such response from me.

The smoking crater of what had once been Archangel sent my heart tumbling into the pit of my abdomen.

"Welcome to the family."

I looked away from the aftermath of my escape and met the man's gaze. He dropped the hand he had extended to shake when I didn't move to take it.

"Family?" I shuddered involuntarily, making him laugh.

"You'll see," he promised, turning away from the base. "Come on, Rourke's waiting with a helicopter in the valley."

Numbly, I followed as he led me away from Archangel, or rather what was left of it. I should have felt freed—I had just been given a second chance at life, a completely new start. But I couldn't shake the feeling that I had just awoken a sleeping giant.

Taking one last glance over my shoulder, I saw the cloud of black smoke rising from the desert. The man came back to my side and offered an encouraging smile.

"I know it's a lot to take in. Don't worry, Rourke's going to take good care of you." He held out his hand again. "I'm Jason."

I pretended not to see it, ignoring the gesture of friendship.

"What am I supposed to do now?"

Jason chuckled.

"Survive."

Part Two

It's in the eyes

Chapter Four

Five Years Later

London, England – September 19th

Pulsating music could be heard four blocks away from the thriving *Wicked Baby* club and tattoo parlor. Lightning flickered ominously on the horizon foreshadowing a storm as I spun the steering wheel of my Corvette, hands sliding over it with a lover's touch.

People lined the pavement ahead, milling about in their elegant cocktail gowns and funeral black suits, waiting to be allowed inside. A smile played over my lips as I depressed the brake pedal and came to a coasting stop just past the red carpeted front entrance.

I reapplied a thick layer of vermilion lipstick in my rearview mirror before shutting off the engine. After scooping up my black leather clutch from the passenger seat, I opened my door and slid out. A gust of ozone-charged wind blew past me as I straightened to my extended height in custom-made high heels. Inhaling deeply the city's aroma of smoke and adventure, I smiled as I rounded my car and stepped onto the red carpet. Gazes turned to watch me as I sauntered to the front of the line. The bouncer braced in front of the door nodded to me, lifting the scarlet rope in silent invitation.

"Keep her warm." I winked, tossing him my car keys. "I won't be staying long."

"Ma'am." He nodded, the muscles and tendons in his bare arms rippling as he returned the rope to its place behind me.

High-heels clicking, I waltzed right through the yawning doorway into the overwhelming display of disco lights and ear-shattering music.

Tell the wolves I'm home.

Four was the grand total of how many times I had visited the *Wicked Baby*. None of which were visits of pleasure.

Slipping through the crowd, I found a secluded corner out of sight of the video cameras placed over each doorway. A location my former visits had discovered. The shadows converged on my form, hiding me.

"I'm in position," I murmured, fingers brushing the ear-comm I wore. A short burst of static followed.

"Excellent, I'm launching Giselle's GPS tracker on your phone," a male voice announced into my ear. Keyboard clicks sounded and then my cell phone buzzed inside of my leather clutch. "You'll be able to find her on the moon now."

"Perfect," I replied, taking a step further into the shadows as a trio of women in tight-fitting costumes walked past. Their bloodshot eyes did not drift to me.

"Give me one more second and I'll have control of every camera in the building." I pictured Rourke's hacker, my equivalent to a CIA analysis, hunched over his computer in the dark office he kept at our base of operations. There would be a cup of cold coffee forgotten at his elbow, an energy drink or snack within easy reach.

"Take your time. I'm in no rush," I batted my eyelashes at a young man as he drunkenly stumbled past.

His companion swerved toward me, his drink sloshing in its glass to spill on the floor at my feet. I effortlessly removed the beverage from his clammy hands and pushed him back toward the bar.

"A shot of vodka," I said, depositing the confiscated drink onto the tray of a passing server.

She nodded, again not meeting my eyes.

"Drinking on the job is never a good idea, Quinn."

"Naff off, Garrett," I hissed, watching the girl wade back into the melee of cliental. Rourke's money had bought the building, but I wondered if it had also bought the staff. Blood money always bought more blood.

The serving girl returned and handed me the shot glass. I took it in gloved fingers and tucked a ten-dollar bill under an empty bottle on her tray. As she wandered away, I tipped the drink back and felt the buzz of alcohol charge through my system.

"Are you all set yet?" I asked Garrett.

A loud beep sounded in my ear in answer. "All set. Give 'em hell."

Oh, I plan to.

Pushing off of the wall, I emerged from the shadows to slide past the bar and into a dark hallway leading away from the loud music and drunken dancers. Neon lights strung from thin wire on the ceiling barely illuminated the way as I meandered past several closed doors. Signs nailed to them read *Employees Only*, *Dressing Rooms*, and *Storage*. According to the GPS readout on my phone, my target's dressing room was the third door on the right.

Its sign read *Giselle*.

Light streamed out into the hallway through the half-open door. I stepped closer, listening. There was one person speaking, as if on the phone.

Perfect.

I stepped through the doorway into a psychotic romance movie. Pink fringe, powder puffs, corsets, lace, and wine glasses lay scattered on the furniture. Lipstick and candles covered everything except the overstuffed closet throwing up clothing. The sickening stench of perfume, cologne, and sweat hit me like a truck and I gasped, trying to breathe through my mouth.

My target stood in the midst of the chaos chatting on a bright pink phone—what other color could it be—and holding up a red manicured fingernail in the universal sign for 'wait just a moment.'"

No rush. I had all the time in the world.

"All right, that's fine." The woman listened to whoever was on the other side of the line and shifted, her corset and silk dressing gown rustling with the movement. "Yeah, sure I'll be there."

Another pause. Her hair was put up in curlers, with a cream colored cloth tied around her brow in an interesting fashion statement.

"The usual? Wonderful. Talk to you later, babe. Bye." She hung up, turning to me as she tossed her phone onto a devastatingly pink daybed.

Putting her hands on her wide hips, she narrowed her eyes and looked me over from head to toe. In a pair of billowing see-through pants and a black blouse stopping at my navel, I probably looked like the Angel of Death to her Pink Phantom.

"You're back." Where a beautiful silk voice should have been, years of smoking and heaven only knew what else remained. Botoxed lips twisted into a smirk that could have frightened a bulldog.

"Giselle," I said in forced gentility. "Is that any way to treat a beloved guest?"

"Yes," she snapped, accent clipped. "Especially when I have ninety-nine problems and *you* are all of them."

Smiling softly, I relaxed my hands. "I promise this is the last time you'll ever see me. Courtesy of Rourke."

"Good!" The relief on her face was painstaking.

Her exhale was enough to send her shoulders slumping forward. Crossing to her dressing table, the woman unstopped a crystal decanter and poured two glasses of gin and tonic. She opened a small refrigerator and retrieved two slices of lime to put in the beverage.

"To what do I owe the presence of your company one last time?" Giselle inquired, handing me one of the drinks.

I took it, watching as she took the first sip.

"I didn't poison it if that's what you're thinking." She chuckled, expression bored.

I twirled the black straw in my cup then stabbed the lime until its juice bled out into the liquid. Giselle finished hers as I mulled over the message Rourke needed me to deliver.

"Well?" she demanded when I set my untouched drink down. Her eyebrows lifted expectantly. "What does he want?"

"Rourke's changing the management of the club, Giselle. You're being replaced."

My words were a bolt of lightning slamming into her spine like a whip. On cue, she gasped and took two steps backward, her eyes dilating in unmasked fear. The relief so evident a moment earlier was completely erased.

"*What?*" Her hand rested over her heart. "That wanker. He can't do that. He promised that this place would be mine."

I sat down on the daybed, coyly patting the seat next to me.

I wonder what I look like in your eyes. Am I terrifying yet?

The woman relaxed and sat beside me gingerly, careful to scoot as far away as possible. I resisted the urge to chuckle at her pathetic fear. She knew from Rourke how dangerous I was, and yet she didn't know even half of the truth.

"He promised you a place to live and work in payment for all that you've done for him, yes, but only if you continued doing what he asked."

"But I have," she swore venomously, eyes flashing.

Tilting my head to the side, I pursed my lips in a mocking sympathetic smile. "Then why does he want me to kill you?"

Giselle's reaction to my announcement was to shriek and strike at my face, fingernails extended for blood. I snagged her wrists, stopping her movement mid-lurch.

She cried out again, "I didn't betray him." She strained against my grip. Beads of sweat broke through the layer of make-up on her face. Her cheeks were bright red from terror and sudden exertion.

"Come on, Giselle, don't lie to me. What poor idiot did you spill Rourke's delicious secrets to?" I released her when she made one last attempt to jerk free.

She looked away from my gaze. Keeping the movement small, I slipped my knife out of the sheath inside my boot. Twirling the weapon in my fingers, I let it catch the overhead light. Giselle froze, paralyzed in place as I laid one hand on her thigh. Any movement to stand up was cut short when I dug my fingernails warningly into her skin. I lazily examined the razor-sharp blade, feeling her squirm against me.

I do very bad things and I do them well.

Giselle tensed, her hand inching toward the edge of her skirt. She whipped out a small Smith & Wesson revolver and brought it up toward my head. I swung my leg, kicking it out of her hands and across the room into her belching closet. Lunging to my feet, I pinned her left arm to the daybed with my boot and drove the knife through the sleeve of her pink dressing gown.

Both arms trapped, Giselle went utterly still as I

leaned over her. Tauntingly, I drew the identical twin
to the weapon embedded through her sleeve. The steel
blade caught the overhead light, glinting. I lowered it
to rest against her throat, six inches of razor-sharp
steel poised to tear flesh from bone.

"Tell me," I hissed.

She trembled, but remained silent.

Without warning, I buried the knife in her thigh
and Giselle screamed, her body arching off of the
cushions. The air tanged with the scent of blood. I
waited until she ran out of breath and fell back against
the cushions. Eyes wide and fearful, but still unbroken,
Giselle glared back at me.

"Who did you tell?" My fingers curled around the
hilt of the weapon.

Rourke never made a mistake, but the people he
used to launder money and other resources tended to
make plenty of them. Especially when they were
female and warmed his bed on the odd occasion. Not
that I could judge Rourke for finding companionship
wherever he could—our lives as assassins were
beseechingly lonely at times—and even I had my own
relational vices.

*Keep making messes. It's greedy bastards like
you who keep assassins like me doing janitorial work.*

Giselle sucked in a sharp breath as I twisted the
blade ever so slightly. Again, she screamed, her cry
echoing in my ear as she thrashed beneath me. Thanks
to the club's incredibly loud music and the din of its
patrons, no one would be coming in answer to the
woman's cries for help. Perhaps that was Rourke's
original intention when soundproofing the walls.

I watched her shaking uncontrollably from pain.
Deep down I knew that her agonized expression
should have twisted my heart, but it didn't. Something
kept me from feeling. I released the knife and felt her
sag with relief, only to curse me viciously the next

moment when I produced a serrated blade from another sheath inside my boot and hovered it over the hand I had pinned down.

"Pick a finger," I said.

She whimpered and shook her head.

"*Pick a finger*, Giselle."

No response.

I set the blade against the base of her thumb and she squeaked.

"All right! Enough! I'll tell you everything."

I smirked and stepped back, tearing my knife free of her leg. She didn't scream, just moaned and pressed her hands over the bleeding wound. Her once spotless pink daybed was now splattered with blood. I rather thought it an improvement on the décor.

"I told my partner, Jim," she panted, pain heavy in her voice.

"Who the hell is Jim?"

Her expression twisted in sorrowful regret. "Nobody really, just another man."

"What did you tell him?"

"He's a small-time arms dealer, you know." She glanced up at me. "I thought I could make more money if we worked together. A nightclub selling companionship with weapons on the side for the right clientele has a nice ring to it. It was a perfect plan until he wanted to know who Rourke was."

"And was it the love of him or the love of money that loosened your lips in the end?" I spat.

"I don't know really, it was all a blur." Hands bloodstained, Giselle pushed a strand of hair back from her brow.

I rolled my eyes at her dramatics.

"Did you tell anyone else?"

She shook her head so sharply I heard a bone pop in protest.

"And where can I find your Jim?"

"He's got a place in Marseille. The address is in my phone over there." She nodded toward her dressing table.

I sighed. "Anything else I should know?"

"You'll need the password to get inside."

I arched an eyebrow, a silent command to finish.

"Amour."

A smile floated across my lips as I let Giselle breathe, her face twisted in pain as blood continued to leak from her wounds.

"Now, that wasn't that hard, was it?" I crooned, allowing a hint of kindness to creep into my tone.

Giselle watched me with pained, suspicious eyes. "That's it?" Her voice warbled feebly with a false sense of hope.

I sighed. They were always so hopeful. But she'd been honest, so I'd make it quicker.

In one smooth motion, I embedded my blades into her abdomen. Two slivers of steel twisted into her lungs. Giselle gurgled on her own blood, fighting to breathe. Her gaze locked on mine, her bright-pink lips parting as she gasped.

"Y-you've no chance... " she stammered, ending in a gut-wrenching cough.

"I know Rourke... you have no chance... against him. No one does."

"I don't plan on going against him," I said, spine stiffening at the mere thought.

"Y-you will," she whispered, shuddering. "They all do. You will see what he is really planning. And then you will know... *everything*."

She tried to laugh, but stopped as her facial features froze in terror. Her bloodied hands reached out, grasping—the move of a person afraid to die.

With one final shudder, Giselle went still.

I bent to check her pulse and admire my handiwork. Two perfect entries into her lungs, the ideal placement to allow for any final words. Her nonsensical babble was of no concern as I cleaned my blades off on her daybed and sheathed them back inside my boots before turning for the door.

They'll do anything to escape death for a few extra seconds.

Chapter Five

The Paris skyline was breathtaking during the day but utterly awe-inspiring at night. I perched on a rooftop, my black shawl fluttering in the breeze as I watched the street below. On nights like these, when I was alone—a wraith of another world—the thrill of bloodlust burned the hottest through my veins.

A man emerged from the quiet pub on the street below. Continuing to watch him, I rose and stretched my legs.

Do you even know that you're the prey this time, old friend?

I didn't move as he crossed the street and let himself into the flats for lent directly below me. The night air shifted as I started toward the fire escape.

Like a shadow, I descended, an avenging angel in the night.

When the fire escape reached the fourth floor, I left it, palming two knives from my boots as I leapt the protection of the metal railing. My feet braced against the wall of the building as I drove the tanto blades into the cracks between bricks. With a deep breath and surge upward, I started climbing. Each moment was slow going, but I reached the designated window and paused. The dormer hung open to let in the evening's cooler temperatures. I slipped through easily and stalked across the dark living area.

Tyrone Algeria. A name I knew almost as well as my own. A face from another time and place so far away that it seemed like another world.

Framed in shadows and leaning against the doorway to the kitchen, I watched the soldier turned civilian as he read a letter just a mere six feet away. The only light came from the moon and a lamp next to the front door. It was enough to make out Tyrone's features, but not give away my presence.

I pursed my lips. Five years had passed since I had last seen the man, but I would always remember the way we both looked in our uniforms the day I was arrested for killing our commanding officer.

Rourke liked to say that I had been wasted in the Army—my talents unused by those who gave the orders. But it was worse than that. My boredom and rebellion led to unsanctioned missions and a growing list of dead bodies in my wake, the likes of which couldn't remain secret forever. The only soldier to leave Archangel before the night of my escape, Tyrone had been there when I ended Wyatt's life.

You're going to regret turning me in.

My target flipped the letter in his hands over, reading the other side totally oblivious to the assassin standing a few feet away. His face was lined with seriousness and determination, his hands scarred from his deployment on the front lines with me.

Too bad Death is a woman tonight, and I'm only one dance away.

Finishing the letter, Tyrone's gaze lifted to settle on me. I smirked as his eyes widened and his hand shot for the pistol holstered underneath his jacket—or at least a pistol that should have been holstered there. Spying on him before his dinner had allowed me to see that he hadn't concealed a weapon under his clothes before visiting the pub. A mistake I intended to exploit.

"Relax," I purred, pushing off of the doorframe.

"How did you get in here?" He backed up against the counter, snatching a kitchen knife from the block.

I chuckled. "If you don't want uninvited guests you shouldn't leave your windows open."

"You climbed four stories?" His sun-kissed skin paled.

"They always think height will keep them safe, that no one could possibly get to them." I released a loud sigh, faking a disapproving tone.

"Who are you?"

"Don't you recognize me, Tyrone? I thought you of all people would remember my face after all these years." I smirked, taking a step forward.

The knife in his hand trembled. "It can't be." His eyes widened. "You're dead. You're supposed to be dead."

"Well then, surprise. I'm not dead. So sorry to disappoint you." I laughed.

"How?"

"The Army lied to us, Tyrone. They gave us two doors, obey or be punished. I found door number three and I took it, without a moment's hesitation."

"You're her, aren't you."

It wasn't a question. Not really. He knew. No one—and everyone—knew who I was. The infamous Dragonfly, once a soldier and now a heartless killer.

Thank Rourke and Garrett for that sterling reputation.

"Yes." My hand slid under my shawl to draw my pistol.

"I haven't done anything wrong. You of all people should know that." Tyrone's chest heaved in fear.

I loved the pure thrill of being utterly in control. I was high on the adrenaline I kept from pulsating through my veins.

"Oh, I'm afraid you're wrong." I pulled the trigger twice.

Tyrone's body collapsed to the floor and his

blood started to create a puddle around him. The man was still alive, but only just. He moaned in agony as I took a step forward. I didn't even have to ask, his last words were already fresh on his lips.

"You're... on the wrong s-side." He choked. "You will lose. Terrorism has no place in the world."

"And yet terror runs wild in the hearts of men." I smirked, watching him take his last breath. "What cruel irony."

Returning my gun to its holster, I approached his prone form. Memories from my past life in the British Army were spiraling back to me as I stared down at my former comrade. We had been friends once.

"You should have killed me when you had the chance," I whispered, closing his eyes with my hand.

There was a static buzz from my ear-comm before Garrett's voice sounded. "Wrap it up, Quinn. You have three minutes before the maid knocks on the door."

I groaned loudly. The only thing I hated more than being shot at was being rushed. "Who the hell hires a maid in the middle of the night?"

"Probably someone who doesn't have the moral high ground," Garrett replied with his typical sarcasm. "Get going. I'm not bailing your carcass out of jail again."

"You've never had to bail me out of jail, Garrett," I hissed, rummaging around the floor to extract the bullet casings from the shots I had fired.

"Honduras, two years ago."

"I wasn't in jail, I was in quarantine." I walked to the far wall and used one of my knives to pry the two bullets out of the sheetrock.

"Same thing," he grunted in annoyance.

I pocketed all of the evidence of my crime and strode to the open window. My gloved hands held onto the edge of the dormer as I flipped out of sight, just as there was a knock on the flat's front door.

"How is quarantine the same thing as jail?" I whispered, pushing myself upright.

"Because I had to hack a satellite, a federal office, and two judges before I busted you out. I would have to do the same thing if you were behind iron bars," the hacker replied.

I rolled my eyes, the Paris breeze hitting my back as I lifted my gaze to the glow of the horizon.

"Your private plane is waiting at the Charles de Gaulle Airport."

"Tell the pilot I'm going to be a little late," I said. My boots found traction on the building's roof as I started walking upward from Tyrone's window.

"Where the hell are you going?" Garrett demanded as I reached the opposite fire escape and paused on the first step. The lights of the city illuminated the readout on my watch as the second hand ticked forward. Right on cue, there was a horrified scream from the room I had just vacated. A grin tugged at the corners of my lips as I started down the steps.

Lucky maid.

"It seems a shame to leave Paris without drinking a bottle of Romanee Conti on the Eiffel Tower." I laughed to myself, disappearing into the night as dawn blossomed overhead.

◇

London, England – October 11th

Advertising was our disguise. Assassinations were our game.

I stood on the fiftieth story of the Shard, the tallest building in England. The wall of windows at the back of my spacious office gave the best view of the city anyone had to offer—a special present from Rourke, the master assassin himself.

Arms crossed, I leaned against the glass, breath steaming it over as I looked down at the helipad on the roof of the building below. Rourke's private helicopter had just landed and I watched him step out onto the tarmac. The brand new Eurocopter EC145 gleamed a metallic grey in the afternoon sun. It amused me greatly to watch my mentor, and employer, walk across the helipad, midnight black suit and shining dress shoes half the sum it took to purchase the Mercedes-Benz helicopter.

You've always had a flair for dramatic entrances. Why stop now?

Reaching the runway leading to the building, Rourke stopped. His chin lifted, head tilting backward as his gaze searched for me framed by dozens of windows. There was no friendly wave, no smile, but the gesture of taking a moment to look for me was enough of a greeting.

Smiling to myself, I turned from the window and crossed the mahogany floor panels to sit at my sprawling desk. My iMac's screen flickered to life as I touched the mouse. A melodious thrill welcomed me back to my email inbox where thousands of unread digital letters waited to gather dust from cyberspace. In the ninety-four floors of the Shard, below and above my office combined, hundreds of people diligently worked away at their jobs—the majority of them oblivious that an organization of assassins lurked within their midst.

Sprinkled throughout the real offices of *London Advertising* were a dozen fake ones, identical to my own.

Rourke insisted our cover story be as good as the CIA's, if not better, and whatever he demanded he received. Dozens of employees ran the company like a well-oiled machine 24/7. Only his beloved assassins were free of the arduous workload *London Advertising* required. Luckily, I was one of the few.

"Knock, knock," a voice said as someone rapped on the partially closed door to my office.

I glanced up as the speaker stepped inside. The assassin looked out of place in his sleeveless shirt and sweats. My office could have come off the pages of a luxury design magazine, not the local gym. He shrugged, hands in his pockets, the spider web tattoos covering both of his arms shuddering with the movement. I spotted the file folder tucked under his arm immediately and felt my heart flutter.

"What is it, Matt?" I crossed my arms over my chest.

"You busy?" He smiled, brown hair tousled and damp with sweat.

I shook my head, closing down my computer and pushing back from the desk on my roller chair. Standing, I met him in the middle of the room.

"I was leaving the training room and Garrett asked me to deliver this personally," he explained, extending the file to me. My heart did another Irish jig in my chest as I accepted it with eager hands. Garrett having sent an assassin instead of one of the advertising company's interns meant that it was Rourke's business inside the document and not for the weak of stomach.

I flipped it open to the first page and frowned. A single blank sheet of printing paper lay inside with a sticky note written in Garrett's handwriting. The message read: New assignment. See Rourke to discuss.

Strange for him to be so obtuse.

Closing the file folder, I strode past Matt toward the door.

"Good news?" He tagged along through the

doorway.

"I have another assignment," I said, taking a left down the hallway in the direction of the stairs. Rourke couldn't disable the elevators in the entire building, but he would have if he could. They were nothing more than a death trap that went up and down. To be stuck in one with no way out was a fate worse than torture. The stairs were always a better choice.

"Already? You just got back from Paris this morning."

I nodded. "Speaking of which, did you get the bottle of merlot I left on your desk?"

Matt moved past me to open the door to the stairs. I rolled my eyes at his politeness. Somehow the tattooed assassin still held his gentlemanly ways close even after Rourke's rigorous training. Not that it surprised me in the least. He had always been this way.

"I did," he replied. "But I didn't drink it."

Pausing in the threshold of the stairs, I faced him with a frown. "And why not? I spent a pretty penny for that wine. It nearly cost me 5000 pounds."

"First of all, I know you stole it, and second, I remember what happened to the last person you bought wine for. The doctors are still mystified by how she died."

"Elizabeth, right? I'd forgotten about her." I laughed, "If you must know, I didn't poison the wine. It's safe to drink. If I wanted to kill you I'd do it with a garrote or something equally violent."

"What a surprise, my trust in you still isn't there," he scoffed. "What poor sap *did* you steal it from?"

"No one, Matt, I'm still out 5000 pounds," I turned to the first stair.

"Where did your money go? Because I know you didn't buy a bottle of merlot with it," he called after me.

I reached the first landing between the fiftieth and forty-ninth floor and faced Matt again. My grin pinched my cheeks as I gestured shamelessly to my new outfit.

"I'm wearing it, love."

Chapter Six

I stepped out of the stairwell of the Shard and veered right. Frigid air blasted downward from the vents in the ceilings and ruffled my hair as I walked along the blandly decorated hallway. White walls and LED lights gave the entire place an aura of distinct, cold power. Rourke and Garrett's offices were the only ones on the forty-third story, rarely visited by anyone except myself. They, like me, preferred to work alone and uninterrupted.

I passed an open room humming with computers—*London Advertisement's* main control base and Garrett's beloved technical empire.

The hacker sat before a huge monitor, scrolling down a page of text, completely absorbed in his work. Underneath a mop of tousled brown hair, Garrett's grey eyes were bloodshot and rimmed by dark circles. Scattered across his desk were the telltale empty cans of energy drinks that had failed. I leaned against the doorframe and cleared my throat. He glanced up at the sound.

"I got your note," I said, holding up the file folder. From under a mound of paper, important looking contracts, and more cans of energy drinks, he produced a plastic box containing two bullets and their casings.

"And I got your evidence."

"Is Tyrone's death cleaned up?"

"Immaculately," he said, standing up to walk across his office floor. He dwarfed me immediately, with his tall frame and broad shoulders. While I stood five foot eight in my high-heeled boots, the hacker still towered over me. His strong jaw and deep eyes gave him a mysterious but caring appearance, aided by his easy-going nature.

All were façades when it came to his work. Even I couldn't measure up to his dedication and ice-cold heart where Rourke's assignments were concerned. Garrett's steady personality balanced my fiery temper. While I did the fieldwork, he stayed behind his computer making sure everything went according to plan. Not for the first time was I grateful that we were on the same team. Though he was as calm as an old cow pony, I knew he could explode once his fuse had been spent. Yet another reason Rourke had been wise to pair us together. My act first and ask questions later mentality balanced out with Garrett's along for the ride attitude.

I arched an eyebrow as he opened a cabinet drawer and dumped the box inside with a clank. "But next time you decide to camp out on the Eiffel Tower and drink wine, do it out of view of a dozen video cameras. I've spent all morning hacking into the Police Nationale and Ministry of the Interior. I'm very good at what I do, but don't plan on frequenting the City of Lights anytime soon."

"Oh darn, I was planning on building a summer home there." I tsked, hands on my hips.

Garrett grunted, walking back to his desk and plopping down in his chair. He stretched out his arm and swept half a dozen cans of Redbull into a metal trashcan.

"I see you're wearing the bonus Rourke gave you for Giselle's assignment."

"Do you like it?" I twirled for his benefit, the billowing fabric of my slacks floating out from my legs.

"You're one step away from looking like a hooker."

"After growing up in drug rings and CEO offices, you would know," I replied, sticking my tongue out at him as I flounced out of his office.

Down the hall, I came to Rourke's door. I knocked on it and pushed through. A rustling of papers welcomed my arrival, followed quickly by my employer's silken voice.

"Quinn, love, what a pleasant surprise." Rourke—dark haired, British, and as intense as the day is long—stood up from his leather armchair. He elegantly closed the book he was reading and set it beside a still steaming cup of tea. A bowl of pomegranate seeds rested nearby. One of the master assassin's favorite snacks.

"Rourke," I purred, coming to a halt in the middle of the floor to let my eyes take in his presence. The overhead lights shone off the gel styling his black hair. In the five years I'd known him, I had never seen one hair out of place nor heard him speak one word he didn't mean. His utter control and calculation brought purpose to my life.

Shakespeare was right. The prince of darkness is a gentleman.

"To what do I owe this honor?" He perched on the arm of the chair and folded his hands. I held up the file, and he lifted thick eyebrows, pursing his lips in a smile. A small piece of lint clung to his pant leg, untidying his appearance on further inspection. Mischief flashed in his dark eyes as he looked me over in return for my own silent examination.

Unlike other men when they looked at me, the master assassin's attention was special. I straightened, preening.

"Ah yes, your next assignment." He adjusted the onyx cufflink on his right wrist.

I walked closer, tossing the file onto his clean desk.

"You could have just called me personally. We don't have to go through Garrett or Matt to discuss my assignments," I said, earning another long look from him.

"It's easier to have a middle man in these dealings, Quinn. With the advertising company, keeping the gossip to a minimum is a must."

"But?" I pressed, noticing the familiar expression of withheld information in his eyes.

Rourke chuckled lightly, reaching out to take my hand. "But I don't need a middle man to tell you how pleased I was with Giselle and Tyrone. I couldn't have killed them better myself." He squeezed my fingers in his.

"You know flattery doesn't work on me."

"Says the woman who would kill her own mother for chocolate and a fast car."

I practically bloomed when he winked.

"How did your trip to Afghanistan go?" I asked, changing the subject easily.

The master assassin let go of my hand and rolled his shoulders tiredly. "The International Free Militia gains new members daily, but they are still outnumbered on the scale of worldwide war. We have to keep eliminating the enemies to their cause or all of our hard work will be in vain."

"Which I'm guessing is what my next assignment is about," I said.

"Smart girl." Rourke reached behind him to pick up another folder from his desk. "This assignment is *extremely* important, as I'm sure you know."

He offered me the file and gestured for me to open it. I complied and stared at a picture of a rough-looking man with a huge scar running across his forearm. A scar, judging from the size and shape, only possible from a violent life in the ranks of the International Free Militia.

Interesting. It's been a while since I killed a deserter from the radical terrorist sect.

"Meet Navid Maleate," Rourke began. "He's grown up in the IFM, rising in rank to that of general. But he's a weak piece in our armor. Promised protection and reward from the FBI, Maleate deserted and fled Pakistan to take refuge right here in the United Kingdom." His eyes flashed with anger as he spoke. "We've put a large bounty on his head, but the FBI is protecting Maleate until one of their agents can meet with him. He has scheduled a meeting between himself and a third party to take place in a couple of days. I want you to be present at the meeting to make sure neither man makes it out alive."

"Any specific method?"

Neither of us had room for stupid or useless conversation. I never asked what the targets had done or why it was necessary to kill them. Rourke always had a reason.

He ran his fingers thoughtfully over his chin. "Whatever you feel like, just so long as investigation cannot trace leads back to me."

"The normal way, then?" I smiled.

"My little miracle. My perfect weapon." Rourke stood and laid a hand on my shoulder. "Quinn, you amaze me. It was a gift of fate that led me to you."

I bowed my head and closed the file folder. "Making you proud is the least I can do, since you killed me so that the Dragonfly might live."

"You shouldn't be promoting murder." His sensuous mouth turned upward into a lazy grin.

"We all have our flaws," I replied, spinning slowly on my heel to face the door. "I'll talk to Garrett and deal with Maleate as soon as I can."

"Quinn?"

"Yes?" I turned back to face him, eyebrows arched in silent question.

"I brought you back something from Afghanistan." He crossed the room to his wall safe and placed his hand on the fingerprint lock. "Our discussion the other day gave me the idea to give you this."

A gift? My pulse accelerated as he opened the door and retrieved a small box from inside.

Rourke carried it back to me and his gaze flickered slyly as he offered me the box. "A special reward for your devoted service, like always."

I hesitated before accepting the gift. Rourke looked on, expressionless, as I eased the lid off. At first I didn't know what I was looking at. Nestled in a padding of grey fabric lay a sparkling chain of gold, and in place of a pendant was a bullet.

"What's this?" I asked, lifting the chain and bullet out into the light. While Rourke tended to favor me with gifts after assignments, this was something I hadn't expected.

Stepping behind me, he took the necklace from my hands and clasped it around my neck. The bullet pressed against my sternum, hidden beneath my shirt.

"A relic," Rourke said. "Something I thought you might like, considering it was one of the bullets from your sniper's rifle."

"My rifle?" I gaped, astonished that the master assassin could be so sentimental. "How the hell did you find it?"

"Your old ally or the bullet?" He chuckled, perching on the edge of his desk.

I shrugged. "Either. The last time I saw anything from my past life it was smoldering in the aftermath of Jason's C-4."

"I have my ways." He smiled, a cold expression on his handsome face.

I pulled the bullet out from underneath my shirt, fingers exploring the shape of the object. The metal was warm to my touch, having absorbed the heat of my skin. He had to have a reason for the gift. Rourke always had a reason; he never did anything out of randomness. The trick was figuring out the reason before it had a chance to kill you.

"Take Maleate down any way you want to," My mentor said, voice low and deadly, changing the subject abruptly.

"I will," I said, stepping backward.

"You have a fortnight to complete the assignment." He glanced out his window, his long fingers tapping out a beat on his desk. "I know you won't disappoint me."

"Have I ever?" I retorted, backing for the door as his silent dismissal pushed me into action.

In the hallway, I felt my grin curl the corners of my lips. Maleate wouldn't know what hit him until it was too late.

Garrett stepped out of his office as I passed, walking toward the stairs. He fell into step at my side, typing a few notes on his cell phone before pocketing it.

"How did the briefing go?" he asked.

"I guess you'll find out when I call you to discuss Navid Maleate and the best way to put him down," I replied, not wanting to show him the bullet around my neck.

We entered the stairwell and began to climb the floors between our separate destinations. Garrett's phone chirped to signal a new message. Walking side by side with me, he unlocked the device and hummed as he read the text bubble.

"Good news?"

"Very. Our new ear-comms just arrived at my house." He smiled at me.

"You have your mailman text you when he delivers your mail?" I frowned, my brow furrowing as we turned a corner and started up more steps.

Garrett chuckled. "It's worse than that I'm afraid. I placed a camera on the front porch so that I can see who comes by. It sends a message to me if someone rings the doorbell." He showed me his cell phone so that I could read the message. It read: Mailman. 4:13 PM. One package delivered.

"You really need to get yourself a hobby."

We reached the tenth floor and exited the stairwell for the hallway.

"I already have one. I babysit assassins for a living." He looked pointedly at me as we paused, facing each other.

I sighed, rolling my eyes skyward.

"I don't need you to watch my back, Garrett. I'm a big girl." Hitching the box higher, I placed my free hand on my hip. "Have fun playing with your technology. I have an assignment to prepare for."

"Quinn, you should know something about Navid Maleate before we get started," the hacker said as I turned away. "He's not going to be easy to kill. There's more to his story than meets the eye."

"Worry about your job, Garrett, and I'll worry about mine," I snapped in reply.

Chapter Seven

London, England – October 17th

In my opinion, there was nothing in the entire world like the atmosphere a British pub offered to its wayward visitors. Even before one entered, the building stood welcoming and enticing.

I stepped out of my Range Rover across the street from the same pub I had visited three times in the last seventy-two hours. Leaning against the hood, I took a deep breath of the crisp autumn air. Clouds hung heavily over the city, blocking from view any building over twenty stories and casting everything else into grey shadow. Fried food and gasoline mingled together to create a chaotic symphony of smells. The traffic passing me on the street between my vehicle and the pub was slow and sluggish under the threat of a late afternoon rain. Exhaust swirled around the back tires of cabs and personal transportation.

Taking another breath, I shouldered my bag and started across the street. The pub loomed closer, its dark windows reflecting the low clouds hanging above. I pushed the door open and stepped over the threshold to a rush of voices. Customers were scattered among the various tables and bar stools. I walked up to the bar and ordered fish and chips and a drink. The man behind the counter nodded, rang up the prices, and then accepted my money. After paying, I turned and located a table nearer the door than my previous visits.

I had one more day to scout out the location of the impending assignment before it had to be carried

61

out. And this visit was all about an exit strategy. Because once my targets were dead, I wanted to be in Oxford before anyone even noticed.

The digital clock on my phone read 7:15 as I sat down and dumped my bag onto the chair beside me. In total, there were sixteen other customers arranged at the bar or the surrounding tables. A small amount compared to what would walk in after 8:00 o'clock and continue until Callooh Callay closed.

On my first visit to the pub, I'd sat in the far back of the room and marked every exit and video camera. I had watched the flow of people in and out of the café and decided the best way to complete my assignment would come down to a matter of patience. Navid Maleate and his contact from FBI wouldn't stay out in the open long. In fact, I suspected they would duck out back for some privacy. If they did, it would give me the perfect opportunity to follow, and then maneuvering the hassles of witnesses and blocked escape routes wouldn't be a problem.

My second visit had outlined the general number of people present in the early to late afternoon hours. I painstakingly recorded the actions of the staff and which tables were the easiest to move around in haste. The one thing that never ceased to amaze me about waiters was their acute knowledge of how to monopolize their time. Watching two particular waiters, I memorized the paths they took through the labyrinth of tables. If the need to evacuate the room quickly arose, I would be ready.

In addition to playing the numbers game, I also used my visits to learn just how fast police or emergency vehicles could arrive on the scene.

Fifteen minutes, plenty of time to do the deed and then get free.

The only calculation I didn't have was whether Navid or his contact would arrive alone. The FBI wasn't known for sending one of their own out into danger unarmed and without backup.

"The fish and chips, miss," a server announced, whisking the steaming plate in front of my nose to settle on the wooden table.

Despite myself, I smiled at the two large pieces of fried fish and thick chips nestled beside them on a sheet of newspaper.

Without another word, the server turned on his heel and swooped toward the next table, depositing more food and drinks.

While I ate I let my gaze wander around the room, planning and playing out each exit strategy from worst case to best. It came down to the question of whether Navid would walk through to the back alleyway or remain inside. Whichever he chose, I had three plans each that would allow me to get away home free.

The clock ticked onward as I brought out a small notebook and started scribbling down the details of the pub once again.

Day Three: Twelve tables occupied.

Absently, I picked up a chip and stuffed it into my mouth. The malt vinegar's tang blossomed across my tongue as I chewed, making my mouth water hungrily. I glanced up at the bar and counted the number of people around it.

Average twenty people per hour after 7:00 o'clock.

Two men behind the bar and three serving.

Satisfied, I closed the book and set it down beside my plate. I nibbled on a piece of the fried fish, lost in thought, when someone spoke.

"They told me that the English can't cook burgers like Americans, and unfortunately I didn't believe them."

I jerked at the voice so close to my right side. The

young man who was seated at the table directly next to mine smiled, dimples appearing underneath startling green eyes.

"Please tell me that's better than what I'm having." He pointed to my plate, accent distinctly American. There was a half-eaten hamburger and basket of chips smothered in ketchup at his table. I was too shocked to reply at once, too busy staring.

"I uhh... I'm sure it is," I finally stammered.

Nodding as if in agreement, he pushed his disappointing meal aside and gave me an apologetic smile. "Sorry, I didn't mean to startle you. I just thought I recognized you from one of the universities here. Apparently, I've been visiting too many recently trying to decide on an art school."

"It's been a while since anyone mistook me for a student at university," I said, hesitating before taking his hand.

He laughed, the action bringing more life into his stunning gaze. "Again, I'm sorry. I've been here about two weeks and still don't know my way around the culture or people."

That would explain the nervous tenor of his voice.

"Don't worry, you'll get the hang of it soon." I went to turn back to my own table when he spoke again.

"I'm just visiting for a couple of months before I go back to Alabama and make the decision of which college to attend. Before I came here I thought it would be an easy choice, but now I'm even more undecided."

I forced a half smile, staring at him in building annoyance. Couldn't he see that I was busy?

"Do you come here a lot?" He fiddled with a sketchbook lying flat on his table.

"No."

"You've been here the last couple of days, right?

Sitting over there." He pointed to the exact tables I had occupied the two previous days. My spine stiffened. He couldn't be older than eighteen. Surely he wasn't some kind of spy or agent.

"You have a wonderful memory." I almost choked on the words.

The young man laughed, picking up the sketchbook and offering it to me. "I'm an artist. I'm afraid it's an occupational hazard."

The many pages bearing drawings and sketches held the familiar faces I had seen in the pub, though I'd memorized their faces for an entirely different reason than his. Three pages bore pictures in pen and pencil of me. I couldn't stop myself from recoiling.

"I'm sorry," the young man said. "I know I should ask permission, but people are usually gone before I can finish a piece. And besides, I don't do anything with the pieces when I'm done. I just use the chance to practice."

I made myself swallow the bile in my throat, trying desperately to calm down. The three pieces he had drawn were of me, there was no mistaking that. My facial features were undeniable.

How had he managed to complete two entire pieces of art and start on a third without me noticing?

"I hope I haven't made you angry." He cleared his throat, looking at me worriedly.

"No," I managed to reply, "I'm just surprised that I didn't notice you doing it."

Smiling in relief, he put the sketchbook away and turned to face me in his chair.

His dark curly hair fell over his forehead as he handed me a napkin scribbled over with a line of text. "That's my email address. You can shoot me a message anytime, and I'll send you the pictures when I'm done with the third one. It's the least I can do."

No, it's not. The least you can do is hand over the

damn book before you get hurt.

"Uhh... thank you." I didn't know how to process the information he had given me. For three days straight I'd failed to notice someone drawing my picture. Three entire days that someone had forever marked me down in history. Garrett would have a heyday with my mistake. I would never hear the end of it if I told him.

"I really hope I didn't offend you," he pressed again.

Apparently, I had dropped off into silence. Meeting his gaze, I shook my head. "Not at all," I lied, reading the name on the napkin, "Nathan Holmes."

"And you are?" He lifted a pencil to write my answer down on the latest drawing he was making in my image.

Damn.

"Isla"—I grasped for one of my aliases—"Isla Taylor."

He scribbled it down on the paper with a nod. "Perfect. Thank you."

"No, thank you," I mumbled, grabbing my bag and getting to my feet as if in a trance. It was time to leave—and possibly rethink my entire plan.

<>

The Shard, London – October 18th

"You don't have time to make other plans!" Garrett shouted at me, voice bellowing throughout his office. "Navid's going to be at the pub in two hours, Quinn. This is a now-or-never chance. If we miss it, the FBI has the secrets of the IFM. Do you want that to happen on your watch?"

"I'm just saying that the location is terrible. I think we'll have better success if we wait." I fidgeted, looking anywhere but directly at him. He didn't know about the young man who drew portraits. Nor was he likely to hear it from me, but I had to try all the same to push for another assignment date.

"Quinn," Garrett muttered tiredly, "Rourke just left for Afghanistan. He's going to tell the IFM that they have nothing to worry about. Navid's supposed to be dead by the time he lands in Kabul. That's only going to happen if you stop this nonsense. What's gotten into you? You seem spooked."

I am spooked. Some American kid spied on me and I didn't even notice.

"Are you listening to me?" Garrett snapped to get my attention, and I growled at him. A warning.

"Fine." I turned for the door. "We'll do it your way, but if something goes wrong it's on your head."

"When has anything ever gone wrong when we're at the helm?" he called after me.

Pausing at the door, I glanced back at him. "Come to think of it, never."

"See? Everything's going to be fine."

◇

Callooh Callay Pub – October 18th

It was raining when I parked in the lot opposite the pub. Shutting off the engine stopped my windshield wipers mid-beat, so I sat in the vehicle and strained to see the street through the waves of raindrops. I dug through my purse until I found the new ear-comms Garrett had ordered. Adjusting it inside of my ear, I heard it beep and then the hacker's voice come over the connection.

"I just tagged Navid on Curtain Road, Quinn," he announced.

Not for the first time did I wonder if the hacker

continued talking even if I left my ear-comm off.

"He's walking fast. ETA less than ten minutes."

"I'll be inside before he arrives," I replied, opening my door and stepping out into the rain. Shrugging my coat collar up against my neck, I hurried across the street and ducked into the pub.

Fewer people occupied the tables. The noise level was lower, either due to smaller numbers or the storm brewing outside. I ordered something to drink but didn't touch it when a server dropped it off at my table. My fourth and final visit to the pub was entirely for business. No more scouting. No more planning.

This is the performance now.

"I have control of the cameras," Garrett said suddenly.

I ignored him, fiddling with the pair of thin black gloves I was wearing. None of the other customers looked familiar—a different group since it was slightly earlier in the evening. And Nathan with his sketchbook and pencils was nowhere to be seen, thankfully.

"Navid's coming in now."

I glanced sideways in the direction of the front door as a man entered, burrowed into his coat. Water dripped off of him, pooling at his feet as he stood in the doorway for several moments longer than someone might normally hesitate. His gaze roamed the room, searching. I saw him settle on a man in the far back corner and start toward him.

"He's here," I whispered. "Navid's making contact with a man now."

"The FBI agent no doubt."

In the far corner to my left, I saw the video camera swivel and smiled faintly. Garrett was using his own *eyes* to scout out my targets.

Navid Maleate was slumped in his chair, leaning close to his companion, expression strained. He kept glancing over his shoulder at the door as if expecting someone to walk in and find him at any moment. The agent, however, either didn't notice or didn't care that they were practically out in the open. I couldn't hear what they were saying, but I got the gist of it reading their body language. Navid was worried and angry, and his companion was trying to reassure him. I flipped open the menu on my table and casually browsed through it, keeping watch on the two men.

"There are too many witnesses inside, Quinn," Garrett said. "You're going to have to take this outside."

"Tell me something I don't know," I muttered under my breath. My earlier estimate that an outside takedown would allow for the easiest hit and run still held true. But how did I get the two men to leave the comfort of a warm pub for a rain-sodden alleyway? That was something I hadn't planned for efficiently.

Navid and the agent were both soaked through, heads bent close together as their gestures grew faster and more urgent. Time was running out and I had no idea how to move them into the back alleyway.

"I can trigger a fire alarm," Garrett suggested.

"That's a rubbish idea." I snorted. "They'll charge out the front door."

"Then you'd better think of something, because they look about ready to blow," he retorted.

I turned back to watch my targets, when they suddenly both stood up. The agent placed a hand on Navid's shoulder, guiding him toward the back door. A devilish grin curled my lips. Problem solved.

"You're in the clear," Garrett relayed. "Give 'em hell."

I pushed back from my table, shouldered my bag, and followed the pair through the pub to where a narrow door marked the back exit. I paused by the toilets to dig out a cigarette pack and lighter from my pocket. To anyone looking, I was a desperate addict and most certainly *not* following the two men before me.

By the time I exited the building, Navid and his companion were already at the end of the alleyway, the street just a few feet beyond them. I ground my teeth together, stepping aside to squint up at the roof. The walls were too bare to allow for an easy climb where a sniper might have an advantage.

The rain had stopped, leaving heavy fog over the city and keeping any potential witnesses inside. My targets stood next to the dumpsters, Navid practically hopping from foot to foot, his expression anxious and pained. The two men huddled together, bowing their heads as they continued speaking in hurried, wild gestures. I was still too far away to make out their conversation, but judging by Navid's pale complexion I knew he was scared.

And you should be.

I backed up a few paces, focusing on the cigarette in my hand. Lighting up, I stepped into view of the two men and exhaled a cloud of smoke. The buildings on either side of me blocked us from view. Only the road presented a problem, should anyone happen to glance our way.

Navid looked over at me, eyes worried. I gave a curt nod in return, looking away to take another draw of my cigarette. As expected, my target and his companion wrote me off immediately as nonthreatening. I smirked, lips pursing around the object between them.

Using the guise of a woman desperate for a fix, I edged closer to the men, nudging bits of trash that had fallen out of the dumpsters with the toe of my boot. The closer I strayed, the more I could make out what they were saying. Navid was terrified, not just scared, and the other man was indeed trying to calm him down. But in vain.

While the agent was trying to get him to talk about the IFM, Navid had clammed up. He had to know about the bounty on his head. Rourke wasn't a merciful man when it came to betrayal, and neither were the terrorists. The agent, however, seemed at ease in the situation. Oddly so.

I crept closer to my targets, still drawing on my light. The two remained deep in conversation, oblivious to my presence as their tones lifted. Maleate cursed in Urdu and shoved his companion in the chest. Cigarette poised at my lips, I watched the two launch into a shouting match. They didn't even glance at me until I drew within five feet, the dumpsters to my right and rear wall of the pub to my left. I had two escape options once the deed was done. One, a quick dash into the traffic of the street. And two, reentering the pub. I could reappear inside as if nothing had happened and waltz out the front door unhindered.

It's time.

I cleared my throat and both men whirled on me, surprise on their faces. The agent squinted at me, eyes narrowing, but Navid just glared. I took a final draw on my cigarette before flicking it away.

"Do either of you know where I can buy a box of lights?" An innocent question meant to relax both men.

"Try the shop on the corner, lady," Navid snapped, accent thick. Annoyance written on his face, he turned back to his companion.

I smirked to myself. *Cocky, arrogant, fool.*

I dropped my bag, bending over as if to tie my shoe. Navid again distracted the agent as I palmed the two tactical knives from inside my boots. I twirled them in my fingers, baring the sharp blades. A smirk curled the corners of my lips as I lunged.

Neither man could react as I crossed the distance

between us and stabbed through Navid's back, piercing his heart.

The agent didn't even get a chance to blink as I wrenched the blades free and sidestepped. Navid's body thudded when it hit the pavement between us. I pressed ahead, setting one blade at the agent's throat and the other at his abdomen.

"What deal did you make with him?" I hissed, pinning him against the wall of the pub.

His eyes widened and his chest heaved for precious oxygen as my blade to his throat left a shallow cut. Blood trickled down to his collarbone as he stared at me.

"What deal did you make with Navid?" I pressed my blade harder, a thin line of blood appearing along his neck.

"W-Who are you?" He gurgled.

"You know who I am," I purred, watching the flicker of recognition in his expression. I was the stuff of legendary nightmares, thanks to the one assignment that still haunted me at night.

At least it hadn't been in vain.

"What was Navid planning on telling you? What kind of information did he share?" I kept my tone cold.

His body trembled as I pressed the blade to his stomach hard enough to draw blood. Gritting his teeth, he closed his eyes, steeling himself against the pain as I tilted the weapon at his throat deeper.

"I—I promised him safety." He swallowed against the pressure at his windpipe. "I promised him safety if he told us—told us... "

"What information did he give you?"

"Nothing!" He gasped, squirming for escape.

In a single strike, I slipped my knife upward between the fourth and fifth rib. The man's eyes flared in agony.

I twisted the weapon, leaning close so my lips brushed his neck as I spoke next. "I'm only going to ask this once more," I whispered. "What did Navid tell you?"

He coughed, blood staining his teeth.

Choose your next moments very carefully. You don't have many left.

"Nothing." He swallowed. "I swear it. He told me nothing, you have to believe me." A sob made his body tremble in my grasp. "Navid wouldn't tell me anything, not until I got him to safety."

Relief sprang into his eyes as I pulled the blade free of his chest. He doubled over, blood staining his hands, craning his neck to stare up at me. Duty, regret, and hope were so alive in his gaze that they were blinding lights glaring back at me. He wasn't lying. Navid Maleate had been too smart to give up valuable information before his own life was guaranteed.

Crossing my weapons before me, I sliced two lines across the agent's throat. The man's face froze in shock as he toppled to the side, revealing a young man framed in the alleyway. My heart stopped in my chest.

The American from inside the pub.

Nathan?

Face the color of ash and green eyes as wide as goose eggs, the young man staggered back a step as he stared in horror at the two bodies at my feet. The sketchbook in his hand crashed to the ground. My pulse thundered through my veins as his lips parted, his expression terrified.

"Isla?" His voice broke.

No, no, no, this can't be happening.

"Hold it right there. Hands where we can see 'em." Half a dozen FBI agents in full SWAT gear burst out of hiding at the mouth of the alleyway.

What the hell?

"Drop the weapon." An agent leveled a Glock 22

at my chest as the others moved to encircle me.

Nathan whirled to face the agents, hands going sky-high immediately. I tightened my grip on my knives.

My escape routes were both cut off, one blocked by six agents armed to the teeth with automatic rifles capable of firing thirty rounds in five seconds, the other by a witness. A witness who had three drawings of my face.

Dammit, Garrett. You said I was in the clear.

There were no words to describe my rush of fury. I was going to punch the hacker into kingdom come when I got back to *London Advertising*.

"Drop the weapon," the agent said again, face hidden behind a black visor and helmet.

I didn't budge—didn't breathe.

No wonder the FBI agent had seemed so calm while talking to Navid. He had backup, and not just any backup, he had men able to arrest Navid for not cooperating. Or more importantly, who could kill the deserter without much of a fuss and with just a limited paper trail.

"Young man, walk forward slowly," the agent instructed, speaking to Nathan. As the artist took his first tentative step toward the agents, I realized that I had a split second of opportunity to act.

Here's to improvising.

Lunging forward, I wrapped my left arm around Nathan's torso and pressed my blade to his chin.

"One more step and I'll kill him." I jerked Nathan against me.

He froze, his heart pounding against my arm. I'd never let a witness survive his first look, but right now he was more valuable to me alive.

The agents stopped, the closest man lifting his hand in a signal for his men to wait. I could feel his hard eyes on me through the tinted visor of his helmet.

He gauged the situation, obviously trying to figure out if my arrest was worth the casualty of my hostage.

Time to go.

With a flick of my wrist, I sent the knife in my right hand arcing up to embed into a gas pipe above the agents. It hissed and fizzed, and with a *pop* the pipe opened to spew gas into the midst of them. They made the mistake of looking up.

After scooping up the sketchbook, I bolted for the street, dragging my hostage along. Behind us someone shouted, followed by a gunshot, the bullet barely missing my head.

Bollocks, I hate running away from a crime scene.

I rounded the side of the building and sprinted for my car. Another gunshot. I ducked, pulling Nathan's head down. He tripped on the curb and I stumbled, hoisting him back upright roughly.

"L—let go of me!" He tried to shove away, but the knife I held against his throat weakened the movement. I yanked him ahead, seeing my car.

Reaching the vehicle, I threw open the door and dove inside, pulling the young man after me. The agents wouldn't shoot and risk killing him. At least I hoped his life was worth more than that, but just in case it wasn't, I had other plans. I tore open the glove compartment and removed an explosive device the size of my palm. Jason had designed it personally, claiming it was small, yet potent. We'd find out. The agents were twenty feet away and closing.

Switching the bomb's timer to ten seconds, I sent it sailing into their midst. They lunged in all directions as the bomb hit the street and rolled.

Crawling into the driver's seat, I *felt* more than saw the bomb explode. The brightness of the blast reflected on the windows as I cranked the key and stomped on the gas. Car brakes screamed and horns blared as we launched forward like a rocket ship and bounced out into the traffic.

With a squeal of tires finding purchase on the asphalt, I yanked the steering wheel to the right. My hostage slid across the passenger seat, clutching the door, as the cars around me slammed on their brakes and swerved out of the way. I punched the gas pedal harder and we raced past them.

Two patrol cars turned onto the road ahead of me, lights flashing and sirens shrieking. Nathan cried out as I pulled a U-turn so hard we came up on two wheels. He was thrown all over the place again. I straightened the wheel and floored the gas of my Range Rover. We took off south.

In the rearview mirror, I saw another patrol car join the other two and come after me. Nathan was totally silent next to me, mouth hanging open. He seemed to be concentrating on staying in his seat. I was concentrating on accelerating as fast as I could.

Traffic was mercifully light, but the closer I got to any large road the more obstacles I would run across. Winding the car up to seventy miles an hour, I tightened my hands on the wheel until my knuckles turned white. I wove in and out of the traffic, going too fast to glance at my tail in the rearview mirror.

"How far back are they?" I asked my hostage.

He didn't respond. He was slack with shock and crushed into the corner of his seat, as far away from me as he could get. He stared through the windshield, right hand braced against the door. He had pale skin and long fingers—fingers stained from paint. An artist's fingers.

"How far back?" I asked again. The engine roared in my ears.

"You killed them," he said. "You just killed them."

"Answer the question," I snapped.

"You killed them."

"How far back are they?"

"Those men—the FBI... oh my... " Nathan trailed off, clutching his head as I wove through traffic, barely avoiding collisions on either side.

"Shut up," I shot back, focusing on keeping the Range Rover steady. "Just tell me how far back they are."

He stirred, turning around to look out the back window. "Hundred feet. One guy has a gun out the window."

Right on cue, I heard the pop of a handgun over the roar of car engines.

"Under your seat," I hissed.

"You should stop."

"Not a chance in hell," I yelled. "Look under your seat."

He turned again and fumbled, reaching under his seat to retrieve what he found hidden there. A Glock 19 slid out of its padded sleeve, ready for use. Shiny, black outer case, fully loaded. I took it from him and wound my window down. Shifting sideways, I made sure that my right shoulder was steadied against the door. An intersection loomed ahead as I glanced at the young man sitting next to me.

"You might want to get down," I said, slowing dramatically. He stared at me with wide, terrified eyes. "I'm serious. Get down if you don't want to go careening through the windshield."

He slid into the space between his seat and the glove compartment, arms wrapped over his head. A second later the rear window exploded. His cry of fear faded in my ears as I slowed down, watching through my rearview mirror as the patrol cars started catching up.

You're not going to like this next bit.

The intersection arrived in a blink of the eye even

after I had applied the brakes as much as I dared. Gun in my right hand, steering wheel in my left, I turned the car to the right.

The engine surged and tires screamed as I slammed her to a stop in the middle of the crossroads. Gun pointed out the open window, I fired twice into the windshield of the first patrol car. Blinded, it swerved to run into another vehicle. Another two bullets into the radiator of the second car and two into the front tires of the third stopped my tails dead in their tracks. I dropped the Glock into my lap, hit the automatic window button, and stomped on the gas. We barreled forward again. The young man said nothing, just slowly pushed back into his seat. The broken window made a strange moaning noise as the air sucked out of it.

"All right," I said. "Now we're good to go."

"Are you *insane*?" At first I didn't realize it was Garrett's voice in my ear-comm that had spoken.

I frowned, accelerating hard. I ignored him, hearing the whir of helicopter blades overhead and sirens behind. A quick glance in the rearview mirror showed six more patrol cars, one FBI force van, and a helicopter.

Dammit.

Garrett had been right about there being more to Maleate's story. The FBI weren't there to offer him safe passage. They were there to extract information and kill him. I had just gotten in the way and murdered one of their own.

My hostage yelped as I wove through traffic, clipping a minivan's side mirror. The speedometer showed ninety miles an hour. I clenched my jaw. My pursuers were catching up, red and blue lights flashing and sirens blaring. The ground troops weren't a concern—I had plenty of experience evading them— but the helicopter was a different story entirely. I was in no position to shoot one down.

This day just keeps getting better.

"What the hell are you doing?" Garrett shouted, static flavoring each word through our comms.

"I'm a little busy to chit-chat, Garrett." I swerved around a taxi with an inch to spare. The roar of engines droned out the sound of my thundering heartbeat.

"Dammit, Quinn, the entire Scotland Yard is on your tail—"

"Tell me something I don't know or hang up." I changed lanes to avoid rear-ending another taxi. Garrett sighed and his demeanor changed instantly—going into calm, rational, casualty-avoidance mode.

It's too late for that now, you clod. The damage is done.

"There's an exit ramp ten miles ahead. If you take it you can shoot across town and access a motorway out of London. But you have to lose the chopper first. Alleyways and side streets are your best bet with air support."

"I know that," I growled under my breath and zipped between two police cars closing in on both sides. My hostage looked greener than Yoda. "Talk me through this, Garrett."

"Steady," he said. "On my mark, take a sharp right."

I nodded, my mouth dry and hands sweaty on the steering wheel. This was worse than the United Nations incident—*much worse*. Nathan moaned, and I glanced over at him. I had never seen someone look so ill.

"Stop, please." Nathan clung to the car door, gasping.

I ignored him, gnawing on my bottom lip.

The traffic on the motorway cleared a convenient path for me as they pulled over for the police. Would it be enough? In a moment, I'd have a clear shot at an exit ramp.

Should I take it?

"Stop!" Nathan's tone pitched as he looked behind us. My speedometer read one hundred and five miles an hour. I gripped the steering wheel, fighting for control.

Bollocks.

"Don't even think about throwing up in my car," I warned. The cacophony of sirens and roaring engines around me escalated, droning out all else including my hostage.

"Turn now," Garrett's voice boomed inside of my ear. I yanked on the steering wheel, grating my vehicle against a Ford Fiesta as I bounced onto the off-ramp of the motorway. There was a shrill scream of brakes and then the sickening thunder of vehicles colliding behind me. I risked a look over my shoulder. The patrol cars closest on my tail lay in a pile of steel.

That'll hold them for a few minutes.

"Take a right up ahead and disappear into the first alleyway," Garrett said, his voice calming. "I'll talk you through the city."

I swallowed hard and ran through a red light, ignoring honks of protest

"Ahead make a left and hang back, there's another patrol car heading north toward you."

I complied and heard the sirens pass. "Okay, now what?"

"It's a straight shot except for that helicopter. Change vehicles and get the hell out of there."

"Change vehicles?" I glared at my car speaker. "Do you know how much this car cost me?"

"Do it. You don't have a choice." Arguing with him was futile when he used that tone. I cursed under my breath and pulled into another alley beside an SUV, the driver just getting out from behind the wheel. It would have to do.

I screeched my Range Rover to a halt and shouldered open my door. Grabbing my bag, I ran out and around the back of the vehicle and yanked the passenger door open. I jerked my hostage out of his seat and threw him to the ground at the feet of the astonished driver, where he promptly threw up.

At least it wasn't in the car.

The driver opened her mouth, but I grabbed her right wrist and opposite shoulder, slamming her head against a parking meter. I let her fall to the ground, unconscious. After retrieving the woman's keys, I grabbed Nathan by the arm and shoved him into the SUV.

"Try not to throw up in here too," I growled, sliding behind the wheel.

He groaned, eyes wide as they met mine through the rearview mirror.

"Are you going to kill me?" he whispered.

"Is this one of those times you want me to lie to protect your delicate emotions?" I retorted, throwing the SUV into reverse and pulling out of the alleyway. The vehicle swap had taken a total of fifty-two seconds.

I must be getting old.

"Keep heading west for another couple of hours before switching vehicles and doubling back. It'll confuse your tails." Garrett's voice came on over my cell phone as I headed toward the motorway on-ramp in the distance.

"There are seventeen ways that could have gone better," I spat, knuckles whitening as I gripped the steering wheel. "Seriously, I'm counting them right now."

"But you made it."

I rolled my eyes, glancing at my hostage where he held his sketchbook in pale hands. "Yes, I made it.

And lucky you, I've got some dental work with your name on it. When I get back, we're hooking up so that I can give it to you."

Chapter Eight

"W—what happened?" My hostage's voice came out groggy and slurred as he sat upright in the passenger seat of the stolen SUV. I glanced over at him, taking my eyes off of the road as he squinted in confusion at his surroundings.

Four hours had passed since I'd let Navid's dead body hit the pavement outside of Callooh Callay. Four hours in which I had been jumped by FBI agents and forced to flee with the young artist in tow. It was safe to say they were four of the worst hours of my life.

"Where am I?" His brow furrowed.

I took a deep breath. The time had passed too quickly to pause and dump his body. My training didn't allow for a break in the action. First and foremost was getting away; any other loose ends came when I was safe. Nathan was just going to have to tag along until it was clear for me to kill him.

"What happened?" he asked again, turning to squint at me.

I licked my lips, forcing them into a humorless smile.

"Good morning, sleeping beauty," I said.

His eyes narrowed into a frown.

"You're the person from the pub... " He rubbed his head and refocused on me. "You killed those two men... the FBI... *the FBI...* "

The realization hit him like a freight train and his face paled to porcelain. His green eyes bulged in fear as he lurched backwards into his seat, getting as far

83

away from me as possible. He went for the lock on the door, but I already had the child safety on. He wasn't going anywhere.

"One and the same," I replied. "Nice to meet you."

"What am I doing in your car?"

I chuckled and changed lanes, carefully plotting my course through traffic. "I kidnapped you."

His eyes widened further, his skin turning to ash—he looked white as death.

And I would know.

I skirted around a cab to take an exit off of the motorway. Garrett had told me to create such an erratic course back to *London Advertising* that no one—not even he—would be able to follow it. So far, I was definitely living up to my instructions. Leaving town only to come back was the perfect ploy—it was the last place anyone would look for me.

"Kidnapped?" Nathan's question made me hopeful that he had a concussion, perhaps even slight amnesia.

"Don't you remember?"

He fell silent, watching me with glazed eyes. His expression said everything his tongue failed to. He remembered everything. I inwardly groaned. Having a witness on my hands was the absolute last thing I needed after the FBI had tracked me down.

No thanks to you, Garrett.

After going unnoticed by the law for so long, hidden by Rourke and Garrett, it chilled me to think a government agency knew who I was and what I had done. Killing Navid and an FBI agent would launch me into the top wanted category. I was one small step away from tumbling off of the ledge to prison bars and the death penalty.

Again.

Shaking those thoughts from my mind, I

tightened my grip on the steering wheel. Thinking about it would only make my situation worse.

Rourke will handle the FBI, and I'll handle Nathan. This whole mess will blow over in a few hours.

"Your name isn't Isla Taylor is it?" My hostage's voice was deep and serious, reserved.

"No, it isn't," I said.

Glancing away from the road again, I caught my hostage's gaze. He swallowed hard, fidgeting.

"What is it?"

"Just behave and do exactly what I tell you, and we might both see tomorrow." I turned on the radio to signal the end of the conversation. The first strains of Halestorm's Mayhem boomed over the speakers and I cocooned myself into the shrieking melody.

◇

Nottingham, England – October 19th

The flashing red and blue lights behind me livened the mood in the car considerably. I glanced at the digital clock mounted in the SUV's dashboard. It read 5:58 a.m.

For miles I'd been driving without any unwanted distractions or unexpected developments, Navid and the FBI fading in the distance in my rearview mirror. Apparently, my luck had finally run dry. A quick glance at my speedometer showed I was correct.

Pulled over for speeding, what are the chances?

My chest tightened as the patrol car grew steadily closer. In his seat, my hostage perked up, worry and hope etching his brow.

Guiding my vehicle to the side of the road just past the off-ramp of the motorway, I glanced back through the car window. We were the only cars on the road.

Perfect odds for something dreadful to happen.

I pulled my gun out from under the seat and placed it discreetly at my side. "Don't say anything," I told Nathan in an even, steady voice.

He froze, eyes widening by the second as his chest expanded and fell rapidly. The patrolman got out of his car, ticket book in one hand, the other resting on his holstered gun.

"Whatever happens, remember I won't hesitate to kill."

If I played my cards right, and Nathan kept his mouth shut, I could get away from the law with just a ticket for speeding and no blood on my hands.

"You're not going to shoot him, are you?" Nathan's voice trembled.

I said nothing. The patrolman approached my door, his hand on the grip of his weapon. I rolled down my window.

"Ma'am, I need to see your driver's license." The patrolman's eyes looked straight into mine.

Compliantly, I reached into my bag and pulled out the required document—forged, courtesy of Garrett. Handing it to the man, I saw him give Nathan a long look. His eyes narrowed as he lowered them to study my ID.

My jaw clenched, catching the instinctive twitch of his fingers half a second before he snapped his head back up to stare at my passenger. I knew I was screwed. My cover was blown.

"Show me your hands!" The patrolman went for his gun.

I didn't flinch as he drew the weapon and pointed the barrel between my eyes. He swallowed hard, Adam's apple bobbing up and down. I lifted my hands for him to see, rolling my eyes.

So much for a bloodless speeding ticket.

"Step out of the vehicle," he said, taking a step back as I opened my door. He knew exactly who he was dealing with now.

Or so he thinks.

Nathan shook visibly as I slowly stepped out onto the pavement, hands still held aloft. Gun in the car, I faced the officer. He looked me over, double-checking that I matched the description of Nathan's kidnapper. Disgust appeared in his eyes, sending a stab of familiar pain through my soul.

"Face the vehicle." He kept his gun pointed at me.

I turned to face the SUV, smirking. Putting my hands behind my head, I allowed the man to come closer and force my torso over the hood. I grunted as he crushed my face against the warm metal. His hands searched every place possible to hide weapons before he straightened.

Foolish, foolish man. If he'd stopped to think he might have saved himself. I was an assassin, trained to conceal weapons from any kind of search or surveillance—trained not to need weapons at all. His pat down was insulting. Surely, he thought I was better than the common criminal.

As the officer reached for the radio clipped onto his uniform, the weight of his hand pressed against my back lessened, giving me a split second of opportunity.

I didn't hesitate to take it.

Twisting, I planted the heel of my boot on his instep and intercepted the hand reaching for his radio. I grabbed his wrist and spun under his arm, my shoulder connecting with his elbow. The satisfying crack of bones breaking followed.

My ears ringing with the man's scream of pain, I dropped to my knees and used his own weight to flip him onto the ground. The breath rushed out of his lungs and he gagged.

Nathan cried out from inside the car as I grabbed the officer by the collar, hauled him to his feet, and slammed him down on the hood of the SUV. Our positions reversed, he stared up at me, eyes wide, as I drew my last remaining knife from the padded sheath inside my boot. The one place he'd failed to search.

"No!" Nathan shouted, stumbling out of the car.

"Don't move," I told him, weapon poised over the officer's heart. He was fumbling at his hip, trying desperately to draw his gun, veins in his neck bulging with strain.

My hostage froze.

"Please don't hurt him." Nathan reached for me, the gesture pleading.

"I'm not going to hurt him." I smirked.

He practically sagged in relief.

"I'm going to kill him."

Nathan lunged for me as I slashed my knife downward. I saw the flash of a bullet out of the corner of my eye and felt the heat of it against my stomach. The officer's pistol slipped from his grasp, useless, as my knife hit his carotid artery. Blood spewed.

"No!" Nathan's scream was muffled in my ears as I released the officer.

Turning, I sunk back on one foot and clenched fingers into a tight fist. Nathan's head snapped backward as he ran right into my punch. His body reeled, sprawling on the asphalt at my feet. My lips twisted into a disgusted sneer as Nathan clutched his bruising cheek and tried to rise.

Stay down, kid.

Turning away, I cut the radio free of the dead officer's uniform and smiled at his still open eyes.

"You were just pulling me over for speeding, weren't you?" I whispered. "Just doing your job."

Sighing heavily, I ran the back of my hand across my forehead. Blood smeared against my skin. I retrieved my guns and bag from the SUV and deposited them into the patrol vehicle. Nathan knelt on the road next to the dead man, staring at some point on the lightening horizon. I picked up the officer's radio and handcuffs and stopped beside the young man as he turned to me, blood staining his hands.

"Don't do this." He sobbed, a tear running down his scraped cheek. "We can help him. We can *save* him."

I shook my head, pointing at the body. "Leave it, he's already gone."

Nathan's horrified expression etched itself into my memory as I seized his arm, snapped the cuffs on his wrists, and dragged him away. I shoved my hostage into the back of the patrol car. He sat, frozen in place, shock and confusion wrinkling his forehead.

"You're a monster," he gasped.

I look alive, but I'm just as dead inside as those I kill.

"Yes," I said, my knuckles white as I gripped the steering wheel. "Yes, I am."

He lay down on the seat, and the single glimpse I saw of his eyes haunted me. I had never seen such an expression as I did then in his emerald orbs.

Before starting the engine, I allowed myself a moment to take a deep breath. My hands tangled through my hair. Never in my five years of working for Rourke had I left such a bloody trail behind.

"You're bleeding." My hostage's voice startled me out of my thoughts.

I looked over at him and followed his line of sight to the stain of crimson that was leaking from my side. A sigh vibrated my lips as I turned the key in the ignition.

"I guess it's a rubbish time to mention that I've been shot," I murmured.

This has to end, and soon.

A few miles down the road, I managed to access the patrol car's computer. As far as the people running the station knew, the man I had killed was back on duty, safe and sound. They wouldn't know anything was wrong until hours later, when I was far, far away. The fingerprints left behind wouldn't be a problem. Thanks to Garrett, I didn't exist in any records. I was a phantom—a ghost.

Rourke sent me because I didn't exist.

I glanced back at my hostage, who had fallen into a silent stupor. He stared out the window, expression unreadable, green eyes dull. I didn't mind the silence. It gave me hope. The young man was going to be my bargaining chip the next time I ran headfirst into the law, and that was a good enough reason to keep him alive.

For now.

Chapter Nine

London, England – October 19th

Wisps of shadows danced around my parked car as I peered through the windshield at the hotel before me. The architecture was clean and colonial. A sign on the front of the building read *The Goring*.

"Are you sure it's clear?" I asked, gnawing on my bottom lip.

Nathan shifted in the seat beside me, avoiding eye contact.

"All clear. I just swept the building's security with a virus and killed their surveillance. If you go in now you'll be a ghost," Garrett replied, tone steady and reliable in my ear-comm.

Normally, I wouldn't have hesitated after hearing the hacker's seal of approval, but the day's events made me paranoid. While I trusted Garrett with my life and knew he was the best—Rourke wouldn't have hired him otherwise—the FBI team waiting with Navid had arrived completely out of the blue. There was no reason Garrett shouldn't have known about them in advance. Something he had said to me at *London Advertising* kept replaying in my head.

"Quinn, you should know something about Navid Maleate before we get started. He's not going to be easy to kill. There's more to his story than meets the eye."

How much had Garrett known? How much was mere coincidence?

I wasn't sure I wanted to know the answers.

A couple walked down the pavement in front of

us, clearly more interested in themselves than anything else around them.

"I'll take your word for it," I finally told Garrett. After driving all day and most of the evening with blood on my clothes and hands, not to mention my injury, I couldn't wait for a hot shower and long nap. Any suspicion I had developed would just have to wait. There was no sense in staying out in the open any longer than necessary. I still trusted Garrett not to lead me into a trap. The hotel would be the perfect place to lie low and deal with my hostage.

Nathan stirred from his trance-like state. Muttering, he sat up as I pulled the vehicle into the car park at the back of *The Goring* and killed the engine.

My entire body ached. The events of the day came crashing down on my shoulders as I grabbed my bag and made sure that my Glock 19 and corresponding magazines were still secure inside. I watched Nathan out of the corner of my eye. There was no emotion in his gaze.

"What are you going to do with me?" His voice, barely above a murmur, made me pause.

I sighed. I had a pounding headache and all I wanted was food and sleep. And the bullet wound to my side would need medical attention, even if it was just a graze.

"I'll deal with that tomorrow." I stepped out of the car, shouldering my bag with a wince. The night air reeked of car exhaust and rain as I took a breath.

"Your reservations are under the name of a Mrs. Gail Simmons," Garrett's voice said in my ear. "Matt should be arriving any second now to take up his guard on the roof. If anything happens, he'll alert you ahead of time."

Without responding, I removed my ear-comm and tossed it into the bottom of my bag. I knew Matt would keep me safe while on lookout, our friendship having begun long before Rourke ever entered our lives.

I escorted Nathan from the vehicle and walked toward the back door of the hotel. As we stepped up onto the pavement, I glimpsed a shadowy figure approaching quickly. My hostage tensed under my touch, but I merely waited as the man approached.

Right on time.

"From Garrett," Matt said, extending a black duffle bag. Camouflaged for hiding among shadows, the assassin wore a black jacket and hood that cast his face into darkness. Long sleeves and leather gloves covered every inch of his elaborate tattoos.

His gaze lowered to Nathan, but he didn't comment. "The room key is in the front pocket," he told me. "I will be on the roof all night."

He started to turn away, but paused. "Don't worry about a thing, Quinn."

Nathan's eyes flicked to me, hearing my name. I nodded to Matt, knowing his reassurance wasn't part of the speech Garrett had scripted for him to deliver. The small comfort he offered made my spirits lift ever so slightly. Steering my hostage into the hotel, I watched the assassin fade back into the night.

The fifth-floor suite Garrett had reserved had a lovely view of the city, which was lit by the haze of streetlamps and skyscrapers. Nathan didn't protest when I steered him into one of the bedrooms with an adjoining bathroom. After making sure that the windows would remain locked, I crossed back over the threshold and pushed a heavy cabinet in front of the door.

Hostage secured, I blinked in the dim lighting of the hotel accommodations. Exhaustion clung to my limbs like chains.

I closed the curtains with a snap, shutting off the only light source. I bumped into the TV stand as I headed for the second bedroom, duffel in hand. My clothes peeled away from my skin as each step disturbed the blood that had dried on them. How had my life gone from flawless control to chaos in just twenty-four hours?

Must be some kind of record.

After dropping my bag on the bed, I pulled the Glock 19 out and set it on the nightstand. I placed a switchblade under the pillows, taking comfort in the ritual, before laying a cigarette lighter next to the handgun.

Just in case. I don't want Russia to happen all over again.

I stripped down to my undergarments, pausing to examine my wound in the bathroom mirror. Thankfully the officer hadn't been a crack shot or the shallow graze could have been a more severe injury. I wet a washcloth and began the tedious process of cleaning the skin. The white material of the cloth was stained crimson by the time I was finished.

After pressing a thick bandage across my side, I crawled into bed with a heavy sigh. A shower could wait until morning. All I wanted was to close my eyes. Matt and Garrett were watching my back—I could afford a few hours of unworried rest.

<><

The clock read 2:27 a.m., and the thermostat a stifling 81 degrees despite my relentless tampering with it. Standing over the AC unit, I put both hands on my hips and swore.

Screw you, air conditioning.

Kicking the broken unit for good measure, I gave up on sleeping. I walked across the soft carpet to pull on the hotel's complimentary bathrobe. Its stark white color stood out in the darkness as I pillaged the mini bar underneath the television stand. Drinking had never been my vice of choice, and drinking alone was even worse.

Taking the entire stock of small alcoholic beverages with me, I stuffed my Glock into the front pocket of my robe and headed for the roof.

Matt looked up from behind the rifle he had swiveled to point at me upon my arrival. Pushing open the emergency hatch, I stepped out into the night as he lowered the weapon to rest beside him. I nodded a silent greeting and padded over to him with an easy smile.

"You should think twice about sneaking up on someone armed with a loaded M24," he said.

I shrugged indifferently. "I knew you'd recognize me fast enough not to pull the trigger."

"I thought Garrett told you to get some rest." He arched an eyebrow as I took a seat on the power box next to him.

I rolled my eyes, producing the two cups I had stashed in my other pocket.

"Contrary to obvious popular belief, I don't need Garrett to mother me. I'm quite capable of taking care of myself." I tore the plastic covering off the cups with a jerk.

The glow of the city glinted off of the black tattoos on Matt's hands as he crossed his arms, his gloves resting comfortably on his thigh. A knowing smirk crossed his lips as I set out the array of mini bottles. "Lonely?"

I gave a little shrug, selecting a bottle of bourbon. "It seemed a shame to waste all of it on myself."

"You seem to forget that I don't drink," Matt pointed out as I started to pour the bourbon into his cup. "Jason's the real alcoholic."

"You don't drink?" I paused, glancing at him sideways.

He shook his head, shifting, expression uncomfortable.

"Not since a drunk driver killed my older brother."

Bloody hell, how could I forget that? I was at the funeral after all.

"Crikey, Matt, I forgot," I muttered. The bottle of merlot I'd given him suddenly felt like the worst gift ever. I knew, better than most, what it was like to be reminded of painful times. "I didn't mean to bring up old memories."

He waved me off, forcing a smile. "That was ages ago. I should be past it, but I've never been one to forgive and forget easily."

Setting aside the bourbon, I tossed the contents inside the cup onto the roof at our feet. Matt watched me silently as I reached for another bottle, this one containing vodka.

"Are you sure that's a good idea?" he asked, raising an eyebrow as I popped open the cap.

Ignoring him, I started to lift the bottle to my lips. Matt's fingers caught my wrist, stopping us both mid-motion, before I could take a sip. I stiffened at the connection.

When was the last time someone touched me?

Matt never touched me. In fact, no one in Rourke's organization touched me if they could help it. My reputation as the master assassin's best and brightest tended to scare my companions into leaving me alone. Something I was rather proud of even if it wasn't normal.

This isn't normal. This isn't the way normal people live, and I don't care.

"Are you sure that's a good idea?" I hissed in warning, eyes narrowed.

His fingers twitched around my wrist, but he didn't let go.

"How about we skip the drinks tonight, Quinn?" Matt whispered, his words strained as I pulled away from his touch. "I don't like the idea of you drunk."

"What makes you think I would get drunk?" I blinked soulless dark eyes at him.

He swallowed hard and gave a low laugh, scooting back from me a couple of inches.

Good choice.

"After the kind of day you've had, I'd already be four bottles in." He smiled, a bit nervously.

"No." I laughed then, breaking the tension between us. "If you'd had the kind of day I've had you'd be dead."

I returned the cap on the vodka and turned the bottle over in my fingers. A gentle breeze picked up, rustling through my hair as I looked out over the capital city.

"How much did Garrett tell you?"

Matt frowned, his jaw clenching underneath the day's worth of scruff on his chin. The question was a loaded one—I had meant it to be—but I needed to know just how much Garrett knew and how much he was willing to share about my troubles.

"Not much." Matt crossed his arms. "He said there were complications on your assignment and that you had to go on the run. My orders were to stand guard at this hotel until you or Garrett told me to leave."

There were no lies or deception in Matt's eyes. Perhaps Garrett didn't know as much as I assumed he did. But there was one thing I couldn't get over. The hacker *had* indeed hinted that Navid's assignment wasn't normal.

Did he know about the FBI or not?

Sighing, I ran a hand through my hair, rubbing my aching temples. Somewhere below me, Nathan was locked in a bedroom—the only mistake I had ever made that might actually cost me everything.

"You can't trust Garrett to know everything," Matt said abruptly, catching me off guard.

I glanced up at him, narrowing my eyes. "Matt, his only job is to know everything." I got to my feet as a gust of wind fluttered my bathrobe.

Matt shrugged. "He's only human, just like us." He spoke softly so as not to disturb the monster in my blood.

I snorted and turned to go, leaving behind the mini bottles of alcohol.

Off in the distance, an ambulance siren wailed. Matt stood to watch me walk away, hands in the pockets of his black jeans. He was wrong about Garrett. The hacker was supposed to be able to predict the future. Rourke had hired him to make sure we never got caught. If the master assassin could trust the hacker, then I saw no reason for him to make such a huge mistake. If he knew about the FBI hunting Navid, then he had purposefully put me in jeopardy and Rourke would be the first person I talked to about it.

Reaching the stairs, I looked back over my shoulder. "We aren't human, Matt. Rourke doesn't train us to be human, he trains us to be killers. Monsters."

The assassin shifted, lips pressing together in a firm line as I continued staring at him in thought. Mere hours earlier, Nathan had accused me of being a monster and I rapidly agreed. It seemed appropriate, if not obvious.

"Damned if you do, bored if you don't, right?" Matt called, voice traveling on the wind as car horns blared in the night. "You forget that I've been there too, Quinn. I know what it's like to lose everything and turn to a savior to find your way home. You were the one who pulled me away from death. A long time ago... " He looked down at the concrete roof under his feet. "I owe you everything I am, just like you owe everything you are to Rourke."

Swallowing hard, I nodded in acknowledgement before opening the roof hatch and stepping into it.

When did life get like this?

I returned to my suite and locked myself in my bedroom, Glock lying across my lap. The cold metal and rubber grip gave me an anchor to hold onto as I looked into the dark and found, not for the first time, that I wasn't afraid.

◇

The Goring Hotel, London – October 19th

My phone vibrating on the nightstand next to my head woke me sometime after seven o'clock. I peeled my eyes open to squint at the hotel room. The shapes of furniture gradually took on form as my stomach grumbled hungrily. A distinct craving for an English breakfast and cup of strong tea overwhelmed my senses, and then I remembered—

Nathan.

My phone buzzed again.

Body protesting, I rolled over in the warm nest of pillows and blankets. Picking up my phone, I pried my eyes open long enough to read the two new texts.

The first was from Matt, telling me that he'd stick around until eight thirty before leaving.

Did you have to wake me up to tell me that?

The other—from Garrett—assured me that though I still had to wait to leave, my tail was clear. No FBI agents or police were after me.

Well, that's nice to know.

I pictured him seated behind his wall of computers at *London Advertising* sending millions of web crawlers into the FBI's database and local surveillance. Any mention of the assassination at the pub and kidnapping would disappear within mere hours. The only reason it hadn't been cleared up already was the unexpected arrival of the FBI. I sighed. Garrett wouldn't be moving from his rolling chair until everything was erased, and similarly I wouldn't be leaving the hotel until he had done so.

I sighed and begrudgingly climbed out of bed. After checking that Nathan was still locked in the other bedroom, I walked into the bathroom and turned on the shower as hot as the tap would allow. While it heated, I redressed my injury before withdrawing a bottle of hair dye and a make-up kit from my bag. I set them beside the sink, ready to use. The woman who eventually emerged from the hotel wouldn't be the same person who had entered it. And neither would her hostage.

One thing could be said about the Dragonfly. I was a multitude of faces and personas. Quinn Rogers had no core identity, nor would she ever, in my opinion. There were some jobs you showered before and some you showered after, but I had a higher standard than mixing day-old blood with fresh when I could help it.

The coffee and tea bar on the first floor of *The Goring* smelled brilliant—the same couldn't be said about the taste. I nibbled absently on a banana nut muffin and watched the television news, faking a bland interest. The chatter about the events at the pub was front and center, but thanks to my makeover no one paid me any notice. Garrett's duffle bag had everything needed to complete my transformation from the Dragonfly to just another ordinary British citizen. A pair of black, lycra spandex jogging bottoms and gunmetal grey exercise jacket to match was the perfect disguise in plain sight. The only thing I'd carried over to my new wardrobe was my black heeled boots. A woman should never have to be parted from her favorite shoes—a mantra I took to heart.

After eating and taking a few minutes to memorize the layout of the hotel, I took two muffins and a bottle of water up to the suite for Nathan. Not bothering to knock on the bedroom door, I pushed it open and entered unannounced.

My hostage was sitting cross-legged on the floor, hands clasped together in front of him and bound by the handcuffs. His head was bowed, eyes closed, and his sketchbook balanced on his knee. The pillows and blankets on the bed remained untouched.

I set down the water and food, crossed my arms, and arched an eyebrow. He knew I was there. His lips moved, but no sound came out, as if he were talking to someone else. He was praying to some divine entity for rescue I realized with a start. Just my luck, I had a religious hostage. I growled under my breath and snapped my fingers loudly to get his attention.

Nathan lifted his chin, dark circles under his eyes. A flicker of confusion crossed his gaze as he took in my new hair color and style. The black dye was at odds with the strawberry red Nathan had first associated me with, further changed by the shorter shoulder-length cut I sported.

"I brought you breakfast." I pointed to the food on the television stand.

He hesitated, most likely assuming some sort of trick or poison awaiting his hungry response.

I rolled my eyes and waved a dismissing hand at him. "Poisoning you would do me no good now, trust me."

Whether or not he truly believed me, he reached up to grab the water bottle, the chain between his handcuffs jingling.

After he had downed the contents, his sad eyes

found mine again. "Thank you," he whispered, voice hoarse.

There's a surprise. What kind of hostage thanks their captor?

"What are you going to do with me?" Nathan licked his lips, eyes wide and bloodshot with worry.

"Depends." I shrugged, leaning casually against the doorframe.

"On what?" He dropped his gaze, but not before I saw his look of resolve.

What a strange kid.

"On how I feel and what *you* do."

"Are you going to kill me?"

"Do you feel like dying?"

An expression I'd never seen before flashed in his green eyes. He looked away and gave a small shrug. "I'm not afraid to die."

"Everyone's afraid to die." With a huff of disgust, I spun on my heel and stalked out of the room. He wasn't going to last much longer.

Let him pray, it won't do any good. Not this time.

Chapter Ten

The Goring Hotel, London – October 19th

I stood at the window, blinds peeled open with my fingers as I watched Matt leave his perch exactly half past eight. My expectation of receiving an "okay" from Garrett when the assassin left was squashed when no word came from him. Five hours later I still hadn't heard anything.

For the fifth time in less than five minutes, I changed channels on the sixty-five inch Samsung, trying in vain to pacify my nerves. My weapons, both knives and guns, lay beside me on the couch thrice cleaned. Crossing both legs on top of the room's coffee table, I leaned back against the couch cushions and shut off the TV. I muttered under my breath, checking my phone for the awaited text from Garrett. Nothing.

As per our routine, the hacker had been in touch immediately after my assignment to kill Navid. He had confirmed that the assassination was successful and helped me get to a safe location when the FBI became an unexpected complication to our plan. According to our routine I shouldn't have been waiting for another call. He had done his job, but I knew this wasn't a normal job. Far from it. I had a hostage, and that made everything once black and white fifty shades of grey.

I uncurled from the couch and grabbed a handful of cash from my bag. With Nathan safely locked inside the second bedroom, I figured I had a little freedom to stretch my legs and sweep through the hotel again. Besides, I was craving chocolate. Leaving the *do not disturb* sign hanging on the door handle, I headed for the stairs.

The lobby of *The Goring* was quiet and empty, save for the desk clerk and myself. I selected a bag of peanut M&Ms, two bags of crisps, and a soda from the alcove next to the elevators. All comfort food—and a convincing cover that I was just another traveler spending the day answering conference calls or napping in her hotel room.

Goodies in hand, I turned to purchase them at the desk and stopped dead as my gaze landed on the revolving doors ahead of me.

Oh, not again.

The glass door whisked open and spun as six men entered, expressions grim. My heart performed a strange half-flutter against my ribcage. I took a step back into the snack alcove as the new arrivals swarmed the older male clerk standing behind the front counter. They might be dressed in plainclothes, but I knew better. The way they walked and surveyed their surroundings—making sure that one man hung at the rear of the pack to watch their backs—set off loud warning bells in my head.

The men were FBI agents. You couldn't miss the thick soles of their combat boots made strictly for running and stability.

I'm going to kill Garrett.

At the front desk, one of the agents flashed his badge. The clerk's face went pale. How had the FBI found me? And where the hell was Garrett? The ear-comm I still wore and the cell phone in my pocket stayed silent as I slipped out of the snack bar and hurried down the carpeted hallway of the first floor. I brushed past a maid with a cart of cleaning supplies, her exclamation of annoyance dull in my ears. I swerved around a corner to find the stairs, then barreled through the door and accelerated up the steps two at a time.

Check out time at this hotel.

After reaching the fifth floor, I hurried down the hallway, nodding to a man as he stepped out of his room. He said something in greeting that I ignored.

At my suite, I flashed the electronic key in front of the reader and saw the flash of welcoming green. I shouldered open the door and shut it quickly behind me. The deadbolt and chain slid into place with a metallic clink. Across the floor in a second, I shoved the cabinet away from Nathan's bedroom door before throwing it open.

The door banged against the wall, plaster showering from the ceiling due to the force. My hostage jumped, eyes wide.

"We have to go. *Now*." I grabbed his arm with an iron grip and dragged him into the main room of the suite.

"Wait—what? What's going on?"

I released him and shouldered my bag in one smooth motion. I tore the sketchbook from his hands and stuffed it inside.

"Change of plans. Our reservations have been compromised." I glanced back at the door as footsteps could be heard in the hallway.

A knock sounded.

Nathan froze, lips parted. I swore under my breath and drew my gun. My hostage took a step backward, leaning away from the sound of the second knock.

"What's going on?" He edged behind me.

Wise move. Anything putting me in danger is twice as bad for you.

"Open up. We need to ask you a few questions," a gruff male voice shouted through the door.

I backed away from the voice, my gun held in front of me. The odds weren't in my favor.

I'm good, but not "six-on-one in a sardine can" good.

To escape the mousetrap I was in, I needed to level the playing field. Easier said than done. *Unless...*

"Who is it?" Nathan whispered and stared at me as I moved to the window.

"FBI agents," I muttered, deep in thought.

His eyes brightened and I chuckled dryly, throwing back the curtains on the window. "Don't get your hopes up. I'm sure they have orders to kill me on sight, and you're going to be my shield."

He paled as I turned to peer through the window. Outside a shallow ledge ran across the building to the fire escape.

"How are you with heights?" I arched my eyebrow at Nathan, speaking over the angry demands of the FBI agents on the other side of the door. They'd come in soon enough.

Backing away from the window, I grabbed hold of the sixty-five inch Samsung television and yanked it away from its stand. The weight and bulk of it meant nothing as I sent it careening into the window. Glass cracked and then shattered, exploding outward with the ruined television. I smirked. The agents would definitely be on their way in now.

"All right, here's the deal." I turned to Nathan. "If you get on that ledge and do exactly what I say, I won't push you off."

I produced the key to his handcuffs, unlocked them, and let them fall to the floor between us.

"Push me off?" he exclaimed. "Are you *crazy*?"

"I'm an assassin, the jury's out." I shrugged and shoved him to the window. He gulped as I gestured for him to climb out through the window onto the ledge. "Go."

"Go?" Nathan glanced back, as if hoping I'd change my mind.

"Get out. Now." I gave him a push in the right direction. He carefully straddled the windowsill and then lowered himself onto the ledge. For a breathtaking moment, he swayed, before regaining his balance.

"Go to the fire escape," I hissed, climbing out after him with considerably more agility and grace.

But then, I have much more experience climbing in and out of windows.

Nathan slid across the ledge, one foot at a time. I buried the strong urge to push him off. Time was slipping away too quickly.

From inside the hotel suite, the door crashed open as the agents burst through.

"Go!" I shoved Nathan onto the fire escape.

A bullet ricocheted off of the metal railing beside me. With a cry, Nathan fell onto the first platform of the stairway, covering his head.

"Come on." I hauled him to his feet and shoved him *up* the stairs.

The men were close. Too close.

Feet pounding on the metal steps, we climbed two flights and reached the roof. I flipped up onto it, pulling Nathan after me. He rolled into a full-body sprawl, breathing hard. I straightened, hand pressed to the bullet graze across my side. The bandaging had held, but I could feel warm blood seeping to the surface.

Lightning flickered across the overcast grey sky. No rain yet, but thunder rumbled like war drums in the distance. The beat fell into place with the thumping of my heart. We had a few precious seconds before the agents, too, arrived on the roof.

"Get up," I snapped, walking past my hostage. "We have to go."

He groaned, coming up to a sitting position. I stuffed my gun into its holster, peering over the ledge of the roof for any sign of the agents. For all they knew, I had lured them up onto the roof for a trap. Which, in a way, was true.

I just had to set the trap.

The drop to the street below would kill me. If I had the time, I could scale the walls to climb down, but there wasn't nearly enough time for that option. My mind automatically shifted from looking for exits to searching for resources. The four industrial AC units to my right were very promising.

Thunder roaring in my ears, I swept past Nathan, ignoring him as I crouched next to the units. The wiring was ancient, the rubber covering it rotted away by the elements and careless maintenance over the years. Along with the new clothes I was wearing, Garrett had supplied a new knife in the duffle bag Matt had delivered. I drew the weapon from my boot and easily cut away the rest of the corroding wire's rubber coating. Nathan's stare was hot on my back as my nimble fingers flew, connecting cords and severing others.

In seconds I had the unit's wires in a heap, which I lit with my cigarette lighter. The stripped rubber melted, making a perfect bowl to support the lighter. I left it there, hoping Jason's training hadn't fallen on deaf ears.

"Is this all a game to you?" Nathan spat out suddenly.

I glanced at him as he got to his feet, hands clenched into fists, face flushed with anger. His clothes were dirty and wrinkled, and the rip in the knee of his pant leg flapped.

I left the AC units to finish my plan on their own and crouched down in front of him, sheathing my knife only to draw my Glock.

"Listen very closely, Nathan."

He swallowed hard as the barrel leveled at the

point between his eyes.

"This isn't rocket science."

Lightning crackled in the sky, followed by the boom of thunder. Electricity filled the air, rippling over my arms and making the tips of my hair stand on end. Nathan shuddered, his earlier temper wavering in the face of death. His fingers pressed against the roof and mine curled tighter around the trigger. I could do it. I could shoot him and escape even as the agents piled onto the roof and an explosion greeted them.

The softest of creaks sounded from the metal fire escape. The agents were on their way up.

Too late.

I surged to my feet and yanked Nathan's body in front of mine. Right on cue, the first agent stepped up onto the roof, bringing an assault rifle to bear on me. His five companions crested the fire escape after him. They formed two rows, walking toward the middle of the roof, the front three agents training their assault rifles on us. I grinned wolfishly, placing my gun under Nathan's chin.

Thunder roared in the sky above us as a bolt of lightning split the dark clouds in a jagged line. A gust of wind slammed into my back and I felt its groping fingers move along my skin. Nathan squirmed in my grip.

"Please don't do this," he muttered.

I squeezed my arm tighter around his torso and he went rigid.

"Took you long enough." I grinned at the agents.

"Let him go, and we can settle this without bloodshed." One agent stepped through the first row of his comrades. He had the gait of a soldier, but the look of a negotiator. I liked him immediately—he would be the first to die.

I tossed my head back and laughed as another gust of wind wailed past. "No bloodshed? But that's the best part, soldier!"

"Release him or we *will* shoot."

I really laughed at that one. Sauntering backward to the edge of the roof, I stopped only when my legs steadied against the three-foot high barrier that kept me and Nathan from falling to the pavement below.

"You won't shoot. You'll hit the boy first, and even if you miraculously miss something vital, my shot *will* kill him." I paused, tilting my head and pursing my lips. "Nice try, though. Please tell me that doesn't usually work."

The agents fidgeted, but didn't rise to meet my verbal assault. A stalemate. If I made a move they would light me up—but if they shot me, Nathan would die too.

No one moved and no one spoke. Only the sound of the wind whistling past, distant car motors, and Nathan's heavy breathing could be heard. His hands grew sweaty around my arm, a pathetic attempt to latch onto something—to keep the weapon in my hand from killing him.

Judging by the agents' lack of complete confidence, I suspected no backup was coming for them.

That's odd. Why aren't they working with the rest of the agency?

I half expected a helicopter to fly overhead at any moment to break apart our stare down. But the sky remained empty—the air silent and taut. My brow furrowed deeper with each passing second. Were these men the same ones who had jumped me at the pub? The lack of air support and ground troops answered the question positively. Perhaps they were rogue agents. An elite group separated from the rest of the Bureau.

That would explain why they were planning to kill Navid Maleate, not save him. They're a hit squad, completely off the books.

The impending explosion I'd created with the AC units would go off at any moment, and I had yet to think of a way to get off of the roof. The backs of my legs braced against the rough concrete of the retaining wall. I tried to think myself out of the situation—and failed.

Just when I resigned myself to doing something crazy, I caught a flicker of movement behind the agents. A figure scurried forward, crouching as he ran at the unsuspecting men. Recognition struck me at once—Jason.

What on earth is he doing here?

Shadows converged on his form, shifting as the lightning illuminated him for a split second. Nathan's chest hitched as he gathered breath to call a warning. *Not today.*

I slammed my foot into the backs of his knees and they buckled. He went down with a yelp, any warning call silenced. Seizing his opportunity, Jason dashed forward and lobbed a dark backpack at me.

"Catch!" he shouted. I snagged it out of the air, slipping my arms through the straps and pushing a button on the handle.

The surprised agents split to fire at Jason as he threw a Molotov Cocktail at the AC units. Had he been watching me the entire time? Flames illuminated the night, eating into the fuel and attacking the units. The agents jumped back, shielding their eyes from the bright flash of light. A perfect distraction.

"What the hell is this?" I shouted as Jason ran full-tilt at me.

His eyes were wide as he shrugged the backpack on, pausing for a second on the ledge of the roof.

"What does it look like?" he shouted, voice falling as he dove forward. "I'm rescuing you!"

I ducked, bullets whistling past me as I held

Nathan between the agents and myself. Plummeting, Jason pulled some strap on his backpack and a dark glider sprung into the air from it.

How very typical of him.

"Let go of the boy!" an agent demanded, hiding behind his assault rifle.

I glanced over my shoulder at them and smirked. "Sorry boys," I called. "It's not happening today."

I stepped backward onto the ledge, dragging Nathan with me, one hand on his collar, the other pulling on the backpack. He called out as we toppled off of the roof, but whatever his words were, they soon turned into a scream as we plunged into gravity's hold. The glider unfolded from the backpack, catching the wind.

Locking my right hand around my wrist, I hugged Nathan's back to my chest as we looped around the side of the hotel. Gunshots rent the air, the agents' bullets ricocheting harmlessly off of the bulletproof shields sewn into the flaps of the glider's wings. I rolled my eyes. There would be no living with Jason now.

"Look up," Jason called, twisting to glance back at me.

I craned my neck to see beyond the edge of the glider.

A rumble echoed the thunder and the roof of the hotel exploded in fire and smoke. Jason's Molotov Cocktail had finished my plans for the AC units. The night went livid with seething flames that seared my back as we swooped toward the street below. Jason whooped and Nathan stiffened as I held him against my chest, arms under his shoulders. Something like relief tightened my grip. Wind roaring in my ears, the clouds opened up and began to release their torrents of rain as the ground rushed up to meet us.

Across the street from *The Goring*, Jason landed

first, glider folding into the backpack. He turned just in time to snatch Nathan as I released him. They tumbled to the ground in a tangle of arms and legs. My feet hit the pavement and I jogged to keep my balance, glider heavy against my pull.

I twisted, scooping up the material as Jason joined me, my hostage in tow.

Meeting his gaze, I narrowed my eyes.

"Don't think about it too much or your head might explode," he said. "Come with me."

He disappeared around the corner of the building into a patch of shadows. Nathan looked like he might throw up. Taking him by the arm, I pulled him after Jason, jogging through sheets of dark rain.

We only stopped running when we reached the assassin's parked car several blocks away. He grabbed our backpacks and stuffed them into the boot of the vehicle, while I forced Nathan into the back seat.

I climbed into the passenger seat as Jason slid behind the wheel and, with a crank of the key, pulled away from the curb. We turned onto a road and headed south, away from the hotel, as the sound of emergency vehicle sirens drew nearer.

"What the hell are you doing here?" I broke the silence.

In the backseat, Nathan stared at me, eyes wide and unblinking.

"It's good to see you too, Quinn." Jason chuckled, pushing back his sweatshirt hood.

I bristled at the trademark air of casualness radiating off him.

As Rourke's favorite in an organization of cutthroat assassins, I'd never been a beloved character among my rivals. Not that I minded. They were a necessary evil to my job and what I did in the cover of shadows. Jason, however, liked to play our history together like a winning card in a game of poker. Since aiding in my rescue from the Army, he always went out of his way to speak to me—and show up in unexpected places just to say hello.

"How come you get all the fancy toys? Garrett never gives me a thing."

"It's my charming personality. You should try it sometime." He smirked. "Though I hear Rourke gives you anything you want and then some."

"Lot of good that did me against six FBI agents." I rolled my eyes.

He chuckled and tilted his head at Nathan in silent question.

"It's nothing."

Jason ran a hand through his damp brown hair, spiking it in all directions. "Garrett gave me a tip about some guys trying to hunt you down. He thought they might try and strike again. Turns out he was correct."

Typical Garrett, arranging Matt to take the graveyard shift and Jason to be the back-up cavalry.

"I guess that means I owe you one."

"Nah." He winked at me. "I think it was my turn to pay up, but next time I'll take my pound of flesh."

I leaned back in my seat, massaging the bridge of my nose. Underneath my jacket, I could feel the distant ache of pain coming from the bullet graze. I almost wished I had been shot. At least an actual puncture wound created an excuse for pain. Grazing merely presented an annoying hindrance—like a bee sting.

Closing my eyes, I ground my teeth together, forcing the pain from my thoughts. "Can you drop me off at my house?"

Jason nodded, angling into another lane of traffic. I peeked in the rearview mirror at Nathan. He was staring out the window, blood trickling from a gash near his hairline.

It had only just dawned on me that I had saved the young man's life instead of letting him splatter on the pavement outside of *The Goring*. Why had I done such a stupid thing? My plan had been to get rid of him and the agents in one fail swoop. What had happened to the plan?

Shaking my head in disbelief, I closed my eyes again. My head pounded as if a herd of horses were stampeding over it. Silence and the rolling motion of the car lulled me into a daze where memories lurked. I felt them creeping into my dreams as my senses slipped away into slumber.

Chapter Eleven

Five Years Ago

Maine – June 9th

One by one the lights inside the lakeside bungalow blinked out. I straightened from my crouch beside the water's edge, brushing the row of dense shrubs beside me. The scent of honeysuckle freshened the air. Oh, how that sweet smell made my heart ache for times lost.

For three hours I'd waited for the family inside the vacation home to turn in for the night. A fog rolled over the lake, creeping into the forest along its borders to aid the darkness of night in hiding me. I waited silently, content to be patient and shake the pins and needles from my legs.

Their time would come. No need to rush it.

Twenty minutes. I moved forward, my gloved hand wrapping around the hilt of my knives, fingers slipping tighter around the hilt. Rourke had seen to the details of outfitting me for this assignment meticulously. It was to be my final test before completing my training with him.

My initiation assignment.

The hardest assignment I would ever face. I studied my hands and wondered if I was ready to have blood on them, if I was ready to kill someone again. Weapons curved like wings, they were the perfect matches to the tattoo scrawled across my back. Once it had been a symbol of hope, now it would be of death.

It's my turn to use... my turn to hurt.

Unsanctioned Eyes

I passed through the fog, no more than a sliver of darkness. Frogs near the shore of the lake continued chirping, oblivious to my presence. Wind whispered through the canopy of leaves above me, playing in my hair. I breathed in and the smell of damp earth and pond algae met my nose.

Strange what little details I noticed and remembered as I approached the little house. In the fog I could still make out the fireflies that had been dancing above the lake since dusk.

The rear windows of the bungalow were open to admit the cool night breezes. Deathly silent, I slithered through one, rolling into the combined kitchen and living room. No sound disturbed the house as I stood up in it.

I crossed the open floor, avoiding the couches, tables, and chairs spread throughout. A pair of tennis shoes on the floor appeared out of the darkness and I sidestepped nimbly.

I paused at the mouth of the hallway, straining my ears. Faint snoring came from the master bedroom to my left, and I turned that direction. My new knives felt good in my hands as I tightened my grip around the hilts. I pushed open the bedroom door and it squeaked faintly. Stalking closer, I could see the husband and wife, lying beside each other in the bed, outlined in the moonlight.

Fredrick Montclair was no more than thirty-five, and his wife, her raven hair framing her beautiful and peaceful face, slept soundly in his arms. My stomach clenched as I lifted my weapons, the cold steel catching a ray of faint moonlight. I leaned over the wife, blocking out the feeble light like the very shadow of death.

I'm sorry it had to end this way. Forgive me.

My blades slit their throats as fast as the strike of a cobra. The battle-hardened nerves in my body didn't allow for me to show my horror outright, but my heart trembled.

Leaving their blood seeping into the sheets and mattress, I left the bedroom and stalked back down the hallway.

The little boy's room at the very end of the hall was oddly clean. Light from a night lamp illuminated the numerous drawings of stars, constellations, and rocket ships taped to the walls. A stack of books sat on the floor, all of them related to astronomy. Plastic glow-in-the-dark stars glimmered on the ceiling, a pale imitation of the real thing.

I stepped into the room and spotted the aspiring astronaut collapsed in a beanbag chair at the foot of his twin-sized bed. Another stack of books lay at his side, a large one open and spread across his lap. Sheathing one of my knives inside my boot, I stared at him, taking in his peaceful features as he slept.

The dark hair that shaded his face from the lamp's light was curly just like his mother's. His button nose made his full lips seem doll-like. Pure and innocent—perfect. He couldn't be older than eleven, and he had the innocence to prove it.

I don't know what I am becoming.

My heart was in my throat as I hideously stole inside his very dreams. The toe of my leather boot bumped a toy rocket ship model, and it clunked in the silence. With a soft exhale, the boy shifted in his sleep. I almost groaned at the pain that flared up as my lungs hitched on their next breath. His fingers slipped off of the book in his lap and it fell to the floor with a muffled thud.

Eyelids fluttering open, the boy woke. I tensed, watching him lift his gaze to me. Confusion, and then fear, overcame his expression, followed by a cry of terror.

Is this what Dawn looked like?

119

"W—Who are you?" His breath came in panicked flutters, his emerald green eyes wide and reflecting the streams of light.

The lampshade star cutouts painted shadows on the wall, like I was standing in space—weightless, timeless. The only reality before me this child and the bloodstained knife I held in my hands.

I stepped closer and he shrank back, sinking into his beanbag chair. My stomach lurched. The fear in his eyes was like a dagger pricking my heart.

Dawn was only a few years older. Sweeter.

My fingers curled into fists as I remained still, staring at him in remembrance. The memories hurt, but knowing what Rourke would do to me if I failed was worse. Much worse. He owned me.

I have no choice.

Pressing my lips together in determination, I advanced even as the boy scrambled to his feet, stumbling on the stack of books. They spilled over the floor and sent him sprawling. Terrified, he twisted to look back at me, pushing himself to his feet as I reached him.

"Please stop," he gasped. "You're scaring me."

I grabbed his wrist as he tried to run, subduing his wild swing at my nose. He thrashed, fighting against me as I pinned him with one arm. He kicked me in the shin and then stomped on my foot, but my hand over his mouth squeezed his screams into nothingness.

I shoved him against the wall and held him in place. His lips parted, chest heaving for air, and he stared up at me. Terrified.

My targets always had a story to tell in their final moments, and I read them through their eyes. Regret, grief, pain, fear, anger, and resignation. I had seen it all before. But this boy—I saw only horror and it made my blood run cold.

Who is in control?

My fingers tightened around the hilt of my blade until my knuckles turned white. Only then did I realize I was trembling, gasping for air that felt like syrup in my lungs. The boy shook violently in my hold, his hands trying to pry mine away.

"Please stop," he whispered again, brilliant green eyes filling with tears. "You're scaring me."

I blinked, fighting the wave of tender emotion ripping at me as the tears trickled down his pale cheeks.

His eyes—I would never forget his eyes.

"Please." His murmured plea hung in the empty space between us.

Heart pounding, soul shaking, I felt my ankles lock as if they wanted to bolt the other way. But Rourke's instructions had been too clear for me to fail. Either I completed the assignment, or he would finish the job and then finish me. I had worked too hard to fail now.

Breathing hard to keep the tears at bay, I lifted my blade, moving as if someone else controlled my body. A flick of the wrist, a pull across flawless skin, and the warm spray of blood hit my face. The warmth of scarlet spilled over my hand from his throat.

I felt the boy's life seep out of his body and instinctively moved closer, catching him in my arms as he collapsed.

Nothing could stop the tears now falling from my eyes as I cradled the child in my arms.

Eyes open, the boy stared up at the ceiling, the stars he loved so much looking down. Blood soaking my clothing, I sobbed, weeping over the innocent life I had taken. My heart twisted with each sob, my stomach churning, bile rising in the back of my throat. My knife lay on the floor and I stared through blurry eyes as the lamp's light danced in the crimson pool of blood.

I swallowed hard and wiped my eyes, smearing blood on my cheek. I gently closed the boy's eyes with fingers that trembled. The life and hope and terror that had been so alive in his emerald eyes were gone. He would never graduate from high school, never get the chance to choose a college degree. His friends would mourn the loss of his presence, and the woman who might have won his heart would never meet him.

And it was all my fault.

Just like Dawn.

Struggling to my feet, I carried the shell of the boy to the bed and bent slowly to lay him down. His curly hair tousled over his pale brow as I gently arranged his small hands on the mattress. The smell of death permeated the room as I stared down at the life I had stolen—the heart I had stopped from beating.

What have I done?

A flicker of light drew my gaze away from the dead boy to a Mason jar sitting on the corner of his nightstand. My throat caught on my next inhale.

Fireflies fluttered inside of the glass container, their little glowing lights flashing sporadically. The sight of such childhood innocence set my jaw hard as steel.

Dawn used to catch fireflies in our backyard. I clenched my bloodied fingers into fists as agony flared through my veins. We'd catch them and then play that we were fairies.

Memories of a distant night in my past trickled in through my thoughts, sending my heart galloping in panic. What had I done?

I took one more look at the boy's face frozen in the cold, cruel clutches of death. The surge of raw pain burned through my limbs as I struggled to my feet. I had done what needed to be done, but at what cost? My hand hit the Mason jar and sent it careening into the far wall. Glass shattered, raining down onto the floor. One by one the fireflies lights blinked out as I stood in the middle of the bedroom, weeping and shaking.

Lifting my chin, I took three deep breaths to calm myself. Rourke had sent me on this assignment for a reason. He knew my past—knew what I was trying to escape. He knew what I had to keep running from for the rest of my life. Picking the child and his parents for me to kill had been the point my master was trying to make.

There would be no room for compassion in my line of work. Shadows and screams, blood and death, they were my only friends and feelings now.

My boots crunching on the broken glass, I wiped away tears, retrieved my knife, and left the bungalow as fast as my feet would carry me. The blade felt like lead as I carried it over the threshold and back into the night. I couldn't leave the haunting images behind. They followed me, clung to me like the boy's blood on my skin.

Reaching my car two miles down the road, I slowed to a halt as my hands found stability against the window. My head spun, the rest of my body numb. Vaguely, I was aware that my hands were leaving blood-smeared handprints on the car as I opened the door and slid inside. The moonlight streamed in through the windshield as its lucid beams pushed away the fog that covered the lake. Fireflies danced over the water, lights flickering and glowing happily.

Was I ever happy? Even with Dawn?

My stomach heaved a warning as I closed my car door out of instinct alone. The images of the boy left in the embrace of death overwhelmed my thoughts as I leaned my head back against my seat and closed my eyes. How? How could I have killed the boy?

Killing the boy was unforgivable, even if Rourke had ordered it. Killing corrupt politicians or self-righteous aristocrats was one thing. I had been trained to murder terrorists and deserters. But slaughtering a child went beyond evil. It was monstrous.

Rourke remade me just to break me again. The pain... the horror... it's all part of his plan.

Sitting there in the moonlight, covered in the boy's blood, I took my hate and wrapped it around my heart. The pain eased, but in its place remained an empty void drained of emotions.

Rourke had sent me to the bungalow with specific instructions to kill the family and find my motivation. Well, he should be happy. I'd found my motivation, and lost my humanity.

I'm so sorry I couldn't save you.

I didn't know if I was apologizing to the boy or to Dawn.

Opening my eyes, I felt a single tear escape to roll down my cheek. It dripped off of my chin as I started my car. Rourke would know how to help me—what I needed so I could cope with what I had done. He would be there for me just like the darkness in my soul. And to thank him for my salvation I would become the killer he desired.

I would become a harbinger of Death. The Dragonfly—the name the world would learn to whisper in fear.

Chapter Twelve

"Quinn?" A distant voice broke into my subconscious.

I stirred, trying to curl onto my side. The smell of honeysuckle faded, as did the blinking light of fireflies. Darkness closed in where the bungalow had once been in front of me.

"Quinn?" The voice again, this time accompanied by a gentle poke to my shoulder.

I groaned and turned away. *Naff off, I'm sleeping.*

"Quinn, wake up. We're here."

My eyes snapped open as the voice finally registered in my mind.

Jason.

I broke free of the lingering grip of my nightmare, sitting bolt upright, only to be jerked back by my seat belt. Jason chuckled, while fiddling with the AC dial on the dash of the car.

"We need to talk about your life choices," he said when I looked over at him.

"What?" I squinted, slowly pushing into a sitting position. My tangled hair flopped into my eyes and I yawned, pushing it back.

"We need to talk about your life choices," Jason repeated. "You haven't called me in four months. I take that very personally."

I shrugged, giving him a confused look. "Jason, I've been on assignments in five of the seven continents in the last four months. How did you expect me to call you?"

"A phone would be the most efficient way I

suppose." He turned the steering wheel and the vehicle rolled onto a gravel road.

"How old are you?" I glowered at him, stifling another yawn.

It was his turn to shrug as I glanced over my shoulder at Nathan. The young artist sat huddled against the car door, eyes downcast and complexion pale.

Sighing, I looked back to Jason. "How long has he been like that?"

"Since you nodded off about thirty minutes ago," he replied.

"Good, I'd rather not deal with questions right now," I muttered.

"That might not be an option."

Frowning, I arched an eyebrow as we parked in the driveway of my house and Jason left the car engine idling. His eyes didn't leave my face.

Don't do what I think you're about to.

"If I don't ask the obvious questions, you know Garrett will, Quinn," Jason began. "Who's the kid and what the hell is he doing in my car?"

"It's a long story." I dropped my gaze. "And if you value your life, you won't ask me about it."

Shouldering open my door, I straightened from the vehicle and stretched, my back popping with the movement. I walked around to the other side and opened Nathan's door, then grabbed his arm and drug him out. Our rain-soaked clothes had dried during the drive, but it left our hair hanging in tangled strands over our gazes. He drew a sharp breath as I took a tighter grip on his arm. His face tilted to mine, and for a moment I couldn't feel my heart beating.

His eyes. A shudder raced down my spine.

It can't be...

Nathan's emerald eyes stared at me, mirroring the boy I had killed five years earlier during my initiation assignment. No wonder the nightmare had snuck up on me.

"Quinn?" Jason rounded the car, forehead furrowed as he looked between Nathan and I quizzically.

No wonder my hostage was familiar. I was holding the ghost of my first assignment.

How? How is this happening?

"Quinn?" Jason spoke again, tone hardening with concern.

Shaking my head, I forced a smirk for his benefit. "If you say another word, I'm going to beat you up and steal your car." Tugging Nathan with me, I strode to my front door and unlocked it briskly.

Jason had no choice but to get back in his car when I didn't offer him an invitation inside, muttering something dirty under his breath.

"What's going on?" Nathan whispered, stiff as a board beside me. I ignored him, sliding the deadbolt into place behind us.

The smell of pine and undisturbed space greeted my nose as I marched Nathan down the hallway of my house.

How long has it been since I was last here?

Dropping my bag onto the kitchen counter, metal buckles clicking against granite, I turned to survey the bay windows overlooking the backyard. Nathan remained silent, a wise choice, as I mentally debated what to do next.

"Is this your house?" he finally asked, voice soft and reluctant.

I nodded, then led him over to the breakfast nook and sat him down.

"One of many," I replied.

Nathan nodded in acknowledgment, chin lifting as he looked at the ceilings where the bare rafters supported the ceiling. I knew there were thousands of people who would have killed for the refurbished farmhouse I only occupied a few weeks out of the year. Unlike the ordinary populace, I couldn't stand to be tied down to one place too long.

One of the many reasons I'm in this mess.

"My uncle owns a farmhouse like this."

I started when Nathan spoke again, freely this time.

"He raises chickens and cows."

What am I supposed to say to that?

Over one hundred acres separated me from any neighbors, providing a nice privacy shield. The sprawling brick house was three stories tall, including the basement I had turned into a training room and shooting range. The money Rourke poured into my accounts after every assignment needed to go to something besides my shoe collection, and it made me feel vaguely *normal* having a place to call home. I had never thought to actually use the land for anything except hiding the occasional evidence I needed to bury or burn.

Sighing, I ran a hand through my hair and squinted at Nathan. He didn't move, merely stared back. His eyes were bloodshot and rimmed with dark circles, but that did little to conceal the bright green orbs.

He looks just like the boy. But how is that possible?

His expression wasn't one of fear—or even feeling. He looked numb, as if he didn't care what I did to him any longer. To be honest, I had no energy left in my body to kill him. The harrowing drive from the pub and back to London had sucked all of the adrenaline and death lust right out of me. Not to mention the painful reminder of my past whenever I met his gaze.

"Are you hungry? Thirsty?" I walked over to my

refrigerator.

He didn't reply, just looked on warily. I pulled two bottles of water from the door of my fridge and tossed one to him. From my pantry, I grabbed a bag of dried apples. He flinched as I sat down opposite him at the table.

"Tell me about yourself." I opened my bottle with a jerk.

"What about... ?" He trailed off, cheeks paling and eyes saddening.

"We can get to that later. For now, pretend I'm not the assassin who is going to kill you."

Nathan fiddled with the bag of apples. I took a sip of my drink and wished for something much stronger.

"My name is Nathan Holmes."

Reaching across the table, I opened the bag of apples and took a handful. "How old are you, Nathan?"

"Eighteen."

"Eighteen, huh?" I said. I would never forget the year of my eighteenth birthday. It had been the year straight from Hell. "What do you plan on doing when you grow up?"

He pushed the apples away quickly, swallowing hard as his gaze met mine. "Does it matter?"

He had a point. It didn't matter in the least, but he baffled me. Perhaps he was related to the family I had murdered five years ago. That would explain the uncanny similarities.

Taking another sip of my water, I cleared my throat. "Are you still breathing?"

"Yes."

"Are you still alive?"

"Yes... " He hesitated, sliding his drink from hand to hand.

"Then you should continue living as if life is going to continue. Seize the moment, especially if it is your last." I took a long swallow of my water and leaned forward on the table. "Tell me who you are, Nathan Holmes."

His slack jaw clenched and he gave me a single, curt nod. I watched him continue to shift the water bottle from hand to hand. The silence in the house stretched on as I waited.

"I was homeschooled until last year when I graduated. I love music and painting. My parents thought it would be a good idea to spend time abroad before picking the college I want to attend." He paused, eyes dimming.

"Sounds like your parents really trust you," I mused, leaning back. *Mine were too trusting, and they shouldn't have been.*

Nathan actually smiled. "Either that or my younger siblings grew enough that there wasn't room in our house anymore."

I had to hand it to him. He had a spark of nerve that didn't seem to balk in the face of imminent demise.

"And your art?" I produced his sketchbook from my bag and flipped it open to a drawing of my likeness. He studied me intently, and I tilted my head to the side.

"It's a hobby."

I traced the outline of the drawing, once again amazed at how lifelike I looked memorized on paper. "An impressive hobby. Perhaps a talent?"

"I actually prefer music. Some friends and I already have a garage band of sorts started. We're going to do our first gig when I get back... "

For a moment I thought he was going to start crying, but he took a deep breath. His expression settled back into one of determination.

"You're rather confident for someone who's going to die."

"I'm not afraid of you, you know." He shook his head, sincerity shining in his green eyes. "You can kill me, but I know where I'm going."

Well, damn. I've heard a lot of last words, but nothing like these.

"What makes you so confident?"

"My faith in God." His voice was merely a whisper, but it seemed to scream in my ears.

I flinched and gripped the neck of my water bottle. The room grew cold as Nathan watched me, the smile on his lips and kindness in his eyes terrifying. I shifted and forced a lazy smirk that sent his smile dashing away.

"Doesn't matter." I lifted an eyebrow. "What are you going to miss most about life?"

His eyes widened, inhaling sharply as I pulled my gun. I was done toying with him. My thoughts stilled as I realized what I was doing, perhaps for the first time.

Mercy—I was giving him mercy.

Resting my elbow on the table between us, I leveled the barrel of my Glock at his forehead. His lips parted, fear widening his emerald eyes and cute face until he looked like a startled porcelain doll.

My finger curled around the trigger.

"Danger Alert."

A shrill security alarm filled the house, an automated voice repeating "danger alert" with obnoxious conviction.

My blood went cold at the same time Nathan jerked, looking around him, an expression of pure confusion and fear wrinkling his brow.

"Danger Alert," the alarm repeated, the siren shrieking in my ears.

My radar security system had only gone off one time before, and it didn't end well for anyone involved. It took four entire boxes of Mr. Clean Magic

Erasers before the bloodstains came out of the cabinets.

Spinning on my heel, I left Nathan behind in the kitchen as I ran through the living room. My priorities shifted like sand—Nathan's life and death were secondary, my own much more pressing. I pounded up the stairs and down the hall to the office-turned-control room. I dropped into a rolling chair in front of my iMac computer and servers and typed in a code on my keyboard, silencing the alarm.

Should have picked the silent alarm, my ears wouldn't be ringing right now.

"Damn." I pulled up the live feed from my security cameras. A black helicopter was flying in low on the horizon, straight for my house.

I doubt they're coming for afternoon tea.

I quickly typed out the command for a full-house lockdown—only I could get out, nothing could get inside, at least not without some form of nuclear warfare. Taking out my phone, I dialed Garrett just as Nathan burst into the room, pale and disoriented.

"Hello?" Garrett picked up on the second ring.

"I've got a chopper homing in on my house right now." No time to waste on greetings. Not when I was about to be blown to kingdom come.

The alarm started going off again, and I glanced back at the screen. The blinking words of the new alert read: Dangerous Explosives Onboard.

I'm not going to catch a break as long as I have Nathan, am I?

"Garrett, I have a helicopter headed this way!"

"You have got to be kidding me."

I shut off the alarm. "I wish."

"There are no military updates requesting manhunts or bombers in the area. Who could they be?"

"I don't know." I glared at the phone. "You're the one who's supposed to know everything!"

The chopper grew rapidly larger in the calm sky. My pulse skyrocketed as I gripped my cell phone tighter.

"I'm coming to you, Quinn," Garrett said. "Did you hear me? I've already alerted Jason and I'm going to launch our helicopter and be there in twenty minutes."

"Hurry, Garrett," I muttered, hanging up.

Twenty minutes would be too late. The helicopter would be directly overhead in less than ten.

I'm on my own. How typical.

Nathan stared at me, his lips pressed together in a firm line, chest expanding and falling rapidly. I sucked in a sharp breath and stood, then I opened my gun safe with the fingerprint sensitive lock and stepped inside. I retrieved one of my most prized possessions from the wall—an Army regulation M240 machine gun. I slung it over my back and emerged from the safe. Nathan tensed as I grabbed his arm and dragged him out of the office.

"I hope you can save our lives again."

"What's going on?" he asked, face ashen.

After propelling us down the stairs and out into the garage, I opened the driver's door to my truck.

"I'm going to bring down a helicopter, but I need you to drive," I told him gruffly.

"You're what?"

"Get in." I shoved him inside and slammed the door. Hopping into the pickup bed, I threw open the crew cab window and tossed the keys to Nathan. "Start the engine. Do you want to get blown up or not?"

He shook his head, turning the key in the ignition. The engine roared to life and triggered the garage doors to open. I began setting up the tripod as Nathan backed out into the driveway.

"Faster!" I pointed toward the empty field behind my house. "Get us over there."

He accelerated as we left the paved driveway and bounced onto the grass. I gripped the side of the truck bed, eyes trained on the helicopter. It was close enough that I could make out the pilots.

We're not going to make it.

"Nathan, step on it!" The truck lurched and shuddered as he complied, apparently more afraid of me than crashing the truck.

I snapped the tripod stand into position and lifted the machine gun, bracing it with my shoulder. The roar of the aircraft drowned out all other sound. My ears rang as I pounded on the cab of the truck.

"Stop!"

Every wheel on the truck locked as Nathan stomped on the brakes, throwing me backward harder than I was expecting. Cursing, I scrambled to set my stance again and aim the M240 at the helicopter. The side doors of the chopper flung open as they pushed a bomb out of the cabin.

Bleeding hell, not on my new landscaping.

The impact of the explosive rattled the ground like an earthquake. Every inch of my new, and very expensive, landscaping exploded. The pickup cab windows shattered, imploding in on Nathan. Vaguely, I heard his muffled cry.

Taking aim at the rotor mast, I squeezed the trigger of the M240. It kicked back into me, butt-first again and again.

Another explosive hit the garden shed several yards away, spraying shrapnel and debris into the air. It rained down around the pickup as I continued my barrage—bullets feeding into the M240 and empty casings ejecting. I saw the man ready another bomb, leaning out of the open bay to spy his target. It only took a second to change my aim for a single shot—his death cry overshadowed by the roar of the chopper as he fell out through the open doors. Smoke shot up in plumes from the rotor mast as I returned to my original target.

That's for my cactus plants, you bastard.

The helicopter dropped one last explosive that landed twenty yards past us—dirt and grass flying up into the sky to mingle with black smoke and flames. My barrage had taken its toll on the metal beast. It listed to the side, spinning straight into the ground.

The crash shook the earth, spitting flames into the air in a final upheaval. Ducking behind the tailgate of the truck, I grimaced as the heat of the explosion rushed past my skin with a gust of wind. Debris slammed into the truck, denting and scratching it, and a metal rod punched through the tailgate inches from my right hip.

I know my insurance isn't covering that.

When at last the earth stopped bucking and the flames died down, I lifted my head to peer out at the hulking piece of destroyed metal. I slumped back against the cab of the pickup, letting the machine gun settle to the floor of the truck bed. Nathan's shaky voice murmured a prayer from inside the vehicle and it resonated inside my own chest in the form of my heartbeat.

The opening of the truck's door sounded like a gong in the sudden stillness. Nathan staggered toward me, mouth open, face white as snow. Trickles of blood painted his face where the glass from the truck's windows had left shallow cuts. He stared at me, gaze dropping to my torso.

"You're hurt." It was the second time he had noticed my injuries before any nerve could do the alerting for me. I glanced down at myself, spotting the injury to my right side. Blood trickled over the piece of shrapnel embedded in my flesh.

Funny, I don't feel any pain.

Without a word, Nathan clamored up into the

truck bed. His hands shook, as if resisting the urge to help me. He stood there, three feet away, staring at my bleeding wound. I ignored him, drawing in a lungful of air. The overwhelming coppery smell of hot blood and the cold acid stink of gun smoke hung in the air. Another inhale. The smoke stung my nostrils.

I took hold of the shrapnel, fingers slipping at first due to the blood coating it. Judging by the feel of the metal, both inside and out, it was embedded at least two inches. Perhaps slightly twisted at the hidden end.

This is going to suck.

Closing my eyes briefly, I gritted my teeth and pulled. There was a wet *slurp* and the metal tore out of my flesh. A fresh sheet of blood bubbled to the surface, another rush of its tang filling my nostrils. I bit down on my lip, pain flaring through my nervous system. Nathan gagged and looked away.

I unzipped my jacket, wincing with the movement, and pressed it against the narrow hole. With a little pressure, the bleeding slowed. I relaxed, the tension in my neck popping.

In no immediate danger of bleeding out, Nathan and I sat in silence, the smoke from the bombs and downed helicopter darkening the sky.

I've missed the smell of explosions and smoldering debris.

At the loud whine of a car engine racing down the road, Nathan perked up, glancing over his shoulder as a blue Corvette swung into my driveway spitting gravel. Jason cut the curb as he bounced onto the open field and headed our way.

Smash my mailbox again and I'll definitely take your car away.

I exhaled, hoisting myself upright. Blood had soaked through my jacket, staining my hands. Gingerly, I lifted a hand away and looked at my palm.

It was rimmed with blood, all the scars and grooves outlined in scarlet. When was the last time I had been so severely injured? Bullet grazes were one thing. This wound would require stitches, and soon.

Nathan stepped closer as I swayed on my feet. The Corvette's brakes screeched as Jason threw it into a halt next to the truck. His window buzzed down a second before he stuck his head out.

"You all right, Quinn?"

"Peachy."

His gaze dropped from my face to the bloodstained jacket. Before I could protest, he had shouldered open his door and leapt into the truck bed.

"Let me look at it," he said, prying away my jacket to inspect the wound.

I tried to slap his hands away. I had lived through much worse.

"Easy now, the bleeding's started again."

Stop fussing, mother hen. I'm fine.

I tried to push him back, but it was like shoving a mountain. Rolling my eyes, I gave up and let him finish the examination.

"What's that?" Nathan was still pale, but alert. I followed his gaze to the much smaller helicopter flying in low on the horizon.

"Garrett," I said.

Jason glanced over his shoulder. "He'll be here in a minute, Quinn. Stay still now, you'll be okay. The shrapnel didn't embed *too* deeply."

"Fan-bloody-tastic." I snorted, finally managing to push his hands away.

Garrett landed the helicopter half a football field away, avoiding the craters in my yard left by the explosives. Jason went to meet him, and the two went to work putting out the fires started by the attack.

I'm never spending another dime on landscaping. It's hopeless.

Chapter Thirteen

My House – October 20th

The smell of antiseptic and peroxide stung my nose as Jason poured a generous amount of the medical cleaner into a thick swab of gauze. I winced as he stretched toward me and ran the gauze over my injury. He glanced at me apologetically.

Ignoring him, I closed my eyes and leaned my head back against the couch. I knew how to clean and dress a wound—there was absolutely no reason for him to be helping me. But, there was no arguing with Jason. Some days he was more of a nursemaid than an assassin.

"Where did you learn to down a helicopter like that?" Garrett glanced over his shoulder from where he stood at one of my breakfast room windows, gazing out at the smoldering wreckage.

Without opening my eyes, I knew exactly what the smoking hull looked like. Memories I hadn't dwelled on for years from my time in Afghanistan rose to the forefront of my mind. My life with Rourke was a much better place than the Army had ever been.

"When I was in Afghanistan there was a specialized group of IFM terrorists that used machine guns to take down our aircraft. Especially the Apaches. I learned by watching their patterns." I shrugged, grimacing as the movement aggravated my injured side.

"You learned well," Garrett said.

Jason's fingers poked the raw nerves around my injury as he swiped the tender tissue with peroxide. I jerked, and he pulled back.

"Sorry," he gasped.

I growled a warning, but let him get back to the task at hand. We were opposites when it came to pain. While I could inflict any level upon myself, having someone else cause pain somehow doubled the agony.

Trying to distract myself, I glanced over at Nathan. He looked completely foreign to me. Gone was the happy young artist I had met at the pub. His face, neck, and arms were gashed open from the shattered cab window. Crimson stains marked both skin and clothes.

Blood is not his color.

"There," Jason announced, "all done."

He secured the thick bandage around my torso and gave me a wink. The wound was deep enough to warrant stitches, but that would have to wait until we had more time. We had no guarantee that the helicopter was a singular attack. For safety's sake, we needed to leave my house as soon as possible. Jason turned to pack away my first aid kit, but I grabbed his wrist, stopping him.

"Don't forget Nathan."

Garrett turned from the window at the name, spotting my hostage at the same time Jason turned to look. Apparently, Jason hadn't noticed him until my request. And apparently, Garrett hadn't realized we were four in company instead of three.

Jason hesitated, glancing at Garrett before obliging me. Ignoring them, I set a hand on my bandaged side as I struggled to my feet.

"Who the hell are you?" Garrett demanded, glaring at Nathan.

He flinched, averting his gaze as Jason began working on his minor injuries. Not receiving an answer, Garrett turned to me. "What the hell is this?"

"This is a hostage situation, Garrett," I replied,

voice low and exhausted.

"I know what it is, dammit! What the hell were you thinking?"

His tone didn't surprise me. I'd been expecting it.

"I was running for my life. What have *you* been doing?" I retorted.

Jason cleared his throat, swabbing at Nathan's neck with antiseptic. The tension in the room was so thick I could have carved it with a spoon.

Just say it, Garrett. We both know what you're thinking.

The hacker licked his lips, eyes narrowed. "Witnesses are supposed to be *dealt with* at the scene of the assignment. By kidnapping him, you failed your assignment."

"I didn't fail anything. Navid and his contact are both dead. The kid was a bargaining chip that I used to get away from the FBI alive, Garrett. Not telling me that I had competition to kill Navid wasn't the greatest call you've ever made either."

"Okay, I deserved that." He took a step back and ran a hand through his hair. "But I swear I double-checked everything. No FBI team was supposed to be in London."

"And then again at the hotel." I crossed my arms, unmoved by Garrett's miserable expression.

"Have I ever failed you before?"

"I don't know. You tell me."

"So, I made a mistake this time," he said. "Or somehow the Bureau has gotten smarter. I don't know. Either way, it won't happen again and won't be a further problem." He shook his head. "According to Jason, there's no way they got out of the hotel explosion alive."

Good. At least I had one less thing to worry about.

"I thought you were going to kill him." Jason

spoke up, straightening from Nathan's side, task finished.

The young man fidgeted, eyes wide and uneasy.

"I was," I growled, irritation sizzling up my spine. "But an armed helicopter escaped Garrett's notice and nearly blew me to smithereens. I thought, given the circumstances, Nathan's execution could wait."

"All right, Quinn. But he is a liability to you as long as he is alive."

I laughed. He didn't need to tell me what liabilities I had in my life. The FBI agents and helicopter had been a clear enough blow upside the head.

"Don't worry about me. I can take care of myself." I nodded out the window to the smoking hull of the helicopter. "Worry about *your* job."

Garrett's jaw clenched. My jab had hit home— maybe it would do something to stop all of the uninvited visitors in my life.

Without another word, he turned for the door. Jason and I shared a look, expressions furrowed. We both knew it was extremely unusual to see Garrett so upset, but he *had* failed to alert me to multiple life threatening attacks.

"Quinn?" Garrett looked back to me.

I straightened, wiping my thoughts off of my face with practiced ease. "Yes?"

"Stay off the grid until I can find out who tried to kill you. Find somewhere you aren't known. Keep the kid alive if you want, or kill him, just remain out of sight until I tell you otherwise."

I nodded. Garrett exhaled heavily, his shoulders slumping.

"They can stay with me, Garrett." Jason stepped forward, shooting me a firm glance meant to quell my instant protest. "My flat is safe, and Quinn's never been there before."

Jason was right. His flat was the perfect option, but I couldn't help thinking that he had been waiting for just such a moment to pounce. He was the kind of man who would save a damsel in distress. Well, if he thought I was in distress, he had another thing coming.

Garrett nodded to Jason and left through my front door.

"Come on." Jason turned to me. "Get what you need. We should clear out of here as soon as possible."

"Take Nathan to the car. I'll meet you there."

Chapter Fourteen

Jason's Flat – October 20th

My house was as far out as you could possibly get from the city without leaving London's city limits. Jason's flat, however, was smack dab in the middle of downtown.

Just like him to prefer the center of the action... and attention.

His flat was on the top floor of a huge complex. With hundreds of neighbors, he had no peace, but for some reason he enjoyed it that way. I was a solitary creature—a lone wolf. Jason fed off of the vibrations of a crowd and loved hunting at the risk of being spotted.

His decorating style mirrors those feelings a little too well.

I stared across his small living room at an ACDC album poster. A record player stood in the corner with an untidy stack of retro vinyl waiting to be played. The built-in TV cabinet showcased far too many souvenirs from various completed assignments.

I wonder if the women he brings back here know where all of the trinkets come from.

"I got those diamond earrings from the jewelry box of a very wealthy Duchess." Jason chuckled, entering the room with a first aid kit in his hand. "She obviously won't miss them since she's dead."

I rolled my eyes as he pulled up a chair next to me and began sorting through the kit, laying out items on a corner table to his left. Betadine, hot water, gloves, thread, a curved needle—

A low sigh rattled through my lungs as I leaned

forward on my knees, clasping my hands together.

Jason observed the movement out of the corner of his eye and gave me a reassuring smile. "Don't worry. Garrett will take care of everything."

Shifting on the couch, I rubbed my hands together quickly, creating a pocket of warmth between them. The incident at my house had only just begun to set into my nerves. I felt on the edge of a mild breakdown—the first in years—and the memory of my reoccurring nightmare did little to help.

"Quinn, are you listening?"

I hummed in response, earning a pointed look. He seemed genuinely hurt I didn't trust him. Not that I cared—I had no reason to confide in him. I didn't feel like sharing my deep, dark secrets with a fellow assassin even if we did share a complicated backstory. Some things only Rourke needed to know about me. And others only myself.

As soon as Garrett sorted out how the FBI knew where I was, and I got rid of Nathan, everything would return to the way it had been.

Then I won't need Jason, just like always.

I glanced over at my hostage, who'd curled up in the most hideous armchair I'd ever seen. His eyelids were lowered, but not closed. He was breathing steadily, but not deeply. His chest lifted and then fell in a regular pattern. *He's in shock.*

"I'm going to give you a shot for the pain," Jason said softly, "and then stitch you up." He picked up a sterile syringe even as I ignored him. Nathan's breathing stuttered as he turned his head to face into the chair. The bright neon green cushions reflected the overhead lights and distorted his complexion.

I wonder what he's thinking.

"Here we go," Jason announced, lifting the syringe.

It was equipped with a long needle and filled with

a yellow tinted liquid. The sight of it glistening in the light made my skin crawl.

Needles and I weren't on speaking terms.

"You're not doing this." I took the syringe from his hand and laid it down on the table unused. Jason pursed his lips, sitting back as I dug through the medical kit until I found the surgical staples. They'd hurt more than stitches, but I preferred pain to needles any day.

Anything but needles... I can handle anything but needles.

"You want me to do that?" Jason arched an eyebrow as I pulled off my shirt and followed it with the bloodied bandage. I clenched my teeth at the sight of the open wound.

"No"—I pinched the skin together—"I've got it."

I worked slowly, holding the torn edges of my skin together to staple back in place. Jason winced at each pop of the gun until he finally got up and left the room. When he returned, bearing a clean shirt, I had finished sealing the shrapnel injury and was cleaning away the blood. He didn't speak as I wrapped swatches of gauze and then tape over the throbbing wound.

"You know that's going to be one hell of a scar, right?" he asked, voice low.

I handed him the stapler and picked up the shirt he'd laid beside me.

"What else is new? I have quite the collection already, what's one more?" Pausing, I saw Jason's eyes flick from one of my scars to the next before coming to rest on my shoulder where the edges of a tattoo were visible.

"Cool ink."

I said nothing.

"You and Matt should open a tattoo parlor or something together," he said when I ignored his compliment.

Unlike our fellow assassin, my tattoos weren't for status or pride. They were reminders. Most of them of things I didn't want to remember.

"Did the wings come before or after you became the Dragonfly?" Jason asked, picking up a roll of gauze and returning it to his kit.

I glanced at Nathan again before answering. His breathing was slower. Perhaps he was dozing.

"Before." I felt the phantom edges of the wings that stretched from the top of my upper arms, across my shoulders, and down my back to finish below my waistline. My tattoo had been the last time I could stand needles. An incident while working for Rourke had ruined all interaction with the objects ever since.

Jason watched me pull on my shirt, the movement tugging painfully at the staples in my skin. Offering a hand, he finished putting away the medical supplies and then started mopping up whatever blood I had left behind.

"Thank you." My words surprised me, but Jason just turned to study my face. He was less than a foot away from my nose. The nearness of his presence put my senses on high alert.

Don't even think about trying anything stupid.

The last man to make the mistake of caging me in had lost more than just his life in the end.

Jason shifted back and smirked. "No problem."

"May I use your bathroom?" I raised my chin.

The abrupt change of subject lifted the tension in the room.

"What's mine is yours." The assassin spread his hands.

I stood and retreated down the hallway without another word.

Jason's bathroom was just as rubbish as the rest of his flat. While I liked to keep my job and interests a secret, my fellow assassin seemed to prefer boasting it to the world.

Typical.

I locked the door and pushed aside an oriental jade statue to lean against the sink counter. From somewhere behind the toilet, an air freshener let out a burst of automatic spray. The stench of roses and lemon verbena filled the room.

Exhaling, I lifted my face to the mirror.

Tired, ragged, and completely defiant. What looked like a normal human being on the outside was anything but beneath skin level. I combed a shaky hand through my hair.

"What are you doing, Quinn?"

I turned on the tap and plunged my hands under the cold flow, the events of the day crashing down on my shoulders like a mudslide. After splashing water on my face, I grabbed a towel as my cell vibrated in my pocket.

Blocked Caller ID.

"Hello?" I lifted the phone to my ear expecting to hear Rourke's familiar voice on the other end.

Someone took a heavy breath. I frowned at myself in the mirror.

"Miss Rogers, you are going to regret bringing down my helicopter." It was a deep and soft male voice. The man had a strong Middle Eastern accent.

Not Rourke.

The towel in my hand slipped through my fingers to the bathroom floor and I backed into the sink counter, knocking the jade statue to the floor. It shattered into a million pieces across the tile and my boots.

"Selah?" I gulped. *It can't be.*

"Surely you didn't think you had seen the last of me." He chuckled.

I dug my nails into the palm of my free hand.

"When I left your camp in smoking ruins, yes, I thought I had seen the last of you." The hair on the back of my neck stood on end.

He was alive—a ghost from the past come back to haunt me with a vengeance.

First Nathan and his green eyes and now Selah, am I stuck in déjà vu?

"What do you want with me?"

"Let's just say there is some unfinished business I have been alerted to, Miss Rogers. And you know how I feel about unfinished business. You will see me very, very soon I am afraid."

My phone blinked as the call disconnected.

I knew the people who had come for me. I knew them *very well* indeed. Chest heaving, I leaned against the door.

"Quinn, are you okay in there?" Jason knocked on the bathroom door.

I couldn't bring myself to muster the words to answer.

"Quinn? Are you okay?" he called again, more urgently.

I opened my mouth to respond as the door swung open. Jason came barreling inside, but stopped abruptly as he saw me, a key in his hand.

So much for locked doors and privacy.

"Whoa, easy there." He took my elbow. "You don't look so good."

"You think?" I gasped, my head spinning. He guided me into the bedroom across the hallway, and I couldn't find strength to resist. Sinking onto the bed, I grimaced as my wound flared in pain.

"What's wrong?" Jason pulled up an armchair and dropped into it, frowning.

I massaged my wrists, unconsciously concealing the faint scarring from the last run-in I'd had with Selah. There was only one way to break me. Rourke knew it. Selah knew it. And both had used it to gain what they wanted in the end, but only Rourke's version of captivity granted him greater access to my heart. Selah's cages and bargaining for my allegiance had led to his death. Or so I'd thought—and hoped.

Taking a deep breath, I spoke. "I know who sent the helicopter."

"We all know," Jason assured me. "The FBI."

"No, Selah."

"*Selah?* You can't be serious." Despite his adamant dismissal, I saw the color leech from his face.

"He called me, Jason. He told me he was coming, and that whatever this was today isn't over." My pulse thrummed faster in my veins.

First the FBI and now Selah—bleeding hell, I was in serious, serious trouble. How had Garrett failed to pick up on either party tracking me?

"Don't worry, Quinn. You've bested Selah more than once, and you can do it again. He's an amateur. He's not a threat to us." Jason's words did little to help my nerves.

"His men nearly blew up my house and me along with it." I pressed a hand to my side. "But why surface now? What does he hope to gain from it?"

"He asked you to join him when they captured you in Sudan, right?"

I nodded, and he frowned. "Maybe he didn't take kindly to your response."

"No, it can't be. That was ages ago. If he wanted to kill me he would have done it before now." I shook my head, standing up to pace the floor. "His attack today has to have something to do with Rourke. We are so close to achieving his goal. Selah will want to stop him."

"Calm down, Quinn." Jason leaned back and crossed his arms. "As soon as Garrett gets back we'll tell him about Selah. He'll know what we need to do."

Garrett had never failed me before, but I couldn't shake the nauseating feeling that everything was changing and I wasn't in control anymore. Garrett had failed to alert me to danger far too many times for it to be a coincidence. *Is he hiding something?*

"Where is Garrett?" I raised an eyebrow at Jason.

"He went to go do some digging on the attack at your place. He should be working on covering everything up. Heaven knows we wouldn't want a random passerby or cop to stumble upon the battleground in your backyard." Jason stood up.

"No, we don't want that," I muttered absently.

"Relax"—he winked and stuffed his hands into the pockets of his skinny jeans—"I'll keep an eye on Nathan while you finish cleaning up. When Garrett gets back we can worry about Selah. For now I'll keep you safe. Call if you need anything."

He had a point. There was very little we could do about Selah and the FBI without Garrett. I sighed and slowly pushed to my feet. A shower sounded brilliant.

As I passed Jason, he grabbed my wrist, stopping me.

"Yes?" I glared up into his eyes.

"What you're doing with Nathan... " He paused, shaking his head. "I think it's the right thing."

I jerked my hand free. "Well that makes one of us."

◇

Jason's Flat – October 21ˢᵗ

"Please don't," he *whispered, brilliant green eyes filling with tears.*

I blinked, fighting the wave of tender emotion ripping through me as the tears trickled down his pale cheeks.

His eyes. I would never forget his eyes.

I snapped awake, my lips parting in a silent, gasping scream.

Choking on the bile in the back of my throat, I curled into a ball as a hot tear slipped from my eye. The wound in my side made me clench in pain, but I shoved it away, struggling to escape the lingering nightmare. The boy's terrified eyes stared back at me—I felt my arm perform the death stroke.

Five years and dozens of assignments later, I had yet to resolve the immense guilt that inhabited the hole where my heart had once been.

I flipped onto my back and gazed up at the ceiling, steadying my pulse with slow, deep breaths. Sunlight streamed in through the blinds on the windows. Jason's king size bed was off of some kind of TempurPedic commercial for people with far too much money and ego. Perhaps I would buy one myself after having a test run in it.

Pictures of modern art hung on the wall, concealing a high-tech sound system. Jason even had one wall reserved solely to display his vast weapons collection. He really had some issues. But, then again, I woke up nearly screaming from nightmares about my past. Maybe we were both crazy.

I pushed myself out of bed, staggered into the adjoining bathroom, and examined my injury with careful, probing fingers. The staples had made it through the night. Slapping on the lights, my gaze landed on a pile of clothes with a note scribbled in Jason's nearly illegible handwriting. The note read: Hope these clothes fit.

I smiled. Jason might be completely different than me, and had an utterly different approach to life, but he was a loyal and helpful asset.

I hope Jason doesn't change. I need something stable with everything spinning out of control.

The outfit he had bought for me, however, was anything *but* under control.

The soft grey sweater dangled off my shoulder on one side to show the black tank top underneath, as well as part of my tattoo. I pulled on the pair of skinny jeans, followed in quick succession by a black beanie that matched my undershirt. The word "Rebel" was stenciled in thickly over the brow of the hat. I rolled my eyes. Jason had fully enjoyed dressing me, that much was clear—the sneaky devil. He'd turned me into a punk assassin. The hat wasn't even the worst part.

Instead of my usual black boots, a pair of thick wedge sneakers lay in wait by the bathroom sink.

"Oh, you have got to be kidding me," I hissed, stepping into the first shoe. "How am I going to be able to run in these?"

"The same way you run in those damned heels you love so much," Jason's voice announced from the doorway.

I whirled to face him, the second shoe in my hand ready to be used as a weapon. Grinning, he held up his arms in mock surrender and sauntered farther into the room.

"Is knocking too old school for you?" I raised an eyebrow.

He didn't grace my jab with an answer, but instead looked over my outfit with a critical eye. "You look stunning."

"Rubbish, these clothes are all naff."

He grinned. "You could be a fashion model if the assassin gig doesn't pay well enough."

"I could be a lot of things." I shouldered past him to reenter the bedroom, picking up my knives from the nightstand.

Jason followed, smiling. "I tried to find something that had a low enough waistband to avoid your staples," he said, gaze focused on my hips. "Do the jeans work?"

Ignoring him, I sat down on the bed and scooped up my boots. The skinny jeans he had selected were perfect, their stretchy waist resting well below my navel and giving enough room for the thick bandages I had wrapped over my injury. As long as I didn't move in a hurry, the outfit would work perfectly. However, I wasn't about to let Jason dictate which shoes I wore.

Quinn, one. Jason, zero.

I stepped into the boots, zipping up the sides and double-checking the laces. The thick heel supported my foot as I secured my knives into their hidden sheaths. Jason plopped down on the bed beside me as I finished. He offered me my Glock 19, hilt first. Facing him, I accepted the handgun.

"Where's Nathan?"

"In the guestroom." Jason laced his hands behind his head casually. "I got him to talk to me."

My eyebrows lifted. "Oh, really? What did he say?"

"Please and thank you."

"That's it?"

He shrugged, standing up and leading the way into the kitchenette. A TV sitting next to the sink played a motocross competition as Jason picked up a large mug of steaming coffee from the counter. He crunched down on a piece of peanut butter toast as he leaned against the cabinets.

"Want some coffee?" He spoke through the mouthful of toast just to annoy me, holding up his mug as advertisement. The once bright red and blue Union Jack painted on the ceramic had chipped and faded with overuse.

"Never," I said. "If you ever see me drinking coffee, I'm either contemplating suicide or signaling for help."

"I will never understand you Brits." He shook his head in disapproval. "Fix me up with six cups of good coffee and I swear I could move a mountain."

"You wouldn't be able to do anything with that much caffeine in your veins. You'd be an absolute mess." I crossed my arms.

He winked. "But a hot mess."

"Where's the tea, Jason?" Scoffing, I turned to open the first cabinet I came to.

He laughed from behind his mug, eyes alight with genuine amusement. "In the cabinet to your right."

I stalked around the kitchen and got a tea bag from the specified cabinet. Jason boiled some water for me and supplied a large mug. Once I had enough caffeine in my system to keep from punching him, I met his gaze once more.

He took the eye contact as permission to speak. "How did you sleep?"

I sat down on a barstool and crossed my arms over the granite countertop, resting my chin on them.

"Well enough. Cheers for letting me use your bed." I stared into my tea. The milk and sugar I had already mixed in tainting the inky color. "How did Nathan sleep? Was he any trouble?"

"He didn't sleep a wink. You gave him a good scare yesterday." He took another bite of toast and wiggled his eyebrows at me. "But he did want to know if I had a Bible."

I arched both eyebrows. "A Bible?"

"You sound surprised he'd want one. I figured you'd be more surprised to learn I actually own one."

He had a very good point. I was honest-to-goodness surprised. I'd never pictured Jason as the religious type. More of a Zen-yoga man.

"Do you want some breakfast?" He crossed over to the stove. "I have toast and eggs, or we can go pick up donuts."

156

"Garrett said we should stay off of the grid. Somehow I think buying donuts wasn't what he had in mind." I lifted my mug from the countertop to take a long, comforting sip.

"Do you really think Garrett means everything he says? I mean, heck, if he did I'd have disobeyed more than half." Jason laughed.

I frowned at him. We definitely didn't see eye to eye on *that* subject.

"Of course he does, Jason," I retorted, pushing my tea back and forth across the countertop.

He popped the last piece of toast into his mouth and dumped his plate in the dishwasher.

"Our line of work is very subjective." He winked.

"It's amazing you're still alive."

He shrugged and gestured to a loaf of bread. "Toast?"

Chapter Fifteen

After a quick breakfast that didn't involve a trip to buy donuts, I went to check on Nathan in Jason's small upstairs guestroom. The blinds had been left open and morning sunlight illuminated everything with a golden hue. I stepped past the doorway and spotted Nathan sitting on the floor, flipping through a book.

So, Jason wasn't kidding. He really does have a Bible.

Nathan glanced up and smiled at me as I approached. Strange kid. I perched on the edge of the bed and looked over his shoulder. It was page after page of what the Christians considered the holy word of God. I only saw paper and ink. How could he stand to read it? Didn't he know everything written inside was a lie?

"How was your night?" I watched him curiously as he closed the book and set it aside. I really couldn't care less, but small talk had never been my strong point and I needed him to open up.

"All right"—he looked at me intently—"you?"

"Jason's bed is the size of a small country, but it's too soft."

The curves around his mouth twitched into a small smile, as if he was remembering something. "My uncle came back from a deployment overseas and said something similar."

"Sleeping on the ground and rocks will do that to you." It had taken me a long time to adjust back to

159

mattresses after my tours in the military. Even still, I often slept anywhere but a bed. Had I really adjusted in the end? An assassin's life really wasn't that much different from a soldier's.

"Is this the same uncle as the chicken-raiser?"

"You remembered." Nathan's dimpled smile appeared like the sun slipping out of cloud cover.

"I remember a lot of things," I muttered. *Way too many things.*

"Why did you join the Army?"

My eyes widened in surprise at the open question. *How does he know?*

"Because I needed to," I replied stiffly. He was good. Oh, he was incredibly good. From one small comment he had known I was a former military member. My secrets weren't as hidden as I thought, especially with his prying eyes and listening ears.

"No one needs to join the Army." He closed the Bible, keeping one finger holding his place. I bristled, fighting against the memories that threatened to overwhelm me.

"Everyone is running from something," he murmured, as if to himself. "My uncle joined after 9/11. He'd never actually say it, but I think he went to look for something. He didn't need to go overseas to fight or find it, but he thought he did at the time."

The room closed in around me. Bone-aching anxiety chilled me to the marrow as I closed my hands into fists. I found it impossible to breathe. How in the world did Nathan know the precise words to drive into my heart? It was uncanny how he knew so little and yet seemed to know everything about me.

"Did he... " I licked my lips. "Did your uncle find what he was looking for?"

The question hurt to physically speak into existence, as if each word tugged on my own broken heartstrings.

Nathan's expression became wistful as he shook his head. "Only when he stopped running."

I almost swore. He had to know about my past—had to know what I was running from. There was no way on earth that his comments were random.

Nathan tilted his head and watched me with endless pine-green pools for eyes. I pressed my back against the doorframe, trying to calm my pounding heart. One phrase—one question—repeated inside of my head until I thought I would go mad.

How does he know me?

"Have you decided what to do with me yet?" He spoke as if we weren't in the same room.

My back throbbed as I pressed back against the door. I wanted out, but couldn't bring myself to actually leave.

I shrugged away the comment and moved to turn the doorknob behind me. He knew too much and yet I *knew* none of it was rehearsed. What he said was a mere coincidence. It had to be—for my own sanity.

"Jason has some new clothes for you." I opened the door wide. "Shower and get dressed. You can eat something afterward."

End of discussion.

He nodded, standing up to lay the Bible down on the bed. I tensed as he walked past, and then he paused.

"Can I have my sketchbook back?" He looked to me expectantly.

Mouth dry, I nodded once in agreement. Anything to get away from him. "I'll put it in the bedroom for when you're done changing."

"Thank you," he said, moving forward again.

As soon as he closed the bathroom door behind him, the lump in the back of my throat started to ease, but the churning in my stomach remained.

I returned to the kitchen and poured myself a

second cup of Irish Breakfast tea. It was that kind of morning. *Oh joy.*

Chapter Sixteen

Hyde Park, London – October 24th

The fish and chips Jason insisted we take on a picnic in Hyde Park tasted bland and unseasoned to my tongue. Every bite dried out my mouth almost as much as the entirely one-sided conversation Jason was supplying for Nathan and my benefit. I had tuned him out a long time ago, instead focusing on lifting each morsel of food to my mouth and chewing slowly. Despite its taste, the meal warmed my insides against the stiff northern breeze.

Seated beside me, Nathan stared at his untouched food. It was a huge risk to be out in public, but Jason had won me over. Four days of being locked up in his flat had everyone on edge, not just me. The first excuse to be outside and moving had been accepted.

Thanks to our disguises, no one will notice us. Not that that makes me feel any better.

Another bite. More chewing.

Nod occasionally.

Blink and repeat.

Jason continued rambling on about the weather, the news, our new disguises and looks, his cars, sports, and other trivial nonsense. I didn't think he'd even noticed we hadn't said a single word in response.

I nibbled on a mouthful of potato, surveying the park around us with mild interest. Jason had parked his car on the street some twenty yards away. Two couples strolled along the park trail to my left, and a woman walked her dog beyond our table near the trees. Fall was in the air, but none of its severe chill.

Yet.

The atmosphere was so peaceful that I almost didn't react to the sudden feeling that someone was watching me.

Over the years I had learned never to ignore instinctive feelings. In the face of a life and death situation, instincts kept you alive. Straightening, I frowned, looking past Jason's shoulder at the road. The hair on the back of my neck stood on end as the feeling intensified. Someone was staring at me.

I surveyed our surroundings again—this time more intently.

The grove of dogwood trees to our right, shading our picnic table, rustled in the wind. Aside from that there was no sound. The birds had stopped singing—a definite sign of trouble. I flicked my gaze to the path. The two couples were gone. Only the woman and her dog remained. With the road nearby the park wasn't completely isolated, but the chances of a passing driver hearing a gunshot were slim.

Isolated. Secluded. The perfect drive-by shooting location.

"When was the last time you went on a picnic, Quinn?" Jason interrupted my thoughts with his hopeless chatter.

I ignored him. Something was definitely wrong—it wasn't just a hunch any longer.

Stiffening, a chill raced up my spine. Nathan felt my tension and glanced at me, brow furrowing.

"How about you, Nathan? You ever go on a picnic?"

Insufferable man. It was a wonder Jason hadn't been brutally murdered on an assignment yet.

"Quinn?" Jason's voice was distant in my ears.

A cloud passed over the sun, bringing with it a sudden gust of wind that blew my hair into my eyes. I quickly pushed it away, spitting strands from my mouth. Jason stared at me as I swiveled on the bench seat, looking around urgently—searching. He seemed to finally understand my uneasiness. Out of the corner of my eye, I saw him go for the gun concealed underneath his shirt.

A man dressed in a suit and tie sat at a park bench a few feet away. He looked up from reading something on his iPad. Our gazes met and my hand went immediately to the grip of my own handgun, holstered behind my back. Jason said something that I didn't hear.

The man's jacket blew in the wind as he lifted his chin, gaze locked on me. He was dressed too heavily for the weather. The jacket was thick enough to hide any number of objects between it and his undershirt. I tensed, Glock halfway drawn.

Our table was silent—ready.

As if receiving a signal, the man stood, dropping his iPad on the ground at his feet. I shot upright, Glock fully drawn as he reached into his jacket. Jason cursed and Nathan ducked. Black metal glinted in the air as we fired our weapons at the same time. Gunshots boomed through the park. Blood puffed into the air as the man sprawled on the ground, pistol skittering a few inches away from his outstretched fingertips.

Nathan crawled to my side, and I latched onto his forearm. His chest rose and fell unevenly, his face etched with fear. His instinctive reaction in the face of an attack was to go to me for protection.

Maybe he isn't as stupid and naïve as I thought.

Keeping him close, I looked for the next threat. The only problem was locating the source of the attackers. I had to find it or future advances could prove fatal.

"Where are they?" Jason muttered to himself, his back to mine, so we covered each other's blind spots. "It can't be a lone wolf shooter."

Another gunshot answered his question a moment later.

I grabbed Nathan by the shoulder, throwing him to the ground beneath me as Jason dove over us both.

It was the woman with the dog who had turned, sporting an Uzi with practiced ease. I wiggled my legs free of Jason and Nathan and kicked at the edge of the picnic table. It flipped onto its side. Tucking Nathan close, I rolled us both behind the impromptu cover. Jason copied my movements exactly as bullets ripped through the rough wood.

"Keep your head down," I hissed in Nathan's ear, one hand locked around his collar, the other holding my gun.

He nodded, breathless, eyes wide.

The woman stopped shooting, most likely to reload. Jason and I glanced at each other over Nathan's head. He gave a small nod.

On three.

Jason held up a single finger. *One.*

Nathan curled into a ball, squeezing his eyes shut. *Two.*

I brought my legs up underneath me. *Three.*

Without so much as a sound, Jason popped into a crouch, firing over the top of the picnic table. The distraction. I heard the Uzi's barking reply and saw Jason flinch as a bullet whizzed by his ear. He fired again and I made my move. The attack.

Standing upright, I caught the woman's attention instantly. She jerked to aim at me, but too slow. Her last desperate and final mistake.

Jason and I both fired, our bullets hitting her at the same time.

I lowered my Glock as the woman hit the ground. An ominous hush descended upon the park.

"Got your six," Jason said, once again taking up position facing away from the road.

I nodded, eyes searching the trail and road for another shooter.

"Get up," I said to Nathan, offering him a hand without looking down.

There was a moment of pause before he accepted and stood shakily at my side.

"Jason?"

"Right behind you," he confirmed as I stepped around the overturned picnic bench. Nathan stuck beside me like glue as Jason followed three steps behind. The park was silent and still. Empty after the sudden attack.

All clear. Or is it?

It was too quiet. Too still. A single shooter was unlikely, a duet more common. But these killers knew who we were even if they were unprepared.

Who would send two gunmen after the likes of us? I would have sent at least three, and probably more for a guaranteed kill.

"Get Nathan to the car. I'll cover you." I motioned for Jason to replace me.

He turned, taking Nathan's arm, and then it happened. The third attack my instincts told me was coming.

A bullet splintered the air where, a second before, Nathan's head had been. Jason swore, scrambling backward as I whirled to face the trees behind us.

The shot had come from a sniper in a tree fifty yards from us.

That's more like it.

For the second time, Jason and Nathan dove for cover. I remained standing, calculating the wind and distance to the sniper.

It all happened in slow motion, but I fired before he could adjust his aim. He cried out and toppled out of his perch. Dead before he hit the ground.

Amateur. You missed your target and gave away

your location.

Two ground troops to move us into the sniper's scope. Distraction, follow through, and execution.

"All clear now," I said, turning back to face the road. I stalked past Jason as he hauled Nathan to his feet.

Nathan looked at me, gaze bewildered. He knew without a shadow of a doubt where the sniper had been aiming. I didn't need to tell him that I had just saved his life.

"Th-thank you... " He shuddered, knees wobbling as I passed.

"You're all right," I said, making sure to put some reassurance in the words. For some reason my instincts insisted I put him at ease.

"This way," Jason said, moving us forward.

Together we formed a triangle as we headed for his car.

I reached the curb just as a black SUV pulled off of the road and stopped. The window rolled down and I narrowed my eyes at the passenger visible inside.

Hidden behind dark sunglasses and a black headscarf, Selah's face met mine. He smirked and something inside of my chest sunk.

I missed something.

A shot rang out and at my side Nathan jerked. Blood sprayed from his arm in my peripheral vision. Four shooters. There were four shooters.

Distraction, follow through, execution, and insurance. My instincts had failed me, as I was getting distracted by Nathan's wellbeing.

Spinning, I caught a glimpse of the other sniper perched in his tree, aiming for Nathan. Fire roared through my veins. Trying to kill me was one thing, but this was something else entirely.

This was an assassination, and Nathan the target.

I stepped in front of Nathan as he bent over

double, clutching at his bleeding arm and gasping in pain.

Selah wasn't there for me.

He was there to kill *Nathan.*

The sniper, hidden by a dark grey mask, hesitated as if waiting for a signal from Selah. I growled deep in my throat.

You've made your last mistake in this life.

I felt Jason turn to point his gun at the SUV, guarding my back again with Nathan sandwiched between us. I tensed. The sniper mirrored my movement, waiting for me to make the first move. Selah had abandoned him to fight on his own. He wasn't going to win this battle.

Nathan swayed on his feet as I set my stance, right foot behind, both knees bent. More than twenty paces separated the sniper from me, but it felt like a Wild West duel. Except with a Barrett MRAD sniper rifle and 9mm Glock instead of revolvers.

Just like the Old West indeed.

It wasn't my finger or the sniper's that made the first move, but rather Nathan, when he fainted. He was upright one minute and the next slumping against the backs of my knees. I saw the sniper move. My finger squeezed once. A single bullet.

Another man toppled out of the trees, dead before he hit the ground.

Turning, I met Selah's glare with my own. He was no longer smiling. Especially when I shot at the SUV's front tires. Jason joined me as the vehicle screeched away from the curb and tore into traffic. Though he couldn't see me, I flipped Selah the middle finger.

"Is it clear?" Jason asked, slowly lowering his gun.

Clutching my injured side, I checked the area over. No one in sight.

"*Now* it's all clear," I stressed before dropping to Nathan's side.

He moaned as I rolled him onto his back.

Jason swooped in, hauling the young man upright. "Let's try this again," he muttered to me as we started for his car.

I rolled my eyes, my injured side forcing me to limp along at the rear. Blood dampened my fingers, a sign that I had pulled the staples out of my skin. *Perfect.*

Jason got us both inside his car and settled before hopping behind the wheel. He shoved the key in the ignition and took off with a roar of the engine. Forcing my own pain away to a dull throb, I turned to Nathan.

He was conscious again, but drowsy. Blood soaked his shirt and sleeve from the wound to his bicep. I couldn't tell if it was just a graze or something more severe.

"This is going to hurt, but I have to stop the bleeding." I met Nathan's gaze as I took off my cardigan and tied it around his wound.

He nodded in understanding and I squeezed. In the rearview mirror, Jason glanced back, checking on me as well as looking for possible tails behind us.

"I thought Selah was a joke. I never thought he'd come back to haunt us." Jason turned sharply at a stoplight, brakes squealing.

"Skunks always have a hard time staying dead." The scars on my wrists throbbed in memory. My only regret for leaving Selah's camp in smoking ruins was that I hadn't taken the time to check that everyone had been reduced to a pile of ashes.

Chapter Seventeen

London, England – October 24th

My grey cardigan, wrapped around Nathan's
wound, had soaked through, turning the expensive
fabric a black-crimson color, before the bleeding
stopped. Sitting in the back of Jason's car, I remained
tense and silent, thoughts a million miles away in
Sudan.

How did Selah survive?

A voice on the phone was easy enough to fake,
but his presence at Hyde Park stole any possible hope
of a ploy. I would have bet my life in the guarantee of
his death mere days earlier. But he had been there, and
not as a ghost.

The memories his image evoked were too jarring.
I closed my eyes, one hand around Nathan's arm, the
other pressed to my own injury.

How did he survive?

Jason glanced back at us in his rearview mirror,
eyebrows raised in concern. I gave a little shake of my
head and tightened my hold on Nathan's injured arm.
He winced in pain. The amount of blood shed between
us seemed much greater smeared across the backseat
like it was.

"Almost there." Jason changed lanes and took the
first right. Pressing my lips together in a firm line, I
counted the seconds before he pulled into the loft's car
park. We walked inside, careful to avoid security
cameras and Jason's neighbors. Being seen bloodied
and bruised was the last thing we needed.

Jason texted Garrett as soon as we stepped inside

his loft. The hacker had a lot to answer for. Despite extensive appearance changes and disguises, Selah had still found us at the park.

And I want to know why.

I took Nathan into the living room and gently set him down in a chair. His hands trembled as he took a glass of water from Jason. I pulled a stool over to sit in front of him.

"I hope you're not too squeamish." I gently took away my blood-soaked cardigan to reveal his injury. Just a graze. He was lucky. "Being shot the first time is always the hardest."

His nose wrinkled. "How many times have *you* been shot?"

"Too many to count." I laughed, reaching under the couch for Jason's first aid kit. Dragging it out, I found the items needed to clean and bandage Nathan's wound.

He kept quiet as I had him take off his shirt. Blood smeared on Jason's couch in the same spots mine had only a few days earlier.

"You're very lucky those snipers were second best." I used Betadine to clean the wound and clear away the blood.

Nathan gnawed on his bottom lip, pain glistening in his eyes.

Carrying over a basin of hot water, Jason eyed the injury over my shoulder. "It'll scar, but only just."

Nathan nodded. After using an antibacterial ointment, I wrapped gauze and an ace bandage around his wound. Thanks to the many injuries sustained during my career, I was a better doctor than most grad students when it came to traumatic injuries. But I was hopeless when it came to the common cold. *Go figure.*

Closing the first aid kit, I started to stand up. Nathan laid his hand on top of mine, stopping me abruptly.

"Quinn?" He looked up at me.

I felt my pulse stutter at the physical contact. I shifted uncomfortably. "Yes?"

"Those men... they were after me, not you."

It wasn't a question. He knew the answer just as well as I did, but the flicker in his gaze told me he still wanted confirmation.

"Yes." I fiddled with a piece of gauze absently. He exhaled, dropping his eyes from mine as he looked away.

"Who would want me dead? I'm no one important."

"That's exactly what I want to know." I sighed.

Nathan nodded, curling onto the couch to stare off into the distance.

Taking the medical kit with me, I crossed the room to stand in the doorway. It didn't take long for Nathan to drift off into a light doze. When his eyelids closed, I left.

◇

I found Jason out on the balcony smoking a cigarette. I nodded a greeting and crossed the space to lean against the wrought iron railing, looking out over the city. The haze of lights and car exhaust blocked out any hope of seeing stars or even the moon. My side was numb from replacing the staples I had torn out during the attack in Hyde Park. It took twice as long to wash the blood off of me as it had Nathan. But it *had* been both of our blood that was smeared all over my clothes.

Putting out his light, Jason walked over to join me on near silent footfalls. He glanced sidelong at me. "Are you all right?"

Our bodies were too close together for my liking. "I'm fine."

"The hell you are," he said.

"I'm fine," I repeated. "Why wouldn't I be?" I took a small step to the side, adding space between us subtly.

"You stepped in to save Nathan's life." A smile curled the edges of Jason's lips. "Not a very Quinn Rogers thing to do."

My eyes narrowed. He was right, and we both knew it. "Why do you care?"

His gaze intensified, an unnamed emotion lurking below the carefree surface. "I've often asked myself that question." Jason turned away, crossing his arms.

"Nice to see there's some humanity left in you after all." My words came out in a hiss. But he was starting to poke at things I had hidden underneath the surface for too long. The secrets of my past needed to remain stuffed into the depths of hell. Why did he think he had the right to unearth them?

Be very careful where you tread. Demons lie underneath my scars.

A breeze wafted past us, carrying with it his cologne. He scuffed the toe of his boot against the ground. Something was on his mind. He was pretending to look properly occupied with other thoughts, but I knew better. The defiant gleam in his eyes did little to aide in his charade. I opened my mouth to speak, but he was faster.

"Happiness looks gorgeous on you."

I started in surprise. Out of everything he could have said, *that* was the last thing I'd expected to hear.

"Happiness?" I frowned, confused.

He licked his lip, glancing off over the city with a faint smile.

"Jason, the very last thing I could be is happy."

"Don't say that. I've never believed your lies."

"What lies?" I spat, suddenly feeling anger flare across my chest to flavor my words.

174

He turned to face me, an odd gleam in his blue eyes. "When are you going to stop telling yourself lies, Quinn?" he whispered.

I stammered, torn between swearing at him and delivering a slap to his sharp cheekbones. "I don't have a rubbish clue what you're talking about," I hissed, spinning on my heel.

He snagged my wrist, stopping me before I could escape. "Oh, but I think you do," he muttered, exhale warm on my neck.

I stiffened as he stepped closer to stare down at my profile.

We were inches apart, in the perfect position to kill each other if we wanted, but neither of us moved.

When I didn't respond, he spoke again. "Have you really forgotten what it was like before Rourke? Before any of this existed?"

I almost recoiled as he gently threaded his fingers through mine.

"Before we had blood on our hands?"

"You forget, I've always had blood on my hands, Jason. I joined Rourke *because* I had blood on my hands." Eyes narrowed, I glanced up at him sharply. He swallowed hard.

"But don't you want to forget that? Isn't that really the reason you joined Rourke. To have your past erased? To forget it?" he asked.

No. I have to remember. I have to remember the pain because I deserve it.

"You're right," I said, breathless. Lying. "I want to forget. I don't want to remember what it was like before."

He shifted, our joined hands keeping me from making a run for it.

"You look beautiful," he said, changing the subject.

I paused, closing my mouth and forcing a polite

smile. "I know. You've mentioned it many times before."

"So I have." He winked at me and placed a light kiss directly above my knuckles. "And so have many other men I assume."

"If you're trying to accuse me of something, just say it." I glared at him, threatening. "But be careful. We're assassins, Jason, killers, *murderers*. We don't fall in love. We *can't* fall in love."

He kissed my hand a second time, his soft lips lingering a moment longer before he pulled away, confliction in his eyes.

"So you keep reminding me," he murmured, turning for the door back inside.

I swallowed hard, pushing back alien emotions. What had he been thinking?

The number one lesson Rourke drilled into our heads was that assassins didn't get attached to anything or anyone. *Ever.* It was just too hard to do what we did and keep a loving, caring side in our hearts. For me, leaving behind romance had never been hard—in fact, it was far too easy in hindsight.

I had always known Jason liked to live wild, defying Rourke's orders and doing things however he thought they should be done. But, like always, he had gone too far. He was trying to drag me along into his rebellion.

Chapter Eighteen

London, England – October 24th

Seated inside the bell tower of the famous Palace of Westminster, I finally found a moment of peace in the darkness. The smog of the city at midnight blocked out the moon in the sky, allowing only a few slivers of its glorious illumination to show. I pulled up the hood of my black sweater and sunk into its shadowy depths.

Gears and the five giant bells of Big Ben hung around me, oblivious to my presence among them. I closed my eyes and breathed in deeply of the night air. Intermixed with thoughts of Jason were conflicted musings of Nathan's fate. After the events of the day, I was more confused about what to do with him than ever. My hostage had to die, that much was certain, but I continued to put it off. The boy I had killed five years earlier was only half of the reason.

Taking another breath, the scent of sandalwood and musk filled my nostrils. An odd combination compared to the smells of metal and stone. I twisted to look behind me, heart leaping into a faster beat.

A shadow-shrouded figure emerged from the darkness, stalking toward me on silent footsteps. The darkness ebbed around him as if he had been molded from the night itself.

"Emotions are agony, are they not?" Rourke's thick accent coated the atmosphere with a soothing lilt.

He stalked forward, not predatorily, not threatening, but with enough of a presence that the wild animal inside me came to attention. Once I couldn't control my fear when he was near me. Now I knew I could hold my own. He had *demanded* I become that good—wanted me to best him—needed me to be a worthy opponent. Even after our years together, I still couldn't piece together the reasons behind his desires.

"Sizing me up, are you?" He eased down to sit beside me. His black coat fluttered open in the breeze to reveal the outline of his loaded Springfield XDs. A flicker of a memory passed through my mind. The last time I'd seen a pistol on his person was the time he shot me.

Rourke's training methods were extremely unorthodox—if training a person to become a bloodthirsty assassin had ever had orthodox instructions and requirements. In a strange, mysterious way he healed the gaping wounds in my life when Andrea Abrams had failed. By giving me a new identity and second chance I became a miracle, to both of us.

Years later, his lessons had shaped and molded me into an unbreakable, unstoppable, merciless force.

I owed everything to Rourke. He was my salvation.

"What happened, Quinn?" The look in his dark eyes told me he'd perceived the thoughts running through my mind and given me a moment to gather my wits.

"Nothing," I whispered. "Just a momentary loss of identity."

"Have you found it, then?" His fingers tapped out a steady beat on the roof as he leaned back on the palms of his hands. "Not everyone breaks into a national landmark to find themselves."

I smiled and rubbed the bridge of my nose. "I think so, but it's... complicated."

"Tell me." Neither a question nor a demand.

Rourke and I regarded each other silently. I

pursed my lips as I read the flicker of emotion in his eyes. Watching him for five years, I'd learned something about the unreadable, mysterious man. I was the only person who could affect whatever monster was living behind his steel walls of emotionlessness.

We were the same, he and I. Two wild things locked inside the cages of our own bodies. He would never admit to it, but there was the same small seed of regret in our black souls that drove us.

For me, it was the event that had sent me running in the first place.

For Rourke—I had never dared to ask.

"It's nothing, really." Telling him a half-truth was better than a total lie. He knew me too well to accept a lie. "Garrett has me worried. There have been far too many attempts on my life in the last few days by the FBI... and Selah."

The lines on Rourke's face hardened at the name. The hand he had resting in the space between our bodies slowly clenched into a fist.

"Garrett has never slipped up before. And now all of this in so short a time period. Rourke, I don't want to say I don't trust him, but—"

"You don't trust him." Rourke finished for me, his voice inflection never wavering.

I gave him a tired smile. His hand unclenched and wrapped around mine slowly. The heartstrings I'd severed long ago shifted, shaking off dust and cobwebs.

Rourke's hand on mine was a wild invitation. His black soul pushed against mine, urging it to join him in a dance with death. My lips pressed together firmly as my lungs pulled in a gasp of air that made Rourke chuckle lightly. He squeezed my hand before releasing. A thrill arched up my spine. I breathed a sigh of relief as Rourke smiled.

"Don't worry about Garrett. I will deal with him."
He got to his feet, his shoulder brushing against mine.

I ignored it. Our relationship was complicated. I
didn't need the added weight of sorting through the
years of baggage and manipulation. He was a storm—
from far away he looked beautiful and breathtaking,
but up close I could see the true havoc of his affection.
If we ever took the next step we would fall off the very
edge we had been toeing for so long.

In the end, we would destroy one another.

"Rourke?"

He turned back to face me, eyebrows lifted, dark
gaze expectant and interested. I swallowed, uncoiling
to stand opposite him. A breeze ruffled my hair,
obscuring my vision.

"What do I look like in your eyes?" The question
had never been planned, and in fact, unbalanced me. It
seemed to have the same effect on Rourke, because he
smiled, a reaction he only ever let happen in my
presence.

He sidled closer, goosebumps popping up along
my arms as if a magnetic attraction between us called
them into existence.

"Why would you ask such a question?" he
murmured, watching my face suspiciously. "Has
someone made you question yourself, Quinn?"

I shook my head.

"Are you questioning yourself?"

Looking up, I felt the full effect of his intense
gaze as our eyes locked. I resisted the instinctive urge
to glance away and stared back. Rourke didn't even
breathe as he reached out to lift my hands into the faint
moonlight. The pale skin around my wrists that were
forever marked with scars glistened.

"I don't want you to worry about Selah," Rourke
said gently. "I can and will handle him."

I nodded in agreement, gulping. His touch was

soft and yet made my skin burn.

"Focus on what has to be done."

Pulling away from him, I nodded again and smiled in reassurance. "I've never doubted you, Rourke. I have feared you, but never doubted that you could do anything you promised."

He leaned forward to press a delicate kiss against my cheek and exhale warm on my neck. I smiled brighter, relaxing into his mysterious affection in ways that I could never do with Jason.

"When you are ready again, Quinn, I have an assignment for you that I think you will enjoy."

"I know I will." I stuffed my hands into the pockets of my jeans.

"Let me know if you need anything, love. You know where to find me." He gave me a faint ghost of a smile.

I nodded, watching him turn away, and then suddenly face me again. My pulse jumped at the strange light in his eyes.

"Garrett told me you are staying at Jason's loft. Before I found you, I went looking for you there. I heard shouting inside. Be on guard for trouble when you go back."

At first I thought he was joking, perhaps even testing me about Nathan's existence, but that quickly passed when I saw the almost melancholy look in the corner of his eyes. What had Jason done? Whatever it was, Rourke knew and it wasn't good.

"Thank you." I started to back away.

"Quinn?"

I stopped, heart in my throat.

"In my eyes you wear darkness and power equally well. You have always been half shadows and half Hell."

Time seemed frozen around us as we stood opposite one another, camouflaged by the shadows of

Big Ben. I made myself smile. It's what I had wanted to hear after all. Rourke's faith in me still held even if I doubted my ability to do the right thing when Nathan was involved.

He nodded and was gone, descending into the shadows of the clock tower.

Not daring to breathe, I took off as fast as my injury would allow down another set of stairs, my thoughts spinning out of control. I forced myself not to think about Nathan. Yes, he was going to have to die, but that would be at my hand and my hand alone. Leaving him alone had been a terrible mistake.

The blocks I had traveled to get away from the loft complex flew under my feet in a blur as I ran. I reached Jason's and surged up the fire escape to drop down onto his balcony. When no sound reached my ears, I threw open the sliding door and burst inside.

Nathan's muffled shouting greeted me when I entered. At least he hadn't escaped or been killed. I moved to the coat closet and ripped away the chair wedged under the door handle. He burst out, gasping heavily.

"What happened?" I demanded. "Where's Jason?"

Nathan gestured wildly, sweat dampening his forehead—a sign of how long he had been struggling to get out.

Bloody hell, he looks awful.

"I don't know," he said. "He came back in from the balcony, forced me in there, and then ran out."

"Did he say anything?" I gripped both of his arms, leveling my face with his. "It's very important if he did."

He shook his head, and then reconsidered.

"Yes, he muttered something about an 'assignment overdue' that he should have done a long time ago."

"I'm going to kill him," I hissed. My thoughts reared up, bristling at these sudden heroic urges.

Calm down. I'm only finding him to kill him myself.

"Where are you going?" Nathan asked, brow furrowing with concern.

"Jason said something about an overdue assignment. There's only one place he could be."

"What are you going to do?" He frowned.

"Nothing good."

Chapter Nineteen

London, England – October 25th

Jason's Corvette was gone from the loft's car park, but I found his Land Rover in its proper place. Getting behind the wheel, I found the key hidden underneath the seat.

At least he's a creature of habit.

As I pulled out of the car park, I dialed Garrett's cell and muttered under my breath for the hacker to pick up. I still didn't trust the hacker, but he would know where Jason was—or at least, I hoped so. Normally, I never would have been concerned, but something about Rourke's expression and comment had made me pause. His mention of the loft and possibility of danger was on purpose. Why, I didn't know, and that worried me. Rourke never did anything without ulterior motives.

"Hello?" Garrett finally picked up on the seventh ring.

"Where's Jason?" My tone left no room for questions. There was a pause and I could hear the faint clicks of the hacker's fingers on a keyboard. Though he was quite possibly the last person I wanted to call he would know where Jason was. At least I hoped so.

"His tracker says that he's at his loft. Why? What's going on, Quinn?"

I cursed under my breath, fingers tapping out an unsteady rhythm on the gearshift. "I don't know, but he isn't at the loft. I need to know where he's gone."

"That's the only reading he has," he said.

A cold sweat began building at my temples. If

Jason's tracker was still at his loft and he wasn't—

I shuddered. It was the only risky precaution Rourke had ever insisted on having for his assassins. Before we finished our training, tracking devices were injected into our forearms. The devices were no bigger than a sliver and only readable by Garrett's computer software. It was only removable if you carved it out of your body—a very bloody and painful task to be sure.

"He's cut it out," I muttered.

"If he cut out his tracker, this isn't a problem for you, Quinn," Garrett said. "I need to alert Rourke that he's gone rogue."

"No, wait," I snapped, my thoughts spiraling.

"Wait? Quinn, you know the rules."

"Rourke hinted there was something wrong." I shook my head. "He knows already. This is a test."

"Then you need to stay the hell away," Garrett hissed. "You're already in enough trouble."

I didn't need him to say Nathan's name to know that he was referring to my hostage. The fire in my veins built. Anger pierced through my thoughts.

I turned the Land Rover's steering wheel with a sharp crank.

"I'm going after Jason. If he's gone rogue, I can do Rourke a favor and finish him off." I hung up and dropped my phone into my lap.

If Jason is really where I think he is...

"I'm going to kill him," I hissed out loud.

<><>

Twenty minutes later, I was standing outside of an old abandoned warehouse, a particularly favored location of Selah's men who often camped inside to see to their business in the UK. While I had visited the building on an assignment to assassinate three of Selah's operatives twelve months ago, I had a bad

186

feeling that Jason was there for a much different reason.

If he's inside, I'm going to break his nose for being so stupid.

We didn't associate with Selah's men other than to kill each other. The only other reason Jason could have gone into the warehouse sent shivers down my spine.

"Are you sure about this?" I whispered to myself as I rounded the Land Rover.

Garrett knew where I was thanks to my tracker. And Nathan was safe in Jason's loft, and would remain that way until I decided to collect him.

If I survive this.

Leaving the vehicle behind, I headed to the back of the warehouse. From the rear it was a clear shot inside through a loading bay. My conscience kept poking at me.

This is a trap and you know it.

Shaking my head, I bent down to pick the lock.

Damn it all to heck. Trap or not, I'm going in.

Memories of the assignment that had brought me here were fresh and raw in my mind. A mental floor plan resurfaced from my memory. Keeping one hand on the wall, I started deeper into the dark building. My eyes adjusted to the dim lighting until I could make out vague hulking shapes ahead. Broken glass and other debris crunched under my boots. I spotted a door and, finding the doorknob, turned it silently to peek through.

Shuddering fluorescent bulbs from the high ceilings above illuminated pipes, gears, and dozens of scaffolding platforms before me. I slipped through the door and started up the six stairs to the first metal platform. Gloved hand sliding over the railing, I walked the length of the platform and started up more steps to a second level.

Voices.

Dropping into a crouch, I drew my gun. The voices were no more than murmurs as I moved forward, staying low to the platform. When at last I could make out words, I stopped and peered over the railing to the main floor. The sight wasn't a welcome one.

Four men and one woman congregated below around a prisoner—which just so happened to be Jason. He was standing upright, arms tethered above his head to an upended bedframe. Blood stained his sweat-dampened shirt, but I couldn't tell the extent of his injuries from my distance. He was still breathing, but his head hung limply between his shoulders.

Well don't you look handsome.

One of the men below picked up a knife from a table. Spinning the blade in his hand, he sauntered closer to Jason. He said something that I couldn't make out and Jason shook his head. Angrily, the man stepped back, lifting the blade to stab. I lifted my Glock, but paused. The man wasn't attacking—yet. I needed to get closer.

The platform creaked quietly beneath my feet as I flipped over the railing and swung onto a lower level. I tucked into a roll to land behind a stack of wood, my side groaning in agony. The voices were louder as I leaned forward to see the scene before me.

"How can you come back here, cowering like a dog with its tail between his legs?" The man with the knife spoke in a deep African accent.

Jason didn't reply.

"You say you wish to be one of us, and yet you tried to kill us. Now you come back like a prodigal son. What am I to believe?"

If I had any doubt before, I knew then. The people surrounding Jason were in league with Selah. I bristled at the name. Mere hours earlier we had been fighting to kill Rourke's enemy.

What could Jason possibly want here? Surely he isn't playing double agent.

The dangerous thought made my jaw clench. Nothing was past Jason—he was the kind of reckless, stupid daredevil who would play double agent as long as it benefited him. Or got him killed.

I peered farther around the stack of crates I was using as cover, my back sliding against it.

"Maiko, go get the van ready," the man still holding the knife demanded.

The woman, Asian by her name, spun on her heel and disappeared. "Bones, Leroy, go with her. Get the boxes sorted. I will take care of this pig myself."

Two more of the assassins left, subtracting the total of five down to two. Now they were just making it easy for me.

"A double-crossing assassin... " the African slurred, grabbing Jason by the hair to bring his face up.

I gripped the grip of my gun, my finger curling around the trigger gently.

"What is fitting punishment for you, hmm? Death, yes, but how would you prefer?"

The other man chuckled as his companion pressed the switchblade to Jason's throat. To his credit, Jason glared defiantly back, his lips bared in a sneer.

"I'd prefer not to die," he mocked.

With a guttural cry, the African moved in for the kill.

My gun jumped in my hand as I fired it, the shot echoing off of the walls of the warehouse. The man stumbled, his knife slipping through his fingers as my bullet went clean through his chest. Blood splattered the ground at Jason's feet. The other man leapt to his feet as I stalked out of the shadows under the scaffolding. My second bullet shot through his neck.

The silent scream that failed to issue from his lips seared itself into memory. I lowered my weapon and looked over the two bodies at Jason, who was staring at me, ashen.

"What in the world are you doing here?" he gasped.

Shaking my head, I hurried over to him and severed his bonds with two precise slashes of the dropped switchblade.

"Saving you it would appear, you wanker. What are *you* doing here? None of that sounded like an assignment." I freed him from the bedframe, his raw flesh bleeding from the rough cords of the rope. He winced and wiggled his fingers as I examined him.

"Squaring up some business." He refused to make eye contact.

"Business. *Right.*" I snorted. "Because that looked exactly like a business meeting. Since when do you have business with Selah?"

I stepped back to give him room to walk and wasn't prepared for his wobbly step toward me. Jason's knees buckled and he dropped like a rag doll. Instinctively, I grabbed his arms, catching him before he could collapse fully.

"Steady on. Are you all right?"

"Yeah, yeah... never better," he tried to joke, but the pale color of his face gave his true weakness away.

I frowned as he pushed me aside to prove his point. His knees buckled again, and this time I was too slow to catch him. He crashed to the floor heavily on his hands and knees. The muscles in his back quivered as he gagged and then coughed up a mouthful of saliva and blood.

Oh, this isn't good.

I knelt beside him, watching as his arms shook. Head hanging between his shoulders, he didn't look up at me. His heavy breathing was the only sound for several tense moments.

"Jason?"

He looked up at me and gave a weak smile, the expression riddled with pain. Frowning, I sat back on my heels as he propped himself against the upended bedframe. I took a closer look at the bloodstains on his shirt then, noting the way the material hung in tatters. With one swift jerk, I pulled it off of him and recoiled.

"Oh my," I whispered, hand to my mouth.

"I've been working out." He winced, and then gave me a forced grin. "Enjoy ripping my clothes off?"

Of all the absolute imperfect times for crude jokes—I could have slapped him but instead settled on a glare. The mischief in his eyes died. Tiredly, he shook his head.

"It's not as bad as it looks," he said. "I've had worse."

I reached out and gently brushed his torn flesh. He gasped and I drew back, shocked at the brutality of the injury. A swath of skin had been gouged raw, black and blue bruises spreading out from it grotesquely.

"What did they use?" I asked, barely above a whisper.

"A pair of pliers," he said. And then he added, "They had some fun."

"Damn right, they did."

The assassin didn't seem to hear me, because at that moment he reached up to touch my cheek tenderly.

"You've changed, Quinn."

The symptoms of internal hemorrhaging were all there—he was lightheaded and dizzy. Judging by the state of his injury, caused both by stabbing and blunt trauma, he needed immediate medical attention.

"You've lost a lot of blood, Jas," I said, tone

concerned.

"Jas?" He smiled faintly. "Since when do you use nicknames?"

"Now isn't the time. You could die." I pushed his hand away quickly, heat burning upward from the touch.

His face contorted as if I had offended him. "Since when do you care?"

"I don't. I'm completely comfortable leaving you here to bleed out on the cold floor."

"All right, all right, no need to be mean." He grunted, wrapping his arm around my shoulders. The groan of pain that issued from his lips while I helped him to his feet was enough to make me wince.

"Where are we going?"

"Outside. I borrowed your Land Rover."

"You drove my baby?" He gaped.

"You left me no other option."

He tried to chuckle, but the noise sounded pained. I adjusted my shoulder under his arm and started forward. Jason managed to stay with me, but the fresh blood trickling from his wound was extremely worrying.

The walk through the warehouse felt much longer than the actual five minutes it took. Jason's weight on my arm increased with every step, his strength to hold himself up flagging. Sweat beaded on our foreheads from exertion. Glancing over my shoulder every other step, I ground my teeth at the slow progress we were making. Every second we weren't driving for the nearest hospital was a second longer Jason teetered on the brink and Selah's goons had a second chance of discovering us escaping.

"Almost there," I said, pulling him with me.

Jason groaned, eyes closed, head tilted toward mine. Shivers raced across my neck as his hot breath fluttered the hair by my ear.

We staggered into sight of the Land Rover, and I unlocked the vehicle with the key fob. We reached it just as Jason's strength gave out completely and I scrambled to catch him. Opening the backseat, I helped the injured assassin inside. He groaned as I snagged his San Diego hoodie from the back to staunch the flow of blood from his wound. His favorite. He'd probably never forgive me.

After making sure he wouldn't bleed out on the leather seats, I hurried around to the other side of the car and revved the engine.

"There's a hospital not far from here. Just stay with me until then, okay?" I glanced back at Jason as I shifted into drive.

"I d-don't need to go to the h-hospital," Jason groaned. "Just take me back to my loft. I have bandages."

You're going to need a lot more than bandages.

"Jas, you need a doctor. That wound isn't something simple bandages are going to fix."

"You'd be surprised. I fixed your shrapnel injury."

"That's different."

"Don't take me to the hospital. There will be too many prying eyes." Jason's voice was pained.

I hated to admit that he did have a point. A hospital was the last place I wanted to turn up, considering I was barely dodging the public eye myself.

"All right," I conceded. "We'll go to Garrett's house."

He's the best at medical procedures anyway.

Jason laid his head back against the headrest. His fight won for the time being.

"You looked like an angel when you showed up back there," he mumbled, his wink turning into a wince of pain.

I rolled my eyes, digging out my cell phone.

"I was praying for a miracle just before you showed up."

Oh wonderful, he was praying too. One thing was for sure, I wasn't going to be able to handle a lovesick, praying assassin.

It had better be from the blood loss.

"Well, I'm glad I could be of assistance. Although I am curious as to why they said you were trying to join them *and* kill them. You do realize that it was Selah who flew in his helicopter to blow me up, right? And he attacked us in the park."

Jason didn't reply.

"I told you he called me. I told you he said he was coming. Are you playing double agent for him and Rourke?"

"That's a long story, Quinn. Now is not the time." He let out a sigh and closed his eyes.

I rolled my eyes, dialing Garrett's number and putting the phone to my ear. For the second time that night I found myself turning to the one person I didn't want to trust, but there was no one else to call.

He answered right away. "Yes?"

"Garrett? I found him. We are headed to your house now."

"I'm already waiting."

"Good. Get your medical room ready, Jason needs a blood transfusion as soon as possible."

Chapter Twenty

Garrett's House – October 25th

Garrett was waiting for us on the front porch of his house when I pulled into the driveway. During the drive, it had taken me continuously talking to keep Jason from slipping into unconsciousness. While any other time I might have welcomed the fact that he was unresponsive, I knew all too well what falling asleep might do to his condition. The amount of blood he had lost was dangerous. He needed to be awake to fight off the advances of death.

I opened my door, getting out as the hacker rounded the vehicle to haul Jason from the back seat. Without a word, Garrett carried the injured assassin across the driveway, up the stairs of his front porch, and inside. I followed on his heels, holding my breath.

"What happened?" Garrett demanded when we were inside his medical room. He looked over the extent of Jason's injuries.

"Selah's goons," I replied with a hiss.

Peeling away the hoodie from the wound elicited a moan of pain from Jason, his jaw clenched. I opened the first aid kit Garrett had set out in preparation.

There's been far too much time spent in one of these lately.

"I hope you have a blood IV ready." I glanced at Garrett as he opened a bottle of antiseptic.

He nodded in the direction of a medical cart pushed against the wall. "Fresh from Rourke's safe at London Advertising. He won't even notice that it's gone."

"Good," I snapped. "One less thing to worry about."

Jason's eyelids drooped heavily as we inserted an IV needle into a vein and started giving him the needed blood drip. I stayed by his side, making sure that the procedure worked properly, as Garrett began attending the injuries to his torso. It didn't take long to locate the incision Jason had made to remove his tracker. Garrett made no comment about it, leaving the bandage already on it in place. The slow and tedious process of cleaning the raw area of skin on Jason's stomach had me wincing in sympathetic pain. At one point it took two shots of morphine before Jason would allow further treatment.

As the hacker put the finishing touches on a row of precise stitches, Jason drifted off into unconsciousness. We left him to sleep and cleaned ourselves up in the bathroom.

"He'll be all right if the bleeding stops soon," Garrett said, tossing a hand towel over his shoulder.

I looked up from where I sat on the edge of the bathtub, elbows braced on my knees. A similar rag was clasped in my hands, stained pink.

I'm just about tired of having to wash someone else's blood off of me.

"The question is what are we going to do with him if he survives?"

I said nothing, staring at the floor.

"You know Rourke will want him killed for what he did."

"Tell me something I don't know." Clenching my hands around the towel, I slowly got to my feet and faced him. "Jason didn't do anything wrong."

Garrett frowned. "But he—"

"You're the hacker. Change what happened to suit our needs. Rourke warned me about Jason for a reason. It's a test," I said.

"A test?"

I nodded. "For what, I'm not sure yet. But for now we need to act as if nothing happened."

"Are you certain that's a good idea?"

"Someone tried to set a trap for me, Garrett. I don't know why, and I don't know who, but I do know that Jason's the real victim in this, even if he instigated it. If Selah set the trap, then he will try again once he learns that it failed. As much as it pains me to say it, we'll need Jason then." I took a deep breath. "Tell Rourke that nothing went wrong. You'll see that I'm right."

I pushed past him into the hallway.

"I'm not sure whether to hope you're right or wrong," he called after me.

◇

Luckily for Jason, after the harrowing time spent securing his survival, my anger had shifted to focus solely on Selah. And my frustration to Rourke.

If Selah had indeed tried to trap me then Rourke had knowingly sent me there in retrieval of Jason. The master assassin would never want me hurt or killed, but he liked to push the boundaries on propriety and make sure I was at the top of my game. Even if that meant throwing me to the fire and wolves. The trick, as it had always been with Rourke, was figuring out his reasoning before it got you and everyone around you killed.

But I knew one thing for certain. Selah had come gunning for me and then reached to include Nathan and Jason. Who was next on the man's hit list? Rourke? Not if I had anything to say about it.

The living room was quiet where I had taken refuge after stabilizing Jason and bringing Nathan over from the assassin's loft. My hostage was sprawled in an armchair, his head resting on a hand, his eyelids dropping lower and lower with each blink. I lay across the chair facing him, my legs dangling off of the armrest. A mug of Chai tea that had long since gone cold sat at my elbow, but the rejuvenating smell of it remained. To my right, a lamp on a corner table illuminated the room in a cozy, but modern sort of way.

Who knew Garrett was such a homemaker.

"Do you want something else to drink?" Garrett paused in the doorway as he walked toward the kitchen.

I shook my head, glancing over at Nathan.

He didn't so much as stir at the interruption. "No, just a blanket please."

Whether he approved or not, Garrett didn't object to my request and soon brought in a fuzzy black-and-white throw.

"I'm going to be in my office if you need anything," he told me as I stood to accept the blanket from his outstretched hand. His gaze drifted downward to stare at Nathan. "Try not to do anything stupid while I'm gone."

"You know me."

He left the room as I silently crossed the floor to lay the blanket over Nathan's still form. His eyes were closed, lashes lying softly on tanned skin. His sketchbook lay open on a side table, the start of a new drawing taking form. I couldn't help but smile at the way his hair hung over his forehead. He looked so peaceful asleep.

The dark hair that shaded his face from the lamp's light was curly just like his mother's. His button nose made his full lips seem doll-like. Pure and innocent—perfect.

He couldn't be older than eleven, and he had the innocence to prove it.

Pushing the memories away, I sighed and checked the time on my phone. It was late, or early depending on what routine you slept. I pinched the bridge of my nose. Exhaustion suddenly tugged on my limbs and eyelids. It was time to sleep and forget about everything for a few short hours.

I left Nathan where he was and headed to the guest bedroom where Garrett had arranged for me to stay. It wasn't until I was lying down, hands behind my head staring at the ceiling, that I realized what I had done.

Did I really just tuck Nathan in?

Covering him with the blanket had been so natural that even Garrett hadn't seemed to notice I was doing it. What had come over me lately? The confident, merciless assassin in me felt raw.

I sat upright in bed and glanced to the open door. The exhaustion vanished, and in its place numb confusion settled into place. Sighing, I ran my hands through my dark hair and then scrubbed at my eyes. A dull ache started at the base of my skull and began traveling upward. Another sigh. I pushed off of the mattress and padded back down the hallway to the room where Jason was sleeping off his painkillers. Quietly opening the door, I peeked inside to see him stretched out on the bed.

"You awake?"

His eyes opened at my voice, then he blinked and squinted.

"It's me," I said, stepping into the room and going to stand beside the bed.

He smiled, finally focusing on my face.

"Are you comfortable?"

He nodded, easing himself upright with a great deal of effort. I slid a pillow behind his back and earned a weak grin of gratitude in return. Silence settled between us. I kept my gaze anywhere but his.

What am I doing in here?

To break the silence, I spoke. "I still think you need to see a doctor." Gently, I fingered the thick bandage wrapped around his bare torso. It had taken Garrett and I four attempts to wrap it correctly. But the real miracle had been leveling out his blood pressure to where death no longer crouched expectantly at his door.

Though he didn't reply, Jason's eyelids fluttered as he yawned, the effects of the painkiller Garrett had given him kicking in with another bout of drowsiness. I watched his chest rise and fall rhythmically as he drifted off to sleep. The sight of him sleeping made my own exhaustion hit like a cinder block.

Let's try this again.

I curled up on the floor, my head resting against the bed at Jason's side. Amid the lingering smell of antiseptic and morphine, I picked up on the sweet hint of honey and lavender. A candle burned brightly on the bedside table. My eyelids drooped as I yawned. I closed my eyes and the darkness enveloped me in peaceful slumber.

◇

The little boy's room at the very end of the hall was oddly clean. Light from a night lamp illuminated the numerous drawings of stars, constellations, and rocket ships taped to the walls. A stack of books sat on the floor, all of them related to astronomy. Plastic glow-in-the-dark stars glimmered on the ceiling, a pale imitation of the real thing.

I stepped into the room and spotted the aspiring astronaut collapsed in a beanbag chair at the foot of his twin-sized bed. Another stack of books lay at his side, a large one open and spread across his lap. I stared at him, taking in his peaceful features as he slept.

My heart was in my throat as I hideously stole inside his very dreams. The toe of my leather boot bumped a toy rocket ship model, and it clunked in the silence. With a soft exhale, the boy shifted in his sleep.

Eyelids fluttering open, the boy woke. I tensed, watching him lift his gaze to me. Confusion, and then fear, overcame his expression. It was my cry, not his, that filled the night.

Nathan stood up before me.

"Quinn?" His breath came in a panicked flutter, his emerald green eyes wide and reflecting the streams of light.

I started backpedaling immediately as he took a step toward me. His fear vanished and in its place concern appeared.

"Quinn? What's wrong?"

"I'm sorry," I gasped. "I'm so sorry."

◇

Jason's rough, hacking cough jolted me awake around four a.m. I sat bolt upright, my neck cringing in pain, nightmare scattering away. The bed shook as Jason convulsed on top of it, face red from exertion.

Scrambling to my feet, I felt my legs nearly collapse. Pins and needles had set in after sleeping in such an awkward position for so long. I shook them out and hurried over to a side table. Jason continued coughing as I found a glass of water and sprinted it back to him.

"Here." I offered the glass and winced when he wheezed violently.

Spittle clung to his lip as I sat beside him. His expression was pained as I helped him upright, steadying the water while he took several deep gulps.

"Thank you," he said when he could breathe

again.

I set the empty glass down as he collapsed back onto the mound of pillows behind him.

The mattress leaned toward him as I crossed both legs and rested my chin on folded hands. Jason lay with his eyes closed, nose tilted toward the ceiling. He looked haggard with the bandages around his torso, pale tint to his cheeks. The heavy exhale he took made the illusion even worse.

What is he thinking, playing games with Rourke and Selah? A few gouges with a pair of pliers are the best case scenario of what could have happened to him.

"Are you all right?" I spoke gently.

His eyes fluttered open and he turned his head to look at me.

"Yes." It was more of a rasp than an actual tone.

We lapsed into a long, drawn-out silence that escalated into awkwardness. He was all too acutely trying to avoid staring at me while I pretended to be fascinated by the light shining on my hands. Finally, I couldn't stand it any longer. I had to relieve some of the anxiety in the atmosphere.

"Can I get you anything? Food? More water? I think Garrett said we should change the bandaging every few hours." The words tumbled off my tongue in a torrent.

"No, I'm all right, thank you."

Shrugging my shoulders, I stood and turned to go.

At least I tried to make it less awkward.

"Quinn, wait... " Jason gestured for me to sit back down on the mattress beside him. While he scooted over an inch or two—wincing with every shift—I perched on the edge of the piece of furniture. "I owe you an explanation."

"Damn straight."

He took a deep breath, gaze trailing up to stare at

the ceiling. I watched his fingers twitch absently over the bandages on his torso.

"Selah contacted me several months ago," Jason whispered. "He offered me a position with him if I'd leave Rourke's organization. Of course, I said no, but after he attacked us I thought it might be convenient to have a man on the inside to know his plans."

"Please tell me you aren't seriously thinking about joining Selah."

After all Rourke had done for us, Jason was going to jump ship? I couldn't bring myself to believe it—or the consequences that he would endure from the master assassin. Death wouldn't be the only thing he'd face.

"I am serious about it," he said. "I am going to join Selah if they will still take me after the event at the warehouse."

"You're insane. You don't need a doctor, you need a shrink."

"Quinn, please hear me out." He winced as he leaned forward. "Rourke's only goal is to unleash the International Free Militia on a weakened world, and he is close—so very, very close. Selah's presence is a testament to it. But what happens after Rourke is done with the IFM? What happens to us when our jobs are done? What will *we* do then?"

I folded my arms, trying not to take an interest in what Jason was saying. But it was impossible. His questions were the same as my own.

Rourke's plans only went so far as unleashing the terrorist superpower on the world. He was incredibly mute on what would happen when he began to build his better world. What happened next, or to us, was a complete mystery—and a worrisome one at that. Our employer had never been the predictable sort.

"Selah's against the IFM. If you join him, Rourke will destroy you," I said, tasting the bitterness in my tone.

"Selah's plan is to come against Rourke," Jason said. "As soon as Rourke has razed the earth to the ground, he will rebuild it by putting into place the kind of people he supports. I've seen what kind of killers Rourke can put on thrones. Heck, you and I have both helped him do it. What world will it become with Rourke playing puppeteer?"

I stood up, distancing myself from him. Jason's brow furrowed as he studied my expression.

"Selah knows Rourke will go too far, that he won't stop at the IFM. He's going to go on killing and engaging chaos. We're puppets, and he is the master. We have to leave him while we still can. Rourke will burn the entire world to the ground before he is finished proving a point. There is no question of that. We have to do something."

"What are you saying, Jason?" I whispered. "We're assassins, we aren't supposed to save the world."

Garrett suddenly knocked on the door, silencing us and coming to my rescue. "Hey, you two all right in here?"

"Yes, fine." I narrowed my eyes. "Jason, however, needs to get some more sleep."

"You know it's true, Quinn." Jason's expression was serious. A strange oddity compared to his usually carefree features.

I fidgeted, trying desperately to avoid buying into his words.

The truth in my heart was that I had been silently questioning Rourke's intentions for a while, but had never been brazen enough to speak up about it. If he wanted to destroy the world, he had good reason to do it. I owed him my life. Everything I was came from him—who was I to contradict his plans?

"Quinn?"

Shaking my head, I sighed heavily so that my lungs rattled with the exhale.

"I don't know, Jason." I flipped off the lights and left.

Chapter Twenty-One

Garrett's House – October 25th

A knock on the door to the guestroom startled me out of my thoughts. My finger tapped the pause button on my iPad, silencing the lead singer of 3 Doors Down.

Nathan appeared at the doorway. "Want some tea?"

There were few words that could bring a smile to my face immediately, but Nathan had hit on three of them.

"You'd better come in," I said.

He matched my smile and pushed through the door slowly, displaying the steaming mug in his hands. I inhaled deeply the smell of Chai. My grin grew brighter. He crossed the brown and green rug to reach me where I lay on the bed. Sitting upright, I accepted the drink with an appreciative grin.

No matter how wicked I am, my one true weakness is a good cup of tea.

"Garrett said you like it dirty."

I arched an eyebrow as I took a tentative sip. The scalding liquid was blasted full of caffeine and sugar. I could already feel the charge of energy tingling in my veins.

"He also told me that means with a shot of espresso, not alcohol. Although, under different circumstances, I'm sure certain allowances could be made."

"Absolutely perfect." I patted the mattress for him to sit. "You should be a barista."

"Apparently, I should be a lot of things," he said, smiling so that his dimples showed. "None of which are alive."

"Touché."

Exhaling, he sat down beside me, crossing his legs to show off the pattern on his socks. I rolled my eyes. Jason had struck again. The Batman logos around the ankles were altogether too like him to be mere coincidence.

"Nice socks." I took another drink of my Chai. The warmth of the mug between my hands raced up my wrists, raising my body temperature.

Nathan chuckled. "Jason said they'd look better on me."

I had to admit he was probably correct. Putting aside my iPad, I studied him through the steam wafting off of my tea.

No fear shone in his eyes as he leaned forward to read the screen of my device and scroll through my music playlists. I lifted my tea to take another sip, feeling an odd sense of peace and calm. The way Nathan sat next to me, hands casually folded in his lap, posture relaxed and open, made me pause. Baffled, I turned inward to observe myself.

I don't want to kill him.

I started at the discovery that I mirrored his openness, relaxing against the mattress beside him. There was no pressure to end the beating heart of the witness beside me, no desire to kill and torture. I pursed my lips in thought.

How did this relationship sneak up on me? And what's the meaning of it?

When I was with him, I felt as if I were normal—just for a moment. That feeling alone made me want to explore it. Normalcy had never been my life, and until then I had never wanted it for myself.

I took another long sip of my tea. Nathan shifted,

hands clasping in his lap as he turned to look at me.

"Thank you," he began softly.

I frowned in silent question to his comment.

Shifting again, he cleared his throat awkwardly. "Back at the park, I never got to thank you for saving my life. If you hadn't jumped in front of me like that, the sniper would have—"

"Taken another shot," I finished for him.

He nodded, eyes haunted.

"Don't mention it," I muttered into my mug. The steam caressed my face as I inhaled the strong scent of masala Chai. "You can hardly thank me for saving your life when I was the one who put it in danger in the first place."

He dropped his gaze and fell silent. After the events of the last few days I had yet to sort through everything that had happened. But I knew one thing for certain—saving Nathan had changed everything. For better or worse.

"How's Jason?"

I blinked, eyes wide, surprised that Nathan would take such an interest.

"Doing better," I said. "The morphine is keeping the pain down so he's sleeping now, and probably will be for a while."

"I'm glad he's all right." Nathan smiled. Another surprise.

"Are you?" I frowned. "Because I wouldn't be... in your shoes."

"He isn't the one who kidnapped me."

"No." I rubbed my thumbs over the hot surface of the ceramic mug in my hands. More of a therapeutic motion then a conscious one. "I'm the one who did that."

Nathan shifted closer to me, dimples appearing as he smiled. The kindness in his eyes was nearly overwhelming. Abruptly unnerved, I looked away from him. I set my mug down on the side table, needing something to do to keep calm. The way he looked at me was the same way Rourke did—seeing right through me. Except where the master assassin saw my lethalness, Nathan seemed to find *hope*.

"Do you regret it?" His eyes flicked to my face. I could have sworn the troop of butterflies in my stomach twitched at the announcement.

"Do I regret what?" I pretended ignorance to buy time to recover from the question.

"Saving me."

What am I supposed to tell him?

I shifted, fidgeting under his intense gaze and knowing expression. The sound of the clock sitting on the stand next to my mug of tea ticked on, filling the room with an annoying cadence of sound. I swallowed hard, placing both hands on either side of my legs so that they gripped the edge of the bed.

How do I tell someone I'm supposed to murder that they're only alive because I'm afraid? I took a deep breath and forced a tightlipped smile. *Because I'm afraid... I'm afraid to kill my second chance.*

"It all happened so fast," I said. "Kidnapping you and then having to run. At the park... it all went horribly wrong."

"No, Quinn, it went horribly *right*."

How very little Nathan truly knew about my life. I had never done the right thing, even when I was called Andrea Abrams.

My chest tightened, my pulse thumping faster in my veins. I felt defensive and ice cold and helpless all at the same time. But the overwhelming surges of feeling were pushed aside by a single emotion. *Relief.* It felt so unexpectedly calming to be understood by someone. Nathan knew me in ways I didn't know myself, yet he barely knew me at all.

I took a deep breath. *Say something. Anything.*

"I'm just going to keep drinking my tea and pretend you didn't say that." Picking up my mug, I downed the lukewarm liquid in three gulps. The sweetness of the beverage almost choked me.

He laughed, dismissing my comment. "Did you know that Kryptonite by 3 Doors Down was the first song I learned to play on the guitar?"

"Now why would I know that?" I pursed my lips together in thought, brow furrowing.

He shrugged innocently and pointed to my iPad. "I can probably play any song you could ask for from your playlist," he said.

"All right." I leaned forward and smirked. "Play something for me, Nathan. I know that Garrett keeps at least one kind of instrument around here somewhere. He likes to plunk away at making music when he's stressed. Apparently, he used to be in a punk rock band before he discovered the beauty of hacking technology."

"He told me," Nathan replied. "He also gave me his guitar."

I sat back as he popped off the bed and vanished from the room, only to return moments later with said instrument.

He faced me on the mattress, toying with the tuning for a moment before looking at me again. "What shall I play?" he asked expectantly.

I picked up my iPad, scrolling through the songs listed until I landed on the perfect one. Turning the screen, I let Nathan read the title. His lips curled into a wide grin as he nodded in excited agreement.

Flexing his fingers, he winked. "Here goes nothing."

I drew my knives from their sheaths inside of my boots and found a grit stone inside the drawer of the nightstand. Nathan struck the first few chords of *Landing in London* by *3 Doors Down*.

"I woke up today in London, as the plane was touching down." His voice, though young, had an instant drawl that enchanted the melody his fingers birthed. "If this keeps me away much longer, I don't know what I would do. You got to understand it's a hard life that I'm going through."

Knife in one hand, grit stone in the other, I began the relaxing task of sharpening my weapons as Nathan continued singing. I lost all sense of time, eyes focused on my hands, ears focused on the music. The way my toes started tapping to the rhythm made my heart turn back to forgotten memories. When was the last time I'd listened to music and felt *something*?

"Stop."

Nathan's fingers froze on the strings of Garrett's guitar, the strains of sound fading into the woodwork around us. I didn't realize I was gripping my knife with white knuckles until he glanced down and seemed to pale.

"Did I do something wrong?" he asked softly, almost fearfully.

The atmosphere in the room had gone from relaxing to icy.

I shook my head, licking my lips. "No." I struggled to keep my emotions under control. "I uhh... I think it's time for you to get some sleep."

Nathan nodded, getting to his feet without a word. The guitar at his side, he turned to go and then paused. "Good night, Quinn."

I flinched at the kind words, closing my eyes. "Good night, Nathan."

His footsteps trailed off as he left the room. Setting my knife to the side, I stared down at my trembling hands. The music had been too much. It dredged up memories that were best left untouched.

Lying down on the bed, I let my thoughts drift toward Selah, and Jason's confession about joining

212

him. Anything to keep my mind from the truth—the past. I still didn't know what to think. Jason's betrayal of Rourke made it hard to focus on anything else. At least it meant he wouldn't be turning me in to Rourke any time soon. Not while I had this kind of blackmail.

My whole world is turning upside down and I don't know how to stop it.

◇

My socks made a soft padding noise down the hallway as I headed for the kitchen, empty teacup in hand. An hour had passed since Nathan retired to his room for the night, the echo of his voice still playing in my ears. Consequently, the house was quiet, Garrett and I being the only ones still awake.

I walked into the kitchen and crossed the tile floor to deposit my cup in the sink. A package of oatmeal cookies sat on the counter, half of them missing. Garrett walked into the room just as I was taking a bite of one.

"Thief." He chuckled, refilling his cup of coffee.

I wrinkled my nose at him and stole another cookie.

Mouth full, I asked about Jason's condition.

Garrett sighed heavily, sinking against the counter. His expression was strained, eyes bordering on bloodshot. "Sleeping, for now," he muttered. "I'm just heading in to check on him. Do you want to come?"

"No." I took an involuntary step backward.

He lifted an eyebrow. Jason's confession about wanting to betray Rourke and join Selah had left deep marks in my thoughts. Everything I thought I had known about my fellow assassin turned out to be wrong. He wasn't to be trusted, and neither was Garrett.

Was I the only one left in Rourke's organization that hadn't lost his or her mind completely?

"No, I was just heading up to bed actually." I forced myself to explain away my reaction for Garrett's benefit.

"I put fresh clothes in the guest bedrooms for you and Nathan." He pushed off of the counter and crossed to the hallway. "If you need anything, text me. I'll be with Jason, working for the rest of the night I'm afraid."

"Not on him I hope." *Don't make him suspicious.*

"I wish." Garrett rolled his eyes. "My to do list has become a do or die list."

"If anyone can get everything in order before they kick the bucket, it's you," I said, following him out to the hallway.

He sighed again, running a hand through his brown hair.

"Well, that makes one of us. Good night, Quinn."

"Night," I called after him as we split ways in the hall.

While he might have been dreading his nightlong work vigil, it gave me the perfect opportunity to catch up on some much-needed sleep. The soldier in me had never been put to rest. I still relied on the old adage: sleep when you can, because you never know when you're going to sleep again.

Heading back the way I had come, I prepared to go to my borrowed room for the night, but paused.

The closed door to Garrett's personal study beckoned to me from across the hallway like light to a moth.

Don't you dare.

I tried to continue past it, but the temptation was too much. Garrett wouldn't leave Jason's side for hours. Plenty of time to sneak a quick look for my curious mind. I had known the hacker for five years, and yet I hardly knew anything about him. This was a chance to dig up a few skeletons in his closet. Something I had never been able to resist.

Giving in a little *too* easily, I crossed to the door. It was locked.

Challenge accepted.

It took all of twelve seconds to jimmy the lock and step inside the pitch-black office. I closed the door behind me softly, letting my eyes adjust to the abrupt change of lighting. Using the flashlight on my cell phone, I located a lamp and clicked it on.

Garrett's study, suddenly illuminated with light, was completely at odds with the office he kept at *London Advertising*. There, under Rourke's constant surveillance, the hacker's space was business-like and all modern tech. But here, in his own home, keeping up appearances apparently didn't matter.

The study was furnished with a single folding table, stained with coffee cup rims, and a rolling chair. Industrial-type filing cabinets stood in each corner, dust-covered and scarred with Sharpie smears. I blinked in fascinated shock. Where the walls should have supported pictures of decoration, dry erase boards hung. I had never seen such organized weirdness.

Jason's the geek, and Garrett's the serial lone wolf. Why am I not surprised?

Trailing my fingers over the rough surface of the folding table, I walked across the room to the first file cabinet and opened one of the many drawers. Manila folders and envelopes were stuffed inside almost to overflowing. Names and numbers, facts and figures. This was Garrett's work—filing away anything and everything that could become a benefit or a hindrance to Rourke.

Sliding over to the next cabinet, I opened a drawer about chest height and began thumbing through the files. The labels bore the names of people, living and dead, who worked for Rourke.

My file was there, as well as Jason's, Matt's, Garrett's, and in the very back, Rourke's. I cocked my head to the side as my fingers paused on my employer's folder. It was very slim compared to the rest, and a different color than the usual off-white. The folder was black and had a number equation written in thick pen at the top left hand corner with a bright red X over it.

$001 + 12.798/2.3(Cr3Hg7) = Immune.$

The markings made no sense—it wasn't even a real equation. I pulled out the file and flipped through the contents in search of an answer or explanation, but found none. In fact, the contents of the folder were very disappointing. A sheet of white typing paper had Rourke's name and a string of letters on it—maybe code, nothing more.

Replacing the folder, I withdrew my own, which was roughly five inches thick. I flipped it open and laid the heavy documents down on Garrett's table. A black and white photo of me in my Army uniform stared up at me.

If only that girl could see who I became without her.

I set it aside quickly and turned to the next page. The contract I had signed before joining Rourke's organization was dog-eared to the last page where my signature made it forever binding. I stared at it in memory. The slope of the writing was off, unnatural, since it had been the first time I had ever signed my name Quinn Rogers instead of Andrea Abrams. Had I truly known what I was signing?

Shaking my head, I flipped to the next article. A blank piece of paper with a number equation stenciled on it fell out of the file.

$012 + 1.274/3.3(Cr3Hg7) = Immune.$

What did that mean? Frowning, I set aside my folder and grabbed a piece of paper from the desk. I wrote down the equation from my file as well as the one from Rourke's. Taking Jason's documents from the next cabinet, I went through the pages looking for the same thing. His equation was crossed out, but I wrote the numbers down anyway.

$010 + 0.672/0.0(Cr3Hg7) = Immune.$

My brow furrowed deeper in confusion as I flipped through Matt's file to discover the same equation. Tossing it aside, I repeated the process with Garrett's file, only to come up empty-handed. There wasn't an equation in his. What did it all mean? I got up from the chair and walked over to the opposite corner where another file cabinet stood, taller than the others.

Opening the top drawer, I frowned. The first file's tab read International Free Militia. Turning to the first sheet of paper, I froze.

Bloody hell, it can't be.

The biological graphs and charts were unmistakable to my soldier's mind. I had spent countless hours during my service learning the successes, failures, and dangers of warfare styles. The only style to hold my attention indefinitely had been biological warfare—in other words, *plagues*.

I went to pull the file out when I heard a sharp inhale behind me. Wheeling around, I met Garrett's gaze as he stood in the doorway, hand still on the doorknob.

"Quinn, what are you *doing*?" His face said all I needed to know.

"Doing a spot-check on you," I returned, surprised at the confidence in my voice. My years of faking appearances and lying were invaluable in the moment. "I'm going to have to give you a C on cleanliness. Who keeps day old coffee mugs on their desk?"

Garrett glared at me. All six feet four inches of him coiled like a spring in a Glock 9mm pistol. I crossed over to the desk and swept up the files I had left out. He didn't move as I returned them to their places and closed the drawers with a flourish.

Turning to him, I felt his gaze harden suspiciously.

"What are you looking for?" he demanded.

"Oh, nothing really. I was just bored."

"Uh-huh... " He took a sidelong glance at the cabinet across the room from us.

My heart skipped a beat. Surely, I had misinterpreted what I'd read. Garrett would have information about the International Free Militia. Of course, he would.

But why have information on virus outbreaks specifically?

"Rourke has me keep any and all information about the IFM and other terrorist organizations. Past and present," he said.

"I know." I nodded, barely keeping my breathing under control. I had to get away from his suspicious eye before I cracked under the pressure of putting on a façade.

Taking a bold risk, I held out the piece of paper I had copied the number equations onto. "What are these for? What do they mean? All of the files have them, but don't explain why."

"Rourke never tells me." He shrugged.

I raised an eyebrow. There was definitely something he wasn't telling me.

"That's odd. Why wouldn't he tell you? I mean, you're the genius behind all of the records. Shouldn't you know?"

"You shouldn't have come in here."

"I know." What had I been thinking? "Really,

Garrett, I was just curious. I didn't mean to pry."

"Good night, Quinn."

End of the conversation.

He didn't bother to order me out of his office or even turn off the light as he left. He just left. And somehow that made me feel even worse about what I had done—and what I had read. There were too many secrets. Secrets bigger than I could even begin to imagine.

This is all wrong.

My emotions burned as I went to my room, confusion and concern swirling in my thoughts. If I had been suspicious of Garrett before, I didn't know what I was feeling now.

I stripped out of my clothes and changed into an oversized shirt before crawling into bed. The soft grey material smelled of Garrett's cologne, the scent dancing inside my nostrils as I tossed and turned uncomfortably.

Breaking into his office had been a huge mistake. I had seen things I didn't know what to think of—read things I didn't want to know. Closing my eyes, I tried to settle my breathing and convince my body to slumber.

It took forever, but when at last I finally did drop off to sleep it was anything but peaceful. In my dreams I stood in a pitch-black space where numbers and dead bodies waltzed around me and laughed in mockery. They haunted the night behind my eyelids.

Chapter Twenty-Two

Garrett's House – October 30th

The ninja star embedded in the wall trembled. I blinked, fingers quivering as I picked up another shuriken from the table to my right. Twirling the weapon in my fingers, I breathed in the cool comfort and lightness of the metal in my hand. I took a step back and launched the six-point star end over end into the target's bulls-eye.

At least I had aimed for the center of the target.

My shot landed well below the intended black dot and embedded somewhere mid-abdomen on the dummy. Not a killing shot as I had intended, but still a disabling one. I had never been any good at throwing stars. Knives and guns were more my thing.

Sighing, I rolled my shoulders out in vain.

Why am I so tense?

The answer to the anxiety clawing its way up my spine lay in the reoccurring nightmare that haunted my every step.

My initiation assignment was the only murder I regretted committing. The boy whose green eyes were mirrored in Nathan's gaze deserved to live a full life regardless of what Rourke said or what his parents had done to warrant a death sentence from the master assassin. But I had killed him. End of the story—or so I'd believed for five years.

Nathan was the living ghost of the boy who stalked my dreams, the possibility of what might have been if fate, or I, had been kinder. My second chance if I dared to take it.

Throwing another shuriken at the human-sized target, I grimaced when it missed the dummy altogether. Gingerly, I ran a hand over my side, feeling to make sure my staples were still in place. They were, thankfully. I picked up yet another throwing star from the table next to the range and launched it at the target. The weapon dislodged one of the others I had already embedded into the wood. Yet again, far below my original target. My ears picked up on the painfully slow footsteps coming down the basement stairs behind me long before Jason's labored breathing grew close. I ignored him, adjusting my grip on the last shuriken. Five days had passed since his near-death experience. Days in which I'd been trapped inside Garrett's house until the hacker locked down our situation. Everyone was lucky that I hadn't tried to put a ninja star through one of Garrett's laptops out of sheer boredom.

"Trouble sleeping?" Jason sat down on a barstool, uninvited.

"Yeah, you could say that." I flicked my wrist and threw the star. It hit home in the target's forehead. I had been aiming for the neck. A filthy word came to mind as I turned to the assassin.

"You shouldn't be walking," I said. "Having trouble sleeping yourself?"

"I don't sleep," he said bitterly. "My mind has the scary capability of being dark and demented."

"You're afraid of your dreams?"

He gave a little shrug as I walked past to retrieve the blades from the target. "Dreams where you get to watch people you care about die, yes."

Stars in hand, I returned to the now-empty table and prepared to throw again.

"So nightmares then?"

"Almost every night."

I let my eyes roam over his body, searching for

222

clues to his strength and injuries. To the casual observer, save for the dark circles under his bloodshot eyes and the bandages around his abdomen, he looked fine. I knew better.

"I've had one or two of those myself recently." I ran my finger along the edge of the shuriken gently enough not to draw blood.

"Just one or two?" Jason raised an eyebrow.

Sighing, I threw the star end over end in a vicious spiral that struck the target's left arm.

Why can't I throw these?

"Okay, maybe one every night since I kidnapped Nathan." I reached for another blade. "But it comes with the territory. We kill people for a living after all. Nightmares are an occupational hazard."

"You're not throwing your hips into it," Jason mused from his seat, wincing as he straightened. His words dashed my already waning confidence and the star flashed over the head of the target completely.

Grumbling a curse, I faced him, hands on my hips.

"Oh, really?"

He stood and shuffled to me. "Here, let me show you."

Though it was the oldest and most shameless trick in the book, he positioned himself behind me and laced his hand over mine as I held one of the shuriken. His other hand settled low on my hip.

There was a heavy exhaling on my neck and I smirked. Jason's face had become as red as the pair of slippers I was wearing. If I wanted to push him back all I had to do was plant an elbow in his abdomen and monopolize on the severity of his injury, but I refrained. Learning how to finally throw ninja stars with deadly accuracy would be worth a few moments of awkwardness.

"If you don't stop feeling and start instructing,

I'm going to put these stupid things to use and cut off your fingers."

"Harsh." He brought my arm back with his, as if getting ready to throw the shuriken. "Look, all you have to do is... "

His left hand was on my hip, pulling it backward so that my right one moved in rhythm with my throwing hand. With the added momentum and power behind the star, it slammed into the center of the target with amazing accuracy. His fingers stiffened as we walked through the move again.

"I can do it." I shook him off and threw another star. It pinged off the edge of the target harmlessly. Swearing, I barely heard Jason's chuckle as he placed his hand on my hip again. Thrice more I let him help me before he finally removed himself from my personal space.

"See? If you twist your hips with the throwing motion, it'll work. Try again."

And so I did, again and again. Each throw inched closer to my original target until, with a flick of the wrist and shift of my hips, I could land the star exactly where I wanted it. Jason continued critiquing my progress, reminding me of the person who had once taught me how to use butterfly knives.

When I had satisfied my restless desire to destroy the target at the end of the shooting range, I gathered up the stars and sat down beside Jason on the bench. We remained in companionable silence for several minutes until he finally spoke with a question that drove a little too close to home.

"What happens in your nightmares?" The extent of his injuries seemed to have done nothing to staunch his affection and kindness. I took a deep breath, fingering the hem of my black pajama top. I wasn't ready to talk about the most recent dream involving Nathan.

"I relive one of my first assignments," I said. "Rourke planned it with a purpose, and it worked."

He made a humming noise, nodding in understanding.

I turned to him. "How about your nightmares? You said they were about losing someone you cared about. Who?"

Suddenly, Jason's carefree persona dropped. He clenched his jaw, gaze narrowing. I felt the atmosphere bristle as he snapped at me in response.

"It's nothing. I never should have mentioned it."

"Hold up a minute. I told you about mine, now it's your turn. No backing out," I insisted, nudging him with my elbow a little too close to his injury.

He flinched away and eyed me, face giving away none of his thoughts. "My nightmares are about watching you die."

Oh.

"Each night differs, but every time it's my fault. And I can't do anything to stop it."

I looked away. Heat crawled up my neck, painting my cheeks in a blush. To say I regretted pursuing the question was an understatement. But it was too late to turn back now.

"How do I die?" I whispered, eyes downcast from his.

"Does it matter? They're just dreams."

So are my nightmares, but I still wake up screaming.

"I'm the one dying, I'd like to know."

Jason sighed, running a hand through his already tousled dishwater blonde hair. Was he nervous?

"Sometimes you get shot by an invisible killer. Other times it's Rourke, or even... *me* who kills you, okay?" The icy tone he assumed didn't match his earlier personality at all.

"You?" I frowned.

225

Without answering, Jason stood and left the shooting range. I stared after him, my own cheeks burning and my head whirling in spiraling circles.

Oh, this isn't good.

<>

Garrett's House – November 7th

After Jason's confession about his dream and the blatant affection lurking in its wake, it was a struggle to keep pretending nothing had changed between us. I forced my attitude into a neutral state of not caring. My reaction didn't seem to surprise Jason in the least, but I could tell that it disappointed him.

I stayed clear of him, letting his injury keep him locked away and then gradual recovery sending him out of the house. The later he returned to the house every night, the earlier I went to bed. It was a dance of sorts we were performing—keeping to ourselves as much as possible.

To make matters worse, neither Garrett nor Nathan took any notice of the change. They accepted the new routine so easily it made my nerves fray at the edges.

While Garrett left each morning to tend to his work for Rourke, Nathan and I stayed inside. Not that my hostage seemed to mind. The young man had discovered a Bible among the hacker's bookcases and holed up in the living room. He spent hours switching back and forth between reading the book and playing around with Garrett's guitar. It was easy for everyone else to go on through the next three days as if nothing were wrong. Go figure. Even Nathan, who was living under the same roof as three people who had originally wanted to kill him—and one who still thought it would be a good idea—was relaxed and content. Peaceful.

226

I was anything but peaceful.

I was going straight out of my bleeding mind.

Garrett hadn't said a word about finding me in his office since the incident, but the moment was never far from my mind. I didn't know what to expect from him in terms of backlash. In my opinion, he was just as likely to keep silent on the matter as go blabbing to Rourke. I wasn't worried about Garrett telling Rourke, the master assassin wouldn't mind, but the not knowing was taking its toll. I didn't know how to treat Garrett, and worst of all I didn't know what to do with Jason.

Love wasn't in my vocabulary. I didn't know how to handle whatever Jason had brought to the table. Affection wasn't an emotion I was able to embody. Rourke had made certain of that, and I wasn't about to seek a change now. But was I still the heartless killer Rourke adored and favored? Had I turned into something else entirely? Maybe the nightmare of the boy's death was a sign that I was losing that heartlessness. The stirrings inside of me couldn't be meaningless.

I desperately needed to prove that I was still the Dragonfly, if only to myself. And Rourke was more than willing to oblige.

◇

London, England – November 7th

"All right, Quinn, everything's good to go on my end," Matt's voice spoke over my earpiece.

I secured my Glock into the corset holster wrapped snugly around my middle, anchoring my emotions to the pain leeching away from my injury.

Rourke had changed the usual line-up, switching Matt out to replace Garrett for the assignment. I didn't know if it was a good thing or not, but I was relieved to know the hacker wasn't my backup. After everything that had happened, I needed to reestablish my trust in myself before letting him back into the picture.

"I will contact you if anything changes." I opened the door of my Range Rover. Stepping out into the brisk night air, I took a deep breath and brushed a hand over my earpiece, ending the connection with Matt. The Hampton hotel loomed in front of me—a beacon of brightness in the lonely, black night. The weight of my weapons made my steps feel unusually heavy.

Starting across the car park, I relaxed into the steady gait and rhythm my high-heeled boots provided as they clicked against the asphalt. The very shadows trailed in my wake, dripping off my shoulders as I walked into the spotlight of the single bulb illuminating the carport outside of the Hampton. Sparing a glance around me, I spotted no immediate or potential threats. My senses remained at ease as I stalked through the sliding glass doors into the hotel lobby.

My task was simple. Break into a man's room and assassinate him for his work to stop the IFM. Nothing I hadn't done a hundred times. I pressed the heel of my left hand against my sternum, feeling my rapid heartbeat as well as the accelerated rise and fall of my breath.

Why am I breathing so heavily?

I shook my head, blonde wig rustling with the motion, and strode up to the front desk. A red-eyed, sleepy clerk watched me approach with a blank stare. Through blue contact lens, I glanced at the clock hanging to my right over the coffee bar. Two o'clock in the morning.

"Welcome. How can I help you, ma'am?" He spoke in a soft, slurred voice.

"Hello." I faked a nervous, hiccupping laugh. "I'm sorry to bother you, but my husband checked in this afternoon and isn't answering his cell phone. Could you tell me his room number?"

"Of course. What's your husband's name?" he asked, turning to his computer.

"Salwerd, Francis Salwerd." I eyed a security camera lodged in the corner above the desk.

He typed away on the keyboard, paused to read something, and then turned to me. "He is on the second floor. Room 216."

"Thank you," I said, offering my best winsome, relieved smile. "You're a life saver."

The clerk beamed back at me as I sauntered around the desk. Passing the indoor swimming pool, I found the stairs and reopened the connection with Matt inside of the stairwell.

"Smile, Quinn, you're about to be erased from the security tapes. You're invisible in three—two—*one*," Matt announced.

"Rourke and I are both letting you off the leash on this one. Screw it up and I'll split you in half."

"Ahh, just like old times." He chuckled. "Copy that."

The earpiece went silent.

Walking up to the second floor, I checked the hallway before stepping through. I reached room 216 and pulled my phone from the pocket of my jacket. Pressing it against the electronic card reader, I listened for anything out of the ordinary, silently waiting for the FBI to show up. But there wasn't a sound, save for the whirring AC unit at the end of the long, carpeted hall.

Satisfied, I started the decoding app Garrett had installed two years earlier. Numbers flashed past on the screen before my cell phone quietly beeped and the card reader flickered green. I pushed open the door to sheer blackness.

The two-room suite smelled of Italian leftovers and beer. I crept into the bedroom soundlessly, senses alert and probing. Faint snoring echoed in the atmosphere, guiding me to the bed where my target, Francis Salwerd, slept.

I looked down at him, trying desperately to still my pounding heart, and adjusted my tight leather gloves. Taking my garrote out of the pouch on my hip, I crouched beside the bed. Francis Salwerd shifted in his sleep, drawing me up sharply.

What's wrong with me? Why am I hesitating?

I struggled to breathe, my lungs collapsing inward with the rate of my frantic heartbeat. Rolling onto his back, Francis Salwerd's eyes opened—

In a second, I cinched the metal garrote around his neck. The man gurgled, fighting against me in vain. A fist glanced off of my chin as I pinned him between the bed and my knee. The life drained out of his body as his struggling only pulled the weapon tighter around his vulnerable neck. Hot tears stung the back of my eyes as I battled the violent dry sob working its way upward in my throat. With a final shudder, Francis Salwerd went limp. I ripped the garrote away, sucking in a lungful of air. The man's deathly pale face stared up at me as I stood over him and the bed. His body sprawled in awkward angles, his face contorted in fear. Putting my breathing back in check, I holstered my weapon.

The assignment was done.

Pure instinct kept me moving. I dared one last look at the body slumped on the bed. My stomach clenched again in warning. I fled the hotel room through the back doors before I could consider my reaction. I vanished into the night of shadows and blood, trying to sort through my thoughts and emotions, but getting nowhere.

I pressed harder on the gas, flying through the night toward *London Advertising*. I took a moment to remove my wig and fix my hair before entering our base of operations. The halls were dark and silent as I took the stairs to the fiftieth floor, where a single light burned inside Matt's office.

Pausing in the doorway, I looked on as he finished the details of Francis Salwerd's death, cleaning up any traces that could lead back to me, or more importantly, back to Rourke. It wasn't until I cleared my throat that Matt glanced up from his work, eyes wide in surprise.

"Quinn"—he stood up from his desk as I crossed the threshold—"what are you doing here?"

I said nothing. Just waited.

Deep wrinkles appeared on Matt's forehead as he watched me, muscled arms hanging close to his sides in readiness.

Four seconds. It would take the former Special Forces soldier turned assassin exactly four seconds to draw his concealed firearm.

Five seconds total to aim and fire.

But pulling his weapon on me would do him no good. I could cross the floor and come up behind him in less than three seconds.

He'd be dead before his finger could reach the trigger.

"How long would it take me to draw my Glock and kill you?" I whispered, tone flat. Matt shifted, his arms coming away from his sides as if a subconscious gesture to put me at ease. It didn't work.

"I don't know. How long?" he replied, eyebrows lifted.

I shrugged. I could draw, aim, and fire in three seconds flat. One second for each movement. My response time was much less than Matt's.

Much less.

Did that make me more of a monster? More of a killer? I'd been the best sniper during my three years of service. Titles and medals had been given to me as rewards and honors. Things that had been destroyed when I joined Rourke's organization and traded one name for another. Matt, on the other hand, had merely existed in his service to queen and country. The only reason Rourke hired him was to serve as a constant reminder of the hell he had saved me from. Seeing Matt, an old friend from the darkest time in my life turned into a monster just like me, had finally finished Rourke's work. My transformation from Andrea Abrams to the Dragonfly complete with my best friend erased from history to become someone else by my side.

Does war make monsters, or do monsters make war?

"I could do it faster than you," I conceded.

He ran a hand through his brown hair. "Is that a fact?"

Ignoring his question, I approached his desk and picked up a printout of a sample newspaper. The headline read: Francis Salwerd dead, Terrorist Involvement Suspected.

"Is this the story Rourke wants printed about the assignment?" I returned the paper and turned to Matt.

He nodded, expression neutral. "It's a flawless cover-up. No one will be looking for an assassin, just a terrorist from the Middle East."

"How many people have you killed, Matt? In the service and out of it."

The question seemed to take the man by surprise, judging by the jerk of his shoulders and flare of his nostrils.

"What are you really doing here, Quinn?" He took a step backward, concerned. "You had a successful assignment. You should be back at

232

Garrett's house celebrating."

"Tell me."

The words hung between us like a web. Matt cleared his throat, shaking his head. "Go home, Quinn. You don't need to hear this right now."

"Tell me."

"I'm being serious. Go home now," he growled, gesturing to the open doorway.

"What's the matter, Matt? Afraid to bare too much? Afraid I'll laugh at you? Afraid I'll think you're a monster?"

"You know how many people I've killed. You're the one who gave me over to Rourke when my unit was captured in Pakistan. You were the one who arranged everything." He stood stock still, glaring.

"Do you hate me for that?" *Please say yes.*

"No. I don't hate you," he replied "I only hate myself for backing into a corner with no way out but to go to Rourke."

"Under different circumstances would you have still said yes to becoming an assassin for him?"

"Under different circumstances, no, *none of us* would have said yes."

"Not me," I retorted, crossing my arms.

Matt's hard expression shifted from unyielding to grieved. "You and I both know that's not true," he whispered. "If Dawn hadn't died and my brother hadn't been killed, we would be different people today. We would never have needed Rourke to give us a new life... a new chance. We never would have needed to be rescued." His voice lowered as he said the last part.

I didn't want to hear anymore, but I knew I needed to. That's why I was there. I needed to be reminded again of where I had been, of what I had become, and what Rourke had done for me. That was the reason I wanted Matt by my side when I doubted.

He'd always been there, even before my name was Quinn Rogers. Yet another reason Rourke had total control over my life. He knew me. He knew how to break me and how to build me up again.

"But they died and now we are here," I said, voice tired and burdened.

"We don't have to be," he murmured, stepping closer. "All you have to do is say the word and I'll follow you out of this hellhole. I've only stayed this long because you are here."

Smiling weakly, I shook my head at him. "No, Matt, I can't do that. For each person there is a sentence, a series of words, which has the power to destroy him. Rourke knows mine."

"You and I both know that's not true," he whispered for the second time, "*Andrea.*"

Spinning on my heel, I stormed out of the room before Matt could see the hurt in my eyes.

Chapter Twenty-Three

Garrett's House – November 8ᵗʰ

Two assassins, a hacker, and hostage sat around the breakfast table eating and drinking coffee.

It looked like the beginning of a rubbish joke, but the memory of the previous night was anything but comical. Right down to Matt calling me by my real name.

My fingers trembled around the fork I held. Without eating the hash browns I had piled onto it, I set the utensil down and placed both hands in my lap out of view of my companions. They didn't need to see me shaking. They didn't need to know about my unnerving night. The horrors I saw in my nightmares were mine to bear alone.

Garrett's ever-present piece of technology was an iPad and he kept sporadically typing and scrolling on. He had already shown me the published newspaper article detailing Francis Salwerd's murder mere hours earlier. I averted my eyes quickly, trying not to picture my target's prone body in the hotel room.

Get a grip, Quinn, there's too much at stake to fall apart now.

Jason had yet to look up from his coffee and toast. The pieces of half-burnt bread on his plate were smeared with peanut butter and jam. An odd combination I noticed immediately. Jason never had jam on his toast, and he most certainly didn't burn anything. Something was troubling him. *Probably me.*

Beside me, Nathan finished his glass of orange juice before glancing sidelong at me. The black shirt he was wearing had a logo from Bastille, some band Jason adored, and his brown hair was brushed back with a small amount of gel. His dimples appeared as he smiled at me kindly. Although he appeared happy, his eyes told me a different story. Worry lines formed at the edges of his lips. Fear lurking behind his neutral posture.

"How did you sleep last night, Quinn?"

The meal had been quiet up to that point, giving me hope that there wouldn't be any questions directed at me.

So much for flying under the radar now.

I shifted in my seat, taking a sip of tea to avoid answering. There was no way I was going to tell him the truth. I didn't have the guts to see the disappointment—or horror—I knew would come.

I'd lain in bed all night remembering every single person I had ever killed. There was no one, not a single soul, I had let affect me. No guilt, no regret, no remorse.

Until now.

Visions of Francis Salwerd's twisted body and breathless struggle to the end made my skin prickle uneasily. I couldn't shake the feeling of blood on my skin, sticky and hot. Even the shower I took long before dawn hadn't helped scrub me free of guilt.

"Restless," was the only reply I could muster.

Jason still didn't look up from his coffee cup, but I suspected he knew exactly what had happened in the cloak of midnight.

"I hope you can sleep more soundly from now on," Garrett said, glancing at me.

I forced a smile in return.

Though Matt had helped me with the assignment, Garrett knew every dirty detail about it. Despite my lack of trust in him and his discovery of me snooping in his office, he congratulated me when I got back from the assignment on a job well done. I was still the "same old Quinn" he said.

The announcement had set in motion a train of thought I wasn't sure I liked.

Do I really want to be the same old Quinn?

Blinking quickly, I gulped the rest of my tea.

"What are we going to do today? Can we get back in the world yet?" Jason started on his third piece of toast slathered in strawberry jam. Something was definitely bothering him.

"You can, but Quinn's still running hot," Garrett said.

"Great," Jason muttered at the same time I swore.

The hacker paused, his coffee mug halfway to his lips, eyes peering curiously over the rim at us. For the first time in a fortnight, he seemed to pick up on the hidden tension between Jason and me.

"Is something wrong, Quinn?" He frowned.

Though I hated the situation, I knew I'd hate getting Garrett involved even more. Not only did I feel betrayed by his actions after the FBI, but I was afraid he would tell Rourke that I had been in his office. I didn't want to know what kind of punishment Rourke might dream of for that score.

"No, nothing's wrong." I forced myself to look confident and carefree. "I'm just going crazy locked up in this house."

"You should have thought of that before." Jason leaned back and crossed his arms. His words were only loud enough for me to hear.

I ignored them.

"Just a few more days," Garrett promised. "I know staying low has been hard on you. Action is your middle name."

He was right—I thrived off of action. Francis Salwerd's murder taught me I needed to get back into the swing of things. Get my confidence and bloodlust back into working order.

Garrett smiled, sympathy showing in his eyes. I frowned.

Is he trying to reassure or deceive me?

"I can manage a few more days." If he hadn't informed Rourke of my snooping already, I had to suspect he wouldn't for the sake of my own sanity. There was enough on my plate as it was to worry about.

We finished breakfast and Jason left without a word, followed by Garrett. That left Nathan and I alone. I knew that going out in public, even with the best disguises I could muster, might end in disaster. So to save Nathan and myself from any possible attack, I decided to take him back to Jason's loft. It would be enough of an outing for me, but with a limited chance of danger. Besides, I was running low on magazines for my gun and the loft was stocked full of ammunition.

◇

London, England – November 8th

"I can't believe you're going to *borrow* Jason's surface to air missile launcher," Nathan said, eyes glued to the Starstreak HVM I carried proudly into the living room of the loft. "What do you even need it for?"

I smirked, laying the heavy piece of equipment on the coffee table. "You never know when you might need a missile launcher, Nathan."

"I guess not," he muttered, exhaling so that the air puffed out his cheeks momentarily. "But where are you going to put it?"

"This bad boy's going under my bed." I winked.

"I thought you were insane before. Now I know you are," he replied, laughing somewhat nervously.

238

"What's insane about keeping missiles under your bed?" I crouched to run a cloth over the Starstreak's gleaming side. "What do *normal people* like you keep under yours?"

"Dust bunnies."

I paused, missile launcher between us, to look at him over my shoulder. His serious expression didn't last long before a shy smile floated across his lips. Rolling my eyes, I finished cleaning the dangerous weapon before a sudden thought struck me. I turned to face the young man in my crouched position.

"Have you done much fighting?"

His eyes widened, eyebrows lifting. "What?"

"Have you done much fighting? Target practice? Hand to hand combat?" I repeated, straightening.

"I guess, a couple of times," he admitted. "At a family camp I shot a .19 and twelve gauge shotgun."

His voice had a hint of hunger in it that made something inside of me stir, lifting as if from a deep and troubled slumber.

"Would you like to try it again?" The light flaming to life in his eyes made me laugh and break into a wide grin.

He nodded, dimples melting my cold interior. Walking across the room, I extracted the key to Jason's gun safe from the top shelf in the closet where I knew he kept it hidden.

"Then follow me. We'll grab some snacks and then head down to the firing range. We might as well enjoy the day while Garrett's grip on our leash is loose," I said, beckoning to Nathan.

He followed me into the kitchen. "What firing range?"

"Jason owns this entire building. It's part of his cover story or something," I said, grabbing a plastic tray from a cupboard over the stove. "He installed a soundproof firing range in the basement so he can practice."

"And no one's noticed?" Nathan's eyebrows knit together in confusion.

"If anyone has, Jason's dealt with it." I laughed, tossing two bags of crisps onto the tray. "But despite his many flaws, he keeps his firing range a secret. It's funny, really. Garrett, Jason, and I all have our own practice rooms. It's not like we don't have access to one already."

Adding some cheese, pretzels, soda, and chocolate to the tray, I thought of the gigantic firing range Rourke had installed in the bottom of *London Advertising*. When was the last time I had utilized its offerings?

A long time ago. I prefer to work out of Rourke's sight.

While Nathan carried the food, I led the way to the front door. We took the stairs.

Apparently Jason and Garrett like their privacy too.

◇

It was no wonder no one had ever discovered Jason's secret firing range. I found out just how pervasive his covertness really was when Nathan and I stepped into the dark room. The fingerprint scanner on the other side of the door beeped as it returned the heavy bolt into place in the wall behind us. A moment later light flickered to life overhead. Loud clicks of electricity announced the sequential flashes as the bright LED bulbs came on all across the fifty-yard room.

Nathan's jaw dropped. "Wow."

"Well, bugger me," I muttered, gobsmacked, walking forward into the video gamer's lab. The walls were littered with graffiti and graphic posters of Halo and World of Warcraft. It was impossible to mistake the room for anything other than an addicted gamer's playroom—except I knew better.

The gun safe in the far wall was concealed by a wet bar, but I knew what I was looking for. Leaving our refreshments tray on a table between two recliners, I headed for it, high heels clacking loudly on the expensive wood flooring tiles.

"What is this place?" Nathan asked, staring wide-eyed at the six television screens mounted on the wall beside the bar.

I grunted, unlocking the safe. "The meth addict's lair."

"What?"

I ignored him, pulling an AR-15 and two Glock 9mm handguns off of the wall mounts in the walk-in safe. Nathan stared as I laid them on the wet bar.

"What do you want to play with first?" I asked, popping a crisp into my mouth.

He glanced at the TVs again.

I rolled my eyes. "Well?"

He shrugged, cheeks a slight pale tint. Maybe he realized just how dangerous his situation had become. It took a strong constitution to be alone with a killer in a place no one knew about where a little, or lot of, blood wouldn't matter.

"I'm not an expert, but I do know we shouldn't be *playing* with firearms."

"You're adorable." I laughed, handing him the AR-15.

He accepted the weapon as I ushered him to the end of the range.

I found a control box mounted next to a promotional poster of Fallout and pushed a red button. A few mechanical clicks later, targets descended from the ceilings to drop into place down range. Nathan gaped in amazement. I wasn't sure what he found more intriguing—the secret gun range or the obsessed assassin who had a shrine to video games.

"At least you know how to hold a rifle," I noted, surveying Nathan's hands along the grip and barrel of the AR-15.

He nodded in acknowledgement, lifting it to his shoulder. I took up position behind him, one hand on his back.

"Take a deep breath," I advised, feeling a shudder race up his spine. "Be confident. Now take aim at the center of the target."

Nathan did as he was told, sighting down the gun as I stood close behind him. I marveled at how naturally his stance came. He would be a sharpshooter in no time with the right instruction.

"Is this right?" He glanced back to get my approving nod.

"Yes, fire when you're ready."

There was a moment of pause before the booming gunshot. The bullet missed the target entirely, and Nathan groaned in disappointment. A life-size cutout of some troll had a bullet hole through its knee.

Hopefully Jason won't notice that his Warcraft memorabilia has become a causality.

"Try again," I said. "You're too tense."

True enough, he was better once he started breathing into the movements and relaxing his death grip on the AR-15. No more of Jason's merchandise was wounded as we transferred to handguns.

Nathan listened carefully to my teaching and implemented it, much like I had learned years ago. Within three hours, Nathan and I were having competitions to see who was the better shot. Thankfully for my pride, I had thousands of hours of experience.

"This isn't fair, Quinn. You've been shooting for years." Nathan glared at me after I beat him for the fifth time in a row.

I grinned, holstering my pistol against my thigh.

"You should have thought of that before you bet twenty M&Ms on winning." I laughed, gesturing for him to make the proper trade of candy.

Begrudgingly, he shifted the bet into my bowl and I popped one into my mouth, grinning at him.

"Can we try something else? Something I might be able to win?" An innocent curiosity and interest sparkled in his gaze.

A surge of playfulness welled up inside of me as I started toward the other side of the basement. I couldn't resist glancing at the bookshelves of Marvel comics.

When did Jason get to be such a nerd?

"How are you at hand-to-hand combat?" I threw over my shoulder.

"Since I don't think you mean fighting my brothers with Nerf guns and plastic swords, I'm going to say terrible."

Oh, I was going to enjoy knocking him around— in the best way possible.

He followed me to a large area of gymnastic mats set up. A punching bag hung off to the side, along with a table displaying a karate gi, belts, and boxing gloves.

"Take off your shoes and socks and I'll show you a few tricks." I bent over to slide out of my boots and he complied while I also shed my gun belt and cardigan. Rolling my shoulders, I stepped onto the mat and faced him.

His eyes narrowed, steps hesitant as he joined me.

"You're enjoying this, aren't you?"

I hopped in place to loosen my muscles. "Tosh, what makes you say that?"

He watched me carefully, mimicking my movements as I stretched out my calves, arms, and hips. "The look in your eyes. It's not murderous, it's *mischievous*."

"Oh?" I laughed. "It's true. I am enjoying this. I get to teach you how to get your hands dirty. Come a little closer."

We circled each other on the mat slowly as I gauged his natural rhythm and movement. I caught the excited gleam in his eyes and smiled, my body lapsing into its natural fighting stance.

"The first thing you need to learn is defense." I lunged at Nathan. He ducked, but only just. I lunged again and he moved quicker, dancing out of my reach.

"Good!" I drew up short so that he could relax the tension in his back. "Now, try blocking a punch. Don't worry, I'll go slow."

"You know, if you were still trying to kill me this would be the perfect opportunity." He chuckled, bouncing on the balls of his feet. "But since you're teaching me how to fight, I somehow doubt that's your plan."

I cocked my head to the side and smirked. He barely dodged the left cross I threw at his jaw.

"Stay focused, big guy." I lifted an eyebrow. "If you were fighting someone else you would be dead right now. Killers don't mess around, and neither do I. A fight ends when someone gets dragged away in a body bag."

Chapter Twenty-Four

Jason's Loft – November 8th

Sweaty and knackered, Nathan and I returned to the loft kitchenette after five hours of training and goofing around. I set the ammunition I had gathered by the garage door with the missile launcher as Nathan toweled off by the sink. He flashed me a dimpled grin—green eyes alight with joy. And despite myself, I couldn't resist returning the gesture.

We had worked on the speed and accuracy needed with firearms, and the clever thinking, observation, and strength needed for hand combat. My hostage now knew the basics of a myriad of fighting techniques—knowledge that could keep him alive.

A new feeling had crept up on me while we playfully trained in Jason's tricked out video games lair. There was something different in the way I wanted to keep Nathan around. I didn't want to kill him any longer. I didn't even want to keep him around to ensure my own safety. I genuinely wanted to spend time figuring him out.

Even the most deadly of assassins have little siblings at one time or another. Adopted ones, too.

"What are we going to do now?" Nathan asked me, wiping the sweat from his brow.

My stomach gurgled—a sure sign that we had positively gorged ourselves on M&Ms and other junk food.

"What do *you* want to do now?" I tossed him a water bottle from the refrigerator.

He shrugged.

"Well, think about it. I'm going to grab my jacket

from upstairs. Wait right here."

Without thinking it through, I left the kitchen and jogged up the stairway to Jason's bedroom and guestrooms. Just as I was grabbing my jacket and shrugging it on, I heard the unmistakable noise of the front door being kicked down.

I froze.

A wave of shock and fear washed over me so sharply that I couldn't take my next breath.

Nathan.

"Shit," I cursed, slapping off the lights and drawing my Glock. My level of stupidity was through the roof for having let my guard down. *Again.* I had let someone sneak up on me. *Again.*

Growling with rage, I flew out of the room. The Dragonfly would never have been caught unaware, and I was losing count how many times Quinn Rogers had been.

Pausing on the top stair, I listened. Slow, methodical footsteps came from below, moving away from the front door and into the living room. I counted six different sets and swore silently to myself. The way they walked in formation screamed strategy and singled them out as FBI agents. Apparently the Bureau was getting better at their job—and having a hard time staying dead.

I'm going to fix that problem once and for all.

Nathan would be hiding somewhere, unsure who was sneaking inside. After what we had been through together there was no way for him to know if the intruders were hostile or friendly. But even though he was clever and hidden, the agents were trained in finding people like him.

I started down the stairs, gun in hand and murder on my mind. Rounding the corner into the living room I saw the kicked-open door beyond, but no agents. I inhaled quietly and moved toward the kitchenette, the last place I had seen Nathan. The sound of footsteps faded and I momentarily lost track of the intruders. Where was Nathan? He wasn't in the kitchen or the breakfast room, and neither were my uninvited guests. A chill arched across my shoulder blades.

Come out, come out, wherever you are.

Stepping around the corner into the hallway on the first floor, I halted. There was the faintest of clicks—someone nearby had just shifted their grip on an assault rifle.

I spun around, throwing the door of the coat closet open. The agent hiding behind a bookcase leapt from his cover, weapon lifted to fire. His first bullet hit the open door. His second was too slow as I surged forward, hands locking around the barrel of the gun. I shoved it up to point at the ceiling. Surprised, he didn't block the kick I delivered between his legs as I tore the gun from his hands. A howl escaped his lips as my movement broke his finger.

Stepping back, I turned his own weapon on him and sent a bullet flying into his abdomen where his bulletproof vest would be weakest.

One down.

At the loud squeak of floorboards, I glanced behind me. Two more agents breached the doorway and fired at me, hitting nothing but empty air as I dropped into a roll.

I fired back: two shots, two guys, two seconds. Game over.

I've still got it.

I lunged over their prone bodies, trying to escape the hallway turned kill box. One man rolled onto his side, blood spilling from his abdomen where the bullet had gone through and through. He saw me coming and fumbled for a knife. I was one step away, speeding up to jump into the hallway as a tremor passed through my veins. One more shot—a head one this time—and he'd be dead. I couldn't do it. I couldn't kill the man who made a feeble attempt to stop me when I swept past. My boot connected with his temple and he went limp.

Stopping, I glanced back at the three injured, but still breathing agents. They would be fine if medical attention was gained in a timely manner.

Why didn't I kill them?

I didn't have time to answer that question. I had to find Nathan and get the blazes out of the building before the rest of the agents converged on me like a flock of vultures.

Run first. Ask questions later.

Around the corner, two more agents emerged in my way. They saw me. An adrenaline rush charged into my blood as they lunged forward. The gunfire already exchanged had broadcasted my location to anyone inside of the loft, so what was a few more shots?

I lifted my gun, taking one agent down with a bullet to the knee. He cried out and collapsed as I took a running leap, launching myself at his companion and wrapping my legs around his neck. Our bodies slammed together and my momentum carried him straight into the wall to his right. His head thudded sickeningly against the solid support, and I swung down and to the side, pulling him to the ground. The butt of my gun connected to his temple as I moved on.

His partner struggled to his good knee, blood trickling from the wound I had inflicted. I hissed, driving the side of my hand into his throat. He gurgled, tipping over to the side.

I turned and came face to face with the final FBI agent.

"I'm only going to say this once, Dragonfly," he said, rifle aimed directly at my heart. "Don't make me break you."

Tossing the hair back from my eyes, I flashed him a grin.

He stood a foot taller than me and two times bigger across. His muscled arms bulged in the sleeves of his uniform. I watched his finger twitch on the trigger. In his dark eyes I could see the raw desire to reduce me to a breathless pile of ash.

"You're the one sending these bastards after me, aren't you? Didn't you get the message when I blew your men up on the hotel roof?" I chuckled, rolling the words off of my tongue in a seductive purr. His shoulders bunched with tension as he balked in suppressed anger.

"Stomached enough of seeing your men die off one by one? Decide to get your own hands dirty?" I licked my chapped lips.

He didn't take the bait. The man was like forged steel—dark, cold, deadly, and unyielding. If he had been anyone else, I would have allowed myself to like him and appreciate his demeanor.

"I'd like to shoot you right now, but people higher up have questions that need answering." His jaw clenched. "So we can do this one of two ways. Either I can make this as painful as possible for you, or you can do as I say willingly and without pain."

"I'm not going willingly. So you'd better get ready to shoot me."

But I was the one who fired first.

Clearly expecting it, he dodged with ease, my bullet just grazing his shoulder. My opponent distracted for a second, I launched myself at him. He stepped back and his returning shot went wide as I reached him and shoved his arm. He had no time to avoid the kick I planted in his stomach. Grunting, he slammed into the wall, his gun slinging away. I kicked his jaw. The vertebra in his neck popped from the momentum of whiplash. He ducked under my guard, punching my solar plexus with a fist. I gagged, winded, and he hit me again, this time cracking his weight down on my right wrist.

Cursing, I dropped my gun and pulled my throbbing hand back.

Deep brown eyes met mine as the agent punched and I dodged. Smooth as silk, I palmed one of my knives, crouching out of his reach. Undeterred, he lashed out with a series of kicks that sent me scurrying back. His confidence built as I retreated, and he didn't realize until too late that he had made a deadly mistake.

He was too close to me to dodge my next move. I stabbed for his leg, and the blade sunk in deep. He cried out, body arcing backward as I wrenched the weapon, his blood flowing freely from the wound. The man staggered against the wall as I prepared to finish him off.

Our gazes locked. My feet rooted themselves to the floor. I couldn't look away. Bile caught in my throat. Only one person in the world could make that expression. One person I never thought I would see again.

"Trent?" I breathed in disbelief.

His eyes widened, jaw going slack. I straightened to my full height, mesmerized in horror. It took a moment, but I finally saw the realization hit Trent, his whole body sagging as if I had drained every last drop of life from his limbs.

"Andrea?" he whispered.

I took a step back at the sound of my old name. Even the air was stricken with tension. Finding it hard to swallow, I let my lips part to gasp in shallow gulps of oxygen as Trent stared at me in fear.

This can't be happening.

Chapter Twenty-Five

Jason's Loft – November 8th

"Andrea, what are you... you're *still alive?*" Trent's brow furrowed in confusion.

I blinked—once, twice, three times. He couldn't really be there—it was just an illusion.

A nightmare.

I lifted my knife to attack, but found that I couldn't move. My knees buckled beneath me. Collapsing, my arms caught me, but only just.

My hands shook, the weapon slipping through my fingers. I couldn't catch my breath, my heart pounding against my ribcage. Trent moved painfully to stand before me, setting his firearm to my head. Black dots danced at the edges of my vision, encroaching inward. The cold weight of the gun barrel pressed to my temple sent a spike of white-hot ice shooting into my spine.

"You can't be her. Andrea died in Afghanistan. She died a good person," he spat. "You're nothing but a *monster*."

My mind was utter chaos as Trent moved to strike me down. One blow to the back of the head and I would wake up in handcuffs and a cell. Or one slip of the finger and I would never wake again.

The split second of hesitation told me what he would do next.

I wouldn't see another sunrise, or sunset. His finger curled around the trigger.

I closed my eyes—

"*No!*" Nathan's shout sucked me back to the

present, ripping me from my thoughts just in time to see him tackle Trent.

The gun to my head scraped away and hit the floor, the bullet missing its target by an inch. I jerked as Nathan scrambled to his feet, shoving Trent back down to the ground where they had crashed.

"Run, Quinn. Go!" He scooped up Trent's gun and dumped it into my hands. "Come on, *run!*"

Nathan pushed me ahead of him out of the loft. Our mad dash to the bottom floor was a blur until he shoved me into the passenger seat of my parked Range Rover. Instinct told me to pull the door closed as he slid behind the wheel. I glanced at him. His face was pale, his lips trembling as he started the engine.

Traffic be damned, he accelerated into it amid a chorus of horns. My numb fingers lost their grip on Trent's assault rifle so it clattered against the dashboard and floor.

"Trent." The name tasted familiar and violent on my tongue as I whispered it to myself.

Nathan turned out of the driveway, leaving behind Jason's loft and the FBI agents. He glanced at me, expression worried, when I repeated the name.

"Quinn?" he questioned, voice fading in my ears.

Children's laughter filled my head, beckoning me into the memory on the borders of my thoughts. Leaning back in the car seat, I closed my eyes tightly against the searing agony inside of my chest.

◇

"Higher! Higher!" I cried, kicking my little legs in a vain attempt to send the swing soaring up into the air.

My brother laughed, giving an extra push so that I flew farther into the blue sky.

The tree limb the swing was tethered to groaned

252

*under the old ropes secured around it. Sunlight
illuminated us as we played, setting slowly in the west.
The smell of honeysuckle wafted across the green lawn
from the bushes by our house.*

"Higher, Trent!"

*"Higher? Aren't you afraid of falling off?" he
asked, hands pushing against the small of my back so
that I swung forward again.*

*"I can't fall! You'll catch me." I giggled loudly,
pigtails flying in the breeze.*

*Trent snagged the swing as it swung back to him,
bringing me to a sudden halt. I bolted off, running with
a delighted squeal as he gave chase.*

*The two of us crested the top of the small hill
overlooking our house. As one, we tilted off of the
ledge and threw ourselves rolling down it amid a
chorus of wild laughter.*

*Coming to a stop at the bottom, Trent crawled
over to me, grinning, as I propped myself up on an
elbow. Grass stuck out of our hair and stained the
knees of our pants. But we didn't care—we were much
too young to care about silly things like that.*

*"You can always count on me, Andy. I will
always be there to catch you when you fall." He
winked.*

*I smiled. Shifting closer to him, I picked a
dandelion flower from the green yard and stuck it
behind my ear.*

"You promise?" I whispered, staring up at him.

He offered me his pinkie finger with a grin.

*"I promise," he said, as I curled my little finger
around his.*

*"You promise to look for me at the ends of the
earth?"*

"Of course!"

*I picked another flower and twirled it in my
fingers thoughtfully. "You promise to find me no*

matter what adventure I am on?"

"Why would I let you have all the fun without me, hmm?" He tapped my nose playfully.

I giggled and twisted away from his tickling fingers. We shared a co-conspirators grin.

Reaching out as fast as lightning, I tickled his side, earning a quick pinch that had me howling in mock pain.

We fell into another fit of laughter, unable to control ourselves. When Trent finally managed to gather himself back together, his eyes locked onto mine with an intensity that startled me. Even though we were only four years apart, he had always been the mature one. Our mother liked to say he was born old. And wise.

"As long as I'm around, nothing bad is going to happen to you."

I tilted my head to the side, contemplating the meaning behind his words. They were much too deep for an eight-year-old. Just as he was about to say something else, a shout came from the porch of our home.

"Andrea! Trent! Time for dinner!" our mother called.

We were on our feet in an instant, racing each other across the yard for the house.

◇

I blinked, coming out of the flashback dizzy and disoriented. For seventeen years, Trent and I had been the best of friends—completely inseparable. Partners in crime, we watched out for each other's backs every hour of the day. But that was before my decision to enlist in the Army and the incident that spurred such spontaneous action.

Trent had never forgiven me for that choice,

refusing to acknowledge my existence after I left basic training. He never wrote letters. Never called. And neither had our parents. But their cruel avoidance hadn't been nearly as hard to bear as Trent's cold shoulder. They had an excuse. Their grief nearly killed them both.

I would never forget the night before I left for my first deployment. Trent had confronted me about running away—the first time we had spoken since the night that started it all.

My brother knew the real reason I wanted to be behind enemy lines carrying a lethal weapon. And I had seen firsthand how the knowledge made his blood run cold. However, nothing he could do would keep me from going.

He was just as bad, after all—running away from reality just like me.

Most people joined the military for one of four reasons. One, military service was a family legacy. Two, your blood ran charged with patriotism. Or three, you wanted a legal way to kill people. Eighteen-year-old Andrea had joined for the fourth and final reason—a reason that quickly catapulted me onto a pedestal of fame because of my fearlessness in the face of death. I didn't want to live—didn't have a reason to keep on fighting. I dared death to come and get me. I was ready to give up and give in. That same desire sent me running to Rourke.

Trent knew exactly what he was talking about when he called me a monster. I was one—I'd always been one. What kind of person taunted death like that? I had been young and hurting, but I knew exactly what I was doing. And that was the hardest burden to bear of them all. I had failed and given up too many times to count.

Moaning, I laid my head back against the car's headrest and closed my eyes.

"Quinn?" Nathan demanded suddenly, breaking the infernal silence in the car. "What's going on? Who was that?"

I opened my eyes, blinking away the memory of Trent's face. My fingers clamped around his rifle to conceal their shaking.

"Come on, Quinn. You're scaring me. Who was that back there?" Nathan pressed, shooting quick glances at me. "You knew him, right?"

"Once," I croaked, licking my lips nervously. "But not anymore."

Chapter Twenty-Six

Kensington Gardens, London – November 8th

The honeysuckle bushes next to the park bench weren't blooming due to the fall weather, but that did little to stop the memories they stirred up inside me. It had been years since I'd contemplated the good times with my family—years upon years since I'd last thought about Trent.

Nathan shifted beside me on the bench, his hands clasping and unclasping anxiously. He could barely keep his eyes off of me—the fear and worry in them too heavy to bear. Consequently, I avoided his gaze, the statue of Peter Pan surrounded by fairies keeping my attention halfway distracted.

The gardens were empty at two o'clock in the afternoon, the city alive all around us except for the piece of greenery. A cover of clouds masked the sun, bringing with it a breeze that rustled the leaves above our heads. I smelled pine, rain, and dirt.

Focusing on my surroundings seemed to be the only thing helping me calm down—that, and the alien sense of comfort Nathan offered. My hands were only just beginning to steady after the shock of seeing my brother again.

"Quinn?"

I glanced over at him and turned away just as quickly. The look in his eyes was too acute.

His eyes—I would never forget his eyes.

Words failing him, Nathan reached out and took my hand. I gasped as he squeezed tight enough to send the memory dashing from of my thoughts. Glancing over at him again, I watched him fidget beside me.

"Are you okay?"

I pursed my lips, unsure how to answer such a pointed question. *No, I'm most definitely not all right, but how can I say that out loud?*

He had saved my life without hesitation, risking his own life in doing so. My hostage had stepped in to save me. Just like I had done for him.

As if reading my thoughts, Nathan gave a half smile, his eyes flashing with a determination and affection that surprised me.

"Thank you."

He shrugged, and then gently smiled teasingly. "Don't thank me. I was the one who put your life in danger in the first place."

How long ago was it that I said those exact words?

"Besides I wasn't ready to watch you die. Neither was God. You still have things to do."

The certainty with which he spoke almost brought tears to my eyes. I blinked and forced a weak smile.

Maybe he was right—maybe there were supernatural forces at work that I couldn't see. I definitely knew Death was very real and more often than not appeared as a person or being. But was he right about God? Was there a higher power that loved us—the lying, cheating, betraying killers that we humans were?

"Who was that?" he asked in a gentle tone.

There was no need to explain who he was referring to, I knew all too well. I shook my head in refusal, grip on the bench beneath me tightening.

"Quinn?" Nathan prompted, not taking no for an answer.

"All right," I said, giving in. "He was my brother once upon a time."

"Your brother?" I looked up just in time to see

Nathan's astonished expression fade quickly into understanding. "What happened?"

I shook my head again.

"Tell me about your brother."

"He's not my brother anymore. I left that life behind a long time ago."

"Quinn," he murmured. "*Please* tell me about him. I don't believe for a minute that you truly left him behind. I saw the look in your eyes. It was—it was... "

Everything within me wanted to finish the sentence. Deep down inside, I knew the perfect word. The look Nathan had seen in my eyes was pure, raw *pain*.

Coldblooded murder was my business, but there were things that once lived in my heart. One of which was Trent. He had been my whole world. But that was before—before my whole world had come crumbling down with the news that two FBI agents brought in the middle of the night.

My mother had opened the door, Trent and I a few steps behind her when she started to cry. She's gone, they had said, she won't be coming home tonight. Or any other night.

She's gone forever.

"Drop it, Nathan." I shook my head. "Trent lost his sister in Afghanistan five years ago."

Getting to my feet, I started to walk off when he snatched my arm and jerked me back around to face him. The move was so surprising that I almost retaliated, swinging my arm toward his head, only to pull up at the last second. He flinched. It appeared he'd forgotten whom he was dealing with. His green eyes pleaded with mine—searching and seeking deep inside of my own gaze for the answers.

I hoped that he would find them and be able to tell me, because there was nothing inside of me except cold, black numbness.

"What happened to you?"

Sighing, I stuck my hands into my pockets and forced a smirk. "You don't want to know."

She's gone and so am I. Too far gone now.

We headed for the car and I got behind the wheel as he slid into the seat beside me. Without a word, I started the engine and shifted into drive. Kensington Gardens faded in my rearview mirror, but the image of Trent's face stayed etched in my thoughts. I desperately prayed to whatever force was out there listening that Garrett would know what the hell was going on. Far too many unanswered questions swirled around inside of my head.

A headache throbbed in the backs of my eyes, making it hard to focus on anything for longer than a few seconds. Seeing Trent had dredged up memories that would have been better left buried forever.

<>

London, England – November 8th

Garrett and Jason both called me within the hour when they discovered what had happened at the loft. I ignored their messages and silenced their calls. Garrett was smart. He would figure out what to do next, and he didn't need me to get any further in the way. Besides, I had other things to do.

Walking shoulder to shoulder with Nathan, I gazed listlessly ahead as we wandered around the streets of downtown. I had no concern for Nathan running away anymore. His selfless act of sacrifice to save my life told me he wasn't going anywhere any time soon.

"Shouldn't you answer that?" Nathan nodded at my cell phone as it started ringing yet again.

I glanced down at the screen, expecting another

call from Jason, but instead finding a message from Matt.

I read the address Matt had sent me and memorized it.

"Quinn?" Nathan bumped against me gently, eyebrows furrowed.

"Bugger off," I growled in warning, walking faster to cross the street. "You know I don't want to talk about it."

He had to jog a few steps to meet my stride. My gaze lifted to read the green sign positioned at the next intersection. We were practically standing on Matt's rendezvous.

"Quinn, please—" Nathan's plea was silenced as a lone figure stepped out of an alleyway ahead of us and stopped.

I halted, throwing my weight backward to keep from colliding with the man. Nathan wasn't so lucky. He ran right into Matt's solid chest, paling as the assassin caught him in a vice grip.

"We need to talk," Matt said, ignoring the young man in his arms.

I nodded, in no mood to argue with him.

Taking Nathan by the bicep, Matt led the way back into the alleyway. Smoke from various pipes filled the air overhead, swirling into vapor clouds and then getting whisked out of sight. Dumpsters reeked of rotting, leftover food and trash. My high heels clicked on the stained pavement as Matt turned a corner and continued onward.

A stray vagabond passed us, her overloaded shopping cart rusted, its right front wheel squeaking relentlessly. Matt paid her no mind even as Nathan craned his neck to look back.

I walked faster, catching up to them as Matt finally came to a stop in an abandoned doorway.

"I know what happened at Jason's loft," Matt

said, looking only at me.

I shrugged. It was easy enough knowledge to acquire. The circles we ran in were very small indeed. Definitely not worth singling me out over, especially with a secret rendezvous.

"Did Jason tell you to come find me because I wasn't taking his calls?"

"No, I'm working on my own here, Quinn," he replied, eyes flickering.

I said nothing.

"I know that Trent was there."

Several streets over, a police siren shrieked, echoing the bells screaming inside of my own mind.

"Quinn?" Nathan sidled up to my side, worry pitching his tone.

Across from us, Matt didn't move.

"Did you know that Trent was hunting me?" I whispered.

Matt shrugged, tattoos concealed by a leather jacket and fingerless gloves. "I knew he was hunting someone, but I didn't hear any names," he replied slowly, mulling the words over with great care. "After you recruited me for Rourke, I made it a priority to keep tabs on Trent at all times."

My eyelids lowered heavily as I remembered the day I had been reintroduced to Matt as Quinn Rogers. Until that day, he'd only known me as Andrea. Now he was the only one who knew what she had become and wasn't afraid.

"Trent's heading up a new branch of the FBI, a kind of rogue team that specializes in avoiding red tape. His orders aren't in any database, but that doesn't mean there isn't a paper trail if you know how to find it." Matt unzipped the front pocket of his jacket and retrieved a folded document. He handed it to me grimly. "If you need proof for Garrett about Trent's team, it's all in there. Names. Dates. Locations.

Current targets." His gaze hardened with emphasis.

Tucking the still folded document into my own pocket, I gave a curt nod. "Thank you, Matt," I said.

The assassin nodded. "I'll keep an eye on Trent," he promised, "and let you know if anything changes."

Taking Nathan's arm, I steered him away, ending our rendezvous. Matt followed us to the street corner where our paths split. He headed off toward the Tower of London, while I led Nathan back to my Range Rover. He was quiet as we got inside and I pulled into the traffic.

London flashed past in my windshield as we sped out of downtown and turned onto Garrett's street. With my house and Jason's loft both known locations to the FBI and Selah, Garrett's house was the only place left for us to congregate. Much to my dismay and suspicion.

It was dark outside by the time I pulled into the garage and hustled Nathan inside. Garrett was in the kitchen reading an email when we arrived. From down the hallway, Jason appeared as we burst into the house unannounced.

Neither even had a chance to say hello before I launched into my verbal assault. "Lying won't do you any good, so you had better start explaining."

Garrett looked at me like I had lost my mind, his fingers poised over the keyboard of his laptop.

"What are you talking about?" he replied, brow furrowing in confusion.

"Why did an FBI team find me today? Are you tipping them off with my location? Or are you just ignoring the fact that they even exist?" I slammed my hand down on the tabletop.

Both Jason and Nathan jumped at the loud thump. "And don't you dare lie to me this time."

"This time? What do you mean this time? I don't lie."

I snorted and crossed my arms. "That's what I thought, but apparently I need to be more objective about accepting what you say as the gospel."

"What the hell are you talking about?" He looked from Nathan to me and then back to Nathan again.

I pulled the documents Matt had given me out of my pocket and flung them at him with a sneer. Garrett caught them, eyes wide.

"What do you say to that?" I asked coldly as he unfolded the pages and began to read.

Knowing how Matt worked, I knew that everything Garrett needed for proof that I was right was on those pages.

It was all there—orders for tracking the illusive, deadly assassin known only as the Dragonfly. Orders that dated back three years.

"How did this happen?" Eyes haunted and death-like, Garrett looked up at me, papers clutched in limp fingers.

I stabbed my finger into his chest. "That's what I was hoping you would answer for me. How in the world did an FBI agent learn about me, Garrett? How was he able to form a team and pursue me for three entire years? And how the hell didn't you know about it?"

"Quinn—"

"Were you trying to keep something secret from me, Garrett, or did you truly not know about this?" I cut him off again. I was going to be the one asking questions, not him. He didn't have that luxury. Not now.

"I swear I knew nothing about this." Fear flickered in his eyes as my hand curled into a tight fist.

"How am I supposed to believe that? How do I know what you're telling me is true?"

"Have I ever lied to you before?"

"I don't know." I narrowed my eyes. "You tell

me."

Garrett crumpled the documents in his fists and lurched to his full height. Undaunted by his size, I lifted my chin to meet his glare. For a moment, neither of us spoke, and neither of us backed down. I struggled against the rising anger that always led to a killing calm that made me do very, very bad things. Seeing my brother again had unearthed all kinds of unwelcome feelings. One wrong step from Garrett and I wasn't sure what I would be capable of doing to him.

"If you can't believe me, then I don't know what else to say, Quinn. I will see what I can do with this new development."

He turned and left the kitchen. I almost grabbed his shirt to drag him back to face me, but restrained my temper. I would give him time to prove himself. If it came to killing him, I didn't doubt for a moment I could take him, and make it slow.

Turning to Nathan, I listened for the front door to slam shut. It did, with resounding clarity. Jason exhaled, turning back into the hallway and disappearing.

"Now what?" Nathan questioned as I sunk to my elbows against the kitchen counter.

◇

Garrett's House – November 9th

The delicious aroma of pizza lingered in the living room long after Nathan and I had devoured the large deluxe Greek goodness. Along with my soldier's rule of always sleeping when I had the chance, eating fell into the same category.

Eat, sleep, and clean your weapons when and where you can, because you never know when you'll have another chance.

All through our meal, Nathan and I had been quiet. Whether or not he approved of me cleaning my Glock and sharpening my knives at the coffee table, he didn't say. The only sound between us was contented chewing and the metallic ring of steel against stone.

Satisfied with my weapons, I put them away and got up from my seat on the floor, lounging against the couch. Nathan had gone to bed earlier, leaving me alone to clean our mess and entertain myself. Garrett had yet to return, and Jason had followed him out the door shortly before dinner, and with them, it seemed, were all the answers to my questions. I felt like I was drifting between reality and whatever level of Hell I had stumbled into.

I went back to Garrett's guestroom and lay down against the mound of pillows on the bed. Darkness had fallen outside, making the house eerie and extremely quiet. A small, nagging thought had popped into my head while Nathan and I ate dinner. It plagued me, but I couldn't fully entertain the possibilities it would hold.

I didn't want to think of Garrett in that way. He had never shown any signs of being an enemy of Rourke. In fact, he had helped the master assassin start his organization and find talented young killers like Jason and myself. But I also would have thought Jason incapable of playing double agent. My perspective of people seemed askew as of late, especially since there was hard proof stacked against Garrett's seemingly loyal nature.

Clearing my mind, I tilted my head back, focusing on the darkness through the skylight in the ceiling. A flicker of a shadow flashed across it and I jumped to attention, the bedframe rattling underneath me.

I tuned in to the sounds of the house at once, hearing the hum of the refrigerator, the whir of the

AC, and the ticking of multiple clocks. Nothing out of the ordinary. I closed my eyes and used my other senses. There was no sound, no movement besides my own breathing. But I could feel the change in the air.

Something was out there.

My instincts guided me out into the hallway, knife in hand. The narrow staircase to the second level of the house was silent and empty as I paused to listen. Even if Garrett wasn't an assassin, he still acted like one. Every window and door of his house had been purposefully tampered with to squeak when opened or closed. It was one of the upstairs windows that squeaked, breaking the condescending silence. I dashed from the room, running up the stairs two at a time.

Turning into the short hallway, I found no one. A window was open, letting in a gentle wind that kissed my face. I caught the faintest scent of cologne. Twirling my knife parallel with my forearm, I slunk through the darkness, prowling for the mysterious intruder. I reached the stairwell and heard a floorboard creak downstairs.

How? How did they get around me so quickly?

I raced back down the stairs, taking them two at a time until I leapt over the last four and landed in a crouch at the bottom. Tossing my head back, I glimpsed a shadow disappearing around the corner. It was uncanny how quickly the intruder moved—

Almost as if they know their way around.

Pursuing, I moved through the kitchen toward Garrett's bedroom at the rear of the house. The bedroom door was open and I entered to find nothing. Not even a hint of a presence to guarantee that someone had been there seconds before. Fury leapt into my throat as I wheeled around and stormed into the living room. Empty as well. Spinning in a circle to survey the first floor, I frowned. The house was large, but the odds should have been tipped in my favor of finding an intruder. Somehow, whoever was inside kept evading me.

A foreboding atmosphere descended upon the house and grew thicker by the second. Abruptly, there was another tread on the front stairs. I crept silently through the shadows. The smell of faint cologne reached my nose again as I paused against a wall. This time the scent was different—more of a fruity musk. Taking a deep breath, I tightened my grip on my weapon, knowing that whoever was on the other side of the wall could be a trained, armed hostile. I swung around, knife coming up to point at the intruder's face. His hand slammed into the side of my blade, knocking it to the side. He stepped behind me, clamping a hand over my mouth. I thrashed, bucking against his body as he pulled me to him.

"Shhh. It's me." Warm breath hissed in my ear. Jason removed his hand and I glanced up into his shadowed face.

"What the hell?" I demanded, breathless.

He nodded in the direction of the front door. "I came in a minute ago and heard someone moving around."

"So did I." My instincts bristled and I grasped the grip of my knife tighter. Jason shook his head, then he moved to a closet, pulled out a baseball bat, and hefted it to his shoulder. I eyed him thoughtfully.

Since when are you a Yankee hitter?

"What?"

"You're still recovering. Let me handle that." I took the bat from him in exchange for the knife.

Together we started forward, armed and ready.

Upstairs, I caught the trail of the intruder as he held back, pausing so that we could see his shadowy figure ahead. My pulse stuttered when I realized he was stalking toward Nathan's room. I glanced at

Jason, who was two inches away, breathing heavily, raised an eyebrow. He shook his head and pressed on.

What have you been doing all day while I've been fighting for my life? I lifted the bat to my shoulder. He looked knackered and weak from his injuries. *Surely you haven't been straining yourself.*

There was a loud creak of floorboards as the intruder stepped into the bedroom where Nathan slept. Jason and I froze. Sheets rustled as someone in the bed sat upright.

"Quinn?"

Crap.

There was another, softer squeak of the boards.

"Quinn, is that y—" Nathan's voice cut off in a startled gasp. I was already flying forward, Jason on my heels.

Bursting into the room, I glimpsed Nathan's form as he cowered in bed, the mysterious figure standing over him. My gaze saw the flicker of the knife in the intruder's hand. I let out a loud cry, lunging forward. The figure jerked, glancing back.

His first and last mistake.

In the darkness, the moonlight streaming through the window reflected in the intruder's wide eyes. I swung the baseball bat at his head, the jolt of impact jarring my bones. His eyes rolled up into his skull as the sickening thud echoed in my ears. The man toppled backward into the wall and lay still.

Light abruptly flooded the room and I whirled around, bat at the ready. Garrett stood in the doorway, his hand still resting on the light switch, his face looking haggard. I turned back to Nathan, who sat in bed, staring at the limp body.

"Are you all right?" I asked, surprisingly breathless.

He glanced up and nodded quickly.

Jason and Garrett passed me, going to the man

and pronouncing him dead. I swallowed hard, letting the bat drop from my hands to the floor.

"Geez, Quinn, remind me never to piss you off at a baseball game."

Jason's joke made my jaw clench. Looking at the dead man, I didn't feel the usual tingle at taking a life. Instead, I felt tired and dirty. I gave Jason a very forced smile and sat down next to Nathan. He was staring into space, looking like he might have had a heart attack. I touched his hand. His frightened eyes locked onto me.

"Hey... " I trailed off.

There was no response from him.

My throat seized up on its next gulp of air. "Everything's all right now, you're safe."

He nodded, but I knew he didn't believe me.

"Who do you think this guy is?" Jason nudged the dead man with his foot.

"Doesn't look like FBI material. Your guess is as good as mine." I shrugged.

Garrett was rummaging through the pockets and folds of the man's clothing, but had yet to come up with anything helpful. I gave Nathan a sidelong look. His coloring was gradually returning to normal.

"Thank goodness you and Jason heard him." Garrett moved to the doorway empty-handed. "I can't imagine what he'd want with Nathan, though."

"Maybe he wasn't after Nathan, and he just got lost and thought he'd take everyone in the house down?" Jason rocked back on his heels.

I went to shrug again. Movement caught my notice out of the corner of my eye. My mouth opened, but my warning cry was too late.

Not again.

Chapter Twenty-Seven

Garrett's House – November 9th

With a tremendous crash, the windows of the room shattered. Nathan cried out, covering his head with his arms as I threw my body away from the flying glass. Three men dropped to the floor of the room, crouched, weapons in hand. Under an unspoken command, they split apart, each going for a different target.

Nathan startled, leaping backward as I lunged to my feet, placing myself between him and the attackers. Jason straightened, throwing my knife at the nearest intruder, but too slowly. He was knocked backward as one of the masked men charged, tackling him to the ground. The third went after Garrett.

Divide and conquer—a seemingly perfect strategy. It was suddenly obvious that the men were amateurs, or at the very least did not know their targets—us—intimately. Dividing rank worked on the battlefield. It even worked in a street fight or bar brawl, but not when your opponents were assassins and were at the top of their game fighting one on one. They had just signed away their defeat without knowing it.

I smiled as one of the men rushed me.

Feigning backward, I let my opponent plant a solid punch to my ribs and follow it through with a knee to the hip. I jerked instinctively. The man bought my performance and moved to finish me off. I took a step back to brace myself and shoved upward, tucking my shoulder under the man's chest. He rolled over me and hit the ground hard. Whirling on him, I dropped all of my weight into the knee I planted on his sternum.

"Dasvidaniya," I crooned and snapped the man's neck.

At another crash I twisted to see Jason get slammed into the wall again. His eyes flickered, the light in them wavering with the trauma. My body uncoiled like a spring, flying across the bed. Jason saw me coming as he reeled from a wild upper cut to the jaw.

My feet hit the floor behind his opponent. I grabbed the desk chair and swung it upward. The masked intruder gasped in pain as Jason kneed him in the groin, backing him right into my space. The chair collapsed on the intruder's head and his body crumpled like a puppet with severed strings. He dropped at my feet, draped over Jason's legs.

"All right?" I asked, holding out a hand to him.

Jason nodded, grimacing and gasping in pain as he took my hand and stood. The fingers he brushed over his stomach came away smeared scarlet. It didn't take a PhD to know that his stitches had pulled out of his injury.

"I'm fine." He waved me off.

"Quinn." Garrett's voice pitched when he called my name. I knew before I saw him that something was wrong. I knew without any explanation that someone was about to die.

Frowning, I turned and met the hacker's gaze. My breath caught.

Garrett stood stock still, the barrel of a Beretta M9 clamped under his chin in front of the only surviving attacker. All movement in the room ceased. Every breath held—every sound silenced.

"Hands where I can see them," the attacker barked, voice deep and gravelly.

I glanced at Nathan, still huddled next to the bed out of the way, for now. Jason winced beside me, face contorted with anger. Slowly, I lifted both of my hands by the sides of my head. Jason copied the movement.

With the bed between us and our weapons scattered out of reach, any counterattack Jason or I tried would take too long to prove successful in saving Garrett's life. While we could cover the distance in two seconds, it would take less than a second for the attacker to pull the trigger. The man would kill Garrett long before we ever reached him.

"I'm going to enjoy this." The attacker chuckled, tightening his grip on Garrett's arm. He looked right at me, sizing me up, gaze lingering a little too long.

A feline growl escaped my lips.

"Rourke's precious harpy. The Dragonfly herself."

"In the flesh." I smiled, performing a mocking bow, arms spread at my sides. "Who are you?"

"No one of consequence."

Oh I doubt that's true.

"Who sent you?" Jason demanded, stalling for time.

I could easily tear the attacker limb for limb, but I needed to know Garrett would do his part by getting out of the way first.

"No one of consequence," the attacker slurred again.

My nostrils flared as the masked intruder shifted his weapon to rest a little harder against the hacker's throat. Garrett didn't even flinch.

I frowned at him, as he remained completely frozen at the mercy of his captor. Though he wasn't an assassin, he was just as good as Jason or I when it came to self-defense. Growing up on the streets and then running a drug ring had seen to that. He knew going still was the last mistake you would ever make in a fight. Especially in a hostage situation.

Why isn't he struggling?

Well, if Garrett wasn't going to make a move to save his own skin, I certainly was. No amateur hit man was going to kill Garrett on my watch. I claimed that right for myself and Rourke.

I shifted my stance, widening it so that I could bend my knees in preparation for a sudden lunge forward. Nathan's subtle gesture out of the corner of my eye caught my attention. I glanced to him for a second—long enough to see him nod toward the baseball bat within *his* reach.

A grin tugged at the corners of my mouth. Oh, he was clever. He was conniving, and brilliant. I read his thoughts as clearly as my own, a plan to free Garrett snapping into place at once.

The attacker opened his mouth to speak, perhaps sensing our unease. He never got the chance to finish. I nodded at Nathan and we made our move—

Time slowed as I saw the attacker stiffen, his body seizing up for a moment as panic gripped him. He saw me lunge for him and knew Death was knocking at his door. His body jerked, finger tugging away from the trigger as if afraid he would accidentally pull it. At the same time, the bat was in Nathan's hand as he surged upward, swinging it at the intruder's arm. Bone crunched as the hard wood connected with the side of the man's elbow. Howling, the attacker released Garrett and his gun immediately.

My foot hit the ground and I was across the bed in a blink. The attacker righted himself, twisting for his weapon to shoot at me, but too slowly. I kicked the gun away and popped him in the nose hard enough to break it. He reeled, Garrett a second priority to his own life. I ripped the hacker away, shoving him toward Jason who had moved to join in the melee. With a wild cry of pain and fear, the attacker staggered

274

as I dove into his abdomen to send us both crashing to the floor. Arms and legs and blood were everywhere as I tore into his face and neck with a barrage of punches. It was only when Jason dragged me away that I stopped, panting.

"Easy, easy, it's all right," Jason murmured in my ear, wrapping his arms around my shoulders.

I grasped his shirt in my fists, panting.

"It's all right."

The attacker moaned, slipping into unconsciousness as silence enveloped the room, pushing out the sound of violence. I leaned back against Jason, hands trembling. Garrett sat on the floor a few feet away, head in his hands, gaze downcast. Looking over Jason's arms, I met Nathan's gaze. He dropped the baseball bat to the floor and swallowed hard.

He had saved Garrett's life by his quick thinking. I wondered if that put us all in his debt. I already knew I was.

Slowly, as if relying on me for support as much as I was him, Jason uncurled his arms and released me.

"Should we keep him alive?" he asked, studying my face intently.

Without a word, Garrett pushed to his feet and made a hasty exit out of the room. Jason raised an eyebrow and silently repeated his question.

I nodded, hands still shaking as I raked them through my hair.

Taking off his belt, Jason knelt next to the unconscious attacker and cinched his hands together. I crossed to Nathan, my breathing coming back under control, as he stood paralyzed, eyes wide, mouth gaping open.

"Ace thinking, you saved Garrett's life," I murmured, placing my hand on Nathan's arm. He nodded, swallowing hard as I squeezed gently.

Forcing a smile for his benefit, I turned to face the attacker as Jason finished binding his feet together at the ankles.

"Take off his mask," I commanded.

Jason complied, and I frowned. Dark hair and olive skin completed the Eastern look to the man's facial features.

Strange, he looked somewhat familiar.

"He might be able to answer some of our questions. Put him in the hall for now," I told Jason. "We need to get rid of these bodies."

I turned back to Nathan and started. He had dropped into a crouch, hands holding the sides of his head as he trembled.

"Whoa there, mate... are you all right?" I bent down to touch his arm.

He shook his head and gulped. I knelt in front of him. All color had abandoned his face, making his green eyes stand out like beacons.

"I can't believe it." He moaned as I reached out to touch his arm. "I can't believe what just happened."

What am I supposed to do to comfort him?

Jason shot me a sympathetic look before he disappeared into the hall, dragging the unconscious man with him. Nathan groaned again, clutching his stomach.

"Nathan?" I asked, worried.

Without warning, he lunged past me headed for the bathroom. Moments later, I heard retching and shuddered. Poor boy.

He was an innocent victim of my life and it made me feel guilty knowing that I'd placed him right in the middle of my own dangerous plight. Again. I knew without a doubt that I needed to reverse what I had done. Nathan didn't deserve what I was putting him through.

The bathroom went silent. Taking a deep breath, I

walked toward it. After knocking, I entered to find him seated on the tile floor, pale and breathing heavily.

"Feel better?" I filled a cup from the bathroom cupboard with water from the tap and handed it to him.

Nathan shook his head and blinked rapidly. "I can't do this anymore, Quinn," he whispered.

Unsure what to make of his comment, I sat down on the floor next to him. "I don't think you were supposed to do anything. I'm the one who kidnapped you in the first place." The cold tile bled into the backs of my legs as I stretched them out in front of me. I laid a hand over my side, subconsciously looking for the telltale sign of pulled staples. Nothing. Jason, it seemed, was the only one of us who had come through the attack seriously injured. His stitches would need to be replaced quickly before infection set in.

Nathan sighed, laying his head back against the wall. The cup of water I'd given him sat untouched between us.

"Nathan, none of this is your fault," I said. "I kidnapped you. If anyone is to blame, it's me."

"I know. It's just that I made a promise to myself and God about you."

I tilted my head to the side. "About me?"

"Yeah... " He fiddled with the cup in his hands. "Can I be honest with you?"

Turning to face him, I leveled my gaze with his. I brought my knees to my chest and wrapped both arms lazily around them.

"I think you've earned that right," I murmured, smiling faintly. He took a deep breath, fingers clasping and then unclasping.

"If you don't mind me saying so, you're a bit callous and bitter," he said.

My eyebrows arched at his words. *Well, this is an interesting turn of events.*

"It's all part of my charm I'm afraid." I shifted, the tile floor warming beneath us.

Nathan's smile died too quickly to shed any light into my darkness. Confused, I watched as he fidgeted, playing with a piece of string from the hem of his shirt.

"Does it bother you? I mean, why bring this up now of all times?"

The young artist turned to me and time seemed to stop. All that mattered or existed was the two of us. "Because I think you're more open now," he said.

"Open to what exactly?"

"To my beliefs... " He inclined his head toward me. "And yours... and what makes them different."

He rubbed his wrists absently, exhaling. All the times before he had spoken about religion or God it had raised a sense of anger inside of me, but not this time. This time I could see the lines of faith in him. This time I wanted to know more.

"Do you believe your god has kept you safe from me?" I paused to take a shallow breath. "I could have killed you many, many times."

He shook his head, a wistful smile on his lips. "Every day I prayed for my safety, and every day I got to watch God fulfill those prayers. He really loves you, Quinn, no matter what you say or believe. He wants you to find the truth."

"I'm not looking for truth, Nathan." I smiled, crossing my arms over my chest.

His eyes flicked an even brighter shade of green as he tilted his head to the side, peering at me curiously.

"Really?" He said it doubtfully. "Then why do you run?"

The question caught me completely off-guard. I thought I'd kept my flight instinct hidden. Neither Garrett nor Jason knew I constantly fought the overwhelming urge to run from my problems and past. But somehow it didn't surprise me in the least to know that Nathan had observed my tendencies.

"When you do what I do and see what I've seen, no place is safe from the horrors." I sighed, my lungs compressing as if a deep abyss had just opened where my heart should have been.

Nathan pressed his lips together in a firm line. His curt nod said all of the words he didn't speak into existence. He stared at me as if he could see right through my skin into the jet-black soul underneath.

"It's hard to have a heart when I have stopped so many others." My tongue felt like lead despite the sarcasm I laced into my words.

The dimples in the corners of Nathan's mouth appeared as he flashed me a smile that warmed my very bones.

"I don't think you're as dark as you want people to believe," he said, getting to his feet. "You're not a monster, Quinn. There is good in you. I have seen it."

"You know nothing about me, Nathan," I said, copying his movement to stand eye-to-eye with him.

"You're right," he confessed, leaning against the sink counter. "But I have seen enough to know that you're lost. I don't believe you truly think murdering people is the right thing to do."

I frowned, questioning the very same thing. For years, I had thought it was the right thing; now, I wasn't so sure.

What's wrong with me? I can't be questioning my instincts now. My thoughts turned on themselves—trying to make sense of what I was feeling inside. Half of my consciousness wanted me to call him a liar, the other half was trying to reason with my heart that he was correct.

"I know God put me in the right place at the right time for a reason, Quinn." Nathan laid a hand on my shoulder. The genuineness flowing off of him was enough to make me relax.

I was home, and yet far, far away, begging to explore further—deeper.

"I'm sorry you were dragged into this."

"Hey, I've always wanted an adventure, I just never thought I'd get one like this." He gave a dry chuckle.

I opened my mouth to continue when Jason burst into the bathroom.

"He's awake, Quinn," the assassin announced, eyes dark.

With a final glance at Nathan, I followed Jason out into the hallway.

The bound and now conscious surviving attacker sat against the wall, glaring angrily at us. Just as we halted in front of him, Garrett topped the last stair behind me.

"Well, well, look what we have here." Jason kicked the intruder's foot. "Bastard."

"Jason," I warned softly, as Garrett strode forward. I did a double take, barely able to believe the hacker's alien look of rage.

Never before had I seen such violence in his eyes. Compared to Jason, he was calm and collected—a cool summer breeze. Garrett compared to me was like pitting a cow pony against a lioness. But the fire blazing in his eyes singed.

The intruder looked up at us from under his eyebrows, sneering. He glanced at Jason and winked. Jason frowned.

"Selah's missed you, brother." The man glanced at me next and gave a golden-toothed grin. "He doesn't take kindly to people who mess with his plans of revenge."

"I can imagine," I returned, smirking, arms folded over my chest. "But what does Selah hope to gain from breaking into our house in the middle of the night?"

He chuckled and shifted his seated position as best he could within the bonds Jason had secured. "Annihilation."

We never saw Garrett's fast punch or the follow through of his elbow connecting with bone and cartilage. We just saw the aftermath as the intruder toppled sideways, blood flowing from his broken nose. Even I recoiled.

Hearing a sharp intake of breath behind me, I turned. Nathan had just appeared in the hallway, and from the look he possessed, he had been in time to see Garrett's reaction.

"What the hell, Garrett?" Jason wheeled on the hacker.

Garrett huffed, shaking out his fist. "He was getting on my nerves."

I didn't buy it, not for a second. Garrett possessed patience, and buckets of it. I knelt next to the intruder and felt for a pulse. There was none. Turning around, I met Jason's expectant gaze and shook my head.

"His neck is broken." I ran my fingertips along the twisted vertebrae. "The second blow snapped the spinal cord. It was all torque."

My gaze lifted to Garrett's, glaring.

His nostrils flared, a flash of regret appearing in his eyes before vanishing just as quickly as it had come. I straightened, staring down at the dead man. It wasn't a surprise that Garrett's superior height and weight were enough to disrupt the spinal cord. It was a surprise, however, that Garrett had even hit him in the first place.

"He had more he could tell us," Jason spat, eyes narrowed, fists clenched.

"No, I heard enough. Selah isn't a threat to us, and not someone we have time to worry about. We can handle him easily."

That was the absolute last straw.

Maybe Garrett hadn't understood me the other times I came forward with a problem. Maybe Garrett was purposefully ignoring the issues at hand. Either way I didn't care about the truth any longer. I just wanted a reaction—and results.

For the second time in a matter of minutes, someone swung a fist. Only this time, it was my turn.

My knuckles collided with Garrett's jaw, hard enough it would likely bruise and loosen a few teeth but not hard enough to break it. He gaped, staggering back, spitting blood out of his mouth until it stained the front of his shirt.

"Dammit, Quinn!" He used his shirtsleeve to gingerly mop up the blood trailing down his chin.

I latched onto his collar, pulling him down to nose level. "What do you think *threat* means?"

"What?" Garrett gaped at me like I had grown another head.

"You said that Selah isn't a threat. Five men broke into your house and nearly murdered us. They would have slit all of our throats while we slept if Jason and I hadn't heard them. Selah is a threat, Garrett—a big threat. He's the only man to have ever captured me. The only person Rourke actually feels threatened by. Go ahead. Try and come up with a reasonable argument why he's not a threat."

I heard Nathan shift positions behind me. Garrett just stared at me coldly.

"But you heard them and stopped them. They're dead now, and the threat is dead with them too."

I shook my head. There was something so off about him that I couldn't help but take a step backward. He still looked like the man I knew, but Garrett's eyes were filled with a light I had never seen before.

"Since you don't seem to remember, there have been a lot of threats lately. You keep telling me that you can handle it, yet I don't see a damn difference. In fact, it's getting worse, Garrett."

As if I had awoken him, he turned to look at Nathan. His gaze darkened, drilling into Nathan with a look of absolute fury.

"All of the threats have been because of *him*, Quinn. None of this has anything to do with me."

My blood simmered, barely controlled rage beating at the doors of its cell. Garrett's pointed look and implied threat on Nathan's life made my hands clench into fists. I placed myself between the hacker and the young man, breaking Garrett's stare. His eyes flickered, the fury abating as it took in a threat higher up on the food chain. Setting my stance, I stared him down.

"Is that what you think?" I had a mind to punch him again.

Jason shook his head at me. He, perhaps best of all, knew what was apt to happen when someone awoke the beast that lived underneath my skin. Garrett would die if he didn't back down.

"Where exactly did the FBI team that has been tracking me for three years come from? I didn't kidnap Nathan three years ago."

"I swear to you that I didn't know anything about them, Quinn," he said before spinning on his heel and making his exit.

No one moved as we listened to his footsteps fade down the stairs. Moments later, the front door of the house slammed. I let out a pent up breath and turned to Nathan. He looked even more shaken than before.

"You can use the other guest bedroom. Jason and I will clean this up and make sure the security systems are back online." I paused. "Do you need anything?"

Nathan shook his head weakly, turning to go. I

watched him shuffle into the bedroom I had been using. His slow movements pained me.

Jason stepped up to my side, exhaling heavily. "If he can get his thoughts to shut off long enough to fall asleep, I'll be in awe."

I ignored him and instead asked, "What does it tell you when an assassin misses his target?"

He shrugged and knelt down next to the dead man lying on the floor. I crouched beside him, leveling an intense gaze with his.

"It tells you they aren't really trying, right?" I breathed, thinking out loud. "Five intruders broke into Garrett's house, the Fort Knox of home security, without warning. They obviously knew what they were looking for, and they clearly knew Garrett."

"Do you hear what you're saying?" Jason hissed. "Are you accusing Garrett of being in league with Selah?"

"I don't know, Jason. But I do know that Garrett knew the intruders tonight. He didn't struggle to get free even when they clapped a gun to his head. And they didn't kill him on purpose. They hesitated, not out of fear or inexperience, but out of duty. I lost count how many times they could have killed Garrett and didn't."

"But if Garrett knew the intruders, or even worse, was part of them, why would he kill this guy?" Jason asked, gesturing to the man between us.

I stared at the blood pooling on the carpet—that was going to take a lot of scrubbing to get clean—and reviewed the scene in my mind. He had said *annihilation* right before Garrett killed him.

"I don't know. I'm hoping it was an accident. Too much strength behind any blow can create enough torque to snap a neck."

"Quinn Rogers, you are insane. Garrett's worked for Rourke longer than either of us. He would never be a traitor," Jason said.

"I would have said the same thing about you," I whispered.

He exhaled heavily and went to heft the dead body upright.

"Leave it."

"They'll be a bloodstain the size of Texas if we don't get him out of here soon," he returned.

I shrugged, indifferent to whether Garrett's carpets remained spotless or not.

"Leave it, we need to fix your stitches before you bleed out right next to him." I got to my feet and, without waiting for Jason to agree, started downstairs.

In Garrett's medical room, I had Jason take his shirt off before lying back on the bed. I switched on an overhead surgical light and popped open the medical kit on the nightstand.

"Six," Jason remarked, craning his neck to look down at his injury. "Those bastards ripped out six of my stitches. And you and Garrett worked so hard on them."

"Shut up," I warned, brandishing a needle, "or I'll fill you full of staples instead of string."

He started humming the song from Pinocchio as I bent to the task at hand, distracting my thoughts as best I could under the circumstances. When I'd finished pulling out the ruined stitches and replacing them with fresh ones, Jason picked up our conversation about Garrett again, grimacing in pain with every word.

"All right, maybe you're right. Maybe Garrett is in league with Selah. So what? What does that look like? He'd be the best damn double agent in the history of the world."

I shot him a glare, prepping a sanitized washcloth to wipe away the blood from his wound. The way he folded his hand behind his head to show off his biceps looked too scripted to be an innocent move.

"I think you're just mad at him for failing to see your brother's FBI team hot on your tail." He seemed to be enjoying my duties as nurse a little too much.

I pressed a little harder with the cloth. Jason yelped, shying away from my touch. "Hey!"

I ignored him.

"If I were you I'd be less concerned about everyone else and more concerned about yourself." He picked up without missing a beat. "We need to get back to work, and somehow Nathan needs to be taken out of the picture. You're right about him not being to blame, but he's still a huge liability."

The blood on Jason's torso cleaned away, I tossed the cloth onto the nightstand. Jason gingerly sat upright.

"I want to let him go home," I said suddenly.

Jason made an odd noise in the back of his throat. He looked at me as if I had completely lost it. Maybe I had.

Jason's eyes narrowed, lips pressing into a firm line. "Are you sure?"

I said nothing.

"Letting him go home is the worst possible idea, Quinn. All it would take is one word to his parents or friends and the FBI would be on our trail like it's a war path."

"They're already after me, what else would be new?" I shrugged.

"This would be worse. A lot worse." His words were sledgehammer blows to my weary heart. "You would never be able to rest so long as you lived."

"Between attacks from the FBI and Selah, I'm already wanted and on the run. There is no rest for me. Never has been, never will be."

"You sound like you've already convinced yourself that this is a good idea." He folded his hands in his lap.

I licked my lips, fidgeting.

Too many reasons to keep Nathan locked in my possession nagged at my consciousness as I stared at Jason. I had already broken every rule Rourke insisted upon by keeping the hostage alive for so long. And I could see the reasons Rourke had for such rules. While it had been hard to kill Nathan at the beginning because of complications, it was nigh impossible to even consider the thought after he had gained my respect.

Or is it my friendship?

I didn't want to let Nathan go for a multitude of reasons, both for my own selfish purposes of having someone interesting to talk to and for our own safety as well, but the thought just felt right. I exhaled. Jason's shoulders tensed as I looked up at him.

"I made a mistake when I brought him into this mess. I trust him not to turn us in, Jason. He'll be safer away from me. I have to do this... for him."

"Are you sure?" he asked again.

"Yes," I replied.

After tonight I know I won't be able to stand it if he gets killed on my watch.

"You're never going to be able to convince Garrett to let you do it."

I muttered a curse. He was right of course. The hacker would never in a million years let me do anything to potentially harm Rourke's organization—or myself.

"You'll have to think of some clever way to keep him in the dark about it." Jason wadded his ruined shirt into a ball, straightening to his feet. "Or forget about the whole thing."

"I owe Nathan this."

"You don't owe Nathan anything, Quinn. This isn't a blood oath. You're an assassin, and he's a hostage. We all know he's supposed to die. Most of all him."

The sight of Nathan tackling Trent to keep my own brother from blowing out my brains made me smile.

"Oh, but I do owe him something, Jas." My smile grew. "I owe him his life, and I know just how to pacify Garrett to grant it."

"You're insane." Jason scoffed as I walked past him into the living room.

The house was quiet after the attack. The smell of gunpowder and blood filled the air as I turned on the sink and plunged my hands under the warm flow. Blood washed off of my skin and disappeared down the drain. My thoughts swirled together like the two liquids until they clashed on two specific thoughts.

One, I felt at peace with the decision to let Nathan go, however that would look. He wasn't a threat to me.

No, the threat has always been closer to home.

And two, Garrett was keeping very dangerous secrets.

Chapter Twenty-Eight

London, England – November 10th

The abandoned train tunnel was empty and bathed in midnight darkness. But that did little to quell my anxiety that someone might stumble upon us. In the passenger seat, Nathan fidgeted. He stared through my windshield silently at the sheets of rain obscuring the far end of the tunnel, sketchbook across his lap and a backpack I had prepared for him resting on the floorboard.

Where is he? He can't be late, not to this.

The engine of my Range Rover creaked, growing cold in the night as thunder roared overhead. I shivered, shrugging deeper into my knit scarf. Nathan took a shallow breath. It sounded like a freight train's whistle in the eerie silence of waiting.

Come on, you can't quit on me now. There's too much at stake tonight.

Pressing a button on my phone, I read the time and echoed Nathan's exhale. 12:32 a.m. Matt should have been in place, opposite us in the tunnel, seventeen minutes ago.

"Are you sure this is the place?" Nathan whispered, sparing a sideways glance at me.

I didn't grace his question with an equally rubbish answer. We both knew I wouldn't have made the mistake of mixing up details. Not when both of our lives rested on a very thin wire.

I clenched my fingers into fists in the pockets of my black jacket. Lightning flashed, lighting up the end of the tunnel like a train's beacon. Involuntarily,

Nathan and I both flinched. Our nerves were too taut not to. Another glance at the time. Another rumble of thunder. Another shaky exhale.

Where was Matt?

My mind didn't take long at all to jump to the worse possible consequence of going behind both Garrett and Jason's backs to ensure Nathan's safety. I wasn't sure if an ambush by Trent or Selah would be worse. There was also the possibility that Matt had turned us into Rourke. The master assassin wouldn't even let me see him coming. It would be a single gunshot for each of us and then blood would flow.

I found it hard to breathe suddenly.

"Want to listen to the radio?" Nathan asked.

I shook my head. "No. We can't turn the car on until Matt arrives and you're safe."

Nathan didn't respond, just went back to staring out the windshield. Waiting. I winced as my fingernails dug into the palms of my hands. I was clenching them too tightly, and yet I couldn't let up. 12:45 came and went. I gnawed on my bottom lip, unsure whether it was safer to remain where I was or leave. In the event of an ambush, leaving the old train tunnel was a suicidal decision.

"Are you sure about this?" Nathan had already asked the same thing a hundred times before we got in my car and a hundred times after that.

While I had openly assured him that I was sure, the truth in my heart was much less certain.

One more minute, Matt. I'll give you one more minute before I take off like a bat out of Hell.

Remaining silent, I placed one hand on the ignition, ready for a quick getaway. Another flash of lightning lit up the tunnel. Nathan jerked at the resounding clap of thunder that followed.

I thought the car headlights that appeared ahead were another bolt of lightning until the sleek hood of a

Vauxhall Insignia broke through the camouflage of rain. My shoulders collapsed forward as the tension drained out of me.

Matt.

"Come on," I said to Nathan, unlocking my door and stepping outside.

He followed suit, both of us carefully stepping over the train tracks to meet Matt in the middle of the tunnel.

The assassin wore a brown bomber's jacket with patches across the chest, it matched the pair of old jeans and jungle green t-shirt he was wearing beneath. His gunmetal grey eyes met mine as I halted a few feet away. I could see glimpses of his tattoos crawling up his neck as the storm continued all around us.

"Did anyone follow you?" I broke the silence first, eyebrows arching.

Matt shook his head. "No one knows where I am. As far as Rourke and Garrett know, I'm in Croatia with the daughter of the president." He held up his arm for good measure allowing me to see the incision neatly closed with five stitches. No more trackers.

"Good."

Turning to Nathan, I discovered that words utterly failed me. I blinked as he stared back at me, a half smile on his lips. He was going free. Or as close to freedom as he could get without endangering Rourke's entire organization. Me included.

I looked back to Matt. "Are you sure the safe house in Bucharest is secure?"

"No one knows about it, Quinn. I swear. Not even Garrett will be able to find us," he promised.

"Good," I said again. I swallowed hard.

"I have something for you," Nathan said, offering his sketchbook to me.

"What's this?" I asked, reluctantly accepting the gift.

"I drew multiple pictures of you. Under the circumstances, I think they'd be better off with you not me." He smiled as I flipped open the book and found the first drawing of me from the pub. I didn't know if I hated or adored the likeness of my face staring up at me.

"Thank you, Nathan." I snapped the book closed and made myself smile for his benefit. "Now go, it's a long trip to Romania."

"I mean it," he said. "You really have changed. There's good in you. I've always seen it."

I clenched my jaw to keep from speaking.

"Nathan?" Matt held out his arm in a beckoning gesture.

Nathan glanced at me for permission. My throat constricted as I gave a small nod and watched the young man head for the assassin's car.

It was too dangerous to let Nathan go home to his family, and even more dangerous to keep him with me. A safe house guarded by the only assassin in Rourke's organization who owed me a life debt was the best compromise I could come up with.

He'll be safe with Matt. You know he's one of the best, and he loves kids.

You know that part especially well.

"I'll message you when we get settled," Matt told me, moving to follow Nathan.

I held up a hand, stopping him. "Am I making the right decision here? I mean, is it safe for me to let him go?"

"Safer than keeping him with you," Matt said. "A lot safer if you really want my opinion."

"So I'm not making a mistake?"

His lips twisted up in a soft smile as he looked at me. "The best apology is changed behavior, Quinn. You're letting him go as far as you can. He's a smart one, he knows what's at stake for you."

292

"So it's not a mistake then?"

"What does your heart tell you?"

I stiffened slightly, my pulse stuttering. "You know my heart hasn't been right in a very long time, Matt. Not since... not since..." I trailed off. The memories were too painful.

He took a step forward, closing the distance between us so Nathan, who was settled in the Insignia, would have no chance of reading our lips or seeing our shared expressions.

"Listen to me, Quinn," Matt began. "I was there when you and Trent lost everything, okay? I was there when you left for the Army. And I was there when you started doubting Rourke's sway over your life. I know what you're running from. Hell, losing someone you care about is what got me into trouble too."

"But your brother died fighting for his country," I said. "I never had that kind of closure."

Matt's eyes flickered with sorrow. "Maybe not, but you've got something better now, haven't you?"

I frowned, making him smile.

"You have a second chance with Nathan to make things right. Like I said, the best apology is changed behavior."

"I'm not apologizing," I retorted.

"Not to Nathan, but you're still apologizing to someone. I know you too well to believe your lies." He winked. "Call me if you need anything. I'll let you know when Nathan and I are settled in Bucharest."

He headed for his car, strides long and confident. I stared after him, watching his back and arms move flawlessly with the movement. He was a cat, muscles curling and then stretching with every step.

"Be careful," I called as he reached the driver's door.

He faced me and laughed. "Damned if you do, bored if you don't."

Getting behind the wheel, Matt said something to Nathan before starting his car and backing out into the rain. I watched until I couldn't see them any longer through the storm before climbing into my own vehicle. It started with a low rumble, headlights cutting a brutal path out of the tunnel.

Thunder roared above the roof of the Rover as I pulled onto a road leading back into town.

Somewhere behind me, Matt and Nathan were heading for Romania. When I had eliminated the threat of both Trent and Selah's men, Nathan could go free, but not until I was certain Rourke and I would remain safe. I might have developed some sort of bond with the young artist, but that was nothing compared to the relationship the master assassin and I shared.

An assassin couldn't afford emotions and humanity. They were dangerous. An assassin could kill anything, but emotions could kill an assassin.

I exhaled heavily. *His eyes—I would never forget his eyes.*

Chapter Twenty-Nine

London, England – December 24th

Car exhaust, sweat, the smell of food, and humidity made the afternoon feel like a smoldering blanket tied too tightly around my neck. I jogged along the busy pavement, dodging pedestrians, bikes, and tourists. My workout jacket clung to my hot skin, doing a good job of soaking up my sweat.

Even after running for almost an hour and a half, my body still showed no sign of stopping. With every step I attempted to rid my mind of the memories of Nathan. He was safe with Matt after all. And as soon as I got rid of Selah and Trent's FBI aspirations, he would be out of my life for good. I wouldn't have to see Jason again, as I planned to return to solo assignments. Everything was going according to my plan—or so I tried to convince myself.

It wasn't working.

I slowed to a stop, running my fingers through my hair as I doubled over my legs to take a breath. People skirted around me as I started walking again. Wiping my forehead, I looked through the crowds without really seeing them. My eyes lifted to focus above the heads of the passersby. A store to my right advertised cold beverages.

After crossing the street, I ducked inside to purchase a bottle of water. I downed half of the container before emerging back onto the pavement. Another block down the way my cell vibrated in my pocket. Taking it out, I read the text message with a frown.

Care for a ride?

Twisting to glance along the street, I squinted as the sun glinted off of a flashy sports car idling at the curb. Though it was a different model, I recognized the owner's taste in the luxury of expensive automobiles at once. The presence of the vehicle was already gathering quite the group of onlookers.

Of course.

Stuffing my phone back into its pocket, I took another sip of my water as I started to cross the road.

The gull-wing door of the Lamborghini Veneno swung upward to allow me entrance into the passenger seat. I slipped inside, the door barely having time to close again before the Veneno surged away from the curb. The driver's black suit perfectly matched the dark leather interior of his car.

"New wheels?" I asked, smiling as I surveyed the stunning vehicle.

Rourke chuckled, weaving in and out of traffic with a practiced ease that made my nerves stand at attention as his speed teetered on the edge of insanity. He took a sharp turn, leaving the busy section of downtown. I was a skilled driver, but he was something else entirely.

Kill me in a freak car accident, Rourke, and I'll haunt you forever from beyond the grave.

"You could say that." The look of pure radiant excitement in his dark eyes sent a thrill rushing through my veins.

"I like it," I purred, feeling each word leave my lips in a gush.

Rourke glanced over at me—taking his eyes off the road for a hair-raising second to meet my grin.

For several moments neither of us said a word, the only sound the powerful engine. I licked my lips, watching out the window as the scenery passed. Rourke's cologne, as always, was a perfect blend of musk and citrus. When I first met him, the combination was so starkly opposite to his dark exterior that it had put me off. The better I got to know Rourke, the more I began to realize that he went out of his way to confuse people about who he really was.

Everything he did, said, or wore was to keep his true identity a mystery—a ravaged mystery that I had yet to crack. Not that I wanted to anymore. I'd seen glimpses of what he truly was and knew that the full truth would be too much to bear.

Rourke took a sharp left turn. Out of instinct, I placed my hand against the door to keep from sliding in the seat. I broke the silence then.

"Where are we going?"

He changed lanes quickly to shoot between two slower cars. "I thought you and I both could spare some time to catch up."

"Catch up?" I arched an eyebrow in surprise. The phrase wasn't the kind Rourke commonly used.

What could he possibly want to catch up about? Garrett does all the debriefing.

"You have been on the run for so long that I feel like I've forgotten you." Rourke glanced over at me. The way he used the word *forgotten* had my insides fluttering wildly. "We both need to catch up, Quinn, get reacquainted."

The hint of a challenge in his voice made goosebumps pop out over my skin like the hackles on a dog. My pulse skyrocketed, panic eating at the cage bars around my emotions.

His choice of words was deliberate—meant to unnerve me enough to give away some kind of secret or weakness. I hadn't felt the full effect of his manipulation for a very long time. In order to keep Nathan safe and my own head attached to my shoulders I had to be at the top of my game. Rourke was never easily convinced.

I shot him a coy glance. "Why couldn't we catch up sooner?"

The smile he allowed to cross his lips and the faint nod of his head told me he approved of my response.

Turning onto a quieter street, he remained staring out the windshield.

"I thought you and I could have a go at old times," he said. "Maybe brush up on some techniques before going out on an assignment together. Perhaps dinner can be arranged as well."

"An assignment together?" I nearly croaked, my tone making Rourke laugh.

"Come now, don't deny me the honor of getting to work side-by-side with my best girl."

His tone was scandalously intimate. Visions of dark nights and candlelight floated through my head as he glanced over at me, eyes flickering.

"Of course not," I muttered, uncertain about the feelings welling up inside of me. There could be only one reason he wanted to do a training session with me.

He was no longer positive that I could still hold my own as the Dragonfly.

Well, I would show him a performance he would never forget. My very life depended on it. Rourke had never taken kindly to people who failed to live up to his enormously morbid expectations.

And neither do I.

Smiling at him, I felt the thrum of adrenaline in my veins. "I'm yours to command," I said, wondering if the words were still one hundred percent true.

He smiled and reached into the inside pocket of his jacket. "Then you'll need these."

I held out my hand to accept the black velvet box he extended, his eyes never leaving the road.

"Open it," he instructed when I hesitated.

Using my fingers to part the lid from its counter

piece, I inhaled sharply at the sight of what lay inside.

"Emeralds from Zimbabwe," Rourke said.

"They're beautiful," I murmured, pulling the bracelet out of the silk cushioned box. I could feel Rourke beaming as I examined the perfect stones in the sunlight.

"I think you will find that they complement the gown I have for you perfectly."

"Emeralds, a gown, dinner, and an assignment?" I tore my eyes away from the earrings long enough to look at him. "You certainly do know how to spoil a girl, Rourke Andres."

◇

Four Seasons Hotel, Paris – November 16th

The bathroom of the Royal Suite brimmed with steam as I toweled off and stepped into a silk dress slip. Music from the bedroom of the hotel suite could be heard as I pulled my new gown off its cushioned hanger. The scarlet red material shimmered in the light as I gently slid it on. A sloping back dropped nearly to my waist and displayed the dragonfly wings inked across my shoulders and spine.

Adjusting the straps, I heard the doorknob turn. The music grew louder as Rourke entered. His black tuxedo matched his dark gaze and onyx hair perfectly. An obvious wardrobe choice.

"Well?" he asked, admiring the dress as I turned to face him. "What's the verdict?"

"You have brilliant taste in evening gowns," I replied, running my fingertips across the fabric tight against my torso and hips. The mermaid skirt billowed around my legs as I slipped into a pair of matching gold high heels. "All things considered, I'd give it a twelve out of ten."

"Excellent," Rourke said, taking my new emerald bracelet from its box. He faced me and gently clasped the bracelet around my wrist.

Our gazes met in the mirror. I smiled and he gave an agreeing nod.

"Finish your hair, I'll have the valet bring my car to the front. Our assignment awaits." He turned on his heel and left the bathroom.

My knees wobbled as I slumped into the vanity chair and dropped my head into my hands.

Chin up, or the façade slips.

Forcing my chin upright, I stared at myself in the mirror and exhaled heavily. Beneath the clothes I'd worn into the Paris hotel, hidden inside of my boot, was one of the sketches Nathan had made of me. Somehow having it with me calmed my guilt and regret. Just looking at it put a smile on my face. But having it so close to Rourke made me nervous. How much did he know about my hostage? And how much did he want from me on the assignment that night?

I wasn't sure I wanted to know the answer.

◇

Paris, France – November 16th

When Rourke pulled up to the Louvre, Lamborghini engine roaring, I couldn't help the wolfish grin that stretched across my ruby red lips. The line of esteemed guests in tuxedos and shimmering, diamond-encrusted ball gowns glanced our way as the gull-wings of the vehicle swung upward. I slid my feet down to rest on the pavement as I waited for Rourke to come around and help me out. The weight of many eyes on my bare legs, showing as I held my skirt away from my feet, only increased my smile.

Surveying the crowd from under my thick eyelashes, I watched as the men gawked and the ladies conversed giddily between themselves. While they were rich and had deep pockets, none of them had arrived in a car like Rourke's.

We were the richest at the event, even if our wealth *was* blood money.

Coming around the front of the car, Rourke fixed the buttons on his midnight black tuxedo before offering his hand to me. I smiled coyly as I stood to my full height on six-inch heels.

"You look ravishing," he purred into my ear, hot breath fluttering the curled strands of my hair. I didn't need to see myself through a mirror to know I positively glowed under his praise. It was to be an act, our portrayed infatuation with each other, and Rourke wasn't missing any time stepping into character.

Curling my arm through his, I reveled in the feeling of my silk gown brushing against my skin. Rourke wasn't the only one who could play this game. A role I had starred in countless times, I prepared myself to be his Jezebel.

My end, however, will be a victory.

Together, Rourke and I crossed the pavement and entered the museum where a benefactor ball and dinner was being held.

The sights and sounds of excitement and riches collaborating to make the event spectacular were nearly overwhelming. As a thank you to its generous sponsors, the Louvre had organized a spectacle that already had my blood pumping. Coupled with an assignment, I couldn't wait to let the real *fun* begin.

My fingers curled tighter around Rourke's arm as we entered the space that would serve as the evening's ballroom. A sharp breath hitched in my lungs as I surveyed the room.

Hundreds of people in their best dress gathered in

the area under the light of chandeliers and ancient paintings. Music played over the speaker system, creating a noise level that masked most of the conversations. Tables with spotless white tablecloths were spread down the hall, candles and elaborate place settings decorating them. It was to one of the tables that Rourke guided me with a gentle hand.

He pulled out a chair for me to sit and then leaned down to speak. "Remember what we discussed," he said, leaning so close that his lips tickled my ear. To anyone watching, the gesture would have been seen as a lover's caress and not the ominous instruction it really was. "Our targets are two weapon contractors to the French Presidency. They will be arriving at any time during the evening. You must be ready to act as soon as you see them."

"Are you sure you want this to be so public?" I asked, watching as food was served to those seated at nearby tables.

He moved closer to be heard over the din of the room. My senses seized at the nearness of his powerful body.

"Yes, those who oppose us must be dealt with, and swiftly. This is to be our last assignment before the real war begins." He slid his hand to my thigh and shivers raced up my spine at the touch. The lines blurred between playacting and reality.

"Will you tell me what the real war is?" I whispered, craning my neck so that I could look him in the eyes. I had lost count how many times he had referred to our next mission as *the war*. No matter how many times I asked, he always refused to answer.

"You will know soon enough, love," he crooned, smiling silkily. "You have until ten fifty-nine to finish off your target, as Jason is set to detonate the bombs at eleven o'clock. Everything is planned perfectly. You kill your man and I kill mine. The explosives will cover our tracks as we escape."

"It seems a shame to destroy such beautiful pieces of art," I whispered.

He shook his head, gaze searching the crowds as more wealthy guests arrived. "Everything for the greater good."

The smell of food and alcohol made bile build at the back of my throat. My eyes blinked rapidly as spots appeared in the corner of my vision, thanks to the flashing lights bombarding me. A shuddering breath overtook my lungs and Rourke frowned, feeling my exhale through our closeness.

"What's the matter, love?" He frowned. "You look pale."

I faked a smile and stood. The sweet classical music and laughter of the room was giving me a raging headache. A waiter passed with a tray of food. I breathed in the smell of cooked lemon Salmon and almost gagged.

"I'm all right, I just need to scout out my target. I'll be back," I said, leaving Rourke's side and vanishing into the throng of people.

Elbows and shoulders bumped into my sides as I wormed my way toward the back wall. My head pounded with each step, eyes blurring as I tried to orient myself in the overwhelming sensory display.

Breaking through the mass of people, I spotted a table full of champagne glasses and made a B-line for it. I ignored the couple standing to my right, talking, as I picked up a glass and gulped the bubbling liquid. The tingling sensation cascaded down my throat as I returned the empty glass. At once my headache dulled and my ears stopped ringing.

My breathing calmed as I leaned against the table, a second drink clasped tightly in my hands. People came and went, passing me without a second glance. Dressed in my expensive gown, I was just like them, perfectly invisible to prying eyes as I hid behind the jewels and artifice they gave me.

No one would suspect me until I had blood on my hands and it was too late to scream for help.

My hand trembled as I lifted the delicate flute of champagne to my lips and sipped the bubbling liquid. People had begun dancing, drawing much of the attention in the room as an orchestra took over where the recorded music ended.

I swallowed hard, feeling the faint burn of the alcohol in my nose. Sniffing hard, I set the empty glass down and went for yet another.

"Whoa, now, isn't it a bit early to be doing shots?" an amused voice spoke from behind me.

Turning, my eyes landed on the man immediately. His black suit and matching bowtie reflected the chandelier lights above us as he moved closer to retrieve a flute of champagne for himself. I tensed as he reached around my waist, making sure his arm brushed my side. Winking at me, he tipped the liquid down his throat. Not at all the proper way to drink champagne.

I resisted the urge to roll my eyes as he set the empty cup down with a satisfied sigh. He sidled closer, eyeing me hungrily.

The universe had to be smiling down on me because I instantly recognized the man's face. Mere hours earlier, I had studied his photograph while listening to Rourke's instruction to put a bullet between his amber eyes.

Target acquired.

"What brings a beautiful creature like you out tonight?" he murmured. His American accent was totally unsurprising. In my years of work, I had learned quickly that Yankees made the best contract arms dealers.

I did roll my eyes then, facing him so I could lean

forward. Body language purposefully reeking of a silent invitation, I smiled. The young man returned the gesture with a wolfish grin. Without removing my gaze, I picked up a glass and eyed him over the rim of it.

"I could say the same thing about you," I gushed in a breathy voice that I knew would attract further attention. "I thought tonight was for lightweight people with extremely deep pockets. You seem to be an anomaly, darling. You drink like an alcoholic, and that suit is so last year."

The glint in his eyes was enough to tell me that I had won my prize. His attention was solely attached to me—I had, in a word, captivated him.

Rourke will be proud.

"You've got me." He chuckled, stepping closer under the guise of getting out of a woman's way.

I took a sip of my drink to hide my knowing smirk.

Yes, yes I do.

"I'm here scouting out the rich ladies, but I can assure you that my car is definitely not last year's model."

"Oh? Well, maybe I'll take you up on an offer to go driving... I'm afraid I don't even know your name." I played right along, practically begging for his attention.

"Harold, Harold Summers." He performed a bow, taking my hand and delicately kissing it. Still bending over, he glanced up at me with a charming smile. "And you are?"

"Isla Taylor," I returned as he straightened.

"Beautiful name for a beautiful woman."

"Flatterer," I murmured, ducking my gaze in mock shyness.

Through the masses of people, I recognized Rourke's tuxedo at once. He pushed his way toward me, a mischievous gleam in his eyes. I knew at once that we were going with our already established plan B. His target had yet to arrive, while mine was already primed. We needed to stall for time.

Without missing a beat, I switched to plan B. Harold didn't even notice my momentary pause in conversation.

"Tell me, what model is your car?"

"A Porsche 911." Harold grinned.

I almost snorted at the comical display. He was boasting as if he were the best gunslinger in the room without even knowing his competition. I had a distinct feeling that there was only one Porsche in the car park—and it hadn't been valet parked.

"A Porsche?" Rourke said, joining our cozy party of two. "That's adorable."

My admirer, and incidentally enough, target, went ramrod straight at Rourke's arrival. His eyes narrowed as if sensing a threat. Putting down my glass, I arched an eyebrow. It was always amusing when two males became territorial. Especially when it was over me.

Rourke turned to me and lifted his hand invitingly.

"They're playing our song, love. Shall we dance?" His crooning deep, dark British accent was impossible to resist.

I smiled and ducked my eyes shyly, playing our perfect game.

"Don't be rude, love. I think Harold was just going to ask me to dance." I turned back to Rourke.

"He can go bother a waitress or something. A Porsche, who does he think he is anyway?" Rourke spat, his attitude the perfect interpretation of a jealous millionaire.

I sighed and gave Harold a sympathetic look.

"Perhaps the next dance." I winked at him as Rourke whisked me onto the dance floor.

My hand fit into Rourke's as his arm encircled my torso, touch settling on my shoulder blade. A shiver ran up my spine as his fingers brushed my bare skin. The live band struck up the first few chords of a lilting waltz and I fell into its seductive rhythm. Rourke pulled me close, his lips next to my ear so that we could talk.

"Target one acquired, estimated time of arrival for target two"—he glanced at his watch—"in ten minutes. Can you stall until then?"

I looked over at Harold trying to talk to a beautiful blonde. The way she scoffed at the man almost made me feel sorry for him. Almost.

"I could stall for two hours if I needed to. He's got daddy's pocketbook and twenty-something hormones."

"Good. If I know anything about jealous men he will ask you to dance the next song. After that, go to work. I will be tailing my target," he whispered before spinning me under his arm.

The movement sent my skirt flaring out from my ankles, my curled hair swinging away from my neck. Coming back into Rourke's strong arms, I smirked up at him. "We should dance more often," I purred.

He raised his eyebrows and chuckled. "If we danced more often we would be put right out of the assassin business."

"Are we really that good?" I laughed as he spun me again, this time catching me in a small dip. His mouth was inches from mine, dark eyes glinting down at me seductively.

Oh, what this game we played did to me.

"Well, I am, but you could use some work." He winked, maneuvering us around the other couples dancing. I tilted my head back and laughed at the sparkling chandelier hanging from the ceiling.

As he brought me back to my feet, our noses

brushed. Energy buzzed between us. He was right—whether it was killing people or dancing, we would blow the business sky-high. The chemistry and elegance with which we worked together was like gasoline and sparks.

I was the spark that set his soul burning, and he was the fuel that kept mine going. Together we were unstoppable—together we were *too* dangerous.

It was in moments like this that I felt the thrill of danger and lust of death the most. They called to me, singing enchanting melodies that only my ears could hear. My senses tingled as they charged off of his adrenaline and admiration. My siren song.

"He's watching you," Rourke whispered, gesturing with his eyes.

I followed his gaze and spotted Harold half-hidden by the crowd. The longing on his face made me grunt in disgust.

"Pathetic, isn't it?" I said, and Rourke agreed.

"It's time," he said as the song drew to a close. I almost pined the loss of his arms around me as he stepped back.

I tilted my chin down in acknowledgment as he turned away. The moment had passed—the pleasure was over and it was time to go to work. My lungs hitched as I walked off of the dance floor in Harold's direction, pretending I didn't see him.

Right on cue, my target moved toward me.

"How about a drink? I can take you anywhere you like." He appeared at my elbow. The classic move of a desperate male. He was trying to corner me where Rourke couldn't butt in.

Smiling, I glanced over at him and slowed in the flow of traffic around us. The orchestra drew their song to a sweeping close before launching directly into another one. Through the throng I spotted Rourke.

His expression set in concentration, he followed

another man through the milling people. Target two had arrived right on schedule.

It's time.

"I'm afraid I can't leave, but there is something you could do for me." I turned back to Harold.

His gaze darkened, skin flushing with eagerness. "Anything for you," he confessed, leaning in with an eager smile.

Oh, he was making it too easy for me.

I made a show of blushing and lowering my eyes. "Do you think you can help me win a bet?" I asked, and then rushed to explain when he frowned. "That's the only reason I came here tonight. I bet a friend of mine that I could sneak onto the stage during the museum curator's speech. If I leave and don't do it I will have to pay her twelve thousand pounds."

Harold whistled in astonishment. "That's a lot of cash for a bet."

"What else am I supposed to do all day with my boyfriend's money? Knit socks?" I gave a little shrug of indifference, ever the spoiled millionaire's mistress. "It's not so much the cash as my sense of pride. Do you think you can help me?"

Holding out his arm, Harold offered a sly wink.

"Come with me, I'll make sure you get to keep that beautiful pride."

I curled my arm through his and slid closer to his side. I could practically feel his ego humming as we started walking through the crowd.

Signed, sealed, and delivered. The poor man was as good as mine.

Steering me through the throngs of richly attired people, he led me right up to the main stage of the room. The orchestra was winding down to a halt in preparation for the evening's speeches when Harold paused to whisper into my ear.

"We shouldn't be doing this, but for you, I think

all doors open."

I smirked to myself. Men were so easy to manipulate.

The crowd started clapping as the museum curator appeared and ascended the side steps to the raised platform. He lifted a champagne flute in silent toast to those gathered in the room before going to the podium.

"Greetings ladies and gentleman," he announced in a thick French accent.

"You go first," I hissed to Harold, nudging him forward.

It didn't take another word to send my gallant white knight onto the stage. Every eye turned on us as I joined him, reaching into the folds of my gown for my gun. The real fun had begun in earnest.

The museum curator jerked, blood spurting from his chest as my bullet found a home in his heart. Harold stiffened in front of me, horrified, staring at the man as he toppled over. There was a hideous *bang-bang-bang* as I shot out the orchestra leader and two security guards who rushed forward.

Effectively winning every ounce of attention in the room, I turned my weapon on Harold next.

"On your knees," I shouted, knowing every ear was straining to hear me for fear of what was to come.

Harold jerked again as if I had struck him when I waved my Glock in a gesture to get down.

Slowly, ever so slowly, he went down on his knees and held up both arms. The crowd shifted, still unsure how to respond, paralyzed from disbelief and shock.

I saw the flicker of movement first, eyes darting to track the man barreling toward the stage with a hand on his gun. A security guard—my first true martyr. He never made it past the front tables. There was a chorus of screams from those gathered in the room.

"Stop," Harold pleaded as I walked to stand behind him. The prime executioner's spot.

I smirked, gun barrel pressed to his exposed neck. "Surprised to see me as I really am?" I asked. "Surprised that one of Rourke's assassins would dare to take you down among so many people?"

"Why are you doing this? You know you're on the wrong side, right?"

I made the mistake of glancing out over the crowd. My pulse stuttered a beat at the sight of so many witnesses. The Dragonfly was no longer a phantom of the shadows. She was visible to all and known to the world as a killer—a terrorist.

Hello world, this is the new me.

"You're not going to get away with this," Harold snarled at me, trembling.

Swallowing hard, I pushed myself back into the calm that made it so easy to kill. I had to do this for Rourke. Everything would fall apart if I didn't finish the assignment.

"No? Watch me."

My gunshot rent the silence of the room in two. Harold's body convulsed. Blood sprayed the floor beneath my feet. A woman in the crowd screamed.

Two brave security guards charged the stage. I plucked them out of the crowd like ducks in hunting season. The crowd was screaming en masse then. All hell had broken loose as those thrown into action by the sight of blood moved to attack.

Harold's assassination was a public execution— Rourke's message to the entire world about his power and absolute control.

Blood stained the floor all around me. A man in a tux leapt into the fight and his fist flew by my chin as I ducked out of the way. His stumbling step placed him right in front of me and I grabbed a handful of his jacket, wrenching it tightly to bring his chest down to meet my knee. Fabric tore and I felt the air rush out of his lungs. Two more times I connected with his body and felt bones break.

I threw him to the side and met another man a second later. He spat a filthy word and lunged for my throat, legs bent and ready for impact. My kick swept his kneecap to the side, tearing muscle and tendon. He came up sharply, dropping to his good knee with a shriek of raw pain.

Reaching under the folds of my gown, I drew one of the two blades I had concealed in a thigh sheath and stalked toward him. There was a gunshot, the bullet grazing my right shoulder. Seething, I looked in the direction of the shot. A guard stood in the midst of the fleeing, panicked crowd. Warm blood trickled down my arm. My return shot killed him instantly.

Another guard appeared on the platform as I turned to escape. His face was lined with determination, body bulging against his uniform. I faced him, a moment too slow to put a bullet through his heart.

Sweeping his powerful legs over the ground, the guard slammed them into mine. I went down, barely catching myself on my hands. He took advantage of my disorientation and grabbed a handful of my skirt. Yanking, he tore the dress, but managed to drag me to his level. He head-butted me. My nose crunched and blood started sliding down my upper lip.

Reeling from the blow, I didn't block the punch he plowed into my gut. Bile filled my throat as I gagged and then choked. The man gripped my waist and slammed me onto my back. I groaned as he dropped a knee into my stomach to press all two hundred pounds of his body down.

His fists flew, connecting with my face over and over again. Spots danced in my vision as I fought to stave off the attack. A small voice started chanting in my eardrums as they rung in pain.

Get up. Get up. Get up. Get up.

Between momentary blackouts, I saw Nathan's face as we said goodbye in the railroad tunnel.

You're not a monster. There is good in you.

The words chanted louder and faster, building. At any second, one of guard's fists could connect with a pressure point that would keep me from waking up again.

You're not a monster.

My body sagged, muscles releasing as the guard paused between punches to draw breath.

He was wrong—Nathan was so completely wrong that it broke my black heart. I was a monster. That was the only explanation why I was even in the Louvre in the first place. I wanted to kill people, right?

I wasn't sure I would survive any kind of resumed attack. But something had to be done before the guard pounded the living daylights out of me. I lifted my legs, tipping his body and weight forward so that he had to fumble to catch himself before collapsing on my bloodied face. His strong arms braced on either side of my head as I quickly pulled his elbow down to my chest and pushed us both into a roll. Our positions reversed and I threw a punch that made his eyes cross.

You're not a monster.

I screamed as Nathan's voice replayed in my head. Every instinct, every crouched muscle and tendon, roared at me to kill my opponent. It physically pained me not to do as my body demanded. But there was Nathan's perfect green eyes flashing in my thoughts. He didn't know my past, didn't know my present. He didn't have the right to put such restrictions on me. I belonged to Rourke and no one else. The assignment at my feet had to be carried out.

Anger welled up inside of me and I roared in

challenge. One snap and the deed was done. The guard went limp as I lunged off of him.

Right on cue, a disturbing rumble shook the room.

To my right an explosion tore through the wall, covering a dozen people where they stood and launching debris into the air. Jason had come through—his explosions were on their way in full force.

I raced across the stage, sliding in the puddles of blood. People scattered as I ran past. The explosions cracked and thundered like fireworks, smoke and flames and debris belching into the air. The very earth quaked in fear.

My hands left blood smeared on the metal bar of the door I barged through. Heart pounding in my ears, I stumbled as the floor lurched with another explosion. The din in the ballroom faded as I reached a set of stairs and threw myself up them. Rourke had promised no survivors, and the only way to accomplish such a feat was to raze the entire museum to the ground. My escape routes were limited to one path and the guarantee of my life shrunk with each moment spent inside the doomed building.

The floor wobbled as I broke onto the top floor and careened down the hallway. Gasping for breath through burning lungs, I saw the open window in front of me and forced my legs faster. I pumped my arms at my sides, the material of my torn and bloodstained dress whistling as it buffeted my limbs.

Please be there, please be there, please be there—

The chant died on my lips as I spotted the zip line still tethered to the windowsill. Something inside of me lifted as I bent to scoop up the leather belt lying on the floor. Rourke had gotten out of the building; the fact that only one belt remained attested to it.

Wrapping my hands in the thick leather, I leapt onto the sill and paused for a split second. Black smoke belched out of the building from the floors beneath me as the building shook, crumbling from the inside out.

"Quinn!" Jason shouted from the courtyard below, next to the glass pyramid. "Jump now!"

I dove out of the window as the floor disappeared behind me.

The wind stilled as I freefell four feet to snag the leather belt around the zip line. My body shuddered from the impact and I almost lost my grip as I started racing down the metal cable. Jason backed up several steps, eyes watching me intently as I zoomed toward the pyramid.

Heat erupted at my back and I knew that the Louvre was moments away from being consumed. Ash and flames flashed past as I coughed on clouds of smoke. Somewhere in the chaos my skirt was singed, parts of it burning away. Air lashed at my bare thighs and calves. Burn welts popped out along my skin as I reached the end of the line.

My body slammed into the glass pyramid. I released the belt and dropped instantly, sliding down the side of the structure. What remained of my gown provided a slip-and-slide effect and hurtled me faster. The glass burned and scraped open my skin, pain escalating just like my speed. The impact of hitting the ground rushed up to meet me just as Jason stepped into view.

He was ready to take my hand, his arms outstretched as I pushed off of the pyramid and launched myself into his embrace. Our bodies collided. We collapsed to the courtyard and rolled in a tangle of arms and legs.

"Come on, we have to go," he urged, dragging me to my feet.

Holding me up, he started running away from the collapsing museum.

I twisted to look back just as the pyramid exploded in bright flames and shattered glass.

The force of the blast lifted us off our feet and propelled us into the air. We crashed back down, for the second time rolling in a tangle. I didn't notice we had stopped moving until Jason spoke again.

"Are you all right?"

I was shaking so badly I couldn't move. Lying on top of Jason's torso, I stared into his eyes, speechless.

"Quinn?" Jason asked again, shaking me.

Still gasping for air, I twisted to look over my shoulder at the Louvre as it went down in a final mass of dust, flames, and debris.

"Dear God... " I breathed, wiping my hair out of my mouth and eyes.

Jason gingerly helped me to my feet. The pressure in my veins waned as I slowly stood.

Civilians on the pavement around us had their cell phones out, while firefighters rushed forward in vain with hoses to kill the fires. There was nothing left of the Louvre except for the heap of material that had once been a grand building full of people and priceless art.

Knees buckling, I collapsed to the ground. My shaking arms barely held me up on all fours. I couldn't take my eyes off of the stains of blood on my skin.

"Easy," Jason said, taking hold of my arms to drag me away from the public.

What have I done?

"Are you okay?" Jason asked.

Glancing up at him, I saw the look of horror reflected from my own eyes in his.

"Are you okay?" he asked again.

I jumped to my feet and ran as fast as my legs could carry me away from him.

Chapter Thirty

Paris, France – November 17th

Sitting on the floor of the shower, I watched numbly as the blood smeared across my skin washed off. It pooled around my feet, tainting the water pink, before vanishing down the drain. I had scrubbed until my body was raw, but still the stains wouldn't—*couldn't*—leave my memory.

The events of the last few weeks cascaded upon me like the waterfall from the tap. They pounded on me like sticks and stones thrown by the men and women I had assassinated.

Leaning back against the marble wall, I winced, hand pressed to my side. In the chaos at the Louvre and panicked taxi ride to the first hotel I saw out the window, I hadn't paused to inspect my injuries. A bullet had grazed my shoulder, leaving a shallow cut. Bruising had already begun on my face from the punches and consequent broken nose I had received from the security guard, and would only worsen. A black eye, it seemed, was in my very near future. However, the wound from the helicopter strike on my house was finally showing signs of healing.

Every injury would eventually fade into a nice scar, joining the myriad of others ranging in size, length, and position on my body. They were the tales my eyes were too dead to tell. They told my story— and were my most jealously guarded secret. Not even Rourke knew the number, nor the causes of them all.

I sighed bitterly, letting my shoulders slump forward. Hot water pooled in the concaves made by my collarbones before spilling down my chest and legs. For a moment I found peace in the warm steam filling the bathroom. And then the screams started.

Burying my face in my arms, I tried to shut out the sounds of agony and rage, terror, regret, and sorrow that reverberated inside of my skull. Every scream I had ever elicited filled my eardrums, burning like hellfire. I clapped my hands over my ears in a vain attempt to stop the horrors. Drawing my knees to my chest, I curled inward against the onslaught. I squeezed my eyes shut.

For over five years I had managed to lock the memories away and stuff them into the dark recesses of my mind. I should have known that the stirrings and newfound emotions Nathan had evoked inside of me wouldn't go away as soon as he was gone.

Biting my lip so hard I tasted blood, I jerked my head back against the shower wall and let out the sob that had been building for so long I had forgotten it lived off of me like a parasite.

There is good in you, I have seen it.

I quaked in the knowledge of what Nathan would do and think if he knew what I had done just a few hours earlier.

The terrified faces of the guests at the Louvre were sure to haunt me in my nightmares.

Turning off the water, I wrapped myself in a towel. My entire body felt numb. The mirror was steamed over as I walked past it to slump against the far wall of the bathroom. I curled into a ball on the rug as tears started to stream down my cheeks. There was no stopping them, nor stalling the shaking that wracked my entire body.

I closed my eyes, seeking impossible refuge.

◇

Eyes bloodshot from tears and lack of rest, I left the bathroom dressed in an oversized t-shirt and pair of shorts. It was possible that a random hotel only six miles from the Louvre was the last place I wanted to be after killing Harold, but I didn't give a damn. If Selah or Trent showed up, I wasn't even sure I would fight back.

Settling down on the bed, I tried watching TV, but ended up switching it off as news of the Louvre kept coming up. Garrett called me to deliver messages I wasn't sure I wanted to hear. While most of the people from the Louvre had been killed in the explosion, there were a few survivors who he thought might remember me. Go figure.

"You should probably lay low just in case," he told me. "Sorry to clip your wings so soon after your release."

My body shuddered as I hung up without a word. While I might have been thankful for his concern mere weeks ago, I didn't know what to think about it now.

I tossed my phone away to the other end of the bed and buried my face in my arms. There was nothing in the world but lies and deceit. Death and blood. Betrayal and fear. I couldn't shake the condemning memories that marked me as a murderer—a monster who enjoyed killing.

I just wanted to be done with it all.

Every tendon in my body locked like the brakes on a car. Something inside of me twisted so tightly beneath my sternum that I gasped in pain. What was I thinking? The Dragonfly was the only life I had known—how could I be done with it?

Rourke was the only person who had ever been there for me when it really mattered. I owed him my life—my loyalty, my skills. Selling my soul to him was both the best and worst thing I had ever done. If I hadn't turned to him, chances were I would be dead for the crimes committed in the Army.

Yes, I had made the correct choice. Not the *right* choice perhaps, but the correct one. I couldn't quit being the Dragonfly. There was nowhere else for me to run—nothing else for me to be.

I tugged a hand through my wet hair, trying to bring my nerves back under control. Nathan's sketchbook lay open on the side table next to the bed. I stared at the reflection of my face forever marked down on the paper. In addition to the pieces he had completed at the pub, Nathan had also been busy during his captivity. Ten new drawings filled the book, each depicting a memorable moment in our unlikely relationship.

Portraits of Jason and Garrett were doodled on separate pages, followed by two of Matt. I picked up the book and flipped through the drawings yet again. Nathan had depicted Trent and I squaring off in Jason's loft, guns pointed at each other. The look of acute horror in my eyes was so real I forgot I was looking at a work of pencil.

How do you do it, Nathan? How do you capture my emotions?

Every single piece he had done of me was stunning. Gripping. I couldn't look away from my likeness as I stared at what Nathan had seen through his own eyes.

So this is how I truly look.

Sighing, I closed the sketchbook and returned it to the table. I curled into the mattress, wrapping my arms around both knees. With his talent, Nathan could have gotten all of Rourke's assassins incarcerated, but instead he gave the pictures to me.

The perfect gift. The perfect sign of pure gratitude.

"Knock, knock! Is anybody home?" A voice from the hotel door startled me out of my thoughts abruptly.

Whirling around, I spotted Jason peeking curiously through the doorway. He smiled sheepishly and stepped inside, holding up a lock-picking device for my benefit.

Great. Just what I need.

"Sorry, I just wanted to check in on you," he said, crossing the room.

I resisted the urge to throw something at him—something hard enough to leave a dent in his thick skull.

"You look awful," he remarked, plopping down beside me.

I sighed, the breath rattling in my lungs. My face throbbed and I could literally feel the black eye forming around my broken nose. "Thanks."

"You should have come with me to Sennen Cove to catch the waves and not gone with Rourke to the Louvre."

"You went to the Louvre in the end. Besides, refusing an assignment is a death warrant, you know that." Again, I sighed, this time looking away from him. In my peripheral vision I saw him frown in concern and lean toward me.

"So is not killing a witness."

"Naff off," I hissed, pushing off of the bed and walking to the other side of the room. He held up his hands in surrender, expression apologetic.

"I'm sorry, I didn't mean it. I just know you're freaked out and I want to help."

"You can help by walking back out that door." I pointed to the door.

"Geez, what happened at the Louvre? It was a mission accomplished. You killed your man. Rourke killed his. And I covered your escapes flawlessly. Why do you look like you've seen a ghost and battled a hellhound to the death?"

Maybe because I have?

321

"Your dramatic analogies are terrible, Jason," I retorted, crossing my arms. "I'm fine. You can leave now."

I tried to wave him off, but at that moment the memory of all the blood at the Louvre came rushing back. The dead bodies and the expressions of those watching overwhelmed my senses. I gagged.

"What happened at the Louvre?" he whispered.

I shook my head, closing my eyes as exhaustion sucked the life right out of me. "Can you help me to the bathroom?"

He nodded, supporting me with a hand under my arm. I took a few steps, leaning against Jason as my head spun and pounded. Spots encroached from the corners of my eyes and I slammed a hand against the wall, catching myself before my knees gave out completely. Jason clenched his jaw, eyes filled with concern.

Lifting my chin, I gave him a forced smile—trying to communicate to him that I was fine. But I wasn't, and we both knew it. A moan escaped my lips and Jason's expression shifted to determination. As if I weighed lighter than air, he swept me into his arms, cradling my body like a child. Carefully, he carried me into the bathroom and set me down on the thick rug, where I curled into a ball. He perched on the edge of the bathtub, watching me with a look he might give an animal at the zoo. I gradually steadied my breathing and forced myself to sit up against the wall.

"I'm sorry," I breathed. "I'm sorry about all of that. I don't know what's going on with me right now."

He exhaled, expression sympathetic as he reached out to brush a strand of my hair away from my face.

"There's nothing to apologize for, Quinn," he said, smiling encouragingly.

I chuckled dryly, hands folded over my stomach

as it gave a weak rumble of discomfort.

Jason scooted closer, placing a steady hand on my knee. "You're panicking. I can see that."

I shook my head. "I killed Harold in front of all those people at the Louvre. I-I saw their eyes, Jason. I saw their horror... it was the same expression Nathan had when I killed Navid."

"Come here." He stretched out his arms.

I pushed off of the wall, crawling on my knees, and buried myself in his embrace. Breathing in his scent, I stared over his shoulder.

His eyes—I will never forget his eyes.

The shudder that tore through my body made Jason jerk in surprise, letting me go so that he could stare into my face.

"Quinn?" he asked, brow furrowed deeply.

I tried to force a smile, but it died on my lips.

"I envy you, you know."

"Me?" Jason straightened, staring at me intently.

"You've got this great Zen thing going on that always keeps you calm. And it goes deeper than just your outward appearance. I think you're truly at peace with the world."

He laughed lightly, the sound warming the room. "Well, it isn't a Zen thing, but I've got my own way of keeping my peace."

"Tell me."

Jason seemed genuinely taken aback by my request. His expression went from amused to confused and then concerned. Reaching out, I touched his cheek. He flinched.

"Quinn?"

"Tell me how you do it," I breathed, vision blurring. "How do you keep yourself under control?"

"I don't." His voice was soft just like his exhale on my face. I barely heard him, leaning forward into his gaze. "To keep control sometimes means losing it."

I stopped suddenly, halted by his words. Tilting my head to the side, I memorized the lines of his face, memorized the way his eyes flicked back and forth in his own examination.

"I don't want to lose control," I confessed, "Ever."

It was his turn to lean forward, hand gently caressing my cheek. I closed my eyes, relaxing into the touch as my body gave a painful twinge.

"That's your problem," he said, "Sometimes you have to lose control."

I opened my eyes again to focus on him. He pulled his hand back slowly, still searching my gaze for some unspoken phrase or command.

"Do you ever get the feeling that you're about to do something you'll either regret or remember forever?" he asked, voice breathless. I smiled, no humor in the expression.

"Aren't those the same things in the end?"

He nodded, sitting back. I had the distinct feeling that he was exercising extreme control even if he was preaching about doing the exact opposite.

"Why don't you try to sleep? I'll chase your nightmares away while you do." He suggested. Rolling my eyes, I laid down on the bed as he moved to settle behind me. He tucked a blanket over me with a gentle smile.

"You're hopeless," I told him.

"I prefer to think of myself as a hopeless romantic with a dirty mind." He laughed, draping an arm over me. I tensed. "Don't worry, that's only when I'm thinking about explosions."

"There's something wrong with you," I replied, eyelids drooping heavily. The weight of his arm around me calmed my nerves as I closed my eyes. His even breathing acted as a lullaby, pushing me into a light sleep.

◇

London, England – November 18th

When I woke up the next morning Jason was gone, but in his place lay a bar of dark chocolate. I wasn't sure whether to love or hate him for it as I rolled over and immediately unwrapped it.

Everything hurt. From the top of my head to the balls of my feet I felt like I had been run over by a bus—the driver had also reversed and repeated the action for good measure. I moaned, finding that my jaw was unable to allow for chewing. Not to be beaten by my injuries, I broke off a piece of chocolate and let it dissolve on my tongue. Perhaps it was wishful thinking or my pain-addled imagination, but I thought the ache started to dull.

The taste of the dark dessert was still on my tongue when a soft knock sounded through the door. A moment later, Jason entered, carrying what looked like a brunch tray with two coffee mugs taking up the most real estate.

"Where on earth did that come from?" I asked as he crossed the room.

"I kissed up to one of the maids and she let me into the kitchen downstairs." Seeing the crumbled chocolate bar wrapper, he chuckled. "I'll take that as a good sign that someone woke up in a better mood." He set the tray down on the foot of the bed before offering me one of the cups. "Don't worry, I made tea for you."

I took it, sniffing the beverage suspiciously before taking a sip. "I didn't know you could brew tea," I said, surprised that it wasn't as bad as I'd been expecting.

Jason sat down next to the tray with a grin. "Neither did I."

"What's that?" I nodded to the tray.

"More chocolate in case my first offering wasn't enough, and something I like to call the perfect morning after breakfast."

My eyebrows shot straight up, the fingers I had wrapped around my mug stiffened.

"Calm down, it's just bacon and sausage and potatoes. You're not going to sign your soul away by eating it either. Here." He slid the tray up so I could reach.

Tentatively, I picked up a fried spear of potato with my fingers and popped it into my mouth. Even if he couldn't brew the perfect cup of tea, Jason couldn't ruin the taste of potatoes. I followed the first mouthful with a quick second. The bruises on my face ached, my jaw barely able to function enough to chew the soft potato.

Satisfied with his offering, Jason crossed his legs on the foot of the bed and leaned back on his hands. He looked *too* comfortable.

"So how many times have you made this for a woman?" I asked, smirking wickedly. Even that hurt my jaw. I winced as Jason choked on his coffee, lapsing into a fit of coughing.

"Damn you, Quinn Rogers," he said when he could finally breathe again. "Can't you just enjoy your blasted potatoes?"

I shook my head. "Any man who cooks me breakfast has to answer a few pertinent questions."

"Sounds like you have a script. How many men *have* cooked you breakfast before?" Jason squinted at me.

And so the tables turn back around.

"None of your business." Stuffing my mouth, I cut off the conversation.

The American tendencies of my companion showed through most days, but never as much as in his cooking skills. I was halfway through the meal when

326

he spoke up again.

"Are you going to tell me what had you so spooked last night willingly, or am I going to have to drag it out of you?"

I lowered my mug, watching him over the rim of it silently.

"Look, I'm not blind, okay? I know there's more to the story than an assignment gone wrong where a few survivors might remember your face. Something was seriously bothering you, and my guess is it still is." He smiled reassuringly. "And I'd like to know so I can help you."

"I don't need help."

"No, but you could use a friend. So why don't you tell me what happened at the Louvre?"

"It's nothing, Jason." I tried to put as much assurance in my tone as possible, but my sudden shudder didn't help my con.

His eyes—I will never forget his eyes.

"I understand you being freaked out," Jason said. "We aren't trained to be entertainment acts."

Knuckles white, I gripped my mug in a death grip, fixing wild eyes on him. A volcano of emotions raged inside of me, threatening to explode.

"What would Nathan say if he saw what I did?" The words fell off of my lips before I could stop them.

"What?" Jason frowned in confusion.

It was too late to pretend that the question wasn't hanging between us. Too late to pretend that Nathan was still in my possession.

Straightening, I clasped my hands in my lap and lowered my gaze. "You heard me."

"Where is Nathan, Quinn?" Jason demanded, eyes narrowing.

"Safe, with Matt in Romania."

"You let him go?" he gasped, nostrils flaring.

I nodded, dropping my gaze from his. "It's better

for him to be away from me. He's safer and I can work for Rourke again. When I've gotten rid of Trent and Selah for good, I'm taking him all the way home to America."

"You really weren't kidding when you said you wanted to." Jason leaned back from me, disbelief riding his voice.

"It seemed like the right thing to do." I shrugged.

"Is it? Still?"

"I don't know." I set my mug down on the tray and pushed off the bed to pace the bedroom floor. "After Selah's men attacked Garrett's house that night, Nathan told me that I wasn't a monster."

"So?" Jason looked confused when I paused to face him.

"So? Look at me!" I gestured wildly at myself. "I just killed a man in front of hundreds of witnesses. And I not only murdered him, but I shot and killed innocent people too. I *am a* monster."

"Quinn, stop pacing, you're starting to scare me," Jason urged, on his feet in an instant. He moved as if to touch me, to stop me.

I twisted away from him, backing up against the wall as my heart pounded painfully against my ribs. The fear of being touched was obvious in every layer of my reaction—completely at odds with our night together. There was no hiding it from Jason as he stood watching me with a slack jaw.

My reaction had scared him—but not in the normal way. No, it scared him for my sake. I had never, ever, stepped away from someone in submission or backed down from a challenge.

Quinn Rogers had never shown fear before.

I took a deep, hollow breath. The knowledge that I had been denying since saving Nathan's life came flooding out of my thoughts and into words.

"I can't do this anymore." The exact same words

Nathan had said to me.

"What in the world are you talking about?" Jason demanded, tone pitching. Was he excited or fearful?

I couldn't tell.

He took a step toward me. I pressed my lower back into the wall, my shoulder blades grating together. My lips trembled.

"I can't work for Rourke anymore. I quit."

"Okay, whoa now, Quinn." Jason gripped my shoulders firmly, forcing my eyes up to his. "Let's think this through for a minute."

"Jason, I—"

I was cut off as my phone rang. I bolted around Jason and dashed to the bed, snatching up the device from the mattress. The number flashed on the screen as I answered it.

"Hello?" My voice was higher than normal. Inwardly I flinched. There was a pause on the other end.

"Quinn? Is everything all right?" Rourke asked, tone low and hard.

"Yes, everything's fine." Jason watched me from the bedroom doorway, brow deeply furrowed.

"I have some news for you, my dear."

I gnawed on my bottom lip, waiting impatiently for Rourke's next words.

"The Louvre assignment was a complete success. We have finally launched our open war on those who oppose the International Free Militia. In a few short weeks we will be in complete control of the terrorist sect. My plans have worked and you are to thank for it all. I want you to take over all of the assignments overseas now. We are on the edge of infamy, my dear."

"Rourke?"

"Yes?"

"Is this all you called me about?"

"No... " He trailed off. "I have another assignment for you."

I opened my mouth to jump in with my prepared words of "I quit," but he spoke first.

"Do you remember a certain young man named Nathan Holmes? He seems to have witnessed your assassination of Navid Maleate and miraculously survived. I want you to get rid of him."

Click.

The call ended as Rourke hung up.

What silence followed was deafening. I couldn't believe the words had actually left his lips. But they had, there was no possible way to deny them. I let the cell slip through my numb fingers to the ground. Its crash was muffled in my ears as Jason stepped forward. He pulled me to his chest, folding me into his tight embrace.

Unable to believe what I had heard, I stared unseeing at a point in the distance. I had to find Nathan—had to protect him. Rourke wouldn't take him away from me. I wouldn't let him take away everything I had. Not this time.

This time I have a choice.

Chapter Thirty-One

Bucharest, Romania – November 18th

"Quinn, this is absolutely insane," Jason said for the tenth time in less than five minutes.

I ignored him, concentrating on following the GPS directions to Matt's safe house in the bustling capital city. The assassin muttered something colorful under his breath, fingers nervously tapping away on his knees.

"What's your plan?" he asked, tone an octave higher than usual.

"I'm not going to kill Nathan, if that's what you're asking."

"And I support that decision," he gushed anxiously. "But think for a moment what Rourke will do to you if you don't kill Nathan. He'll never forgive you. He will hunt you like a dog until Hell freezes over."

"I'm not killing him, Jason. I still haven't been able to stop shaking since my last assignment." Leaning against the car door, I rested my chin on my fist, my other hand on the steering wheel.

"You're a killer, I'm a killer, Rourke's a killer. That's what we live for. You had a hard assignment with a witness and then had to go on the run. You were lying low so long I don't doubt it affected you when you killed again. But seriously, you want to quit?"

Jason looked dubious, and extremely worried. I was curious why he had even agreed to come along with me in the first place. Rourke knew everything. I was certain he would know Jason was with me in a matter of mere hours.

If he doesn't already.

"If I remember correctly, I saved your worthless hide when you decided you wanted to leave Rourke to join Selah's buffoons. You even asked me to leave with you. You of all people don't have the right to judge me." I stopped at a red light and glanced in my rearview mirror to see if we were being followed. Nothing.

Jason held up his hands in surrender. The light flashed green and I peeled away with a roar of the engine.

"All right, all right, but just hear me out for a second. Really think about what you are doing. If you leave Rourke in such a bad light he's never going to stop hunting you. He will find you and kill you. Nathan too, if he survives that long. You'll be committing suicide."

"I don't care as long as Nathan is safe."

"But I just said—"

"I know what I'm doing." I cut him off, turning the steering wheel.

"Fine. If you're going to get fitted for an early coffin, better count me in as well," he said.

I looked over at him as he stared ahead through the windshield, a determined, stubborn gleam in his eyes. Now I knew why he had been so eager to come with me to Bucharest in the first place. There was no denying the ulterior motives I smelled lurking beneath his chivalry.

"I would tell you to pound sand if I wasn't walking into my own grave," I told him bitterly, and then relaxed. "Cheers."

"Don't mention it." He winked.

"Now get ready. Matt's safe house is the last building on this street. We need to be prepared for anything."

Heavy thunderstorm clouds had fallen with the midafternoon hours, bringing with them thick shadows and cool breezes. I shut off the vehicle's engine before stepping out into the garage of the inconspicuous A-frame house. The automatic door started sliding down behind me, concealing us from the rest of the quaint neighborhood.

"Matt sure knows how to pick 'em," Jason mused, walking around the hood of the car to join me. The door thudded into place, plunging us into darkness. A second later the overhead lights flickered on with an electric buzz.

Crates, boxes, and a myriad of various tools decorated the garage in a rather film set atmosphere. Everything looked like an ordinary family lived here. There was only one problem. Everything was too perfect. Staged.

"This place looks like a mortuary." Jason shuddered, gaze roaming over the boxes.

I said nothing, leading the charge into the quiet house.

Matt was standing in the mudroom when we exited the garage and walked down a short hallway.

He smiled at me, eyes kind. "Quinn," he said as I stopped opposite him.

"Matt." I nodded.

"What the hell is this place?" Jason demanded, looking around him with wide eyes. "This is the creepiest safe house I've been in. It looks *real*."

Matt chuckled, gesturing for us to follow him into the kitchen. "Seeing as this is my own personal refuge and not one of Rourke's, I decorated a little differently. When we're on an assignment for Rourke and need to lay low we can afford to be isolated. I can't do that when I'm going solo. The neighbors here like to bring over the occasional casserole or fruit cake."

"Holy hand grenades," Jason muttered.

I rolled my eyes, walking past Matt into the common area of the house.

Assassins and their curses.

"Where's Nathan?" I asked, not seeing the artist in any of the rooms Matt had led us through.

"In the back bedroom. Drawing." Matt nodded for me to go on ahead while he turned to watch Jason open the refrigerator.

"Next time I need to lay low I know where I'm coming. You have everything," Jason exclaimed. "Are those Little Debbie crème pies?"

Leaving the two men behind, I strode down the main hallway of the average-looking house, glancing around at all the average-looking furnishings. If you looked hard enough, the photographs and smiling faces in them could be seen as the photoshopped masterpieces that they were. But none of Matt's neighbors would ever be inside long enough to scrutinize the assassin's cover story. It was a foolproof alias he had taken on like a mantle. Oldest brother taking care of his younger sibling, Nathan, while the rest of the family stayed in the country. If I had to guess, I'd say that Matt had even convinced his neighbors that Jason and I were some long lost relatives visiting.

He's thought of everything. Same old Matt. Some things never change.

I stopped outside of the bedroom door and listened. The sound of pencil lead being dragged across paper gradually reached my ears, spreading a smile across my lips.

Nathan.

"Knock, knock," I announced my arrival before pushing open the door.

Nathan twisted from where he sat on the bed

facing a window. His emerald eyes flickered as he grinned at me.

"Quinn," he said happily, hopping off of the mattress to stand upright. "What are you doing here?"

My momentary relief at seeing him and Matt was instantly dashed.

How do I tell him that I was sent to kill him?

"I umm... Jason and I are here checking in on you." I lied, words hissing out through my clenched teeth. "You look happy. Is Matt doing a good job keeping you safe?"

He nodded.

"What did I tell you? I'm a great babysitter." Matt's voice drew our attention as he and Jason appeared in the doorway behind me.

My body shivered. "I know you are," I muttered, remembering a time and place that he and I had both been different and yet still protecting a young life.

He stared at me for a moment, gaze intense.

Jason finally cleared his throat, breaking the silence. "I don't mean to break up this happy time, but we have some work to do." He lifted both eyebrows in emphasis.

I sighed, watching him take a bite of a crème pie.

"What's going on?" Nathan asked, frowning at me.

"You're not safe here anymore," I told him, eyes still locked on Matt. "Rourke knows you're alive and sent me to kill you."

"*What?*"

"I'm sorry, Nathan," I said, reaching out to him and then changing my mind. My hand dropped back to my side limply. "We have to leave."

"Where?"

"I have other safe houses." Matt shifted next to me, staring at Nathan.

I shook my head. "No, I don't want to drag you

any deeper into this. Rourke will know that you helped me."

"Does that really matter anymore?" His words were pointed, acutely spoken just for me.

I lifted my gaze to his and shuddered.

"Quinn, you know what's going to happen here."

"What's going to happen?" Jason had forgotten his crème pie and was looking back and forth between Matt and me.

I had the sense that he knew we were talking much deeper than the present.

"What are we going to do with Nathan to keep him safe from Rourke?" Jason asked.

There's nothing we can do, is there?

I opened my mouth, trying to find the right words to his question when my phone beeped. I nearly jumped out of my skin.

My cell was always on vibrate, always on silent. In my line of work, there was no room for unexpected noises that could result in death. There was only one person who could get past the coding and hack the technology—only one person who would have the urgency to contact me at the risk of putting my life in danger.

Heart in my throat, all eyes on me, I answered Garrett's call.

"Where are you?" Garrett demanded as soon as I picked up. His tone was high with desperation—something I had never heard from him before.

"In Spain, enjoying a much needed spa day." I lied, trying to keep the details as limited as possible. Garrett didn't know that Nathan was still alive and that I was trying to keep it that way.

"Don't lie to me. I know you're with Jason and Nathan at Matt's safe house in Bucharest," he said. "You need to get the hell out of the there. *Now.*"

My blood ran cold in my veins. So much for

keeping secrets. Instinctively, I bent down and unsheathed one of the knives from my boot. Jason stiffened, eyes widening. Backing away from me, Nathan paled. Matt copied my movement and drew a Luger from under his shirt.

"There were several survivors from the Louvre, and they went public about what happened and what you did. This morning the President of France spoke out on your arrest. He's put a huge bounty on your head and he would prefer it if they brought you in dead. And if that wasn't bad enough, your brother's special ops team is on your tail now, Quinn. You've got to get out of there."

Time slowed as my heart started and dove behind my spine. Vision tunneling, I gasped, all other sound fading in the background. The world knew what I had done—the world knew *who* I was.

"Did you hear me?" Garrett shouted across the phone line. There was no one alive who could fake the urgency in his voice. He would have to be the greatest actor in the world to pull off a scheme like this.

Do I risk it? Do I trust him?

"Did you hear me, Quinn?"

I must have stayed silent longer than I thought. "Yes, yes, I'm here," I answered, voice cracking.

"Forget everything and get out of there."

"What about Nathan?" I asked. "Rourke sent me here to kill him. I have to protect him—"

"He's the last person you want to be with you right now."

"But the FBI doesn't know that I was the one who kidnapped him—" Garrett cut me off again.

"No, but they will if the two of you are seen or caught together. Right now, Nathan is the very last person you want anywhere near you. One crime is always easier to run from than two."

I was definitely going to be sick. My head spun

like a top as I took a step forward, stumbling around a chair with my jerky movement.

Only two people in the world had the skills and ability to compromise my entire cover story without batting an eyelash, and one of them was on the phone warning me.

Is Rourke behind this? Is this a warning about leaving him?

I didn't want to finish the thought.

"What about Jason?"

My companion shook his head as if to say *oh hell no*.

Matt's grip on his weapon tightened as he hurried off down the hallway.

"Don't worry about him. Just get out of there."

I didn't take the time to say goodbye before I hung up and stuffed the phone back into my pocket. Meeting Jason's expectant gaze, I let out a pent up breath. Nathan was even paler than before.

"I have to go."

"I know," Jason replied, taking Nathan's arm. "Go. Matt and I will take care of him."

Breathless, I nodded to both of them before taking off at a run for the door. I was halfway to the front of the house when I spotted movement out of one of the windows. Skidding to a halt, I swore under my breath. An FBI van was parked in the driveway, another one on the street. There were at least twelve agents in full SWAT gear surrounding Matt's safe house.

Great, just bloody great.

Sprinting away from the windows and deeper into the house, I burst into the garage.

Matt greeted me. "Take this," he said, holding out the handlebars to a motorcycle. "It'll be more versatile than your car."

Without a word, I accepted the Ducati and

straddled the seat. Matt tossed me the helmet and helped me shrug on a bulletproof vest. I went for the ignition and he stopped me.

His eyes were ice cold when I looked up into them through the visor of the helmet. My hands trembled.

"Survive now. Cry later."

I nodded, revving my engine as he stepped back to the garage door opener. The leather seat underneath me rumbled from the Ducati's powerful surge to life. Matt hit the button to open the door. It started to rise with a mechanical click.

I tossed caution to the wind.

Before the door had even reached the halfway point, I shot under it, my knee brushing the cement of the driveway as I leaned to the side to get through.

Gasoline and exhaust assaulted my senses as I roared down the driveway. The FBI agents whirled to watch me, shouting curses. Gunshots sounded and a bullet dinged off of the metal of the motorcycle. Tires skidding over the curb, I turned left onto the street. Firing my gun once behind me, I saw one of the agents go down. My vehicle of choice wouldn't get me far. I just hoped it would be far enough. Speeding down the street, I reached the main road out of the neighborhood. I paused, glancing back to see the FBI agents jumping in the van to give chase.

Dammit.

I leaned over the handlebars, willing the bike to go faster as I cut across the flow of cars on the road and took a sharp turn. Ahead the traffic light flashed to red. With a mightier engine, the van was closing in on me. I had to use its bulk against it.

Instead of stopping at the light, I cursed it all and streaked straight into the intersection. Blaring horns and screeching brakes were a distant noise in my ears, the blur of cars mere flickers in the corners of my eyes. I held on with white knuckles, leaning so far to the side that my knee was inches from brushing the pavement as I stuck the turn onto the busy motorway.

Straightening my body and the bike again, I sped away. Behind me the FBI van had been stopped in traffic, giving me the chance to disappear.

Several miles ahead, I ditched the motorcycle behind a dumpster, silently swearing to buy Matt a better one to replace it, and hurried into a shopping center, keeping my face down.

In the clothing department, I grabbed a pair of jeans, as well as a blue t-shirt, sweater, scarf, and ball cap. I breezed through the cosmetic aisle with practiced ease, snatching a make-up kit that included foundation, eye shadow, and lipstick, and paused long enough to grab a backpack.

At the dressing room a young girl, hardly older than seventeen, looked me up and down with an unspoken question in her eyes. I quickly fished out the wad of extra cash I always kept on hand for bribes. Her eyes widened.

"I need you to do something for me," I said in Romanian, lowering my voice. "Do it and this is yours."

"What do you need?" she asked, voice piqued and eager.

I rattled off a list: "Hair dye, scissors, a pre-paid cell phone and charger, sneakers, socks, two bottles of water, some granola bars, a couple of apples, and chocolate—lots of chocolate."

She agreed, accepting the backpack I handed her.

"And above all, keep your mouth shut about it." I ducked into one of the dressing stalls.

By the time I was done changing and putting on the make-up, she was back, knocking softly on the stall door. I opened it to find her holding the bulging pack. She had managed to stuff a loaf of bread, an extra t-shirt, first aid kit, and surprisingly—astounding really—a new set of kitchen knives.

What in the world?

She hid a giggle behind a hand as I gave her a questioning glance. My eyebrows shot up at her reaction and complete lack of a worried, scared, or surprised expression.

"Don't worry," she said kindly. "You would be surprised how many women come in here looking to get out of abusive relationships. I've helped one or two of your friends out of tough situations."

I bristled at her assumption of "friends," but didn't contradict her. Who was I to crush her dreams of sowing a good deed? She didn't need to know that she was helping the most wanted criminal in the world. Ignorance *was* bliss.

"Thank you." I took the backpack from her, offering the large roll of cash in return.

She shook her head, refusing.

"I'll cover it." She gave me a genuine smile, taking hold of my hand and giving it a comforting squeeze. "If you need a safe place to go, the churches are always open. God can do impossible things for you."

Her eyes were full of truth and sincerity. Perhaps she had once been, as she put it, one of my friends. Nathan's god might be more real than I originally thought.

Giving the young clerk a smile, I pulled back and shut the door.

Thirty minutes later, I emerged from the shopping center a completely different woman. Thanks to my Good Samaritan, I had food and supplies to last several days.

I went back into the alley and destroyed my cell phone. The Dragonfly was on the run.

Part Three

Even death has a heart

Chapter Thirty-Two

York, England – November 19th

Learning that the world knew who I was and what I had done—that they were actively looking for me—was more than a shock. It had been a complete disaster, and the nightmare was only beginning.

I didn't know where being a wanted criminal, a terrorist no less, put me, but knee-deep in Hell sounded like a good place to start.

The only instructions Garrett had given me were to update him on my whereabouts as soon as I was out of harm's way, or as close as I could get to being safe under the circumstances. But the longer I waited for him to respond to my location, the more I came to realize just how far from *safe* I actually was.

I found one of the dumpiest motels I had ever been in, and that was saying a lot compared to the doozies I had found in my lifetime of crime. Though it was most likely the last place someone might look for me, I was a long way from being in what Garrett deemed a safe location.

In fact, by what the hacker had told me, nowhere was going to be safe for me. The FBI knew who I was—had known for some time, apparently. But thanks to Rourke's assignment at the Louvre, the President of France had issued a manhunt to find me—not to mention promised a bounty to a small handful of professionals that was rumored to triple if I were brought in dead.

I sighed heavily, my lungs rattling, the sound nearly booming in the silence of my room. There were dozens of bounty hunters who wouldn't hesitate to follow the trail of green paper like bloodhounds. When they came after me, my fight for survival would be official—and impossible.

My forearm stung, a thin bandage wrapped around the incision I had made to remove Rourke's GPS tracker from my body. Seven stitches seemed an awfully low price to pay for the ache, both physical and emotional, that came with being separated from it. Had I made the right decision? My heart whispered yes, but my stomach twisted with an uneasy no.

Glancing over to the corner on my left, I scowled at the solitary spider that was my only companion. Its detailed web hung between the far wall and TV monitor. One move and the spider would be tangled helplessly in its own creation—doomed to die trapped and helpless. Exactly how I felt. Someone had swept away the supports of my well-constructed web and now I was stuck. Trapped. The bars of the iron cage I feared the most closing in around me with a click of finality to it.

"At least I'm cuter than you," I mumbled, tilting my head to look at the spider from a different angle. "You look like a Jacqueline to me."

I lay back on the bed, head resting on two pillows I had piled behind me. The AC clicked and gurgled to my right, spitting out tepid air.

"Are you as bored as I am, Jacqueline?"

As per typical spider behavior, my new friend didn't say a word in response. Getting up from the rumpled bed, I walked to the door. I made sure the deadbolt was in place before turning sharply. I caught my toe on the broken baseboard of the doorway. Acute pain laced up through my ankle.

"Bollocks!" I hopped onto my good foot, grabbing at my throbbing toe.

Jacqueline looked on from her web, uncaring. All

eight eyes gleaming in the dim lighting. After hobbling over to the bed, I collapsed with a loud exhale.

"That's the third time I've done that," I spat, glaring at the spider. "You'd think I would learn eventually."

Jacqueline remained silent. *No surprise there.*

"Has anyone ever told you that you have the gift of web making?"

My arachnoid friend blinked eight eyes at me as I got back up, gingerly putting weight on my aching toe.

The hotel room was increasingly quiet as I lifted a finger and swept one of the supporting strands of web away from the TV. Jacqueline jerked, rushing upward out of danger as her beautiful creation came crashing down.

"There." I sighed. "Now you and I are exactly the same, except you can escape and I have to wait."

Jacqueline's sleek black body vanished into a crack in the wall. I turned back to the bed and collapsed onto the mattress. Curling up under the covers, I cradled my head in one arm and played with my Glock pistol with the other. What was Nathan doing? What were Jason and Matt doing? My hasty departure from the safe house had been enough of a distraction to hide them from the FBI agents, I was certain of that. But where had they gone from there?

Are they alive or dead? Safe or in danger?

I closed my eyes and worked my jaw until it ached from pain. Just like my toe.

Rolling over, I tucked my arm under my chin and stared at the rest of my weapons I had laid out on the TV stand. A little smile curled the corners of my lips as I glanced at the set of kitchen knives. The shopping center employee was creative, that was for sure. Unable to turn my body off, I sat up and turned on the television monitor.

The prepaid phone I'd bought buzzed, vibrating the entire TV stand. I leapt out of bed to retrieve it. One look confirmed that it was exactly who I wanted to hear from. A second glance confirmed that it wasn't exactly good news.

Call me when it's safe.

Garrett's ominous text message spurred me to do exactly as it demanded. Raising my phone to my ear, I listened anxiously to the timed ringing.

After four rings, he answered. "That was quick."

"What else would you expect? I'm going out of my mind with boredom and nerves. I'm talking to spiders."

A moment of thoughtful silence, and then a question. "Spiders?"

"I named her Jacqueline," I muttered, glancing up at where my arachnid friend had disappeared. "Not that it matters. What's going on?"

"Nothing good."

Oh for the love of explosions.

"You have got to be kidding me."

"I wish I were, Quinn. I really do."

"What am I supposed to do, Garrett?" I whispered, at some sort of loss. His warning call in Bucharest had worked to put to rest some of my suspicion concerning his loyalties. It would have been easier, not to mention safer, to let the FBI catch me. By calling me, Garrett had managed to win back a small amount of my trust. And dependence.

"Leave. Run. Get as far away as possible in short."

"And Nathan?"

It was easy enough for me to drop everything and vanish in the dead of night, but I had another life to think about now.

"What about him?"

I sighed, pinching the bridge of my nose. "I want

him safe, Garrett. He has to be safe before I'm going anywhere."

"Fine, I'll see if I can arrange something as soon as possible. But for now, get out of town and stay there. Out of the country would be even better," he conceded, sounding exhausted all of a sudden, as if our conversation had drained years of his life away.

"Should I message you when I'm settled?"

He muttered something. "No, I'll message you when it's safe. Good luck. You're going to need it."

"Cheers," I said, voice dripping with sarcasm.

Laying my phone back on the television stand, I looked once more in the direction Jacqueline had gone. "Goodbye, little friend. I hope you can rebuild your web soon. I have work to do too."

I crossed to the other side of the room to retrieve my bag. Packing my weapons inside, I paused to glance out the window. I would do as Garrett said and disappear, but I had something to do first. My trust in him might have returned, but it still wasn't the same, especially where Nathan's life was concerned. Luckily for the boy, I had one last, desperate place to turn to for help.

◇

London, England – November 19th

I found one of the London field offices of the Federal Bureau of Investigation within half an hour of arriving back in the city and spent the rest of that hour scouting out the best place to wait. Deciding to wait on the porch of the building that stood adjacent to the Bureau's, I crossed my legs and leaned back on my hands. A mere ten minutes passed before a familiar van pulled into the alleyway between the buildings.

Wind buffeting my face, I stood and watched the

agents pile out slowly—almost dejectedly.

My steps felt heavy, despite having swapped my boots for sneakers to finish off my disguise. The backpack on my shoulders was a mental hundred-pound burden as I walked toward my brother. If there was any other way to go about keeping Nathan safe, I would have been there instead of where I was in a blink of the eye. However, I would do anything—*anything*—to keep the young man safe. I owed him his life after what I had done, both to him and to the boy I had killed for Rourke five years ago. He was my second chance, and following that same trend I was going to give my brother another opportunity to either help me or kill me.

Stepping into the alley, I spotted the agent I was looking for at the back of the others.

Trent had always had a certain way of walking that made him stand out in a crowd. The confidence he held was a great comfort years ago. And I found it no less encouraging now. He would be able to protect Nathan, so help me.

Waiting until two of the three agents went inside, I stepped forward as Trent pulled a duffle bag out of the back of the parked vehicle. I reached the chain-link fence separating us, then took a quick one-two step and leapt onto it. Trent's head snapped upright as I flipped over the top of the obstacle to land before him.

"What the hell are you doing here?" His hand went for his concealed gun. My brother stiffened, his eyes wide as I sauntered over to him.

"I'm here to make a deal," I replied.

"You have three seconds to say something to stop me from plugging you right here, right now," he growled, gun drawn and pointed at my chest.

I gave an indifferent shrug. "I know where Nathan Holmes is."

He stared at me. Silent.

At least he hasn't shot me yet.

"Promise to keep him safe and I'll tell you how to find him."

He didn't so much as blink.

I took a step closer, breath held as he gripped his weapon tighter. "Look, I know we're not on the same side of the law."

He snorted, the barrel of his gun lowering ever so slightly. "Well, bugger me, that's something we can agree on."

"But we are on the same side where Nathan is involved," I finished. "Protect him. Swear to me that he will be safe and I'll tell you how to find him."

"We will never be on the same side." The utter hate in his expression tore at my insides.

I stepped forward. The cold, hard barrel of his gun pressed into my sternum. One twitch of his trigger finger and I'd be sprawled on the ground bleeding out. My eyes dared him to take the shot.

"If you ever loved Andrea, you will keep him safe," I hissed, holding his gaze, daring him to take the first move.

Reaching into my pocket carefully so that my brother didn't think I was going for a gun, I retrieved a piece of paper with Jason's number scribbled on it.

"Call the number and you'll find Nathan," I said. He didn't say anything as I slipped the paper into the pocket of his pants.

I stepped back and was over the fence and sprinting away before Trent could react. Nathan would be safe. Too bad I couldn't say the same about myself.

Chapter Thirty-Three

London, England – November 20th

Matt turned the key in the ignition of his Insignia as if the world depended on it. Or at least my safety depended on it, which it did. We were out of the city in a matter of minutes under his driving skills. I lay back in the passenger seat, staring out the window instead of looking at my companion.

It had only taken a single text message to bring the assassin charging to my rescue. As I'd known it would. Despite my compromised position, I still had Matt and Jason's loyalty to see me through—and perhaps Garrett as well if his warning phone call was any indication of his allegiance.

Ever since I'd left Trent, a rapidly deepening hole was forming in the pit of my stomach. My energy and thoughts drained right into it.

"If there's one thing we know how to do it's hide," Matt said.

I nodded, but remained silent, my thoughts anywhere but on the task at hand.

I remained looking out the window as we merged onto a motorway headed north. Images of Nathan swirled in my head, replaying everything that had happened. Trent would see that he was safe, I was sure of that, but at what cost? If Rourke wanted Nathan dead there was very little hope anyone would be able to keep him alive for long. I silently prayed that I hadn't doomed both my brother and Nathan.

"Do you think Garrett will help us or deliver us like a package to Rourke?" I turned over to face Matt. My suspicions of the hacker were in hyper drive. His warning call had probably saved all of our lives, but did that cancel out the other times he'd seemingly put us in danger?

Matt smiled encouragingly. "Garrett might have loyalties to Rourke; however, he knows you well enough not to attempt a double-cross."

I tried to return his smile but had no strength to complete the gesture. My gaze trailed back to the window as silence descended upon us again.

"Are you all right?" Matt's gaze was heavy on my back. "Quinn?"

"I'm fine." I brushed his question away.

"Garrett will get this whole thing to blow over in a matter of time. Don't worry about it. You'll be back to handpicked assignments from Rourke within the week. Remember, we have the third world war to look forward to." Matt winked as I glanced over at him.

He meant well, but his timing was perfectly awful, as was his means of encouragement.

"Matt, I don't want to go back to killing people for Rourke. *Ever.* I'll tell you the same thing I told Jason. I'm quitting after this is all over."

I had never seen such astonishment as that which was on Matt's face in that moment. He almost didn't stop in time to avoid a car in front of us as he was too busy staring at me with his mouth gaping open.

"You heard me," I said. "I don't care what you, Garrett, Jason, or Rourke say. I'm not going to do this anymore."

"Well, bugger me, Quinn. When Jason told me I thought he was joking." He whistled. "Are you sure you know what you're doing? I mean, this lifestyle is all you know. How are you going to walk away?"

It was no surprise to me that I couldn't scrounge up an answer for his question. Sighing, I closed my eyes and pinched the bridge of my nose. "I need a phone."

Opening the glove box of Matt's truck, I withdrew the pre-paid cell he always kept with him for emergencies. It came to life with a condescending trill. I opened the keypad and dialed a number I could remember better than my own name. Matt swallowed hard, sparing worried glances at me as I lifted the device to my ear. There was no answer on the other end, and I inhaled nervously as it sent me to voicemail.

"It's me, Rourke."

I faltered as my throat constricted. My fingers clenched the phone to my ear, every bone in my body quaking in terror at what I was about to do. In his seat, Matt's knuckles were white as he gripped the steering wheel, watching me with dark eyes. I licked my lips, unable to speak.

The beep as I ended the call seemed to echo in the silence of Matt's car. I lowered the phone to my lap, staring down at it.

I couldn't do it.

◇

Munich, Germany – November 21st

The doorknob turning woke me. I squinted, trying to make out my unfamiliar surroundings. The LED clock on the bed stand to my right read 8:15 a.m. I blinked and yawned. The dreams and relentless tossing and turning were awful but thankfully over for the night.

Coming around the corner from the door holding a cup carrier and two grocery bags, Matt appeared. He smiled and nodded at me as he passed the bed, going to the room's table and chairs.

"Morning," he greeted after depositing the bags. Perching beside me on the bed, he offered one of the cups. "Hot Chai latte?"

I sat upright and took the hot drink from the assassin. He smiled again, lifting his own Styrofoam cup to his lips for a drink. Not as romantic—or manipulative—as Jason's breakfast in bed, but still the charge of caffeine I needed.

"How does the news look so far this morning?" I frowned at him.

"Well, aside from the fact that everyone and their monkey is looking for you, the news is pretty quiet. They've officially labeled you a terrorist though, so cheers." He lifted his cup in a kind of toast.

I groaned and contemplated crawling back under the blankets. Why in the world had I ever thought Rourke's plans at the Louvre were going to work out? There were a hundred different reasons why we never did any of our assignments in the public eye.

We're assassins, not bloody show ponies.

"Bleeding fantastic. How am I going to outsmart Rourke and the entire world?"

"With me." He patted my back. "We're going to do this together."

"That's just great." I scowled. "Now I know I'm doomed."

His elbow was sharp, but his wink eased the sting. At least I could be thankful I wasn't completely alone.

◇

Munich, Germany – November 25th

Setting down my box of take-out, I looked over my shoulder at Matt, who was reading the latest James Patterson thriller. The two-room loft we had rented for twenty-four hours was sparsely furnished, sporting two twin-sized beds, a table and chairs, and a couch. I exhaled and stared at the cream floating in my coffee mug.

Cold take-out and coffee.
The dinner of champions and fugitives.

"Good read?" I inquired as Matt turned another page in his book. Setting aside my untouched coffee, I folded both arms over the table. The café adjoining the loft hadn't served tea—a tragedy I was prepared to kill for to remedy.

"I'm sure I can find you a copy if you're interested." He smiled, eyes flickering from where they looked at me over the printed pages in his hands.

I sighed. "No thanks. Being locked up in a loft to read, not knowing if I'm going to be attacked at any moment, is a reoccurring nightmare of mine."

He chuckled, returning to his reading while I plopped down on the couch. My weapons were all cleaned thrice over, as were Matt's. They had taken less time than the shower and nap I'd taken earlier. With each passing hour, I became more acutely aware that help was slipping away. I was still on the Most Wanted list after all, with no way to contact the outside world without being picked up immediately. Or shot at.

What's Garrett doing? With his resources, he should have called days ago. I should be able to go home by now, unless...

I sat up straighter on the couch—unless Rourke really had betrayed me. Unless the Louvre assignment had been a set up all along.

It suddenly made sense. I was on my own, sorely outmatched and outsmarted by the master assassin who had trained me. I could only hope and pray Trent hadn't turned on me too. His promise was the only thing keeping Nathan safe—and that was more important than my own life.

"Want to play a game?"

My eyebrows shot up in surprise as I turned to

look at Matt.

"I think I have a deck of cards."

"Are you kidding?" I hissed, sounding harsher than I intended.

His genuine smile fell, replaced by a heavy sigh. He closed his book, setting it on the table before him with an air of finality.

I swallowed hard. Hurting Matt was the last thing I wanted to do, especially when he was taking such a risk to help me.

"I'm sorry, I didn't mean that." I fidgeted in my seat. "I'm just anxious."

Matt nodded. "I understand, it's not like I haven't seen you agitated before."

"Shut up," I warned, realizing exactly what he was referring to and wanting to think about anything *except* those memories.

Matt slid out of his chair and crossed the room to pull up another chair directly in front of me. He turned it to face away before straddling the seat. I leaned against the couch as he crossed both arms over the chair's back and rested his chin on tattooed forearms.

"You need to talk about it, Quinn. It'll kill you if you don't."

"Being dead would be a step up from my current circumstance." I snorted, looking anywhere but directly into his gaze.

"I was there. I know exactly what happened to her. I know why you can't forgive yourself, or Trent."

"We might have been kids back then, a lifetime ago, but we're not children anymore, Matt. The past is not open for debate."

His black tattoos glistened in the overhead light as he shifted, shrugging his shoulders. The movement showed defined muscles across his pectorals and upper back underneath his tight t-shirt. I crossed my arms, defiant.

"You could have killed me in Islamabad instead of recruiting me, you know. Things would have been a lot different."

"I couldn't kill you," I grumbled, my arm cross turning more into a self-comforting embrace. "You were my brother's best friend and an idol to me. I may have been a heartless assassin, but I wasn't going to lose someone else. Not in a million years."

He smiled. "So it wasn't because of my tragic good looks that I was spared by the infamous Dragonfly?"

"Are you kidding? If it were up to your looks alone someone would have finished you off long ago." A wave of relief washed over me at his change of subject.

He knew that the topic of my past before Rourke and the Army was painful. So much so that I still had nightmares about that fateful night.

"I'm proud of you, Quinn," he said. "Keeping Nathan alive is a risky thing."

"But is it the right thing?"

"Absolutely. Everyone deserves a second chance."

I pushed off of the couch, squeezing past him. "You forget, I already had a second chance and I killed it myself."

"Then get it right this time. You won't earn another chance."

Nodding absently to Matt, I disappeared into the bedroom and shut the door. I locked it before facing the two beds and window beyond. A nap sounded wonderful, but I had other things to do. More important things by far.

At the foot of my bed, I pulled my Glock from my bag and stuffed it under the hem of my flannel long-sleeve shirt and grey jacket. I checked that my knives were sheathed properly and then opened the window. I slipped through it and started climbing the fire escape to the ground three stories below.

Striding down the street, I took a right at the first corner and started walking in the direction my feet decided to carry me.

Forty-five minutes later, I was sufficiently turned around after wandering the woods outside of our Munich loft. Beads of sweat trickled down my forehead as I pressed both of my hands up against the rough bark of a tree trunk. Waiting for Garrett to take care of the FBI and Selah had taken everything out of me. I no longer had any patience left to combat the tide of Rourke's manipulation and deceit.

Since the Louvre assignment, I had known something was wrong. Rourke's power was limitless. If he wanted to, he could have cleared my name with the wave of his hand and Garrett's software. The fact that he hadn't confirmed my worst fear.

The master assassin had indeed thrown me to the wolves.

Sending me to kill Nathan only made the knowledge worse. He was waiting for me to make the next move in our deadly game for two. Would I keep running away, or would I race back to him?

Sighing, I pulled my phone out of my pocket and dialed his number. It switched to voicemail.

"Rourke?" I paused. "It's me."

My knees trembled, threatening to deposit me onto the ground. If I said one more word I would forever sever my connection with the man who had saved my life. Rourke would kill me if I said anything else. Once I said my piece there would be no place he couldn't find me—no one to run to and nowhere to hide. The very devil wouldn't be able to help me when Rourke heard the message.

"I can't kill for you anymore," I whispered. "I quit."

Lowering the phone, I let it slip through my trembling fingers to the ground. I'd said the words my heart longed to say since letting Nathan go with Matt. The words that would either kill me or free me—but in all reality, wasn't that the same thing in the end?

It was done. I had ended it.

I took a shuddering breath and lifted my boot to smash the cellular device. Pieces of broken plastic like the shards of my heart shot into the darkness.

Rourke had saved me and cursed me over and over again. He was my savior and my demon all at once. I knew him and he knew me—we were the same side of the coin.

We were nothing more than monsters bearing human skin, and I had the sickening feeling that I'd just struck that monster with a stick.

Oh God, help me.

Chapter Thirty-Four

Munich, Germany – November 25th

I returned to the loft just in time to see Matt bustling out of it, our backpacks in one hand, phone in the other.

"Garrett just called," he said, gulping for breath. Stuffing our bags into my hands, he threw open the truck door and jumped inside. "He knows what you told Rourke."

I blinked in disbelief. "He *what?*"

"Rourke called and notified him that you were no longer in the organization, and that all assignments for you were to stop. He told Garrett not to assist you any longer and to let the world do what they wanted."

"The bastard," I hissed. I had expected nothing less from Rourke concerning my status in his organization, but he could at least honor my time with him by killing me himself.

"Luckily for us, Garrett still has some loyalty to you. He called to tell us that Rourke is in Iran and that we should get to the other side of the globe as quickly as possible."

"Iran?" I frowned.

He nodded, starting the engine as I buckled into the passenger seat. "He's finalizing details with the terrorists. His grand war will be starting soon, whatever it may actually be."

He glanced sideways at me. Apparently, Rourke hadn't kept his plans a secret just from me.

"Rourke's work with the IFM has been majorly based in Afghanistan, although the movement began in

Iran. His war of terror must be finally here."

Matt had a point. I had seen firsthand what kind of work Rourke was doing in the Middle East. If he was in Iran, then his schemes were finally coming together. Another world war was well on its way.

That's just what I need, something else to run from.

We pulled away from the loft and Matt took a right on the first intersection, merging into the flow of traffic on the road. I rubbed the bridge of my nose, a headache interrupting my thoughts.

"Did Garrett say anything else?"

Matt made an odd sound in the back of his throat.

Frowning, I glanced up at him. "What?"

"He said that I'm supposed to keep you alive until he can talk to you," he said. "No matter what happened. He's even sending Jason to help keep you alive."

"Well, that isn't ominous at all." I turned to stare straight ahead at the road before us.

Rourke would let the wolves on my tail dispose of me for him. No loose ends left alive, and I had just become the biggest loose end in his life.

Whoever got to me first—the FBI or some bounty hunter looking for the French President's reward—didn't matter as long as they killed me. My usefulness to Rourke had come to a screeching halt with my voicemail. All that was left for me was my death.

Unfortunately for Rourke, I wasn't the kind of girl to go quietly into the night. If he threw me to the wolves, I would return leading the pack.

"Is Garrett in Tehran?" I turned to Matt, a tenor of strength deepening my voice.

He nodded, changing lanes. "Once he's back he will join us."

"Well, he'll be happy to hear I'm going to save him the extra trip." I watched the German foliage flash

364

by. "When's the next flight to Tehran?"

"I *knew* you were going to do something crazy," Matt muttered. "I should have checked flight times before we left."

I gave a little shrug.

"Why run if Rourke's decided not to kill me himself? Besides, I will be closer to the action. Being in the thick of it always helps me think."

Matt swallowed, his fingers tightening around the steering wheel. "I'm not sure whether to say 'that's my girl' or scream bloody murder. He's so going to kill us."

"You really should have thought of that before you decided to help me." I laughed, earning a wink in return.

Chapter Thirty-Five

Tehran, Iran – November 30th

From behind dark sunglasses, I watched the masses of people moving on the street and pavement in front of the airport. Matt tapped his fingers restlessly on the gearshift. I gave him a half smile and checked the time. Behind me, Jason exhaled loudly.

Garrett was late.

"Are you sure he said he'd be here at two o'clock?" Jason piped up from his position in the backseat.

"Yes, positive," Matt grunted.

We lapsed back into silence, staring at the people flowing steadily in and out of the airport. No manner of shrugging my shoulders or deep breathing could cure my nerves, at least not yet. My fingers drummed on the dash of the Jeep we had rented, joining Matt's nervous symphony.

The three of us had been scouting out the IFM and their dealings for the last four days, plotting some kind of strategy in vain. There was no sign of Rourke, and still no word from him. Knowing Garrett was flying in from Yazd to help us relieved some of the nagging anxiety in my mind. He at least knew how to find Rourke.

"There," Jason spoke again, pointing. "Passing the cart merchant."

Matt and I both straightened in the front seat of the Jeep. My stomach twisted—in relief or concern, I wasn't sure.

Garrett paused at the edge of the street to survey

367

the chaotic busyness of the Iranian culture. People and livestock crowded the road between us, milling about and shouting in native languages. I could smell the stench of sweat and urine through the open windows of the vehicle. Spotting us, Garrett gave a slight nod, and crossed the road. Without a word, he got into the backseat of our vehicle next to Jason, and Matt pulled away into traffic.

Jason, always on his crusade to lighten the mood, spoke first. "Well, well, it looks like we're getting the band back together."

"Pardon me for my lack of excitement, but I'm not exactly thrilled to have the band back together," Garrett said.

All relief vanished with his words.

"Damn," Jason muttered, slumping lower in his seat.

Beside me, Matt pressed his lips together in a firm line. His eyes darkened.

"Never in all my years working for Rourke, and independently before that, have I gone through so many firewalls, background checks, and hacking websites. I've trashed over two dozen computers and twice that many systems." Garrett leaned forward to scowl at me, arms draped across Matt and my seats.

"If I wasn't an assassin I would be tempted to give you a lecture about illegal activity online," Matt said.

"If you think that's bad you should see what our government is up to," Garrett replied. He then added, "You, Quinn Rogers, are famous. Everybody's got a gimmick now."

"What does that mean?" Jason asked the question that was on the tip of my tongue.

Behind the wheel of the Jeep, Matt turned into a narrow alleyway, heading to our safe house. Bells and people shouting outside of the vehicle continued as we drove. In addition to searching the country for Rourke, the three of us had been busy gathering supplies and other intelligence. Both of which were exceedingly hard in a city that terrorists controlled.

"It means it's going to take a damned better hacker than me to clear your name," Garrett stated indignantly.

Jason swore, and Matt tensed. I tried to swallow, my throat constricting to make the movement near impossible.

"That's just great," Matt mumbled.

Rourke had intentionally let people survive the explosions at the Louvre, intentionally let them squeal to the media and law enforcement. This was Rourke's game, and he was going to make me play whether I wanted to or not. He wanted to force me to run back to him. The assignment at the Louvre had been planned all along—a test to see if I really was the same old Quinn. And I had failed. Nathan had left deep marks in me, deeper than I could ever imagine. Running back to Rourke like I had done time and time again when my life was in danger wasn't an option any longer. I couldn't do it. Not without sacrificing Nathan.

Out of everything that could happen, I couldn't let *that* become reality. At least I knew that much to be true.

"Is there a better hacker than you?" Jason turned to Garrett, eager expression vanishing even without a response. If there had been a better hacker than Garrett, Rourke would have hired him. "Just to be sure we're all on the same page... ?"

"Same page?" Garrett growled. "We're not even in the same library."

"Excuse me?"

"I already told you, it's no use." Garrett sniffed. "Quinn either turns herself in to avoid more agony in waiting, holds on with her final breath and goes out fighting, or does what Rourke wants."

I ran a hand over my chin, sucking in a shallow breath. Matt copied my breathing pattern, exhaling evenly through his nose, showing no sign of anxiety or frustration.

"We also have Nathan to worry about," he said. "Whether we like it or not, he's still a factor in this mess."

"What about Nathan?" Garrett frowned.

"I gave him over to the FBI," I said simply. "It seemed the best option."

Sitting up in his seat, Jason tapped on Matt's shoulder. "Find the next dark alley and stop. We need to pick up a few things."

◇

Locked in the safe house Matt had arranged for the duration of our stay in Tehran, Garrett set up his five laptops—making the drab interior look like the security room at Fort Knox. A fact I knew from a previous assignment inside the United States Army post.

With most of the table and floor space commandeered by the hacker, I took over the beds, laying out and inventorying every weapon we had between us. So far, there were six handguns, four knives—not including my own—six grenades, and three hundred bullets spread among the gun models. A considerably small amount under the circumstances.

I massaged my right temple with my middle finger, trying to coax the beginning twinges of a headache to go away.

What I wouldn't give for a valium right about now.

"Quinn!"

I snapped out of my thoughts at the sound of

Jason's voice. His head and shoulders protruded through the window, a medium-sized box braced on the sill.

"This is the last box," he announced. "Quick, come get it before it slips out of my hands."

"Dammit, Jason, be careful," Garrett muttered as I hurried over to the window and extracted the box of C-4. Stacking it with the other four at the foot of the rollout bed, I turned to watch Jason slither through the window. Matt locked up the Jeep parked in the alleyway before following.

Our trip to Jason's specified dark alley had proven fruitful in the dangerous explosives department, but the illegal arms dealer failed to have any guns worth buying. Apparently, you couldn't mess up the process of making things that go boom. Guns, however, were more fiddly.

Hands on my hips, I frowned at the explosives.

"And just what exactly are you planning on doing with all this?" I raised an eyebrow at Jason as he passed me to kneel before the boxes.

"Blow Rourke up, obviously."

Oh, obviously.

I rolled my eyes in exasperation as Matt passed me, giving my shoulder a squeeze. Garrett looked up from his computers long enough to toss the assassin a can of Coke. Dropping into a chair, Matt popped open the can, eyeing Jason suspiciously. Though he was the most skilled out of the four of us when it came to explosives, he seemed like the needed spark to send us all Hell bound. Any wrong move on his part would bring two assassins and a very dedicated hacker cracking down on his knuckles. No one wanted to be blown up by Jason, apparently.

"We need supplies like handguns and food, not C-4. No one is going to blow Rourke up," Matt said.

"Besides, you'll have to take a number for that

job. There will be a very long line, believe me," Garrett added.

Realizing, perhaps for the first time, we were all watching him anxiously, Jason straightened to face us. He surveyed our preparations with raised eyebrows, chewing on his bottom lip.

"You said we needed supplies, but failed to mention what for," I said. "From the looks of things, one could argue you are plotting world conquest."

Jason shrugged and sat down on the floor next to his C-4. I could have sworn Matt winced at the casualness Jason exhibited around the boxes. Garrett stopped typing long enough to glance at him.

"Rourke wants Quinn to play a game, right? His game," he said. "She told him she quit and he threw her to the wind. I think it's time we show Rourke not to play games with a girl who can play them better."

He gestured to his stockpile. "This is going to be our message to him."

As rousing a speech as Jason's was, I couldn't shake the feeling that we were missing something—that we were wrong in our calculations.

"On a scale from one to Australia, how dangerous is this plan of yours?" Matt twisted the top of his soda can until it popped off.

Jason chuckled. "It'll work if that's what you're asking."

"What I want to know is if it will be the death of us," Matt said.

Garrett was back to typing on his laptop, eyes glued to the screen. Jason shrugged indifferently, looking to me.

"Probably," I mumbled, tiredly. "But what else is new?"

"You're taking this awfully calm, Quinn," Matt said. "Care to enlighten us with your secrets? I don't see you doing yoga."

"No, no yoga here," I said. "However, I just realized that I have all of Rourke's best assassins on my side. Even his hacker is here with me. That has to count for something, right? Rourke doesn't have any cards left that he can play that could sway me."

The men around me glanced at each other, thoughtful expressions on their faces. One by one, they seemed to reach the same conclusion. Matt was the first to smile and nod, Jason agreeing with a wink. Only Garrett showed no acknowledgment as to if he thought I was right or not. But I had the distinct feeling he had reached the same conclusion at the same time I had.

This might actually work. I might be a free woman.

I let myself relax for a moment, taking in the reality that I had three people willing to risk their lives to help me save mine. When was the last time I was in the same position?

Maybe in the Army. Definitely not since Trent and I were young.

"We should celebrate," Jason announced, turning to the C-4 piled behind him. "I think I packed some coffee in one of these boxes."

Matt's eyes bulged as he scooted a few inches away from the explosives. I couldn't tell if he was more anxious about the contents of the boxes or Jason.

"Here it is!" Jason held aloft a paper bag that smelled suspiciously of coffee beans, a sideways grin on his lips. "Anybody want a cup of joe?"

"It's probably radioactive," Garrett mumbled, smirking as Matt and I both turned down Jason's generous offer.

For a moment everything was perfect. For a moment the world felt halfway right. I had friends—or as close to friends as I was going to get.

I'm already leading my own wolf pack.

I would survive Rourke's blackmail because he had trained me to survive anything. My head was above the waves just long enough for a breath.

And then the eye of the storm was gone.

My prepaid cell phone vibrated violently on the wooden table at Garrett's elbow. I turned, watching him pick it up. His skin went the sickly color of ash in the space of a breath.

"Oh my god," he muttered, slowly, *reluctantly*, looking up at me.

I frowned, taking the phone from him. One look and I felt my skin heat.

"Quinn?" Jason's worried tone sounded far away as I stared at the picture on my phone, unable to tear my gaze away.

"Quinn, what's wrong?" Matt demanded.

"Rourke has Nathan," Garrett answered for me.

Chapter Thirty-Six

Rourke has Nathan.

The words had no meaning at first. No context as I stared at the picture on the screen of my burner phone.

A figure matching Nathan's build sat in the picture, thick ropes securing his arms behind him around a chair. Blood stained the white shirt he was wearing, most likely from the split lip and gash above his left eye. I blinked. The emerald orbs stared at me through the photo.

His eyes—I would never forget his eyes.

Surely, it wasn't the young artist I had met in a pub. He was safe in Trent's care, surrounded by the FBI. But in my heart I knew better.

Rourke had Nathan.

My Nathan.

"Quinn?" I jerked at the sound of Matt's voice reaching out to me over the void my thoughts had put in place. His face came into focus as I blinked again, looking over my phone at him.

"Quinn, take a deep breath. You're not breathing," he said.

I ignored him, looking to Garrett. For once in his life, his fingers hovered lifeless on the keys of his laptop.

"What do we do?" Jason asked me.

I ignored him.

"What do we do now?" Jason turned his attention to Garrett when I failed to respond.

But Garrett wasn't any more verbal. Matt took a step to my side, extracting the phone from my white-knuckled fingers.

"It's okay," he said. "Look at me, Quinn. Nathan's going to be okay."

He alone knew what had happened the night I heard news much too similar to what had just arrived.

"It's happening again—"

He held up a hand to stop me. "We have a plan. Stick to it."

"What plan?" Jason demanded, looking rapidly between the three of us.

Matt nodded to me, giving my hand a tight squeeze before answering the assassin. "We follow your plan."

"My plan?" Jason gasped. "My plan was rubbish from the beginning. Now it's even worse." He faced Garrett. "What's your plan?"

"My plan was to follow your plan." He stood, stretching to his full height.

Jason opened his mouth, most likely to object, when I spoke first.

"I have a plan."

"Is it a good one?" Jason's eyebrows lifted.

I met Matt's gaze. He nodded, expression dark.

I won't let history repeat itself. Not this time. Not with Nathan.

"I have a plan," I repeated.

Without a word, Garrett swiveled his laptop so that I could see the screen. I stepped closer as he dropped his gaze from mine. He understood exactly what I was about to do.

Taking one look at the laptop, I read the location he had tapped through my phone, barely controlling my surge of fury. There would be a time to unleash it, but not until I had honed it into a blade that would sever Rourke's head from his body. This was my chance to make amends for what I had put Nathan through.

Amends for what Dawn went through and what I did to the boy.

I would make Rourke pay. I would make him pay for everything he had done to Nathan. But I would make him suffer for all he'd done to me.

"I have a plan," I repeated.

◇

I couldn't breathe, couldn't see, let alone move as my companions launched into action around me while I detailed my plan. Garrett selected one of his laptops, stuffing it into a backpack. On the other side of the room, Jason was tearing open the boxes of C-4 and attaching fuses. Only Matt stood still, mirroring me as we stood in the middle of the floor.

"Come with me," he whispered, taking my hand.

Blinking, I followed his gentle tug numbly, so lost in memories that I couldn't decipher reality from the past.

Matt led me into the bathroom of our safe house and closed the door behind us. I didn't even hear the sound of the hinges creaking.

"Breathe, Quinn," he instructed, turning me so that I faced him, my back to the sink and mirror.

I tried to inhale, my lungs burning as I panicked. Gently, he placed his warm hands on either side of my face. I trembled at his touch, close to breaking down in sobs.

"It's happening again," I said, voice stuttering on the words. "Matt, it's all repeating itself."

"Breathe."

"I... I can't," I gasped, eyes widening in terror.

"You have to," he insisted, hands holding my head up.

377

"I can't breathe... it hurts."

"I know," he crooned, pulling me to his chest, chin resting on the top of my head. "I know it hurts, but you have to fight it."

A hiccupping laugh bubbled up through my lungs, catching us both by surprise. Matt let me go, taking a step back to look me in the eyes. I held his gaze, but only just.

"It's a fitting punishment for a monster," I muttered bitterly. "To finally have something worth dying for and knowing that your love is going to be the thing that destroys it."

"Rourke's not going to destroy anything," Matt hissed. "He's not going to touch Nathan."

"That's what they said about Dawn... " I trailed off, feeling the panic surge up again. I couldn't—wouldn't—let that kind of horror touch my heart again.

Pushing forward, Matt stopped when I had to crane my neck to look up at him. His expression was serious, the same look he wore while facing down his targets, but his eyes were soft. His eyes softened whenever he looked at me, as if he saw me differently from everyone else. Because, in truth, he did. He knew what I was running from.

"You have to forget Dawn, you have to forget everything you've ever known." He said it with such intensity that I felt my body shudder involuntarily. "It's time to stop running, Quinn Rogers. You've finally found who you are. Don't let Rourke take that away from you too."

I swallowed hard, my fear beginning to fade. "What do I do?"

"Go," he murmured. "Take him down. Take them all down."

Nodding, I took his hand in mine and squeezed tightly. His eyes were dark and deep, seeing things from a past neither of us wanted to relive.

"For your brother," I said.

"And for Dawn," he echoed.

I released his hand and opened the bathroom door. Back in the main room, we found Jason and Garrett ready for us. The latter handed me an ear-comm while Jason dragged me over to a table. He pointed at a crudely drawn map of a room scribbled over with bright red Xs.

"This is the location where Rourke is now," Jason told me, pointing to the map. "And the Xs are where I'm going to stash the C-4. We'll be able to remote detonate them separately or all together for a distraction or total annihilation. Whatever happens, or whichever avenue we choose, I need you to make sure you're nowhere close to any of these locations."

"What happens if she is?" Matt questioned, walking up behind me. He peered at the map over my shoulder.

"A bullet may have your name on it, but C-4 is more 'to whom it may concern,'" Jason said. "Let's just say that'll be Quinn all over."

"Noted." I swallowed hard, sharing a look with Garrett across the table.

"The ear-comms will make sure we can hear what's going on and adjust your plan as needed." He tossed one of the comms to Matt. "We have no guarantee that Rourke will play by any set of rules."

Or that I will for that matter.

"What about Nathan? How do I make sure he's free of the blasts?" I leaned on the table, wracking my brain to memorize the red X marks on Jason's map.

"That's something I'm afraid you'll have to do by yourself," he replied. "Matt and I will set the charges outside while you're inside keeping Rourke busy. Once they're in place, we blow the place. With Rourke neutralized, it'll be a heck of a lot easier to find

Nathan and get him to safety."

"In terms of success rate, how much of a percentage are we talking here?" Matt interrupted, drawing everyone's gaze.

Jason fidgeted as one by one we turned to look at him. Picking up his map, he tucked it into the pocket of his jeans. "Do you want an honest answer?"

We all nodded.

"About eleven percent."

I sucked in a sharp breath through my teeth, hearing it whistle as Matt swore and Garrett muttered something in disapproval. Silence followed Jason's announcement. I lowered my gaze to stare at the floor. An eleven percent chance terrified me. With Nathan's life hanging in the balance, I knew I couldn't rely on Jason's literal C-4 plan to save us.

A thought popped into my head—an idea that would increase the chance of success to ninety percent. Well, at least Nathan's chance of survival.

If Rourke wants to play games, let him. I have my own rules.

"Quinn?" Jason was waiting for my permission, Garrett and Matt right behind him.

I held out my hand to the hacker. He laid my phone down on my palm, the picture of Nathan clearly visible on the screen. My fingers curled around the phone tighter, the hard case biting into my palm. The picture of Nathan blurred as I let my anger wash away my fear. Matt was right; if I stood any kind of chance in bringing Rourke down, I'd have to forget why I ran to him in the first place. But I knew Rourke better than anyone. If I truly wanted Nathan to make it out alive, I was going to have to give the master assassin exactly what he wanted.

Me—giftwrapped and bloodstained—his precious Dragonfly.

Because after all, this whole thing was about me

and Rourke. All of it was a ploy to ensure that I ended up on my knees before him and he came out on top as always. My savior didn't take kindly to being replaced and was ready and willing to do anything to get me back. I was going to make sure I capitalized on the *anything*.

Contrary perhaps to Rourke's beliefs, I had learned a few things about playing his game.

"Matt and Jason, you place the C-4 while I distract Rourke. Radio me when you're ready. We'll just have to hope and pray that Nathan and I are in position before then," I said, lying through every syllable. "Whatever you do, don't do anything until I tell you to. And Jason?"

He frowned at me.

"Don't set anything on fire."

"Agreed." Jason nodded, scooping up a stick of C-4 from the table.

Matt gave me an encouraging glance before I turned to Garrett.

He smiled softly. "Give 'em hell."

Chapter Thirty-Seven

Tehran, Iran – November 30th

My anger took me to a place where I only knew three things: Nathan had been taken by Rourke, I was a weapon forged to end lives, and if Nathan was hurt, no one was walking away alive.

Rourke had made the biggest mistake of his life bringing Nathan between us. There would be no stopping me now.

The Iranian street was deserted as I stalked down it, black head scarf shadowing my face, but not the death radiating off of the rest of my body. To an observer, I might have appeared to be just another human being, nothing like the living armory beneath my clothing. Every weapon I could fit on my body, I had. From the tips of my boots to the top of my head, I was dressed in black, melting into the shadows I passed.

Night had fallen in Tehran, and with it came the freezing temperatures of darkness. The moon above was full and sent every silhouette around me dancing in its light. Dirt and trash corrupted the otherwise beautiful neighborhood-turned-slums. I opened my mouth to breathe rather than smell the rank air as I paused in the arch of a doorway.

Somewhere in the night, Jason and Matt were approaching the ramshackle building directly ahead of me, C-4 in hand. While I entered through the gate of the six-foot chain link fence surrounding Rourke's location, they would get to work. Time was of the essence, and every second that ticked by meant the odds of Nathan's survival dwindled.

I took a deep breath, watching my exhale vanish in a plume of vapor. The building Rourke's location had led us to looked abandoned, but I knew better than to trust my eyes alone. Rourke wouldn't have posted guards outside, but would have stationed them in the interior as an obstacle to slow me down. He didn't want to stop me, just make sure I had to fight to get to him. To make sure my motivation was genuine.

I ground my teeth, taking two more deep breaths. Rourke Andres wanted a performance, and Hell be damned, I would give it to him.

"I'm in position," I whispered, double-checking that our ear-comms were connected.

A buzz of static followed, then Jason's voice answered.

"We're in position twenty feet behind the house."

"Waiting on you, Quinn," Matt finished.

I squinted into the darkness, trying to make out the figures of my friends, and failing. They weren't going to ever forgive me for the change of plans I'd concocted before leaving the safe house. But I could live with that as long as Nathan survived.

"Garrett?" I said.

"We don't have much time," he replied.

I silently agreed. Stepping over a pile of trash, I started for the fence and building beyond. "Remember, don't do anything until I tell you to."

"On your mark, captain," Jason acknowledged.

My hands silently unsheathed my knives. This wasn't a night for guns and bullets. This night was personal.

I pushed the front door open, not caring that it squealed on its rusty hinges. Rourke already knew I was coming.

Past the threshold, I found signs of recent life. There were several empty rifle casings on the floor. A flicker of movement to the left caught my eye. My fingers tightened on the hilt of my knives as I spun, driving the steel home between two ribs into the man's heart. He gurgled, surprise in his wide eyes, as I wrenched the weapon free with a vicious sneer.

Watching him collapse to the floor, I sensed the next man coming up behind me. I stepped back, driving the heel of my boot into his foot. The man howled and I buried my elbow into his chest, feeling the air rush out of his lungs. As he doubled over, I whirled on him, crossing my blades in front of me and slashing them across skin.

Blinking crimson from my eyelashes, I sheathed my blades. For the first time since the Louvre assignment, my hands were steady. *Deathly still.* The calm that always overtook my body before a fight had come back.

I'm here of my own free will, and my body knows the difference.

I stepped over the bodies at my feet and crossed to the staircase on the other side of the hallway. The blood pumping through my veins was completely cold, just like my frozen heart. I was the Dragonfly—a heartless, merciless killer molded into a monster. There was nothing I couldn't—*wouldn't*—do.

The top step creaked as I stepped on it and crested the second floor of the building. A long hallway opened to my right and I turned, following it into a large bedroom. Five men stood inside, forming a vague semicircle around Rourke. I stopped, gaze locking with his.

"Hello, Quinn darling," Rourke purred.

Don't play his game.

Surveying the confined space, I took stock of my situation with a practiced eye. The five men were a mix of body types, but their distinct stances were the same. It immediately identified them as fellow assassins.

Just by looking into their eyes I knew their orders were not to kill me. Rourke didn't want that. *Yet.* But they would fight back, perhaps to the point of killing me if provoked. I tilted my head so that my chin and nose lifted in the air. The men shifted uneasily. Until Rourke ordered them into action they were alone with their own thoughts and feelings and they were afraid of me.

As well they should be.

Threats observed, I turned to search for the sole reason I was even in the room to begin with. Where was Nathan? Our plans wouldn't work if the young man wasn't in the room with me.

I shifted my feet, placing my right boot behind me so I could push off of it for added leverage. The men noticed the move and mirrored me. Rourke blinked lazily, amusement in his eyes. He knew I would come. He had baited me with something I couldn't possibly resist. What he didn't seem to know was how grievously mistaken he had been to tug on the one thread that made me human.

Nathan was my strength and weakness—the one good thing in a lifetime of evil.

No one moved as we regarded each other. Licking my lips, I put my hands on my hips and exhaled through my nose. Rourke didn't shift a muscle. The other assassins watched us silently face off—each our own force of nature to be reckoned with.

If Rourke was a hurricane, then I was a forest fire.

It wouldn't be a spoken command or even a gesture that would spark the fire I couldn't tame. Rourke's expression would remain the same. None of the five men watching me, waiting for me to move, would shift their stances. Rather, it would be a flicker in Rourke's eyes—a silent challenge—that would send me charging across the room to engage my opponents. My knives would be in my hands as I clashed with the first assassin who intercepted me.

Instead of ruining a perfectly good set of clothes and what appeared to be a relatively stain-free carpet, I decided on a more diplomatic approach.

"Where is Nathan?" Bitterness coated each word like venom.

Rourke watched me with a calculated, emotionless expression. His dark eyes narrowed as I started across the floor to stop directly in front of him. The assassins around us stiffened, hands reaching subconsciously for concealed weapons in readiness.

Rourke unfolded himself from where he rested against a table. The toes of our shoes brushed. Dress shoes against black boots—a perfect sum of our relationship.

"Where is he?" I spat, the muscles in my back cording together.

Rourke chuckled. "Alive... for now."

He slid his hands effortlessly into the pockets of his pants. The casual gesture made my skin prickle like the hackles on a dog and a growl rose in my throat. He was stalling, and we both knew it.

"Name your price."

He said nothing.

"Name it," I hissed.

Reaching behind him, Rourke scooped up an iPad from the table. The sound of his fingers typing in the passcode seemed to echo in the room. My fingers twitched. What kind of game was he playing?

I almost jumped out of my shoes when my ear-comm buzzed. Jason's voice came over the wireless connection, breathless and hurried. "The C-4's in place, Quinn. We're ready to detonate."

No, no, no, not yet.

"I didn't come here to barter, Rourke," I said quickly, knowing Jason would hear me over our comms. "Name your price and you'll have it."

"What the hell are you doing, Quinn?" Jason demanded, tone anxious. "We have to detonate now."

While I was clear of the red Xs Jason had scribbled on his map, I had no way of knowing if Nathan was or not. I couldn't let the C-4 go off until I saw that the young man was safe with my own eyes.

"Where is Nathan?" I questioned, hoping that it would keep Jason from doing anything rash.

Rourke ignored me as he looked up from his iPad coolly.

"My price is simple. A life for a life."

"Whose life?"

He smirked. "Your life for the boy's."

"Stick to the plan," Jason warned over the ear-comm.

I inhaled deeply, shutting out Jason's voice. He didn't—wouldn't—understand what I was going to do next.

"Quinn, don't you dare." It was Matt's voice that came over the comms next.

I gritted my teeth.

You knew this was what he wanted. Just agree to it.

Rourke lifted dark eyes to stare at me, assessing. If I didn't know where Nathan was, I couldn't let Jason blow the C-4, and without the C-4 we had no plan. Swallowing the bile in the back of my throat, I gave him a single nod and played my final card.

"All right."

"All right?" Rourke's gaze flickered, expression frozen in place.

There was a collective inhale from the other assassins in the room. As if they had been holding their breath waiting for my answer.

"All right," I said again. "You can have me in exchange for Nathan. I'll come back to work for you if you let him go free."

"All right? What happened to the plan?" Jason fumed over the ear-comms as I let a wry smile flicker across my lips.

This wasn't your plan, but it was mine all along.

Rourke beamed back at me, his wish granted. Even if he wanted to hide his pride, Rourke couldn't have concealed the raw pleasure and satisfaction shining through his eyes as he beheld me. Despite the fact that I had rebelled against his power and control, the master assassin still needed me. A universal truth I knew would break his will to harm me in the end.

"Gentlemen, say hello to your prodigal sister," he said, gesturing to the others standing around us. "I always knew she would see the light for what it truly is. Lies."

I said nothing.

"Jerome," he commanded. "Bring the boy here."

One of the men left the room, turning right outside the doorway. I exhaled in relief. The plan wasn't completely lost—as long as Jason kept it together and didn't blow the building up out of spite.

Rourke reclined against the table, the iPad back in its original spot. A device used to stall for time, nothing more.

A moment later two sets of footsteps sounded in the hallway as Jerome returned, ushering a bound figure in front of him. I couldn't see Nathan's face due to the burlap sack over his head, but I knew it was him. Something inside of me both ached and let out a sigh of relief. He was alive and breathing, and almost within arm's length.

Without a word, Jerome marched him over to my right to stand against the far wall. I watched carefully as the assassin ripped the sack away and Nathan squinted up at the light. Flinching, his gaze settled on me.

"Quinn?" He blinked, frowning.

"I'm here, Nathan." My voice was raw, reserved. A lump formed in the back of my throat. "You're going to be okay now."

Turning to Rourke, a shiver of anger coursed through my body. My experienced eyes hadn't missed the scrapes and bruises covering the young man's body. Blood stained his shirt and pants, patches of it under his nose and bottom lip. More injuries since the picture Rourke had sent me.

"Deal?" Rourke's eyebrows rose as he looked down his nose at me, inquiringly.

I took a slow breath, letting it rattle inside of my lungs.

"A life for a life," I agreed, stretching my hand out between us. An olive branch, a bridge. My plan all along—to surrender myself for Nathan. Jason and Matt would just have to deal with my decision.

Rourke's fingers were warm as they wrapped around mine, tightening just enough to ensure a firm handshake. My skin prickled as he held on even after I let go. Sliding his grip upward, he took hold of my wrist like a vice. I winced, pulse escalating as he leaned down to whisper in my ear.

"I always knew you would come back." His warm breath tickled my neck. "You do not love, Quinn. You cannot feel. You destroy and you kill, and no one loves you but me."

He drew back with a cruel smirk painted on his full lips. I felt frozen in place, my feet rooted to the floor in front of him.

I nodded, agreeing with Rourke. "I was wrong. I am nothing but a monster, just like you."

"Quinn?" Nathan's voice was small and weak.

I closed my eyes, plunging my newfound feelings

back into the pit of my stomach as fast as I could. I had to keep it together just a little bit longer. As soon as Nathan was safe I could fall apart, not before.

"Let him go, Jerome," I said, stepping back into the position of Rourke's right hand. His prodigy.

The master assassin tilted his head to the side, brow furrowed. Jerome didn't move, hand still on Nathan's arm.

"I said, let him go."

The man turned to Rourke, a silent question in his eyes. Rourke lifted a hand, a dismissal. It was my turn to frown.

"Nathan goes free, that was the deal."

He walked around to stand so that I was on his right and Nathan his left. "He's seen too much, heard too much. If I let him go, my Dragonfly will never be able to fly again."

"But—"

"Kill him now and we can go back to the way things were, no harm done."

Nathan jerked, trying to struggle out of Jerome's grip in vain. I saw the panic in his green eyes and felt my own rise to mirror it. Rourke had never intended to let Nathan go. Not with his life at least. In my obsession to return Nathan home, I had failed to see that no one else would do the same. Nathan had seen too much. He was a liability—one that needed to be dealt with.

"You bastard," I growled. "You said he'd go free."

"And he will. A life for a life," Rourke assured, looking past me to where Nathan stood against the far wall. "Life for you and death for him or death to you both."

Rourke's gaze took in every inch of me, from the beads of sweat decorating my brow to the tips of my black boots. The only sound was our breathing.

Finally, he lifted dark eyes to meet my own. It was a test to see who I would choose, him or Nathan.

Think. You have to do something.

"You don't have to kill him. We can take him with us." As soon as the words were out of my mouth I knew I could never allow that to happen. Nathan shuddered before I had even finished my desperate plea. I didn't want to imagine what sorted horrors he had seen while held hostage by the master assassin.

Rourke chuckled, placing both hands on my shoulders to turn me around. I met Nathan's gaze.

"Let him go, that's all I'm asking you to do, Rourke. Let him go alive and you'll have me," I said. "You'll always have me."

"The boy has seen too much." Rourke snapped his fingers and the five assassins stepped forward, closing their positions into a tight circle.

Nathan and I were trapped.

"Let him go, Quinn. It's better this way."

I said nothing. *Don't play his game.*

"Why are you fighting against the cause that created you?" He tilted his head to the side thoughtfully, almost pitifully. "This is who you are, accept it."

"You don't own me any longer." I set my stance, lifting my face to stare up at him in challenge.

He hummed, amusement coloring the sound. "I've always owned you. Since the day you killed that boy in Maine, I have owned you. Your life is mine."

"No." It was a feeble defense against his manipulation, power, and control. Flickers of a memory blurred my vision as I stared at Nathan.

The boy... the life I didn't save.

"Choose, Quinn, me... or the boy," Rourke hissed, fingers squeezing my shoulders, digging into my collarbones.

I felt my mind release the pressure locking my

lungs into place so that I could breathe again. It was time I made a move to right the wrongs I had committed. Time that I accepted my second chance and ran with it.

Nathan smiled softly, gaze sorrowful, almost as if he knew who I was going to choose. He was worth dying for, I realized.

"You're not a monster," he pleaded. "There's good in you."

Even as Rourke laughed at him, I felt my answer overwhelm me. The ultimate switch—my sacrifice was needed to stop the man who had once saved me.

"Jason," I whispered, "blow it."

Nothing happened.

Rourke laughed harder. "I guess now is as good a time as any to tell you that your *friends* won't be coming to your pathetic rescue."

"What did you do to them?" The blood in my veins turned to livid fear.

He shrugged casually. "What do I do to traitors and betrayers?"

"Death." The word left my mouth before I could stop it.

Rourke smiled, a truly despicable thing to behold.

"The same thing that will happen to you if you do not kill the boy." He held out his hand, gun offered freely on his palm. "Which do you choose, Quinn? Life or death?"

I'm not going to fail someone else.
Not again.

In answer, I bared my teeth and lunged. The gun went flying out of Rourke's hand as I slammed the heel of my palm against his wrist. Spinning, I drove my elbow into Rourke's solar plexus. As he staggered back, winded, my leg came up, and his eyes bulged as my foot slammed into his broad chest. The kick sent him flying, and his body slid as it hit the floor.

The room fell utterly silent. I had just eliminated the leader, the best of us, in six seconds.

Rolling my shoulders, I picked up Rourke's gun, swiveling to look at him as he got to his feet. He applauded slowly, smile genuine, but eyes cold and heartless.

"Well, well, well," he said. "It looks like I have my answer. Pity. I would have rather kept you alive."

He drew back, expression grave as he unsheathed a knife from his jacket. Jerome moved toward Nathan, his own weapon extended and ready.

Rourke lunged, swiping for my neck at the same time I twisted to fire at Jerome. The tattooed assassin stumbled, bullet embedded in his throat.

"Get down!" I shouted at Nathan, ducking under Rourke's knife.

The master assassin lunged again, clipping my left arm with his sharp blade. I yelped. There was no way I would be able to stand up to Rourke for long. He would destroy me before I ever caught my stride in the dangerous dance we had locked ourselves into.

Skipping back, I avoided his advance as he moved too quickly to distinguish every movement. I had forgotten how utterly amazing he was when he fought to kill.

The muscles under his skin moved flawlessly, collecting and launching in calculated attacks. Never hesitating, but always carefully planned. I gasped as he nearly sliced open my throat. Using his own gun, I blocked his stab. The collision of our weapons sent mine flying away against the wall.

"Such a waste," Rourke growled, wiping blood from under his nose on the sleeve of his dark suit.

I took a shallow breath, watching the other assassins out of the corner of my eye. One stood next to Nathan, a pistol held against his temple.

"This is who you are. *Accept it.*" Rourke looked

on as I pulled my knives. He crouched, weapon held parallel with his forearm.

We stared at each other, breathless. Two assassins—once friends—trapped in a tango of sentiment. He wanted my alliance solely attached to him. Unfortunately, I had Nathan's life to consider. My fight was no longer just for me.

"Let us go," I demanded one last time as Rourke's finger tightened around the hilt of his knife.

Mine did the same. His dark eyes held my gaze and his thoughts passed before me. The answer was no. The answer would always be no.

We belonged to each other.

Who attacks first?

"Quinn?" Nathan murmured.

I gulped for breath, arms steady as they held my knives. A bead of scarlet trickled over the assassin's upper lip, matching the stains on his collar and sleeve. He stood straight, mirroring my stance perfectly. The world stilled as I saw the veins in his neck twitch. His only tell as he moved to finish me off.

Kill him first.

"Quinn."

I had only heard that tone of voice, that urgency, once before. It was only after I turned and leapt at Nathan that I realized who had spoken. There was only one person alive who could say something that would make me respond without hesitation. Even Rourke's commands never urged such spontaneous action.

My immediate dive to the floor came from years of working in life-and-death situations with Garrett calling the shots. Though his life had hung in the balance the last time I'd heard that tone, I knew it was mine that was endangered now.

Something sliced open my skin and embedded in my body. Sharp pain laced up my right shoulder as I strained to lunge at Nathan. If I could get to him I could use my body as a shield, an added layer of protection for him, but sudden weight pinned my body down just short of reaching him.

I looked up to meet his gaze just as the four walls around us exploded—

Chapter Thirty-Eight

Tehran, Iran – November 30th

The four walls around the room exploded, blasting inward with a deafening roar. I felt my body lift off of the ground as the force threw me into the air. Acute pain overwhelmed my senses as the object embedded in my shoulder twisted. Crying out, I slammed against a chunk of debris. Flames and dust swirled wildly in all directions, singeing my hair and burning my skin.

A second explosion ripped through the room, sending the dry wall to my left shattering into dozens of pieces. Throwing my arms up, I was too slow to block a chunk of the ceiling from colliding with my already throbbing ribs. I blacked out as my head hit something hard, smoke rushing into my lungs.

Waking up moments later, I groped at my surroundings, trying to orient myself. Smoke and dust, fire and blood were everywhere. The pain in my shoulder intensified as I tried to sit up. Reaching around, I ripped Rourke's blade out of my flesh. The metallic smell of blood momentarily grew stronger than the stench of smoke.

I squinted, twisting painfully to worm my way out from underneath piles of debris. A loud ringing filled my ears. Hot blood spilled down my jaw from ruptured eardrums, my ear-comm gone.

"Nathan," I rasped, crawling across the floor. I unearthed Jerome's body from a pile of debris. Or rather, what was left of him. I shuffled away, clawing through the dust and pieces of ceiling.

Where is he? Where's Nathan?

I coughed, smoke burning my throat and lungs. Each breath hurt to draw as I pushed to my feet. Tears spilling from my raw eyes, I stumbled around, confused and disoriented. Nathan had been next to Jerome. How far could he have been thrown?

Staggering, I left the ruined room and stopped at the top of the stairwell. I barely caught myself with a hand on the wall before toppling down the stairs. My head spun out of control, the ringing in my ears making it impossible to hear anything. Gripping the wall with white-knuckled fingers, I blinked, bringing into focus the figures that materialized below me.

FBI agents led by my brother and followed by Jason and Matt charged up the stairs. SWAT uniforms passed me, disappearing into the haze of smoke billowing out of the room down the hallway. I took a tighter grip on the bannister as my legs trembled, my lungs coughing up smoke.

Voices gradually reached my ears as Jason and Matt rushed to me.

"I thought you were dead," I muttered as Jason grabbed onto my arm.

"Not dead," he whispered, wrapping me to his chest as my knees finally buckled. We both slid to sit on the top step, Matt standing over us as the agents searched for Nathan.

My head rested on Jason's shoulder, throbbing and swimming. For a moment I felt safe. "Why aren't you dead?" I whispered numbly.

He chuckled, stroking my hair. "You have your friend Selah to thank for that."

I frowned, opening my mouth to speak when a loud shout came from the room. The floor beneath us bucked in warning, house groaning in the aftermath of the explosions.

"Nathan?" I asked, gaze lifting to Matt's.

398

His lips tightened. The house creaked again. Jason pulled me tighter against him, standing up as the smoke thickened.

"Get out!" Trent cried suddenly, emerging from the smoke. "Get her out of here!"

It didn't take a second invitation for Jason to scoop me off of the stairs and into his arms. Matt led the way as we fled the building covered in dust and reeking of flames.

"They'll find him," Jason promised in my ear as he carried me down the stairs.

I looked over his shoulder at Trent as he ducked back into the room. There was another groan from the weakened wooden structure around us.

"Nathan," I mumbled, eyelids suddenly a hundred pounds of weight to keep open.

We broke out of the house in time to see part of it collapse. Coughing, Jason laid me down in the street as I shivered from the loss of adrenaline. Matt was there with a blanket from an FBI van parked nearby. He wrapped it over my shoulders as we all turned to watch the house tilt dangerously to the side.

"I told you not to set anything on fire," I said, glancing sideways at Jason.

"Technically, I didn't set anything on fire."

"Of course not"—I craned my neck to glare at him—"you completely blew everything up."

"Destroying everything seemed like the best option." He chuckled, stroking strands of my hair back from my face. The tenderness of his touch surprised me, drawing my attention away from the chaos all around us. Our eyes met. "They'll find him," he said.

The slight break of tension vanished as the building shot another plume of smoke heavenward. I had seen what the explosions did to Jerome. Did Nathan meet the same fate?

Jason took my hand, squeezing it. "They'll find

him," he repeated.

I said nothing, struggling to stay awake as the first agent emerged out on the street. My heart nearly split apart from relief.

The figure my brother carried in his arms was covered from head to toe with sheetrock dust, but I knew Nathan immediately.

Ignoring Jason's suggestion to remain seated, I lunged to my feet and ran to meet Trent. He knelt on the road, carefully laying Nathan down as I reached them. I slowed, looking for any signs of life.

"Is he... ?"

Trent shook his head. "Alive."

"Thank God," I muttered, sitting down beside them as the other agents came jogging out of the building.

We all watched as it gave a final shudder and then collapsed inward. Jason winced, shooting me an apologetic look. I ignored him, cradling Nathan's head in my lap.

"The bodies?" Trent demanded as the agents approached us.

They shook their heads.

"Five accounted for. All dead," one man replied, taking off his helmet.

Five?

I blinked, confused. Counting Nathan and myself, there had been eight people inside the building before Jason's C-4 stockpile was put to use.

"Quinn?" Jason frowned as he saw me staring at the destroyed building. "What's wrong?"

"There were eight of us in there," I mumbled, hands resting on Nathan's chest. "Five assassins, plus Rourke, Nathan, and me. Eight."

Trent's expression darkened, eyes narrowing. "Are you sure there were only five bodies left in the debris?"

His men nodded.

"Unless someone was flung out of a window, yes sir."

Had someone survived the explosion?

"Quinn?"

All of my worries vanished in an instant as Nathan's hand brushed my arm. Looking down at him, I almost burst into tears. He was alive and he was safe. *Finally.*

"Thank you." He smiled, dimples showing and igniting my utter joy.

I took his hand in mine tightly. "No, thank you."

As Trent picked him up and Jason helped me to my feet, I couldn't look away from Nathan. Matt had been right in all of his advice. Nathan was my second chance, third, and fourth chance even, and I had finally made the right choice.

He was never supposed to mean so much to me. He wasn't even supposed to be alive. I was never meant to fall so hard for the young artist who had filled the empty role of younger sibling. But God had had other plans in mind for us. I'd fallen for his contagious smile and infectious faith, and that was the truth. His unconditional love and forgiveness were the only things keeping me going, and I would hold onto him until the very world ended. Because if there was one thing I knew, it was that it hurt like hell to let go.

Chapter Thirty-Nine

The Shard, London – December 24th

"It doesn't feel like Christmas Eve, does it?"

"Hmm?" I glanced up from staring into the cup of tea in my hands, startled from my thoughts by Jason's voice.

He chuckled, standing on the other side of my office. "I said it doesn't feel like Christmas Eve," he repeated.

I fiddled with my cup, looking out the windows over the bright lights of the city. The knife wound to my shoulder was a distant ache, constantly reminding me what had happened mere weeks before.

"No," I agreed. "There isn't any snow."

"I thought you didn't like the cold." His eyebrows lifted as I turned away from the window of my office to face him.

"I don't. It's a bloody nightmare to drive in, but something about it makes the season feel more festive." Walking past him, I surveyed the metal trashcan sitting atop my desk. The embers of the fire we had started inside were still burning the pieces of ash that had once been detailed reports from Rourke's desk.

Jason crossed to my side, tossing another handful of shredded paper into the can. A moment later, he used his lighter to renew the flames. I sighed, the heat caressing my face.

"It doesn't feel right to destroy everything Rourke worked for without knowing what he was planning."

Jason shrugged, pocketing his cigarette lighter.

"He's dead, Quinn. Whatever his plans, they're dead now too."

"All the same, I wish I knew." My tea sat forgotten on the desk as the papers inside the trashcan shriveled into dark layers of ash.

Jason took hold of my shoulders, turning me to face him. "Look at me." He lifted my chin gently. "We're doing the right thing here."

"How can we be sure?"

"Because no one else is going to get hurt as long as we're alive." He tapped my nose, "It's not like Rourke's going to pop out of the grave to haunt us for burning his stuff."

London Advertising was a vast network of offices, both official and illegal. And every office harbored secrets that we couldn't let the world see. While advertising had been Rourke's cover story for us, losing him meant that we were also losing that shield. Trent had already agreed to help us create an alibi in the case of Nathan's kidnapping, but first we had to get rid of every trace Rourke had left. Easier said than done. He'd had fingers in pies all over the world.

"I wish Garrett could have been here to help us do this," Jason muttered, letting me go. "The safes were all programmed to his fingerprints after all. Him being here would have saved me near a million dollars worth of C-4."

Jason grunted, sitting down in my rolling chair. He propped both feet up on the desk that had once been mine.

"Any word from our missing hacker?"

I shook my head. No one had heard from Garrett since Tehran. His last word had been to me alone, and I didn't have the heart to tell Jason.

Garrett's warning cry before the explosions had gone off was enough of an apology and a goodbye. He was gone. Vanished.

"Odd," Jason said. "Although, I suppose he was the last loyal ruby in Rourke's crown. He probably didn't want to meet the same fate as Rourke's empire."

Maybe, maybe not.

Since Nathan's kidnapping and Trent's unexpected arrival on the stage of my life, Garrett had neither acted normal nor loyal to anyone.

"You never told me what happened that night, while you and Matt were setting the C-4." I perched on the edge of my desk, dumping another handful of documents into the trashcan.

"There's not much to tell, really," he said. "Rourke's goons attacked us, but we managed to overpower them in a shrewd move I like to call the Argentina flip."

"But when you and Matt showed up with Trent, you mentioned something about Selah."

He frowned, expression the perfect example of confusion, but there was a momentary flicker in his eyes that caught my attention.

"I did?" He chuckled. "You must have been hearing things. I haven't seen or heard from Selah since *his* goons tried to gouge me to death with plumber's pliers."

"And how did Trent even find us? He showed up just in time to save the day."

Jason shrugged, avoiding my gaze, opening one of the desk drawers. "Your guess is as good as mine. However, I wouldn't stress about it. Nathan's safe and Rourke is dead. What more could we ask for?"

Answers.

He pulled the drawer out of the desk and stood to dump the contents into the trashcan.

I read the heading of one file. "Wait."

Jason froze, looking at me with raised eyebrows. I walked around the desk to pluck the files out of the

405

drawer.

"I'd like to dispose of these on my own." I forced a smile for his benefit.

He shrugged again. "Suit yourself, I'm going to go sweep the rest of the offices on this floor. Are you okay here on your own?"

"Of course." I smiled. "Why wouldn't I be?"

"No reason specifically, I just wanted to make sure." He winked, setting the empty drawer down and striding out of the room.

I collapsed into his vacated chair, ignoring the dying fire as I stared at the files in my hand. This was the second time I'd been given the chance to destroy them and failed.

As part of our promise to Trent to destroy any trace of Rourke, we'd gone through Garrett's home files as well. Matt had led the charge to burn through the contents of his office, granting me the wish of destroying the files I'd found while staying with the hacker. But I couldn't do it. No matter how many times I tried, I couldn't bring myself to burn the documents.

I ran my finger over the files, reading the names written in thick Sharpie on each. *Quinn Rogers. Jason Sanders. Matt Rustler.* And finally, *Rourke Andres.* Was he dead or alive? No one truly knew for certain. Just like no one knew where Garrett was.

Pushing away Rourke's folder, I withdrew my own. I flipped it open to the mysterious equation.

012 + 1.274/3.3(Cr3Hg7) = Immune.

What did it mean?

I pulled out the biological graphs and charts I had saved as well and laid them next to the equation. Plagues. Fatal viruses. What had Rourke been planning?

"Quinn? I found something you might want to take a look at." Jason strode back into my office suddenly.

Jerking, I stuffed the folders into my bag under the desk and zipped it up with a snap. I brushed my hair back from my eyes as Jason stopped beside me. He held up a familiar black box. I didn't need to look inside to know what it was.

"It has your name on it," he said.

"A last present from Rourke," I explained. "A relic from the life I once had as Andrea Abrams."

I couldn't help but feel the sad flutter of my heart as Jason removed the lid and stared down at the bullet and gold chain.

"Strange, isn't it?" I perched on the edge of my desk, scooting the smoldering rubbish can a few feet away. "We both know that Rourke never did anything without definite reasons, but I haven't figured out why he would give me the necklace. It seemed completely random."

Jason hummed thoughtfully, taking the necklace out. The bronze-gold bullet caught the light and glistened. "Maybe he never got the chance to explain his reasons."

"I can't believe he's really gone." I pursed my lips.

Jason didn't say anything, stepping closer to clasp the necklace around my neck. My skin prickled at his nearness, his breath fluttering my hair.

"Still not as pretty as you though." He smirked, moving to admire the piece of jewelry.

I rolled my eyes.

"Don't judge me. I'm a hopeless romantic with a dirty mind."

"Oh, I know all about your dirty mind." I exhaled sharply. "You blew up our employer without batting an eyelash. I'm sure your friends in Selah's brother band were all smiles to hear that news."

Another mention of Selah felt like a kick below

the belt even to me, but I couldn't stop myself from saying it. I had too many unanswered questions. Questions that Jason seemed to be evading purposefully.

"I didn't want to do all the things I did, Quinn. But sometimes you have no choice in the matter." He ran a hand through his tousled blonde hair. "Sometimes we have to do bad things to get good results. When that happens, people often forget all the good you did."

I smiled at him. "If there's one thing I've learned from this entire catastrophe, it's that you always have a choice, Jason. Always."

I hopped off the desk and walked toward the wall of windows overlooking London. Jason followed, his footsteps soft behind me.

The horizon was dark, sparkling with the haze of a billion lights. No stars were in sight. I leaned against the windows, one arm braced above me to rest my forehead against.

Jason exhaled heavily. "Would it really kill you if we kissed?"

My eyes snaked to look at him standing stiffly beside me. He was positively bursting with frustration. His desire wasn't a surprise. He always had the worst sense of timing.

"No, but it would probably kill you."

It was a warning not to push me. With Rourke's death, Garrett's disappearance, and my brother's return to my life, exploring a relationship was the last thing I wanted at the moment. Jason exhaled again, chest deflating. I watched his reflection in the windows turn away from me.

"Jason?"

He looked back at me, expression dimmed.

I faced him, trying my best to smile encouragingly. "I'm sorry I'm not what you deserve."

He took my hand and kissed it. "Oh, don't worry about me. I haven't given up the ghost just yet. You'll come around to me, Quinn Rogers, of that I am certain."

Chapter Forty

London, England – January 1ˢᵗ

Cardinals in the trees above my head chirped, winging about the graveyard as a light dusting of snow dampened the ground and my boots. Hands buried deep in the pockets of my black trench coat, I stood over the simple gravestone that marked the life and passing of the girl I'd once been.

Andrea Renee Abrams, it read. *Beloved daughter and sister.*

Born June 13, 1991 – Died March 20, 2012.

Footsteps amid crunching leaves came up behind me as Trent stopped at my side. I didn't glance sideways at him as he tossed a single rose down on the dead grass before the headstone. It seemed a shame to waste a flower for an empty grave and an equally empty life.

"I hate that mum and dad spent money to bury an empty coffin for me." I didn't intend the words to sound as bitter as they did. Sparing an apologetic look with Trent, I tried to communicate that with him, but he didn't seem to notice either.

"They had to have some kind of closure. This was the only way they could have it, I suppose." He shrugged.

"What was the service like?"

He blinked, eyes widening a little at the question. Frowning, he scuffed the toe of his shoe through the snow. "Simple and elegant, just like Andrea would have wanted."

I didn't reply as my brain simulated a mental

411

image of what might have occurred. The faces of people who might have been present paraded past my mind's eye. Turning away, I faced Trent.

"Was Matt there?"

Being reunited with his former best friend had been almost as much of a shock as seeing me again. Matt and I were both back from the dead, and Trent seemed to be questioning everything he'd ever believed.

"Yes," he said. "Matt got special leave to come back for the service. I don't know who was more distraught over your death, mum and dad or him."

"There's so much I regret." I sighed tiredly, the fight all but drained out of my body. His eyes drifted downward, leading mine to the matching headstone next to Andrea's. Unlike mine, this tomb wasn't empty. This marker in the earth concealed a coffin that I had once stood before, sobbed over, and helped lower into the ground.

This stone belonged to my sister.

Dawn Natalia Abrams, it read. *Beloved daughter and sister.*

Born December 15, 1999 – Died February 29, 2009.

I didn't dare read the rest of the inscription trailing in flowing font beneath the dates. I knew it by heart anyway. No, I stared at that dash line connecting two days in time that were far too close together.

"She should have lived a long and happy life," I whispered. Trent inhaled, a low, drawn out noise that seemed to echo the hollowness of the falling snow. "We all should have."

"Fate is a cruel thing," he said, almost to himself his voice was so low. "To let you come back and not..."

He didn't need to finish for me to understand the meaning behind his words. I swallowed the bile suddenly building at the back of my throat. It had been foolish of me to ever expect a warm welcome from my brother. A fool's hope that we could pick up where we'd left off years ago. He wanted Dawn back, the only thing in life neither of us would be granted.

Our sister was gone—torn from our hearts and lives at the age of ten. I would never forget the horror of seeing her mangled, twisted, and mutilated body when the FBI finally found her. What was left of her.

I blinked back hot tears, sniffing in the cold, frozen air. It was my fault she had been taken, killed. I didn't deserve Trent's forgiveness, didn't want him to even mutter the words. My sins were inked onto my skin literally in the shape of my dragonfly tattoo. A reminder of the mistakes I had made and the precious life those choices had cost.

"There's so much I regret," I said again, lacking the words to put my sorrow and guilt into.

Trent nodded, eyes glazed and distant, matching my strides as we both started walking away from the two headstones. Snow dusted my cheeks as we passed under a grove of aspen trees. Neither of us spoke another word until we were standing at the gate leading out of the cemetery. I paused before leaving the holy ground.

I wasn't finished paying my respects to the dead.

While Andrea Abrams had been buried in the graveyard five years ago, another one of my lives had been laid to rest. No headstone to mark my deeds as the Dragonfly. No one to mourn her spiritual passing into what I hoped would be a better life. But the version of Quinn Rogers I had been while Rourke was still alive was gone. Dead.

Nathan had killed her.

"I'm sorry we had to be reunited like this." I shrugged deeper into my coat, braced against the wind.

"Me too," Trent muttered, breath turning to vapor

in the air. "You would not believe the amount of paperwork I've had to fill out since I found out you're alive."

Nothing remained of the two siblings we had been moments earlier. Only the FBI agent and the shell of an assassin stood looking out over the city.

"That's what I've always dreamed of hearing you say, brother dear." I chuckled dryly. To keep the pain and guilt away I would play our game too. Some wounds went too deep to rip the bandages off yet.

A few cars passed on the road, windshields fighting against the ever-increasing downpour of snow. We stood shoulder to shoulder watching them go.

"Are you ready for what comes next?" Trent asked, watching me out of the corner of his eye. I pressed my lips together in a thin line.

"Not really, but you said so yourself, I don't have any other choice. It's either this or a life on the run for who knows how long until the world catches up to me." I took a breath, trying not to let my emotions run away with me. Trent was doing me a huge favor; I owed him and the FBI everything.

Why does it feel like I'm walking out of one cage and right into another?

"The Bureau knows that it would be a foolish move not to recruit you and the remaining members of Rourke's organization. You're the best of the crop," Trent murmured, "It's going to take your skills and connections to ensure that the International Free Militia comes crumbling down for good."

"I know." The words were hollow on my tongue as an involuntary shudder tugged across the muscles in my back.

Turning, my brother faced me, expressionless. "I was told to give you exactly twenty-four hours to sort out your business before clapping the handcuffs on.

414

The Bureau has everything set up and waiting for when I bring you in. Your friends are already in custody and being relocated as we speak."

A deep sense of relief filled me at his words. Matt and Jason were safe, the newest recruits of the Federal Bureau of Investigation. They would have an easy adjustment to their new lives. Unlike me. Where I was headed it was a long road to be hoed.

First came the very public arrest and then the courtroom full of screaming, angry people who would call for my head on a silver platter for what I had done at the Louvre. Once I plead guilty to my crimes and was locked away the real beginning could occur.

With the Dragonfly safely behind bars, I would be given a new identity and a new job as a private consultant owned by the FBI. Where they pointed I would go.

"Are you all right?" Trent's voice brought me back to the cemetery with a jolt.

Blinking, I glanced over at him and forced a smile. "Of course, I was just thinking about what outfit I should wear to the trial. If the media of the world is going to be present I need to look my best."

"Very funny." He scowled. "I can and will take away your twenty-four hour head start if I have to."

"Don't worry, brother dear, I'll be the model assassin on the witness stand."

"Good," he snapped, starting to walk away.

"Trent?" I called, stopping him before he could reach the curb.

He turned but said nothing.

"What about Nathan? Can I see him again before the trial?"

"Nathan Holmes is safe and out of the picture. No one knows that you were involved in his kidnapping. The Bureau wants to keep it that way. If you set one foot in his direction I have full permission to plug you full of holes."

"I guess that's a no then," I muttered.

"You bet your boots that's a no," Trent replied, "Take my advice and stay away from him. Your paths crossed, but now it's time to move on. Don't forget you have a new life to look forward to once we've put to rest the world's fears of the Dragonfly."

"I'm overjoyed."

"Twenty-four hours," he said, walking backwards to his car, "That's all I can give you before all hell breaks loose. Make sure you're ready."

I nodded, watching him go, not bothering to reply to his comments as he unlocked his vehicle and got behind the wheel. As soon as he was gone and I'd crossed to my Range Rover, my phone gave a loud buzz from the pocket of my coat.

Blocked Caller ID.

"I've been expecting your call," I answered, knowing full well who was on the other line.

"I would hope so, Dragonfly. It is by far time you and I had a proper talk," Selah replied with a bemused chuckle.

I unlocked my vehicle and slid behind the wheel. "I have twenty-four hours before I'll be behind more bulletproof glass and security than the American president. Where shall I meet you?"

My hand lifted to rest on the bullet hanging around my neck, a subconscious gesture I didn't realize I was performing.

"Don't worry, I'll find you," he said.

Acknowledgements

Writing *Unsanctioned Eyes* has taken a little over five years and has been a labor of love created not just by me, but by many, many insanely talented and dedicated people.

My endless and extreme gratitude go to my editor, Jennifer Clark Sell, for her generous help and support getting *Unsanctioned Eyes* ready. Thank you for the countless emails that pushed me in the right direction. The way you understand my vision for the characters and story has been a huge blessing to me.

To my brilliant cover designer, Najla Qambers— you brought the book to life better than I could ever have imagined.

Thank you to my parents, Lisa and Ben, for reading me so many great stories, and then allowing me to pursue writing with reckless abandon. Your critiques, read-throughs, and suggestions are greatly appreciated. Dad, a special thanks goes out to you for (trying) to keep me on the realistic side of fiction. To my little, but much taller, sister, Lillian, thank you for the love and support. I can't wait to see where your journey takes you.

To Amanda Humphrey and Paige Muncy, your friendship and encouragement have meant the world to me both in life and in writing. I love you dearly.

To Jacqueline, my fellow dragon-tamer, for all of the incredible help, encouragement, suggestions, and getting the characters as well as I do. You came along just when I needed you, and my world is now brighter because you're in it. (I, however, fervently apologize for my characters possessing you. Jason still likes your pillows better than mine. Pardon the snores.)

To Chris Lee, your help with the various weapons and fight scenes in the book were enormously appreciated.

Thanks to all of the people who came along just when I started doubting myself—Terry Maggert, Ben Arment, Tonya Whitt, Ashley Olson, Katie Erickson, Bethany Dewhurst, and every single person who clicked the Follow button on Twitter or Instagram. Your notes and advice have meant the world to me. You're the reason I've reached this finish line.

To Ben Powell, I never would have made it past the start without you.

To Blaine Russell (the comma King), thank you for all of the read-throughs in the beginning.

To Sarah White, for answering my endless questions.

A special thanks goes out to all of the authors who have inspired me to chase after my dreams of writing. Sarah J. Maas, Jill Williamson, Jeff Gerke, Shannon Dittemore, Donita K. Paul, Tosca Lee, Mark Wilson, and Daniel Schwabauer: your advice paved the way.

To my characters, who brave whatever obstacle I put in their paths. You have been an inspiration to me, and I hope, to everyone who reads this book. And to God, who told me to "write my story".

Lastly, but perhaps most importantly, thank you to those of you who are reading this. I know I wouldn't be here without you.

Brianna's *Unsanctioned Eyes* Playlist

(Includes notes from the author)

1. "Kill Our Way To Heaven" by Michl. The tone of this song really matched the emotion of the book and characters, for me.

2. "Dragonfly" by Shaman's Harvest. Quinn's theme.

3. "Do I Want To Know" by Arctic Monkeys. Jason's theme.

4. "Daylight" by Foxworth Hall. Nathan's theme.

5. "Solid As Stone" by Stephen. Matt's theme.

6. "Make Me Believe Again" by Nickelback. Garrett's theme.

7. "Bad Dream" by Ruelle. This song helped me get inside of Quinn's head after she kidnaps Nathan and her whole world turns upside down.

8. "You Are My Greatest Creation" by James Newton Howard. And this song was the perfect undertone for the scenes between Quinn and Rourke.

9. "Boy" by John Murphy. A powerful song that's perfect for chapter eleven.

10. "Weapon" by Matthew Good. This song fueled the emotional, sad scenes throughout the book.

11. "Don't Close Your Eyes" by Sam Tinnesz. If I had to pick a theme song for Quinn and the gang, this would be it.

About the Author

Brianna grew up in a small town in Oklahoma learning the language of the wind and trying to survive the heat of summer. She fell in love with all things literary at an early age and the journey from reader to writer followed. With the help of One Year Adventure Novel, she finished her first novel in 2012 and hasn't been able to stop creating new worlds and adventures since.

As well as writing, Brianna is addicted to tea, chocolate, and music. When she isn't reading or writing, Brianna teaches Ballet and Jazz.

She lives in Virginia with her family and spoiled Dalmatian, Valentine.

Contact Brianna

Author's Website:
https://briannamerritt.com

Additional Social Media:
Twitter: https://twitter.com/briannawriting
Facebook:
https://www.facebook.com/briannamerrittwriting/
Instagram:
https://www.instagram.com/briannawriting/
Pinterest: https://www.pinterest.com/bgmwriting/
Goodreads:
https://www.goodreads.com/user/show/59014298-
brianna-merritt
Tumblr: https://briannawriting.tumblr.com